SILK ROAD

SEALS OF DESTINY

SPECIAL EDITION

T.J. MICHAELS

SILK ROAD (SEALS OF DESTINY)

Copyright 2012 – 2013 by T.J. Michaels
ALL RIGHTS RESERVED.
Second Electronic Publication December 2013, Bent West Books
First Trade Paperback and Electronic Publication July 2012
Edited by Tamara Mays
2nd Edition Cover Art by Stella Price
Formatted by IRONHORSE Formatting

ISBN: 0985787473
ISBN-13: 978-0-9857874-7-9

PRAISE FOR THE NOVELS OF TJ MICHAELS

Silk Road

"An action packed thriller too hot to miss!" ~Lisa Renee Jones, national bestselling author

"Silk Road twisted and turned flawlessly. The characters were nothing short of fantastic."
~Booked and Loaded Reviews

"SILK ROAD is an entertaining urban fantasy romance that promises to captivate readers as good, evil, and something in between converge in a real page turner from beginning to end."
~R. Barri Flowers, bestselling Harlequin author of MURDER IN HONOLULU and MURDER IN MAUI

The Vampire Council of Ethics Series

"Interesting new world. Hot stuff!" ~Shayla Black, New York Times bestselling author

"CARINIAN'S SEEKER was a highly erotic, thrilling suspenseful, paranormal read that will blow your mind."
~Fallen Angel Reviews

"It had me rooting for their happy-ever-after as much as cheering their kick-ass assignments"
~Just Erotic Romance Reviews

"T.J. MICHAELS has done an astounding job of crafting a steamy hot suspenseful romance—"
~Romance Junkies

Spirit Bound Novels

"All in all, [On the Prowl] is a fun and delightful story with spicy sex and great suspense both in the love story and the plot."
~Just Erotic Romance Reviews

"Using heat, danger and tension, Egyptian Voyage will keep you glued to that edge of your seat as you go along for the ride. TJ Michaels has written a story that will fascinate, horrify and ultimately delight the reader."
~SensualReads.com

Forever December
"[Forever December] is a highly erotic, touching and sexy novella that will have you reaching for a tall, cold glass of water and a fan."
~Romance Divas

"Explosive love scenes will curl your toes and leave you fanning. Readers who love a flare for the dramatic with paranormal elements will certainly become fans of TJ Michaels."
~Romance Junkies

Jaguar's Rule
"The plot is flawlessly executed and the characters remain true."
~The Romance Studio

"T.J. MICHAELS knows how to write plot and passion in a most memorable way!"
~Fallen Angels Reviews

DEDICATION

To my kids, Tamara and Michael, who forever encourage me to pursue my dreams even while fussing that I work too much (((HUGS)))!

To R.G. Alexander who sat and listened to me ramble about the ideas for this book without once threatening to put a metal bucket over my head and whack it like a gong.

To Lee Iron Horse, my favorite zombie-fighting partner in crime who is always willing to jump in and save my literary bacon.

And to my readers, especially the ones who catch me on social networking sites—You are all so supportive, funny and lively. This writing thing wouldn't be nearly as much of a blast without you. I am so grateful.

PROLOGUE

A page from an excavation journal on display at the
Pergamon Museum in Berlin

Expedition: Archaeological journey to Hierapolis on behalf of
the Berlin Academy of Sciences
Catalogue Date: July 2, 1887
Logged by: Dr. C. Wilhelm Humann
Artifact/Find: Torn pages from a document found during
excavation of the ancient ruins of Hierapolis near Denizli
Province, now modern-day Turkey
Age: Estimate—200 BC
Origin: Unknown
Material: Ink of unknown substance written on parchment
Language: Ancient Greek
Status: Unverifiable
Theory: Believed to be a hoax or part of a written play about
angels. Perhaps it was to be performed by an artist or storyteller in
the amphitheater located in the middle of the city? Hierapolis is of
the Hellenistic period. As such, the ancients of that city believed in
the Greek pantheon and believed that the city itself was founded by
a Greek god—Apollo. Therefore, it is unlikely that anyone other
than a storyteller of that age would write of angelic beings during
the time in question.

Here we have translated the original ancient text to the best of our ability, though various spots on the document are smudged or otherwise unreadable.

"A single jagged tear in the fabric that makes a family can destroy it forever. We felt immeasurable loss as those who had been a part of us since their very creation were ripped away. Left behind is a hole in the landscape of our community, a chasm of emptiness that will never be filled.

Like having an arm twisted from the socket without the luxury of a blade, their severing was agonizing and unspeakably ugly, leaving the exposed tatters of our emotions every bit as raw.

We felt the longing of those who wished to stay just as we'd felt their joys, triumphs and sadness through the ages. It assaulted our senses, even as we were driven to obey, driven to force them out of the only realm they'd ever known.

We beat them bloody, until they were bruised in mind, body and spirit. But we felt the sting of our own betrayal. We'd turned on them. Abandoned them. The pain they felt as they were separated from us reverberated from their minds to ours like the ripples of sound after striking a large gong. It was soul-deep as they looked us in the eye while we landed blow after blow.

"Do not do this to us," they cried. "Do not make us leave you. We will die. Worse, we will die alone."

Yet we had no choice. The smallest seed of rebellion could not be allowed to root or sprout, let alone grow. Could not be allowed to corrupt order.

Even as they fought back, tried to keep what had always been theirs, it wasn't enough. They knew it. We knew it. We pushed them beyond the boundaries of the heavens, beat them back until they were beyond the stars. Even my fellow Watchers, those who inhabit the skies and those who serve on the Earth, observed with awe the utter destruction that we, the Host, delivered without quarter.

Their wings were nothing more than bloodied stumps as we tore away the last symbols of their former status. Bodies, once as bright as the stars, dimmed as they fell.

None would ever be punished such as these, thrown down so that the impact shook the Earth itself.

Some landed on jagged mountain peaks. Some crashed into the seas with such force it was as if they met solid stone rather than water. Some sprawled unmoving in snow to experience an utterly foreign sensation—bitter cold. Some met burning-hot deserts where the rough sands scraped away flesh.

What small bits of their bodies that had not been damaged in the fighting were shattered, rent apart as they made contact with hard earth. And to Earth are they bound until their final judgment.

As if the judgment already given was not enough.

They would never take to the air again. Ever.

What were they to do? What were they to become now that what they had been created to serve was no longer accessible? Would they mend? Of course. They were beings of the stars, celestial through and through, yet that which sustained them could no longer be called upon to replenish them. We are warring angels; injury is nothing new. But for our brethren, what would normally take moments to heal would now take...

Then I realized I had no answer, had never been cut off from the Source.

We watched their expressions of disbelief harden even as their bleeding, tattered bodies began to mend oh so slowly. With the mending of each wound came a new emotion.

Rage.

It affects us, their anger, but we must remain true to our purpose. We must remain connected. The need, the determination to hold on to what is left of our family after we wrought such devastation helps keep us strong.

So we turn our backs knowing that we committed such fierce and lasting judgment, such violence against my own...the agony of it will forever reverberate through my soul.

There is no need to wonder if any who were to be cast out remained. We have been thorough. It is done. Something that none have witnessed before is finished.

The Fall.

As I sit and write this, it occurs to me that it is no wonder my lost brethren continue to despise man. A creature created from the dust of the ground had been given dominion over all the world, a creature they had been expected to bow before. In punishment they were cast down to live among those very beings they saw as beneath their notice.

I never thought anything could cause me to question my

3

purpose, my existence. My masters. Yet doubt lingers as to whether what we have done is...right. But it is a doubt I will never share with another lest I suffer the same fate.

[Illegible writing—smudged ink here]...

We miss them as they were. We will always love them deeply for the rest of our days. Yet we cannot undo their rebellion.

~Larien, Principality and Angel of the Art of War, Watcher and member of the Host"

CHAPTER ONE

A flare lit up the inky night sky. Larien blinked once, twice, fisting his hands at his sides to keep from rubbing his eyes. No way would he give the man now standing in front of him the satisfaction of knowing a permanent image of his ugly mug had been burned into the back of Larien's retinas.

Pansy-assed showoff.

The heat from the blazing weapon in the hand of his kin warmed his Adam's apple. He gave a slight nod and his skin rasped against the edge of the blade.

"Ambriel." It was little more than a drawl, but it was as much as the sanctimonious bastard was going to get.

"What the hell are you doing here?"

"I can't tell you that," Larien replied.

"Do you wish to rephrase that, sulphur breath?"

The insult had him considering his choices—kick Ambriel's ass and get dog piled by his horde of Dudley Do-Right *Seraph's*? Or…damn, it was hard coming up with an "or" just now. But he wasn't here for this. Larien let his hands hang loose at his sides.

"Look, Ambriel, I'm not here for any trouble, believe it or not."

"Not."

Larien smirked. "I have a job to do and I'm not leaving until I do it."

The blade left his neck as Ambriel whipped it backward in a perfect half circle. The steel stopped a hairsbreadth from the curve at the base of Larien's skull.

A warning snarl emerged from Ambriel's throat. "I am not some soft-spoken ministering angel. I am a warring angel, a *Seraph*, and I have no problem kicking your skinny ass if you do not clear out."

Larien's eyebrows rose so high he wondered if they'd left his forehead. "Did you just say…?"

"Yes, I said ass."

"Actually 'skinny' was more offensive than 'ass'. But the real question is since when did you start cursing, cousin?"

"Ass is not a curse, it is a word. But if you like I can definitely curse you, Larien. It would be my pleasure."

Ambriel might not be Fallen but he was far from the pure driven snow he fronted as. And they both knew it.

The warriors of the Host appeared angelic, but they fought with unmatched drive and ruthlessness, even when in human skin. And now those warriors moved in on Larien. In unison, their eyes began to glow the otherworldly blue that signaled an impending transformation. Not good.

Larien slowly reached into his breast pocket and fished out a sparkling piece of parchment.

"Look, here's my hall pass. It's getting late and I need to handle my business."

There was no mistaking who'd written the note, as there was only one person in the entire Universe who possessed this particular parchment. Larien almost smiled when Ambriel's eyeballs grew as large as saucers. It wasn't every day you got to see one of these guys surprised.

"This human, *our* human, is your assignment?"

"If your human is Jayla Protegenu, then yes."

"But you, of all beings?"

"That's what it says, so can you get your gargantuan boyfriends to move now? Pretty please?" Larien stopped just short of batting his lashes.

Ambriel reluctantly lowered his sword, snapped it back into its scabbard with a metallic *schnick* and stepped away.

"Well, you can try to go in, but I cannot be held responsible for what happens. Our girl has spoken the words of protection and called us into position. Look around. We were already camped around her property when *you* showed up."

Ambriel spoke as if the word "you" tasted like piss on his tongue. Larien hoped it did.

"And here we will stay until she releases us." In spite of the seriousness of the moment, Ambriel smiled in admiration as he looked toward the house. Whoever was in there had the *Seraph's* respect? A human?

Larien then followed the asshole's gaze toward the roof where a burly, short-haired angel with skin like newly minted gold sat cross-legged. Suddenly he stood, pointed north and said, "Here comes another one!"

And at the speed of light—which had a whole new meaning when you were standing toe to toe with beings made of the stuff— a black-purplish blur moved with increasing speed toward the house. Ambriel and crew laughed outright when the blur hit a window with an audible *smoof,* and then bounced off the vibrating pane to land with a painful-looking plop on the ground.

Moments later, the blur solidified into a heap of very unhappy demon.

Ambriel tilted his head and said in a whisper out of the corner of his mouth, "She has also forbidden entry to anyone but her guardians. That would be us."

"She did? Really?" Larien hadn't meant to ask the question aloud, but this kind of revelation huge.

"If you are here for Jayla," Ambriel spat, "then surely you already know this."

Larien bristled. He definitely should have known but there was no way in hell he was going to admit that he had *not* been briefed on this particular point.

Feigning ignorance, Larien simply said, "So what the hell did I just witness?"

"She routed every unfriendly entity and forbade them from ever returning. You should have seen the sorry saps filing out the back door, faces all long and sad because they could not bother this wonderful soul in her dreams and thoughts tonight. It made us all ROFL!"

Larien's brows climbed up his face. "ROFL? Really? You know that's a text messaging thing, right, Ambriel? Are you ever going to learn to speak more modern?"

Ambriel ignored him and continued to laugh at the bruised, full-fledged, semi-flattened demon rolling around in agony on the ground.

Though he'd been delayed, one good thing had come of it. He'd received some valuable information—piss off his new charge and she had the ability to send him packing, assignment fulfilled or not.

Larien turned and headed toward her door.

"Hey, I said only her guardians can enter," Ambriel called after him.

Larien just smiled as he moved toward the house. He could, in fact, walk right into her home just like the good guys who stood guard outside. But no need to mention that little fact. The less anyone knew about his reasons for being here, the better.

If word got out, the warriors who were so impressed with this human might not appreciate what she was truly capable of. Lucky for all of them, not even the woman herself had any idea.

And her life depended on that secret remaining just that—a secret.

* * * * *

"Who are you and what are you doing in my house?"

Larien pushed away from the wall and stilled. There was no way between here and Hell this woman could see him. Not only was he cloaked from sight, but in the darkness of the room, *he* could barely pick out the curvy outline of the body underneath the covers. And his vision was…well, super.

The soft swish of linens rubbing against skin snagged his attention.

"I can't see you clearly but I can feel you. I know you're there. Who are you?" said the owner of a feminine and very pissed off voice.

Another second passed in silence. After all he'd gone through to get in here, he hadn't worried about what he would say to the human. He'd planned to duck in, get a look at her, and get right back out again. But something about her called to him. He should have been backing out the door rather than holding up the wall while watching her sleep. But it was as if her energy reached out to his. Held him there.

"Answer me. You have no right to be here. I exercise my authority and I command you to—"

The air around him crackled with power as she threw each word out to the Universe. Fuck.

"*Wait!* Hold on a minute." The energy that had begun to swirl about his body settled...but only just. "Let me explain why I'm here before you throw me out. I was sent, but not to harm you."

"I don't believe you. You don't feel like a bringer of peace to me."

Oh, she was both clever and correct.

"I don't typically bring anything close to peace," he said, "but in this case I'm on a mission of diplomacy. Not mayhem."

God, what I wouldn't give for some good ol' mayhem right now. Scads easier than dealing with a woman.

Her heartbeat remained steady and there was no stink of fear on her at all. She was truly unafraid. How refreshing, especially for a human. Hell, he almost surprised himself to find the thought was genuine, minus the usual smart aleck undertones.

"Stay right there," she demanded. This time the rustling of blankets brought with it the scent of incense as covers were thrown back and stirred the air around her. Nag Champa temple incense from India, if he wasn't mistaken, one of his favorites. Nothing quite like the smell of halmaddi and sandalwood. The woman took her time climbing from the bed. Not bothering with the bedside lamp, she stomped to the bedroom door and flicked the switch on the wall.

The room erupted with light. "Ow! How about a little warning, Jayla?" What kind of bulb was in the overhead fixture, a bazillion-watt floodlight?

She turned away from the wall, faced him and stilled.

So did he.

This woman, this *Jayla*, had an aura Larien was hard pressed to describe. It was a bluish-white vitality that rippled around her in waves—not of purity, but of power. Untapped power.

Just beneath that aura was a woman covered in the most beautiful skin he'd ever seen in his seemingly endless life. It was a deep bronze hue, like a mix of hot coffee, caramel and cream. She looked edible, like something he could come to crave by just having a single taste. Honey-brown irises bled into a subtle mix of darker and lighter green around the edges. Hazel, he believed it was called. Though her eyes blazed with anger, it brought out the unique color rather than detracted from it.

It suited her almost as well as the short, silky-looking number she'd worn to bed. Thin straps held up a loose-fitting royal purple gown that barely fell to the tops of her thighs. Correction—muscular, sleek thighs.

Good God, the woman was, in a word, tempting.

Larien locked his knees to keep from moving toward her. One, he didn't want to scare her. Two—and most importantly—sexy, alluring women had been his downfall. Literally. There would be no straying from the mission.

He squashed the newly blooming attraction as if it were nothing more than a blade of new grass beneath his boots. Reining in his emotions, Larien ground them into the pit of his existence, determined to leave them there to wither and die.

Great. Now you are waxing poetic. A very bad sign.

* * * * *

Jayla couldn't decide whether to toss him out on his butt, stand there and gawk or yell for help.

Unlike the protective *Seraphs* and take-no-prisoners *Cherubs* downstairs, so reverently beautiful they muted their true forms just so she could look upon them, this guy drew her in a purely sensual way.

Energy with a bit of a dark bite blazed off the oversized man. Unmistakably *un*human. Not evil—she knew full well what that felt like—but not quite nice either.

Sporting a stylish leather trench coat, black jeans and scuffed motorcycle boots, this *whatever* was rough-and-tumble gorgeous. Tall and broad with a buzz cut so short it was barely stubble, he looked like one of those mountain man types rocking the almost-bald look. Definitely a man who could woo a woman in ten seconds flat then go out and chop a forest full of wood without breaking a sweat.

And right now he seemed to spill all that maleness all over her bedroom...uninvited. Annoyance at having her private space invaded trumped his yumminess by a long stretch.

"So, let's get down to it. What the hell are you doing in my house? And I don't even want to know how you know my name." Though she did like the way it had rolled off his tongue when she'd turned on the light...

Get a grip, girl. Uninvited guest, remember?

"What are you?" she snapped.

"Which question do you want me to answer first?"

He folded his arms across his chest and huffed as if she'd inconvenienced him, as put out to be here as she was about his unknown intentions. Huh.

"Look, are you going to—?"

"Jayla, my name is Larien," he said, cutting her off.

"Larien?"

"Yes, and I am to assist you in a task."

"What task? And why should I believe you?"

He stretched out his hand. A folded piece of shimmery-looking paper slowly floated across the space separating them. By itself. Neat trick but...

"Too slow," she mumbled as she stomped the remaining distance between them and snatched the note out of the air. "Sorry," she mumbled when Larien hissed something about manners, or lack thereof. Great, and now she was blushing. "While I may not be afraid of you, I didn't mean to disrespect you," she said. "Even if you *are* in my house, in the middle of the night, in my bedroom with nothing more than a piece of paper to recommend you."

The landscape of his face went from amused to taut to wrinkled forehead to slate smooth. She'd managed to confuse a supernatural?

Wow, I am good!

"You look like you're wondering what my deal is. It's all over your face." Okay, the smirk she tried to suppress morphed into a full-on grin. "Well, not anymore. Guess you've gotten your shit together and now you're doing the stoic I'm-a-badass face. No worries."

Goodness, she was doing the feisty thing with an unknown man broadcasting a serious me-no-play-well-with-others attitude. She must need to go work off some energy. First order of business in the morning—go hit a heavy bag at the gym or something.

Remembering the piece of paper in her hand, Jayla read it and cocked her head sideways in disbelief. Along came the curiosity that never ceased to get her into trouble. She read the note again for good measure then flew to the window. With her back to Larien, she was suddenly quite aware of how the little hem on her gown ruffled as she raised the pane and yelled down to Ambriel and his crew in the yard.

"Hey guys, this is rather light on details. Just says he's here on official Host business. Is this for real?"

Ambriel grumbled back, "Yes, Jayla, it is genuine. He is being honest in his intentions…for once."

Well that didn't sound good. She whirled around to face Larien. He didn't look as if he cared in the slightest, but she didn't miss the tail end of a curse or two as he coughed into his hand.

Rather than wary, it made her smile.

Back across the room, she settled down on the bench at the foot of her bed and crossed her arms over her chest. With an expectant huff. "Okay, Larien, I'm listening."

"There is an ancient artifact that you are tasked to find and my job is to help you acquire it."

Genuinely confused, Jayla said, "I'm so not Lara Croft. Seriously, I own a gym and write for the local paper. The university has an archeology department where I'm sure you can find someone more suitable. I've never even been on an expedition before though Egypt is on my bucket list."

"You're more than suitable. In fact, you're the only one we know of that can handle this job. We're after the Seal of Solomon."

"The who of what? I still don't see how that means I'm your woman."

"You are definitely my wo—" He cleared his throat and then pushed on. "You are definitely the woman for the job. The artifact belonged to someone in your familial line. There may be clues in your family's history that can point us in the right direction. Clues an outsider may be unaware of."

"Still," she pushed back. "I just don't think I—"

"Jayla, you were chosen for this task by the Archangel Gabriel himself. If you'd like to tell him 'no' be my guest. I, however, don't have the luxury of such a choice."

When she woke the next morning there was no sign of the handsome hunk who had spent very little time telling her even less about a super-secret mission to recover some artifact seal thingy she'd never heard of.

Damn. No sign of him at all.

CHAPTER TWO

Abaddon sensed Jabon the second he strolled into the stone building. He hadn't yet seen the asshole but was quite aware of every being who came and went from this place. After all, it was Abaddon's to control, to rule. For a time anyway.

The warmth of the female *lilitu* demon writhing beneath him overcame the chill that lingered on his skin, yet he knew it wouldn't last. He was always so cold. Humans thought his kind reeked of either starlight and roses, or brimstone and fire. Yet the cold was the true torment. There was heat, wonderful glorious flames all around him, yet he couldn't get warm. Would never be warm.

Even his erection, though surrounded by the scorching wet flesh of today's bed partner, was just as shy of "icicle status" as the rest of him.

Well, at least he could still come. His strokes increased in anticipation of the wash of warmth that would erupt from his balls and up through his erection. Then the familiar tingle that would spread through his body and blood, bathe him in heat from the inside out. He didn't even care that the pleasure lasted only a few moments. He would take what he could get for as long as he could get it.

Hold on. Hold on just a little bit longer.

Until the pressure built to the point his head, both of them, would blow off.

His partner arched beneath him as Abaddon grabbed a fistful of her thick white hair and pulled her head sideways to bare her neck. Licking a path through the sweat gathered there he groaned when the sweet, addictive taste of her skin hit his tongue. It was one of the allures of her kind—their body fluids bent lover to their will. But it didn't apply to Abaddon.

He ruled this place, was immune to the wiles and weapons of the creatures here. It was heady, the power he wielded in this realm. But not as intoxicating as the body beneath him as it glowed in response to her arousal. Her sharp claws sank into the skin of his back and left stinging trails on either side of his spine. He welcomed the pain, anticipated it just as much as the coming orgasm.

"Yes, yes. Ah God, I'm coming," the *lilitu* gasped into his ear. Slick sugared walls squeezed him. Milked him. Oh, this would be good.

"Excuse me, sir. He said it was important."

Fuck.

Abaddon turned toward the archway that led into his private chambers with a very decipherable snarl. The guard gestured to the guest standing at his side and then turned and ran.

"May I join you?"

Jabon.

At least the idiot had sense enough to wait for Abaddon to motion him forward. At Abaddon's nod, Jabon strode inside. What's-her-name squeaked, wiggled out from underneath him and tore out of the room at the sight of his unexpected guest's extending fangs. Smart woman. With Jabon, you never knew whether you were getting a fuck or a fight. And considering he'd just interrupted the one and only bout of sex Abaddon had time for today, the latter was more likely than the former.

"This had better be good."

No further threat was necessary and they both knew it.

Not bothering to cover himself, Abaddon rose as Jabon moseyed to the other side of the bed chamber, settled into a large throne-like chair formed of black granite and then put his boots up on Abaddon's dining table. Ass.

Why had he ever given this particular Fallen demon the ability to come and go from this realm? It had seemed like a good idea at the time. After all, Jabon was privy to the goings on of both friend and foe. If tossing him through the Abyss gate without a proper order wouldn't land Abaddon in more trouble than he was willing to deal with, he'd drag the idiot down to the gate himself.

Just because Abaddon was tasked with overseeing this place didn't mean he had the same desires or goals as those he babysat. One day he'd enjoy ending Jabon...after the fucker had served his purpose.

The skin at the corners of Abaddon's eyes tightened until they were mere slits as he watched Jabon snatch up a ripe pear and begin munching on it.

But Jabon was no fool. This was important, otherwise he wouldn't be here. After all, this man wasn't just any Fallen. He was *The* Fallen and now a demon on top of that. Jabon and his cohort, Simjela, were responsible for the second Fall. It was they who'd led astray the Watchers—those angels charged with the task of teaching life skills to mankind. The amount of skillful deception required to get all those devoted beings to set aside their duty just to get laid was masterful. Horrifying, but masterful.

Jabon's ability to ferret out information where there appeared to be none was the only reason Abaddon hadn't tossed him out by the seat of his no doubt very expensive tailored pants.

"I heard through the grapevine that someone has been sent to find the Seal of Solomon," Jabon said.

Abaddon stilled. His midday sexual escapade had been interrupted for this?

"Old news, Jabon," he growled. "You're wasting my time. If I can't get the female you just chased off to return, perhaps I'll require you to take her place."

Jabon stilled mid-chew. Classic.

Abaddon moved closer, stalking him with purpose. Everyone knew that Abaddon never issued idle threats. Ever. "Besides, Jabon, someone has always been after the Seal, even when that idiot Solomon was still alive."

Jabon stopped breathing for a moment, and then feigned calm. As expected. "True, but those someone's didn't have the help of Larien or Chelriad—"

"Larien and Chelriad?" No fucking way.

"Exactly."

"What are two Fallen angels doing helping a...a what? What has been sent for the Seal this time?"

"My sources say it's a human."

"Oh please. And I thought you had something important to tell me. Angels have always been charged with helping humans. As for Larien and Chelriad, I'm guessing those two are trying to earn brownie points for fucking up."

Half the pear was left on the table as Jabon wiped his mouth and rose. "It's more than that. Unlike previous hunters of the Seal, this particular human can actually use it."

"Impossible." Abaddon gave an exasperated sigh. "No human can use the fucking thing. Not unless Michael shows up and delivers it personally or—"

"The human is a blood Descendant of Solomon."

"Excuse me?"

"I said the human is a Descendant. A true one though they may not know the extent of their powers. It's said this person may be able to exorcise enough authority to call *Seraphs*," Jabon said silkily.

The Fallen was out of his mind. Descendants were born every day yet their legacy was all but lost. There hadn't been a single one in ages who truly knew what they were or knew how to exercise their special type of magick.

If there were true *knowing* Descendants, certainly they would be protected. Either that or dead.

Patience at an end, a snarling and still-naked Abaddon released his talon-tipped wings. They snapped open with a loud *whoomp* as he bared his fangs. With one hand he stroked his cock and grabbed a paling Jabon with the other. "Your proof, demon? If you have none, I suggest you find some lube and then think twice about barging into my private space again."

Just then, Abaddon's chief of staff poked his head through the archway. "My lord, a word?"

Abaddon turned and frowned fiercely. Not because of the interruption, but because the demon standing next to his chief of staff was black, blue and purple all over...and those were not his natural colors.

Though well over six feet tall, the demon's frame was particularly stooped, and the sword strapped at his hip was bent as if he'd tried to spar with a rock wall. His typically glossy black wings were dull, blemished and rubbed raw in spots.

"What the hell happened to you?" Abaddon demanded.

It took the underling a moment to reply given the swollen mess that was his face.

"Captain Geminon sent me to you to report an incident. I was out hunting in San Francisco when I ran into…trouble."

"What kind of trouble?"

"I saw a spirit, a human spirit glowing in the night. I went to see if I could torment it. It, the human, had a whole troupe of angels, all warriors. They were everywhere."

"And they did this to you?"

"Uh, no."

Abaddon pinned the foot-shuffling demon with a glare, urging him without words to get to the point.

"I approached and the *Seraphs* didn't even try to stop me."

"So," Jabon asked sarcastically, "they kicked your ass from a distance?"

The demon looked to Abaddon before answering. "No, sir. I flew right by them but when I tried to enter the human's house I was repelled. Forcefully."

"By what?"

"That's just it, sir. I don't know what. But something made it impossible for me to enter. Not to mention that whatever *it* was kicked my ass all over the yard until I could get off the property. It was like getting beat down by a cross between the Hulk and the Invisible Man."

"And what of the angels?" Abaddon asked.

"They just watched and laughed, the bastards. We were—"

"We?" Jabon prodded.

"I wasn't the only one. Several of us met up about five miles from that place. All had the same story. That's why Geminon thought I should deliver my report to you directly."

Abaddon waved a dismissive hand and the limping, multicolored bruise-of-a-demon quickly withdrew. Well, as quickly as he was able.

"Jabon, when was the last time we did an inventory of living Descendants?"

"How the hell should I know?"

A growl laced with black intent was Abaddon's response. "It's your fucking job to know!" Abaddon roared. How the hell had Jabon convinced so many of his kind to Fall? Ridiculous. "The next time I ask you a question and the answer is unsatisfactory, you'll not have to worry about my being annoyed with your coming and going. You'll be staying. Right here. With me. Period." His smile was purposely sadistic. "Ah, I see you understand."

Abaddon so enjoyed the sight of blanched skin on a demon. And just now Jabon's gray skin, the evidence of his Fallen demon state, was almost white. Lovely sight, the bastard.

"I'll have someone get on it right away. We've tracked the births and deaths of the Descendants for millennia but there hasn't been one worth notice in ages. Literally. It became a non-priority to continue but we can easily fill in the blanks," Jabon said quickly.

Abaddon stepped close until he was almost nose-to-nose with Jabon. "You'd better."

CHAPTER THREE

Of all the places he'd been over the centuries, Larien had a true love-hate relationship with this city. A place as diverse as San Francisco meant shining examples of culture, pristine architecture and wealth right next to grungy, soot-flavored despair and bloodletting nastiness.

Larien cloaked himself from human eyes and began the hunt for his prey. Sure, he was on a mission for the good of all spirit- and mankind, but he'd been chosen for this task for a reason—unlike his goody-two-shoes *Seraph* cousins, Larien had no qualms about not playing fair. He knew exactly where to go to find what he was looking for, which required a bit of creative thinking, not something his brethren did a lot of. They were made to obey and were quite satisfied doing just that. Larien, not so much.

Now he stood in the middle of supernatural central—the Tenderloin district. It was most densely populated area of the city, filled with families and children. Unfortunately it was also the poorest neighborhood, which meant there was a high concentration of violence and homelessness. Though it wasn't all bad, there was a kind of grittiness here that you just didn't find in many civilized cities these days. It was the perfect place for hunting. There was no doubt that one of the dank, trash-filled alleys of the Tenderloin would get him exactly what he needed.

A whiff of stale urine was overshadowed by the scent of cooking grease coming from the backdoor of a local soul food joint. Larien smiled, loving even the smallest signs of revitalization. The building had been an abandoned coin laundry the last time he'd been here. Unable to resist the spicy creole scent wafting from the place, he ducked inside.

It was no surprise to find a lower-caste daemon working here. The man quickly wiped down the takeout counter and then turned his attention to Larien.

"Are you here for me?" the daemon asked quietly. Fingers shook as he grasped the cleaning rag tightly, but he held Larien's gaze in spite of his obvious fear.

"Not my job anymore, as I'm sure you can tell." Cloaked or not, to other supernaturals, Larien's aura gave him away just as theirs told him all he needed to know about who or what they were. Unlike demons, daemons weren't bad guys. They were neutral and had every right to live on this plane without being harassed.

"Well, others have been tromping around down here, roughing up the locals. They're after someone. Staying out of their way as best we can. Figured if they were here hunting illegally, you might be too."

"Nope. I only want a number nine with extra hot sauce," Larien said, careful to keep his expression calm. He had a good idea who was "tromping" around, but it wouldn't do for this lesser to know that, even though he'd tucked an extra serving into Larien's bag.

A nervous smile accompanied the little one's relieved sigh as he rang up the meal and shooed Larien out the door with a friendly wave. It was closing time. No surprise, even if it was only late afternoon. Hell, it was a stretch for anyone to visit the Tenderloin in the daytime, let alone at night. And with winter closing in, it would be full dark soon.

Chasing the last of his crawfish beignet down with strong chicory coffee, Larien tossed his trash. Quickly, he turned into a dim alley off Eddy Street that let him out in the middle of a block crowded with cans to be picked up the next day.

And that's when he felt it—an unmistakable wrongness, like a sour ripple in the air, in the very fabric of space-time itself. Not all supernatural creatures were on seek-and-destroy missions, but what he picked up now caused a twisted shrinking feeling in the pit of the stomach. Not a sense of dread but simply a discerning of an unnatural and definitely unwanted presence.

He tracked the aura to a church.

Larien snorted. Why did this encounter have to be near some church? It wasn't the old moldy type typically seen in movies but that wasn't the point. It was just so cliché. No building could sway the outcome of any situation. Rolling his eyes, Larien backed away from the church steps, discreetly backed into the doorway of a side entrance and watched the street.

Moments later a man with flame-red hair passed by. Though there was plenty of mid-day foot traffic, the man stood out. The man's energy pulsed and crackled as he moved swiftly by, but everything else about him screamed "human".

Larien stayed where he was and watched him duck into a typical dirt-and-cream colored apartment building across the street. Not far behind were two beings who definitely didn't belong. It was obvious the male had seen them though Larien doubted he'd understood what he'd seen.

Their ridiculous height, the silvery-gray tint of their skin and razor-sharp, glossy-black talons on the tips of deep burgundy wings told a story that was fit for folk tales. Fallen demons.

This didn't make any sense. What would these particular beings want with a "sort of" human male? Prior to their Fall, this class of angel was like the secret service hounds for the higher-ranked Host. Their specialty—interrogation of supernaturals, not humans. Even now, they would still perform tasks similar to that of their true purpose, which did *not* include influencing destruction or mayhem in this realm. It didn't matter what flavor of supernatural you were, every entity was subject to laws, whether universal, spiritual or natural. And if the target of these Fallen demons was the short red-haired guy they tailed into the apartment building, those laws were about to be broken.

Fucking bad guys forever fucking with his schedule. Now he'd have to tip his hand sooner than he wanted to. But as he moved in closer to the human's apartment building, the grin spreading across his lips just wouldn't go away.

* * * * *

Thankful for the thick post-lunch crowd that moved along the sidewalk, talking on phones or to each other, Talan had risked a quick look behind him. No one blinked at the towering figures closing in on him. Were they even cloaked from human sight? Or perhaps they were just sort-of cloaked, letting him see them, but only him? And what the hell kinds of creatures were they?

Fucking supernaturals. He lived in a neighborhood full of them. Daemons, demons, vampires, magic wielders, you name it. While friends with a few, Talan gave the nasty ones wide berth and, in turn, they left him alone.

But these beings were too beautiful for words. Indescribable, really. Surely they looked like angels, though he'd never seen one. Yet these guys exuded a menace that was unmistakable, dark, and damn near panic inducing. The way they walked and owned their space left no doubt that they expected to find and take whatever it was they were looking for. And it seemed that something was him.

Forcing his breathing to remain even, Talan moved past the neighborhood church, walking as fast as he could without running, and threw a prayer toward the building. "God, if you're in there," he said as he passed, "I hope you're available to provide a little bit of help in the next few minutes or so."

Talan laughed. Couldn't help it. A building may hold certain energies, but it didn't keep things out. Only wards could do that, and you had to know what you were warding before you could put an effective one in place.

His apartment building was warded against blood elves, unknown Shadow Priests and a few other beings. Luckily, he had a nice spell in place that would tell him what he was dealing with. Hopefully it would buy him enough time to figure out what to use to fight them. Or banish them. Bind them. Something. *Anything!*

Not bothering with the elevator, Talan walked calmly across the lobby of his building to the stairwell, quietly closed the door behind him and then tore down the steps at a dead run. Adrenaline spiked and his limbs seemed noodle-like. It felt like he was moving too slowly, drudging through wet cement, so he hopped the rails and jumped down to the next landing. Hallelujah for leasing the entire basement!

"Henjiru," he whispered as he moved down the dimly lit hall toward his apartment door. Shadow magic filled the air as the spell unfurled deep in his belly and filled him to overflowing with

power. The flask in his inside jacket pocket warmed in response to the magic's call. He popped the cork, tipped his head back and grimaced as the contents splashed against the back of his throat and burned all the way down to his gut.

Bleh. Why do potions always have to taste like ass?

Apartment door securely locked behind him, he laughed, knowing it wouldn't slow down whatever was behind him. Moments later the snap and hum of the revelation spell rang through him, setting his nerves a-sizzling with the knowledge of what it revealed.

"What the fuck?" Now he knew what tailed him, but he sure as shit wished he didn't. Terror, thick and strangling, bubbled up in his gut. Fallen. Big-assed, mean *demon* Fallen? Most Fallen remained daemon and left his kind alone. If these had made the final leap to full demon, then that meant...

"Fukutsu!" he yelled. The Fortitude spell settled into place over his body just as the door flew off the hinges.

He steeled himself. Turned.

"Fuck!" Massive cement-gray skinned beings took him in with terrifying gazes. Their features were beautiful, flawless. Their builds symmetrically sculpted, like the statues he'd seen in the Polycleitus exhibit at the museum just last week. The blond one raised a hand and beckoned. It was like being wooed with sensuality and punched in the gut at the same time. The other, a dark-haired creature, had locks so silky-looking the urge to play in it was almost overwhelming. Until he smiled.

Fangs.

"Come now, human, this doesn't have to be unpleasant," said Dark Hair.

That voice. So seductive. Tempting. It almost made the lie believable as the words settled in between Talan's ears and rang with a tangible hum. He took a single step toward the bearer of that melodic, beguiling sound then shook himself so hard his brains rattled in his head. No way in hell was he going to fall under their spell. If he was going to die, they were going to fucking work for it.

"What do you want?" But under his breath he mumbled, *"embrace"* and forced his muscles to relax as the healing poised just outside his skin, ready to do its job for the blows he knew were coming. "And what the fuck are you?"

Talan knew the answer, but still couldn't quite believe it. Here in his house of all places.

"We want information about the Seal," they said in unison.

"The what?"

And it wasn't an act. He had no idea what they were talking about.

"We are aware you are acquainted with a Descendent, one who has knowledge of—"

And all hell broke loose.

* * * * *

In the hallway just outside the human's apartment, Larien listened closely. A pungent odor—dried mushrooms perhaps?—mixed with mist and magick seeped through the space where the door used to be. Whatever it was, he could feel it amp up the power that seemed swirled around in the air. It tasted earthy on his tongue, yet not quite of this plane. Interesting. Perhaps his prey wasn't human after all.

Deep breath in.

His ears buzzed then cleared, and his eyeballs vibrated as the scent in the air lit him up like a match, caused him to focus keenly on his surroundings. It was almost like having a whiff of angel crack that enabled a sort of laser-sharp focus. His goal was clear—take out the two intruders without tipping his hand to the pseudo-human. His attention snapped back to the conversation taking place inside the apartment.

"We want information on the Seal," they said. These Fallen—correction, Fallen-turned-demons—wanted the Seal? *His* Seal?

Hell. No.

The next instant, Larien was inside with his weapon clear of its holster. At the same time the human pulled out what looked like a thin piece of wood. Power hummed and then light flared from the tip and flashed around the room. The stream of energy or *something* slammed into the nearest bad guy and wound its way quickly up its body, trapping it.

"Release me at once, human!"

"Fuck you!"

"If you do not give us what we want, we *will* end you."

What the hell was going on here? No supernatural—Fallen demon, demon or otherwise—was sanctioned to kill humans.

Amidst all the yelling, growling and crackling of energy, Larien's keen hearing picked up the red-headed man's mumbled, "Aw, hell, not another one." Larien almost laughed.

At least he has common sense enough to be concerned about my appearance.

"I'm Larien, here to help."

"I'm Talan, here to *not* die!"

All right then.

Larien's weapon sizzled through the air, the black blade glowing with unblessed light. It locked with a clang against the sword of bad guy number two and kept it from slicing into Talan's scalp.

The Fallen demon trapped in the undulating ribbon of gray light from the end of Talan's wand went rigid at the same time Larien knocked his partner back with a solid cut across the chest.

Just before he called up his power to banish the snarling foe, it bent over backward and screamed in multiple pitches so high Larien wondered if it had become several women sometime in the last few seconds.

Out of the corner of his eye, he saw Talan jump back from the one he'd wrapped up in his spell as it opened its mouth and joined its partner in the howling. Their screams were filled with terror, as if they knew what awaited them. But that was impossible. They couldn't possibly know Larien had temporarily been granted the authority to render judgment against anyone looking for the Seal. Couldn't know he could send them to the outer realm, or even through the Abyss gate itself.

So what had put that fear in their eyes? What made them twitch? Made their heavily muscled limbs flex and jerk as if they yanked against some unseen bindings, trying to free themselves?

Eyes bulged and blood flowed from wounds inflicted by neither Larien nor Talan. Though they'd done plenty of damage, it didn't account for the new smoking gashes that appeared across the Fallen demons' bodies like the lines of a map to some unknown destination.

With a final wail of agony, both bodies expanded as if they

were on the verge of blowing up, but instead of gore and guts spraying across the room, they simply disappeared in a rush of nothingness. No wind. No sound. Nothing.

They'd left nothing behind in the torn-up apartment other than the faint whiff of death and burned flesh.

Was it something the human had done with his magick?

Lowering his weapon, Larien turned. If the human's gaping mouth, wide eyes and launched eyebrows were any indication, he was just as surprised at the turn of events as Larien was.

Larien motioned toward the bits of dust floating in the too-quiet room and asked, "Did you?"

"Nuh-uh."

"But you saw?"

"Uh-huh."

"How were you able to see them in their cloaked state?" Larien asked.

"Don't know. Same way I can see you, I guess."

Not quite true. Larien had, in fact, dropped his cloak back in the stairwell. The others hadn't lowered theirs until after they'd entered the building, yet this Talan had known he was being followed long before they'd ever caught up to him.

"It's obvious you're not quite human, yet you aren't eudaemon, daemon or demon. What the hell are you?" Larien asked.

The human buckled under the power of his voice.

He'd forgotten to dampen it, but given the current chain of events he would simply have to apologize later. Right now, he needed answers.

"What the hell's a eudaemon?" Talan asked, quickly recovering and moving around the wrecked space drawing symbols in the air. A hum of energy prickled beneath Larien's skin as the wards began to form.

"A eudaemon is an angelic servant, like guardian angels or messengers. They usually mute their true forms so they can be looked upon by humans, if they wish to be seen at all. They're good guys. Unlike me. How familiar are you with the supernatural?"

"Well you just explained what a eudaemon is. As for the rest, I have daemon friends. Anyone or anything with a celestial spirit can be daemon, rather than those with ethereal energy, such as the various kinds of fae. As for demons, some are born, others are made. Then there are shifters and vampires, which are a whole 'nother story."

Larien crossed his arms over his chest and listened to the surprisingly well-versed human recite the various levels of demonitude as if he'd been born into that world. Impressive.

"Bottom line, hybrids like me keep clear of 'em," Talan continued.

Hybrid? Larien thought. *Hybrid what?*

"And I'd definitely put the two that just blew up into the 'run away from' category. Seen plenty of demons, but never a Fallen one."

And on a dime, the man turned and changed the subject. "So you're a bad guy? What kind of bad guy? You're Fallen but not like those other ones so does that make you only sort of a bad guy? Amazing how many categories of things are out there." Talan cocked his head and eyed Larien as if he'd just stumbled upon a mystery of epic proportions.

Rather than answering the jumble of run-on questions, Larien felt along the thin line between the human realm and the celestial. There was no sign of the presence of the two Fallen demons on either plane.

"Uh, maybe later for twenty questions then, eh?" Talan said, eyeing Larien from the corner of his eye as he moved around the room.

"Anyway, you asked me what I am. I'm a Priest," the human said.

"You don't look like any priest I've ever seen." Larien wiped his blade on a cleaning cloth then sheathed it at his back.

"I'm a Shadow Priest when I need to fight. Otherwise I'm…something else."

Something else? Well, since Larien wasn't about to reveal his own origins just now, he'd let the man keep his secrets.

The power of Talan's wards strengthened and Larien could almost see them weave together like so much fabric in his mind's eye. Time to go.

Without another word, Larien headed toward the door.

"Wait," Talan demanded, raising his wand with a surprisingly steady hand.

"I suggest you stop pointing that thing at me."

"You helped me, but how do I know you aren't some other kind of asshole trying to win my trust only to take me out later?"

"Because I'm not squashing you into the tile like grout."

"Yeah, well, thanks."

The man's smile was genuine as he extended his hand...the one without the wand in it.

Larien accepted the overture. "Anytime. Talan, right?" At the human's nod, Larien said, "Until next time."

"I hope there isn't one of those."

Oh but there will be, my friend. There will be. With a wink, Larien invoked diaphaneity and vanished from the apartment. He didn't bother hiding his grin. After all, contact with Jayla had been achieved, and now target number two had been acquired. Excellent.

* * * * *

Careful to stay out of Larien's sensory range, the unseen meddler patted himself on the back with way too much flourish—even for his dramatic tendencies—and grinned from the shadows of the church. Oh, had he ever put in a stellar performance just now.

A whispered, "Thank ya, thank ya verra much" was followed by an Elvis-esque swivel of his hips. God, he loved human entertainers, even dead ones.

His bottom lip bled from biting on it to keep from laughing. Old Larien surely wondered what the hell had happened to the two Fallen demons. But there were no clues, no leads. And that was just the way he liked it.

He'd been careful to mask his presence as he'd made those red-winged slavering idiots' bodies crack like stress fractures on blown glass. Oh, and leaving nothing behind but floating dust motes? Classic! He couldn't have made a better show, if he said so himself.

Given that the fight had taken place in the human man's basement, he almost missed the faint energy signature that meant Larien had indeed left the building. Just imagining the confused look that must have been on Larien's face was enough to make him want to belly laugh. Instead, he clamped his lips together to hold it back.

Clearing his mind, he conjured a clear mental picture of where he wanted to go, powered up and flashed out.

CHAPTER FOUR

Jayla spun off her weak foot and hit the human-shaped target on the heavy bag that hung from the thick chain in the middle of the boxing ring.

Her cell phone rang. Without missing a beat she tapped the earpiece as she hit the center of the target dead on again and again.

"Hey Chel. What's up?"

"What's up with you, Jay? You all right?"

"Fine," Jayla said with a grunt as she landed another kick followed by a combination of punches. "Just sparring with myself and thinking of a new angle for this story I'm working on. My editor at the newspaper is getting on my nerves. Idiot can't seem to get it through his head that the crap stories he's giving me are, well, crap." She laughed then let out a whoosh of air as her foot made contact with the heavy bag. "So how's the photo shoot going?"

Her best friend was a high profile model on an equally high profile project. Chel was, quite simply, a stunner. No one would ever guess the woman was a total geek with a cache of all the latest gadgets.

"It's going well, though a bit slower than I'd like. Thought I'd check in with you between sessions."

"Aw, aren't you sweet? Girl, guess what? Over the weekend I met—" She bit her tongue at the gaff. "Uh, I *dreamed* this gorgeous hunky guy popped into my room out of nowhere."

Whew, that was close. There was no way she could let slip that she'd met a hunk without revealing the circumstances or secrets behind that meeting. On the other hand, now that she'd had some time to consider the details of the mission, where the hell was her new partner in crime? And had he fed her a crock, considering it had been straight days since he'd come to her? What kind of task was so important that he could take off before they even got started?

"Hunks popping into your room, eh? I myself happen to love those kinds of dreams. So what did he look like?" Chel asked. Jayla could practically see the mischief sparkling in her friend's eyes, even through the phone line. She may not be able to spill all the beans just now, but there were definitely some things she could share.

"Oh, Chel, he was beyond gorgeous. He was all rugged-bad-boy-kick-ass-take names-later gorgeous. Tall, but not too tall for kissing. You know, about six-foot-four or so. Big, brawny, shaved head. Or more like no matter how close he shaved he'd always have a bit of shadow up there. Super square jaw, dark eyes. Permanent frown."

"Permanent what?" Chel asked.

"Permanent frown. You know, it's that look that could stand for 'I'm thinking hard', 'I'm looking at something I don't understand', or an annoyed 'who the hell do you think you're talking to'. I bet if I'd managed to piss him off he'd wear that same expression. Permanent frown. Just, gah!"

Chel's gasp was followed by...nothing. No static. No noise. Not a sound came from the other end of the line. Miss Arlisa Chelton was a regular fuss bucket, though a bit broody at times. Silence simply wasn't her style so she probably had a makeup artist plastering lipstick on her perfect mouth in preparation for the next round of photos. Still the quiet was unsettling as if she were watching a needle ease toward a balloon and anticipating the pop.

"Soooo...anyway," Jayla continued past the unease beginning to bubble in her gut as she pushed the half-lie out with a wince. "In my dream, this guy was absolutely drool-worthy. He was on a mission to find an artifact of some kind, which is ridiculous considering I'm as far from being a treasure hunter or archaeologist as you are from being an ugly-duckling-nontechnical-construction-worker type."

Then her breath soughed in and wouldn't come back out as a group of guys walked into the sparring room. "Oh my god." It slipped out before she could catch it. Jayla wanted to smack herself in the forehead knowing Chel was unlikely to miss the gasp of surprise.

"What? What's wrong, Jay?"

Damn. Lowering her voice to a whisper she said, "Chel, you're not going to believe this, but my dream guy just walked through the doors of the gym." With two of the guardians that had looked after her for as long as she'd known how to call them. Holy crap.

"What do you mean he just walked in, Jay? What's going on?"

Larien had arrived and he'd brought his ridiculous jump-me-now magnetism with him. Bastard. Not fair that he could set her pulse racing while she obviously had no effect on him if he could show up, and then disappear for days without a word when it was all supposed to be so urgent. Bleh.

The small party stopped just outside the boxing ring. Dream guy looked up at her with a bit of devilish twinkle in his cocoa brown eyes. Or was that annoyance? She didn't' know him well enough to tell. Ambriel was talking on the phone and...what the hell? Angels used Bluetooth? No way.

"Hold on, Chel," Jayla said and quickly put the phone on mute. "Why in the world are you guys using cell phones?" Jayla asked, knowing her mouth was wide open and her chin had practically hit the mat in amazement.

"Because we're blending in," Ambriel said with a blinding smile. Not literally, but he sure did have pearly white teeth.

"But no one can see you but me. Why in the world do you need to use a phone and a Bluetooth ear fob?"

"We couldn't have you appear as if you were talking to yourself, so we're in true skin today." This from Barchiel.

"And you're really talking to someone? Not just bullshitting and pretending to have a conversation?"

"Hold on a second, Jayla," Barchiel said. "Yes, we're with her now. I know, I saw his instructions but we aren't leaving him here with Jayla until she releases us from the duty of protecting her. Yep, got it. Okay. We'll check in later." Barchiel tapped his earpiece and laid his sea green gaze on her.

She just couldn't get over it. *Seraphs* were really on the phone. How in the world did supernatural beings know more about technology than she did? In fact, it seemed that *everyone* knew more. If Chel hadn't pre-programmed Jayla's phone to automatically configure the Bluetooth when she hit her best friend's speed-dial number, she'd be hard pressed to make a call at all.

"And what in the world are you two wearing?" Jayla cocked her head to the side in wonder. For a couple of all-knowing, all-seeing beings, they'd missed the mark on fashion.

"This is an exercise facility, is it not?" Barchiel asked, not bothering to hide the smartass in his voice. Jayla laughed. Just couldn't help it.

"Yes, this is a gym, but it's literally freezing outside and raining. So, uh, what's with the...uh...?"

Her brain wasn't properly computing what she was seeing with her eyes.

They both sported tank tops, Ambriel's in neon orange and Barchiel's done in neon green. Short shorts cut so tight they may as well have been Speedos, matched the colors of the tanks. High top basketball shoes in a rainbow of colors she was sure had to be angel-made because no company in their right mind would dare manufacture them. And neither of them wore jackets. Sunglasses? Yes. Jackets? Not so much.

"This is San Francisco. You told us this city loves rainbows. So we dressed accordingly. Once we release our corporeal bodies, we'll go back to our usual armor," Ambriel said.

"Though I must admit that I am really liking jeans." This from Barchiel.

"Oh my goodness, Ambriel. You guys, just...wow."

"Do not hate, Jayla." Ambriel smiled even more radiantly at having found a use for one of Jayla's "silly human expressions".

"Amazing. Angels are not only more tech-savvy than I am, they're trying to be more fashion conscious. Geesh."

"Jayla?!"

Oops. She'd forgotten her best pal was even on the phone.

Unmuting the line while trying to hide the sheepish, yet amazed quality from her voice, she said, "Uh, sorry Chel. Will you be back in town next week? You've gotta come for dinner on our usual night, 'kay?"

"Jayla?" Chel growled warningly.

"I'll fill you in then. Just come to my place when you get back."

"Wait, Jayla…!"

With that she disconnected the call with a light tap to the light earpiece in her ear and stared. Hard.

Larien stood not five feet from her. And he was just as darkly beautiful in broad daylight as he'd been when he'd waltzed into her bedroom at eleven-fifteen at night a week or so ago.

The faintest bit of pitch black hair was a fuzz over his scalp. Perfectly formed black brows over pretty brown eyes that managed to look intelligent and annoyed all at once, and his sun-kissed skin made her think of warriors and pirates. Like a bad boy wrapped in good guy skin or vice versa.

The man was so sinfully dark and otherworldly beautiful it sent a zing of longing through her belly, at the same time a slither of trepidation crept down her spine.

He had the same bad-ass aura and stance as the other warring angels, yet Larien seemed so much…more. He hadn't said a word yet the man both called to and raised caution in her.

She knew he was an angel. He wouldn't have been able to hang with Ambriel and Barchiel if he wasn't. She'd never felt even the slightest womanly urge for an angel before, ever. Yet this one was not only handsome—in truth she'd never seen an ugly angel, not *Seraph, Cherub* or any other rank—but Larien incited a riot of emotion, all of it unexplainable and ridiculously hot.

"Well, if you are sure you are comfortable with this…this rabble, Jayla, we will leave you in his care," said Barchiel.

That earned them both a roll of Larien's eyes.

"Yes, I'll be fine. See you guys tonight?"

"Just call us and we will be there."

With that Ambriel and Barchiel turned and left a scowling Larien behind. Jayla took one look at his scrunched–up, annoyed expression and burst out laughing. There was just no way a man so unmistakably "in charge" should be able to pull off "petulant" so well. Jayla had a feeling he did everything well, whether good or bad. The thought chilled her to the bone.

So why wasn't she running like hell?

* * * * *

Larien watched his escorts walk out of Jayla's gym, but not before they made a few very clear hand gestures to indicate what they would do to him if he didn't behave.

Hurt him? Pfft. As if.

Nothing like eudaemon with a testosterone overload. Geesh. After a few growls and some posturing, he was glad to be rid of Ass One and Ass Two. And now he could turn all his attention to his new best friend—Jayla Protegenu.

She climbed from the boxing ring with an ease and grace that made it clear she spent plenty of time there. Sleek, sweat-sheened muscles flexed as she moved, yet she had curves galore wrapped in a sensuality that was unmistakable. But given his track record, mistaking it was exactly what he should do.

But he hadn't been known for doing the right thing.

Suspicion crept in through the corners of his mind. What the hell was the First Triad trying to do to him, pairing him up with this woman? They had to know he'd take one look at her and want her in his bed. Ulterior motive, perhaps? It didn't seem to be their style, but who knew? Their machinations were known only to themselves.

"So, we meet again?" She didn't sound the least bit happy to see him.

He had to get her to lead him to the Seal, so he could get out from under the last and only thing that could control him. It was a chance he never thought to have. Ever. No way in hell, er, heaven—whatever—was he going to blow it by allowing himself to be distracted.

She was a beautiful woman, vibrant and lively. Larien liked that she had signs on her body of someone who enjoyed life and lived it to the fullest. Scrapes on her elbows. A few cuts here on her knees. An impressive scar on the side of her thigh that looked like she'd gone five rounds with a tree on the way up or down the side of a mountain. At that moment her aura drifted slowly toward him like the smoke of the sweetest incense. It—*she*—called to him, drew his attention like nothing he'd ever experienced in all his long years. He even liked the curve of her belly, wondered what kind of chocolate she liked…

"Is there some reason I'm getting the silent treatment here?" Jayla asked.

"Sorry." He'd slipped into his own thoughts, got stuck there and missed whatever she'd said after "again".

"So you're here because?" she asked with a curious yet less-than-welcoming smile. Seemed as if she couldn't decide whether to stroke him or poke him with a stick.

Hmmm. What a strange encounter this was turning out to be.

"I told you that we're to embark on a mission of sorts."

"Yes, you did. But that was days ago so I figured you were full of shit. Pfft." Followed by a dramatic roll of her eyes.

Guess he really had left a poor impression. And why the hell did he care as long as she agreed to do the job?

"I had a few tasks to see to before we begin our little mission. I'd rather not talk about it here."

Jayla looked around with a bit of a scowl on her face. "What's wrong with here? I spend lots of time here. I happen to *like* it here." Her words were bitten off more and more sharply with each syllable and it was beginning to sound like an impending rant.

Women. No doubt he loved them. But understand them? Not so much. All he knew was that he'd offended her somehow and hadn't the faintest clue how. But he needed her happy. He had a feeling that if this woman wasn't happy, no one would be happy. The thought made him smile.

God, he must be tired.

"I like this space, too," he said. "It feels like a nice place to work out. Well lit, good location and even better energy. Is it usually empty this time of day?"

Her response was to snatch a towel from a pile of clean-smelling linens piled on one of several shelves along the wall. Jayla pinned him with a glare as she wiped the sweat from her body, but didn't answer his question.

There might not be anyone around right now, but it didn't change the fact that he needed to get her out of here. "I can sense others of my kind, but only when they're close. Nothing popping up on my radar, but there's no telling who might be listening," he said, not taking the chance on getting any more specific than that, especially not after his run-in with the two Fallen demons and the

Shadow Priest human a few days ago. If he played his cards right, he'd have all his tools in one place soon, but this wasn't that place. And it certainly wasn't the time.

"What are you talking about, demons? I'm *so* not afraid of demons. Seriously, you have no idea," she said, sounding both bored and annoyed.

"Yeah, well the ones who are interested in what we need to find aren't your garden variety ward-busting frilly frou-frou demons." No, they were big–assed, powerful Fallen who'd made the final transformation to full-fledged underworld-friendly demons.

"Excuse me?"

Larien watched her left eyebrow inch toward her forehead as a frown formed over her previously smooth and lovely features. He started to rein in the snark, but she needed to understand what was at stake here. He sensed that the woman truly was unafraid…but if she had any sense she'd be terrified. Hell, even he was concerned about their coming task and he'd had plenty of experience kicking both angel and demon ass.

Well, once upon a time.

"Look, I didn't mean to be an ass but there are things you need to know about what we have to do. This is serious business. No picnicking or tulip walking."

Her hand curled into a fist and made its way to her hip. The frown remained.

What was wrong with his mouth that it couldn't form a decent sentence in this woman's presence? He was usually more refined. Well, refined for a former warrior.

"Listen, I know you are capable or you would not have been chosen for this task, Jayla." Her chin dipped so she watched him through her lashes, but at least she wasn't scowling and seemed less likely to smack him now. Sort of.

The least he could do was smooth over a bit of the coming sting of their task, because she was sure to hate him through-and-through soon enough.

"Can we discuss this over dinner?" Larien asked.

She looked him up and down and curled her lip as if he smelled less than pleasant. Finally, she blew out a frustrated-sounding huff and said, "Sure." And then she tossed the hand towel she'd used to wipe her neck and stomach into a laundry bin.

"Sure? Just like that?"

"Why not? You showed me your hall pass, as you call it, the other night. And my guardians wouldn't have brought you in here if you were a danger to me. So, sure, let's do dinner."

"Excellent. I know just the spot."

"Fine."

She started to turn away, and then said, "But no snark or assholery, or I'm done. Get me?"

He smiled. The woman was refreshing. He'd literally popped into her life, demanded that she accompany him on an angelic mission and she wasn't running for cover. Instead she stared him down and dared him to be an ass while still maintaining a sweetness just under the surface. Yep, refreshing.

"I can't promise on the snark, but I'll try to rein in the assholery."

Her smile was all teeth and Larien's heart dropped into his boots. Good god, she was adorable…in a feral sort of way.

"I just need ten minutes to change and we'll go, 'kay?"

"No need. I'll take care of it." In fact, he'd been looking forward to it. Larien took her hand and flashed her from the building.

CHAPTER FIVE

"Holy shit." Jayla groaned, doubled over and wrapped her arms around herself.

"What's wrong?"

He couldn't possibly be serious. He'd "poofed" her from her gym into a car without warning and he was asking what's wrong? Obviously good-looking did not equal bright, did it?

If she hadn't been looking at the unmoving pavement just past the hood of the car and people standing in line across the parking lot waiting to get into wherever they were, she would have sworn they were still moving.

In circles.

Rapidly.

Oh God, she was going to throw up.

"Don't you ever do that again without warning me first."

"Do what?" Larien asked, all wide-eyed innocence.

"What? *What?!*" she screeched and then slapped her hand over her mouth in an effort to keep the bile at the base of her throat from bubbling up to the surface. And it wanted out. Really badly. Ewww.

Larien cracked the window on her side. Leaning her head back, Jayla sat up and took in huge gulps of fresh air along with whiffs of Larien. Surprisingly, whatever scent Larien carried—there was no way she could think hard enough just now to figure out what it was—calmed her roiling stomach as thoroughly as the crisp evening breeze.

After a few deep intakes she imagined that the faint green tinge that surely sat beneath her skin began to fade.

"Look Larien, flashing me around without warning falls into the assholery category."

"It's called diaphaneity. It means vanishing."

"Diaph-a-what? Never mind. Repeat after me. Unexpected poofing. Equals *Assholery*. Got it?" And he was grinning. If she hadn't been so relieved that her stomach had begun to settle and her gag reflex was calming, she would have been miffed.

"Now that we've got that straight, I think I can manage to make it inside the restaurant now. But I'd like a glass of wine while you go back to my gym and get my stomach."

She'd been so out of sorts after that whole flash-around thing she'd forgotten that Larien hadn't given her a chance to change. She looked down at herself and gawked. The man had not only changed her clothes, but he'd flashed all the funky sweat off her skin and out of her hair.

She now smelled like she'd just stepped out of the shower and out onto the town. Yanking the visor down, she peeked into the mirror. Her hair was swept up into a stylish French roll and the naturally curly spirals at her nape and ear points tickled her skin as the gentle breeze blew through the car window and cooled her skin.

Yes, the man had style. Now that she could look around without blowing chunks all over the car, correction, the very expensive black-on-black luxury coupe, she took in the scene with more appreciation.

He'd put her in a jewel-blue silk and chiffon number edged in satin piping that made her feel like a sexy starlet walking the red carpet. Matching high-heeled pumps, handbag and wrap done in a light blue Burberry pattern completed her ensemble.

But that's not what had her jaw on par with her toes.

Her angel sported the purple designer label—Ralph Lauren! The dark gray tailored suit and lighter gray band collar shirt complimented his eyes. The planes of his face were granite hard but sinfully handsome. Even his five o'clock shadow made her want to run her fingers across his square jaw and high cheekbones. What an interesting mix of energy he put off. While he was as handsome as any man she'd ever seen, Larien had an edge to him she couldn't place, a ruggedness that called to her adrenaline junkie side. Yet he appealed to another part of herself she hadn't truly explored—the feminine bits. Not that she wasn't in touch with it, but she'd just never had a man truly appeal to it. No one had really moved her enough to make her want to let it out to play.

Then she saw where they were—The French Laundry restaurant in Napa Valley. Taking in the entire package before her—man, car and atmosphere—all she could think of was...Wow! She'd been here to celebrate the launch of her chain of gyms a few years ago. It was a crème-de-la-crème place and the only time she'd worn the super-sexy bra and panty set that Chel had given her as a congratulatory gift.

Speaking of bra and panties...

As Larien got out of the car and walked around to her door, Jayla took a moment to take stock of her clothing once again. Her sports bra was long gone and gym socks had been replaced with sheer thigh high stockings.

"Uh, when you changed my clothes, did you happen to see anything you shouldn't have seen?"

The very *not* angelic grin he flashed was answer enough.

"Perv."

Taking her arm and helping her from the car, he leveled a gaze at her and said, "Oh, sweetheart, you have no idea."

A flush heated her cheeks.

That whole "run for the hills" feeling rushed over her, leaving gooseflesh behind. But where was the fear that should have accompanied it? Instead of terror, she found herself wondering exactly how pervy Larien could get. And if she ran, how long would it take for him to catch her?

* * * * *

They were shown to a private dining room where an impeccably dressed wait staff filed in and began to set the dishes out for them. The guy in charge was a tall, lanky young man with dark brown hair long enough to be pulled back into a ponytail. His easy smile and confident stance said he took great pride in what they'd brought into the room. "My name is Jesse and my team will be taking care of you tonight." His manner was easy, yet confident as he set their napkins in their laps and directed his two wait staff. Fresh French rolls, soft butter and berry preserves were set next to chilled glasses of water and three carafes with different types of wine. Next, salads of greens, fruit and veggies so colorful she was hard pressed to describe them. Wow.

Then the covered dishes were revealed.

"For you, madam, we have sweet butter-poached Maine lobster with king trumpet mushrooms and petite onions." Jayla's mouth began to water the moment she got a good whiff of the meal.

"And for you, sir," Jesse said, "we have the Atlantic cod with Yukon gold potatoes, celery, and parsley and chowder sauce. We brought all your dishes out at once so that you are not disturbed. As you enjoy the salads and soups, please leave the covers over the main meals so they do not go cold. Enjoy, and ring if you need anything." He motioned to a small porcelain bell next to the Zinfandel.

At the first bite, Jayla sat back in her chair. "Mmm. God, that's so good," she moaned.

Larien simply observed. His dark gaze seemed to cut right through her. Sure, he appeared to enjoy his food, yet seemed to enjoy watching her more than eating the sumptuous fare spread about the lovely table.

Was it okay to be attracted to a supernatural being? What if this was just a side effect of being in this particular man's presence? Maybe certain angels affected humans differently?

God, what was she dealing with here? Jayla had no idea. Until Larien, her only contact with supernaturals had been limited to her guardians. Ambriel and his boys were always in and around her house, but they only came when called and simply walked the grounds to make sure that nothing came in that she didn't want visiting. She'd watched them kick plenty of demon ass yet they'd never done anything as normal as share a meal. Never sat and discussed their history with her. In fact, most conversations were had on nights that she couldn't sleep and she did most of the talking from the window that overlooked her small backyard.

They listened politely as she rambled about humans and trends and clothes and whatever else, even when they were obviously bored to tears. It wasn't their purpose to chat.

But Larien was here for a purpose as well. So why did he affect her differently from all the others? Why did he make the bottom of her stomach dance around? Cause her to skin to flush and the breath to catch in her throat as she watched him eyeball her from across the table?

Why did he cause a tingle to flare up in her gut and spread through her body with such precise heat it made her press her thighs together?

Goodness the man was as potent as gold label tequila. No, wait, she hated tequila. Larien was more like twenty year tawny port wine—something so decadent you had it in place of dessert and savored it on the tongue long after you'd swallowed.

Just as they finished their last bites, the door swished open.

"Excuse me, sir, and madam. Dessert?"

Larien looked to her in question and at her eager nod, a slice of cake and a cup of steaming hot coffee were left for both of them. "Enjoy and please let us know if you need anything else," the attendant said, then left as quietly as he'd come.

One taste and she was lost in confection heaven. The lightest lemon cake was layered together with a cream cheese filling laced with toasted hazelnuts and drizzled with Bourbon vanilla glaze. On the side of the gold-rimmed dessert plate sat a small spread of chocolate-dipped pineapple.

She raised a single bit of the fruit, bit into it.

"Oh god," she moaned. "That's so good it's just wrong."

Larien's laser beam gaze heated, zeroed in on her mouth. Lids at half-mast, he lowered his head as his nostrils flared. Her temperature shot up hotter than the coffee the waiter had just poured.

Shifting on her chair, Jayla shoved a large forkful of lemon ecstasy into her mouth. If she stuffed her gob, she'd have to concentrate on chewing and swallowing without blocking her airways rather than the way Larien caused her pulse to skip.

She ground her teeth. *Geesh, Jayla. Rein it in, woman. You don't know anything about him other than who sent him.*

Strangely, that was enough for her.

Besides, it was all about living to the fullest. That meant *not* running from the opportunity to enjoy life, to live and love. Sure she'd had her share of broken promises and broken hearts, but it never stopped her from heading into the next experience free of baggage, or as free as she could be, anyway.

Her mom had taught her that it didn't make sense to punish someone for the mistakes of another, so why shut herself off emotionally from someone who had never hurt her? And if attraction to this man was wrong, guilt hadn't shown up to make her feel bad, so maybe it was okay to be gaga over an angel.

"If you're done we can get to the reason we're here," Larien said. He hadn't touched his dessert. She eyed it from across the small table they shared.

"Uh, you gonna eat that?"

"Nice to meet a woman that actually eats. Have at it." He slid his plate across the table. She lifted a forkful, moaned in a way that sounded sexual even to her own ears. But it was just so good.

"So, Larien, lay it on me." His brow flew upward even as his chin dipped to his chest so he could look at her through his lashes. Predator.

"Oooh," she gulped, "that didn't come out quite right." He had to know where her mind had gone or his smile wouldn't have taken on such a wicked edge.

"I mean, uh, tell me about the mission again."

"We need to recover the Seal of Solomon. As a Descendent of his family line, you've been chosen to help me find it."

"I remember that part from the night you first waltzed into my bedroom. You're not really here to feed me some crap about being the only surviving member of Solomon's family, are you?" She licked some of the cream cheese filling off her fork. Wondered how they'd whipped it so smooth. Almost as smooth as the skin at Larien's throat.

Girlfriend, stop. Keep this up and you'll miss everything he's saying.

"Are you serious?" Larien said. "The man had seven hundred wives and three hundred concubines. No way in hell are you the only one. But you happen to be one of the few who understand the authority you have as his great, great, great however-many-grandchild." He took a sip of his own coffee. "Who taught you to summon angels?" Larien asked.

Cup halfway to her mouth, Jayla was glad the steaming dark liquid hadn't been sucked in with her gasp. A curtain of gray fell over her soul as it always did when she thought on the two people who'd been integral in teaching her about her gift. They were long gone from this world. Would she always experience the pain of their passing anew? Would their memories forever squeeze the air from her chest and clog her throat with tears? This wasn't a subject Jayla enjoyed speaking of. Ever. Yet there was an unexpected comfort in confiding in Larien. It made no sense, all things considered.

"My dad and my grandma taught me when I was little. Why?"

"Are we able to talk to them, find out how they learned?"

"Sure, if you can get us a direct line to heaven…which you may be able to do, though I'm being rather smart-alecky about it."

"Sorry, uh, no. So they've passed on?"

"Yes."

"Anyone else in your family you can ask?"

"No, not really. It used to wig my mother out. So, we, meaning me, my dad and Grams, just kind of kept it among ourselves."

"Any cousins, uncles? Anyone?"

"Sure I have cousins and uncles, but I've never talked to them about summoning angels or anything else. Like I said, mom freaked whenever Grams talked about Solomon and angels and demons and stuff. So, I figured if mom couldn't handle it, I certainly wasn't going to have the entire family think I'd gone bonkers."

"Fuck."

"Did you just cuss? Are angels allowed to do that?"

He pinned her with a glare that made her want to laugh and grumble at the same time. Arching a brow she waited, curious of the direction this conversation would go.

Jaw set, Larien painted on a game face. "Fine, let's get down to business. You eat. I'll talk."

At her nod he began a history lesson in angelology that made her guts wrap around themselves in knots of hope and utter terror.

CHAPTER SIX

Thankful he'd driven them back to the city rather than doing that poofing thing—her stomach protested just at the thought of it. Bleh.

Jayla put her hand in Larien's as he helped her from the car. She almost sighed in pleasure at the warmth of his palm.

"Would you like to come in for a while?" Oops. She hadn't meant to ask quite like that, all 'come hither'. In fact, she'd never had a guy come inside after just one date. But it wasn't a date, right? Just dinner. So this didn't count.

Perhaps it was that single glass of wine that had her just a bit off balance.

That's my story and I'm sticking to it.

"Of course I'm coming in."

Okay, now she was *completely* off balance.

"Excuse me."

"We're glued at the hip until this mission is done."

"Glued?" She gulped. "Why?"

"There are factions out there that don't want you to find the Seal and you don't stand a chance against them alone. At least not yet." His lips softened from a grim line into an inviting bit of a smile. "Trust me, you want me here."

Boy did she ever. Want him, that is. Here. There. Damn, anywhere. Larien was an exercise is pure sex appeal. Perhaps it was an angel thing?

The grim line was back as he looked around her front yard. She swore she heard a growl when he spotted Ambriel. It was a typical sight for any given night—a lawn full of guardians at strategic points, a couple up on the roof and, if she looked in the backyard, one or two sitting on the fence that looked out to the ocean across the street.

"Why are they here?" he whispered as his hand settled at the base of her spine as if she really needed guiding to her own front door.

"I always call them. Habit."

"Well, it's a habit you can break, at least until we're done finding the Seal. I can protect you just fine," Larien grumbled and kept right on walking. Jayla tightened her jaw, held her breath, and even still a quiet snort got away from her. And earned her a scowl from Larien.

He was nowhere near crowding her personal space, yet the heat of his body warmed her back as she unlocked the door. And with that thought came a different kind of heat. Mentally shaking her head at herself, she pushed the door open and kicked off her shoes at the threshold.

Just before he closed the door, Larien turned and said, "Yo, Ambi, we'd invite you in for dessert, but we didn't bring you any." Then he flipped him the bird. And Ambriel flipped it right back. What the hell was going on with these two?

"You are so bad," she whispered, not bothering to keep the incredulity out of her voice.

"That I am," Larien agreed.

That devilish bit of a grin was back, transforming the lines of his too-serious expression to one that was boyish and fun. She felt that grin to the balls of her feet.

Must have been the wrong thing to do because the man went stock still, and then stepped back in a swift move that put more distance between them than she wanted. And the game face was back.

"So, we'll get started in the morning," he said.

"Okay. Where?"

"I'd like to know more about your family, you in particular. I'm hoping something that hasn't been considered before can lead us in the right direction."

"I have a photo album of my family. A bunch, in fact. And then there's my Grams' stuff. She shipped it to me right before she passed away."

"She didn't live here in San Francisco?"

"Nope. She lived not far from my parents in upstate New York. Anyway, it's all crammed in a storage unit on the other side of town." Wiggling her toes against the cool wood of the foyer floor, Jayla started when Larien helped ease her coat off. Fingers skated across bare skin at the shoulders of the swanky dress he'd fashioned onto her body.

She could really get used to this gentleman stuff. On the other hand...

"So what do you get out of all of this?" Jayla asked.

"Brownie points."

"Snark much?"

"Of course." His coat joined hers in the small closet she hardly ever used. "But honestly, does it matter? When Gabriel accosts you for an errand, regardless of the reward, or lack thereof, you're not really going to say no, are you?"

Her temper flared at the fact that he wasn't truly answering her question. "I'm not really qualified to answer that, Larien. A bit out of my league."

He stepped close and whispered, "Oh, I'm definitely not out of your league, Jayla."

He lifted his finger as if he would gently ease it over her chin, and then snatched his hand back.

"I'm sorry. I should not touch you without your permission. Or with it."

"Aw, you're such a gentleman."

"Gentleman?" He laughed. Actually, it was more of a hoarse sounding snort. It went well with his self-loathing expression. She tilted her head and wondered what caused such a pain-filled look, even if it had only lasted a moment. "Having manners doesn't make me a gentleman, Jayla," he said. "Not even close. Trust me. I'm the farthest thing from a gentleman you'll ever meet."

In a blink he was dressed for a shower. Or rather, *un*dressed.

"Really?" It came out all kinds of breathless. It sounded ridiculous but she just couldn't help it. The man was drop-dead sexy even when he was wrapped in nothing but a towel around

49

those lean hips. She closed her eyes against the image of his broad chest and all that smooth-looking skin stretched across it. Then there were the muscles of his stomach that screamed for her fingers to trace the map of ridges and dips. When she raised her lids again the view was even better as he leaned in close.

"Yes. Really." Eyes dark, broody with a hint of mischief. His scent rose from his skin like steam off the water of a hot spring in the dead of winter. So close, yet not quite close enough. Was he going to kiss her? She didn't typically kiss on the first date. Oh, wait. She'd already covered that ground. Not a date.

"And Jayla?"

"Huh?" It came out nothing more than a wisp of sound.

Just a hair closer and his breath fanned her cheek. And along came the same little tummy wiggle that had kicked up earlier in the evening, followed by a honeyed warmth at her core.

"I like it."

"Like what?" she breathed.

"Your scent. It smells even sweeter than what you had for dessert."

"Oh." It was all she could manage to piece together in her fog-filled brain.

With that, the man put his hands on her shoulders, backed her into her room and said, "Goodnight, Jayla. If you want to shower, just give me five." The next thing she knew, the door closed and she was in her room. Alone.

"Bastard."

A soft mirth-filled chuckle echoed quietly down the hallway so faint she'd almost missed it.

"I hope you get blue balls," she muttered to herself.

"I heard that." His voice was loud and clear as the laughter continued to move down the hall and off to the left toward the bathroom.

"Bastard." Funny how the words formed on a grin that stayed plastered in place as she undressed and headed for bed.

* * * * *

The morning sun brought with it the most ridiculous annoyance possible.

Jayla had bounced out of the house and down to the curb where he waited next to the car.

He opened her car door and then stomped around to his side and climbed in.

"Good morning!"

His response was an audible snarl.

"Oh stop grumbling already." It was the sunniest demand Larien had ever received and that only rubbed at him more.

They were going to look for clues in what was probably a dusty, dank storage compartment, not stepping out on the town for a, for a…hell he couldn't even think of where Jayla would go dressed like this.

She wore a pair of bright yellow jeans with a matching fine-gauged sweater that clung to her curves like sunshine poured over some decadent pastry. A pair of high-heeled sandals wrapped around her feet in the same eye-popping shade. Thick hair was pulled up into a cute, curly, poufy thing on top of her head and tied with a yellow ribbon. She smiled at him from behind a pair of Hello Kitty yellow and white blinged-out sunglasses.

Hello Kitty shades? *Yellow* Hello Kitty shades? Really? That old song from the 80's popped into his head.

I'm walking on sunshine. Weh-heh-helll. I'm walking on sunshine. And don't it feel good?

No, not particularly.

Little Miss Sunshine looked so decadent, his cock was as hard as the tire iron in the trunk. It was uncomfortable as hell.

Hard to take my mind off of a sexy woman if my damn cock stays hard from scenting her every-damn-where.

And now, with her dressed like a birthday present ready to be unwrapped, he had a visual that would take some work to clear away. Grrrr.

The woman was going to get them killed. He was so distracted by the luscious picture she painted in that curve hugging outfit of hers that he was sure someone, hell anyone, could sneak up on them and he'd have his heart cut out while he drooled over Jayla. Not that cutting out his heart would do him in, but it would hurt just the same.

While he might be hard as hell to kill, Jayla was mortal, vulnerable. She certainly wasn't trained for this kind of danger, and Larien couldn't allow this kind of distraction. He needed a serious head start to keep all their asses out of the sling.

Pull your head out and get it back in the game.

"What the hell are you scowling at me for?"

The doors were closed and the windows up. And it was too small in this fucking car.

"Diaphaneity will get us there faster."

"Hell no. That poof thing makes me wanna barf." She picked idly at a piece of nubby yarn on her brilliant sweater.

"You get used to it after awhile."

"I don't want to get used to it, Larien," she said sweetly and smiled so large she surely showed all her teeth. "Let's just drive okay?"

He put up a fight, really, he did. But damn if she didn't get her way and Larien still had no idea how. So here he was, pulling away from the curb, driving. He fucking hated driving—a new development since he'd met Jayla. Driving meant he was in close quarters with her, close enough to touch. Close enough to catch her clean, intoxicating scent, hear her heartbeat, the soft sough of breath as it moved in and out of her lungs. Close enough to know when she was aroused. Like now.

He could dial down most of his senses so sounds weren't quite so loud. But there was no way he could shut off his breathing or close himself off from inhaling her scent, catching the warmth of it. And it wasn't because he needed to breathe. It was because he needed to have this connection to her, no matter how small.

But he couldn't have her. He knew that. When this was finished, he would get what he needed and go on his way. Jayla would become a mere memory, like all the others. He was a man who loved women. He'd never regretted the loves of his life, knew that moving on was simply the way of things. Life. Death. Rebirth. If he had to live life over again, he wouldn't have changed a thing.

The result? He was as jaded as the day was long. Hadn't had or wanted a woman for the long or short term in God knew how long. Then along comes Miss Walking On Sunshine and all his hidden buttons started pushing all by themselves.

You are supposed to be good. You are supposed to behave. Keep your hands off the human.

Why, again? Surely there was a reason?

Jayla crossed her legs and adjusted the seat so she reclined just a bit, head tilted to the uncharacteristically clear blue sky visible through the sun roof.

"Unusual to have such lovely weather in February."

Larien didn't respond.

He was trying to keep from looking her direction, keeping his eyes away from the hands crossed lazily beneath her breasts. Thirty-six B-cups, if he wasn't mistaken.

Shit.

"What's wrong with you? You're all snappy and growly. You on your period?" she asked with a totally straight face.

Irreverent woman. He rolled his eyes, bit his tongue to keep from laughing and took a deep breath. Then he wanted to kick himself when the faint scent of a bit of female sex settled more deeply into his lungs.

The drive seemed an eternity with the whirlwind that was Jayla sitting beside him. The woman was an endless store of energy as she blasted the radio and bopped around in her seat to anime tunes, made phone calls to have the staff cover her duties at her gym, promised the editor at the newspaper that she'd get her Op-ed piece done by the end of the week, then invited a friend over for dinner, which he'd thoroughly planned to skip until he'd caught the voice on the other end of that last call.

Now he *had* to be there if his plan was going to play out the way he intended.

"Right here," she said, pointing to a cream brick two story off to the right. A quick glance down to the piece of paper she'd jotted the directions on earlier. "This is definitely the place."

As they parked Jayla's spine seemed to grow more rigid and this was the quietest she'd been all morning. Letting his vision slip to *othersight* he watched her aura flicker and fade from a vibrant yellowy-pink of whimsical joy until there was practically no color at all. "What is it? What's wrong?"

"Nothing," she said, yet her gaze was glued to the glass double-doors of the building's entrance. That single word was full of so much sadness and pain. Deep, raw. It radiated from a soul that had been a shining beacon only moments ago. As the sparkle that had surrounded her all morning dimmed, Larien wanted nothing more than to bring it back. But that wasn't what he was here for.

"Jayla?" She didn't respond and Larien didn't push. He would not yet tell her he felt her grief, *saw* her vibration, because in truth, he shouldn't be able to. Shouldn't feel compelled to care for her.

As was his custom, Larien got out, walked around the other side of the vehicle and opened Jayla's door. Sun shone through a clear blue sky to reflect off of the modern building. Jayla got out and looked up. As bright as the day was, she seemed to suck in the light even as her skin paled. Gaze moved from the white stucco walls to the intermittent painted brick columns to the large one-way glass windows.

Whatever secrets lay behind the doors of this place managed to shake this human; a woman who wouldn't hesitate to stand toe to toe with beings powerful enough to destroy her with a simple thought. Yet here she was, taken aback and uncertain. Larien didn't like it at all.

Once inside the storage building, he was glad to see it was well lit and ventilated. Larien remained quiet as they strode into the large lobby. Jayla dug into her pants pocket, pulled out a small key and handed it to the bubbly green-haired attendant at the front desk who examined it quickly, looked something up on the computer and handed it right back.

"Okay," the girl said with a bit of a Valley accent. "You, like, need to go up to, like, the third floor. Then you're gonna, you know, turn left and go to, like the fourth unit down the hall. The number will totally, like, be on the door. Okaay?"

With a smile that barely curved her lips, Jayla nodded, gave a quiet "Thank you," and headed for the stairs. Foregoing the elevator they padded silently up to the third floor to stand in front of a wide roll-up steel silver door. It reminded him more of a bank vault than a place where an old woman would stash her belongings.

Jayla remained quiet and still.

Ignoring the tight squeeze in his chest at Jayla's discomfort, Larien pulled annoyance over himself like a cloak and peppered her with questions, not knowing what else to do when she was like this. Maybe she'd snap out of it.

"What's in here?"

She shook her head, face devoid of all expression as she stood stock still. After a moment of thick quiet she stepped forward, key in hand.

After her second try at the deadbolt Larien gently pried the key from trembling fingers and she finally said, "I haven't dug through any of this stuff. Grams sent it here and paid up on the storage fees right before she died. I received a letter from the executor of her estate along with the only key. I came right away—"

The words were barely a whisper with an undertone of gray contemplation. A deep breathe just as her aura flickered. A bit of color returned to her cheeks and he knew she bolstered herself, recovered the woman she truly was inside.

"—but it looked like a bunch of big boxes of crap to me. I just couldn't deal with it at the time. So...I didn't."

Once unlocked, they reached down together and pulled. The heavy door rolled up smoothly on well-oiled rails.

Larien cocked his head and said, "Yes, it does indeed look like a big bunch of crap." Jayla's trembling lips gave way to a smile, then a chuckle. The sound, though short lived, lightened her entire countenance, began erasing some of the sorrow she'd walked into the space carrying.

"Look for the lights. It's a bit dim."

Larien agreed...except for the faint glow around some of the boxes. They were alive with their own aura, obviously spells and protections had been spoken over them. In fact, if he hadn't been here with Jayla, he was sure he would have been knocked on his ass trying to get in here.

A quiet click and the space filled with bright florescence.

"Is it normal to have a table and chairs in the middle of a storage room?" Jayla asked.

"No idea. Believe it or not, I've never been in a storage unit, let alone one like this."

"Oh come on, you're an old assed angel. Surely you've done everything by now."

Oh yes, she was definitely beginning to feel more like herself.

The beginnings of a full-out smile tugged at his lips but he teased her back instead with a stern wag of his finger. "I will let the 'old' remark pass, Jayla."

Moving more fully into the large room she said, "It feels more like a living room than anything else. I half expect to see floor rugs and reading lamps. I didn't pay it much attention when I came here before. I was upset that Grams had passed, that I hadn't been there to say goodbye. I didn't really want to hang out here looking through her things. Figured I'd get around to it sooner or later."

"Let's get down to it, shall we?"

With a huff she closed the door behind them and joined him in exploring. Jayla's grandmother had obviously taken great care in giving instructions for her possessions. The room looked more like an ancient temple from a mix of cultures than a twenty-first century building. On one wall hung two thick parochet veils, side by side, as if they led to a doorway to the beyond. The purple silken looking drapes, embroidered with gold thread in the shape of flames called to Larien, as if he'd seen them somewhere before gracing a seat of power. Judging by the antiquities arranged around and about the place, it was quite possible. A gilded altar that appeared Persian in nature sat regally on a low pillar in front of the veils. Replicas of Roman stone columns stood watch in each of the four corners while artifacts of various origins were piled in box after box after box, neatly arranged around the space.

The table and chairs were arranged on a warm brown geometric floor rug in the very center of the room, of good quality but rather ordinary when compared to their surroundings.

Jayla walked across the room, grabbed a dusty but sturdy-looking box and hefted it into her arms.

It glowed a faint yellow beneath her fingers—clear, metallic, shiny and bright. It was the color of power being activated, awakened.

"What made you pick that one?" Larien wondered aloud.

She looked down at the box, shrugged and moved to open it. Impressive. Jayla obviously couldn't see the energy humming around the item in her hands, yet it was clear she'd been drawn to something of importance.

Perhaps she had gifts that neither of them knew of? There was no room for surprises in this game yet....

"Note to self—kick Gabriel's ass for giving me even less details on Jayla than I first believed. Bastard."

He had to figure this out before he said anything about this connection that seemed to hum between them. A connection that made him want to run to her one moment and flee the next.

Though the box was obviously heavy, she didn't ask for any

help. And before he knew it, the chivalrous gentleman he'd denied to everyone he'd ever known poked his head up and had him moving before he could even think to resist.

Grabbing the box from her hands he leaned forward and dropped a quick peck of a kiss on her forehead. "I've got it."

"I can carry my own."

"I know you can carry it, but I like being nice. Well, to you, anyway."

Jayla eyed him sideways. "You are just so weird. One minute you're grumbling like I kicked you in the junk, then you're being all sweet. Good thing you're so nice to look at or I'd ask Gabriel for a replacement."

He actually threw his head back and laughed. The woman was… He'd have to think about it, but whatever it was, he liked it.

After setting her box down, Larien grabbed a few more from around the room that seemed to have stronger protections around them. He placed them carefully on the table, tucked in and got started.

One thing was evident, Jayla's family was thorough. Her grandmother had not only passed down her own knowledge of their heritage and calling, but that of every person who'd come before her. This stuff was centuries old. How had they kept it hidden? And over the years whoever received the knowledge kept the information in its original form – scrolls, books, parchments—as well as transcribed onto the medium of their day.

That meant hours digging through endless papers, books, old pictographs, stenographs, slide projector medium of brown crinkled film, and early audio reels of men and women reading bits and pieces about the Seal in various languages. Then there were the microfiche, eight-track and cassettes tapes. Jayla's grandmother was a bit more up to speed. She'd left her contribution on a stack of CDs and a memory stick.

"Wait, what's that?" Larien held his hand out for the rolled-up aged papers Jayla was about to toss aside.

"Looks like a regular old Torah scroll, you know, like what they'd use in a bat-mitzvah or something. Not sure though. I never did master the language."

"Well, that's obvious. It's not a Torah and it's not written in Hebrew."

Careful not to tear it, Larien unrolled the scroll and felt his stomach drop into his shoes. He'd thought never to lay eyes on anything like this again. Ever. He couldn't decide whether to be humbled, shocked, or what.

"Definitely not a Torah," he whispered, then began to read.

The words rolled, musical and magical, off his tongue. Jayla's eyes widened with each word until her aura practically sizzled a bold indigo blue, the color of intuition, sensitivity and deep feeling, overlaid with yellow as bright as her clothes which meant the woman was full of inner joy, generous at heart and wasn't attached to, well, anything. She was content, right down to her vital energy. What a rare but pleasing quality to see surrounding a human.

Hazel-honey eyes sparkled as her smile made the corners crinkle. The shell he'd cemented around himself cracked just a bit.

"Wow," she whispered.

His thoughts exactly—both the words he'd just read and the beautiful, glowing woman in front of him.

"That was like nothing I've ever heard. I didn't understand a word yet I-I felt it down to my toes. What language is it?" she asked.

"It's the celestial language. The creative tongue of the Source themselves." Something he hadn't seen or spoken since his Fall.

"Uh huh, and you were cussing in it earlier."

One side of his mouth quirked up and he simply shook his head. The woman sure made it hard to remain a broody badass. "Not quite this language, but my native tongue is something close, yes."

He unrolled the scroll a bit more. A piece of paper that seemed much newer than the rest fell out of it and was imprinted with the outline of a ring. Larien grabbed up the newer bits and began to read.

"What?" Jayla asked.

"What, what?"

"You're grumbling again."

"Oh. Sorry. It's a note from your great-grandmother to your grandmother. I'm sure it is information you already know."

"Doubt it." The stiff blanket of sadness she'd shucked off earlier returned. He'd remember to ask her about it later, once they returned home.

Home. It had a nice ring to it, even if it was only for a moment in time. A drop in the bucket of his life. It had been a very long while since he'd chosen to call a place home, especially a place with a female in it. If he were to have a woman, the one sitting in front of him would be the perfect partner.

Sigh.

But that wasn't in the cards. Not for him. Not anymore.

Jayla's gaze remained focused on her fingernails. The man in him wanted to fix it for her, to wipe the frown away and replace it with the smile she'd been wearing earlier as she sang anime tunes at the top of her lungs. But he was here to find a relic, not find a female. And he would not do anything to make Jayla believe he was after what was in her pants simply to get her help in finding the Seal. This woman could never be a part-time lover. No, if she were to become his, he'd want all of her, all the time. And since he didn't do anything by half measure, he would leave her be.

His heart squeezed tight in his chest at the sadness that infused her aura. Just as he reached out to her—and when had his hand decided to do something without direction from his brain?—a metallic *chink* filled the suddenly too quiet room. His gaze whipped up to find the source of the sound.

There on the surface of the sturdy table laid a small badly tarnished, very old-looking ring. It had fallen out of the papers he held in his hands.

And just like that Larien felt Jayla's pain dissipate to be replaced by pure curiosity. He wasn't sure what he was happier about—Jayla being distracted out of her grief or finding yet another clue.

"Yes!" Jayla squealed.

Larien knew better. "Don't get excited. There's no way finding the Seal of Solomon is going to be as easy as it dropping out of a scroll that was written in the celestial language. Especially since this scroll simply tells the legend of the Seal and who was entrusted with it, which we already know—Solomon."

Jayla grabbed for the grayish piece of silver and held it above her head.

"Frodo, you must destroy it on the slopes of Mt. Doom! Mwahahahaaaa!"

He winced at the exaggerated and terribly hokey accent that was supposed to be old Gandalf. Yes, even *he'd* seen Lord of the Rings.

"Uh, no. Just a tarnished old ring, Jay. Sorry."

"You don't sound sorry," she snapped but her words held no heat. The soft look in her eyes made it clear she poked fun at him. She'd swung from sad to sassy so fast he was surprised her head hadn't started spinning. The thought made him smile inside.

"All of this will take some time to wade through. We'll pack up the car. Much more comfortable looking through these things while sitting on your couch instead of this hard-assed chair."

"Not to mention I have food, greedy bastard." She poked at his tummy. Larien went still, cocked his head and wondered. He wasn't sure anyone had ever done that before. And he was surprisingly comfortable with it.

"Well, I wasn't going to say anything, but now that you mention it, yes, you do have food. We'll get a cart or something and load it up. It should be safe enough.

"What do you mean, it should be safe enough?"

"Nothing."

The energy from the cache would certainly draw attention to them. There might be protections over the items while they were in this room, but until they were safe behind Jayla's doors they were vulnerable. Time to move.

CHAPTER SEVEN

"You drive."

"What? Me?"

"Yes," Larien said. "You can drive, can't you?"

"Are you being a smart ass?"

"No. Not at all." His attention was riveted on the load he was stuffing into the trunk and back seat. He seemed so distracted, Jayla wondered if he was aware of what he was saying at all. "Besides, it's not like you have to have a car in this city," he went on as he shoved a heavy wooden crate inside with such force the entire car rocked back and forth. Thank God for emergency brakes. "You can get anywhere." Shove. "At any time." Kick. "I didn't want to assume you could drive, so put your back down, woman."

"Put my back down?"

"Jayla, are you trying to start a fight?"

He would choose now to slam the trunk closed and pin her with a deadpan stare. You know, like he knew the answer already or something.

"Me? I am not!" She bit back a growl because that was exactly what she'd been doing.

"Good. Then *you* drive." And without another word or even a glance he grabbed a stack of books from the abundance of stuff and settled into the front passenger seat.

Buckled up and ready to go, Jayla glanced to her right to check her blind spot. It didn't matter that they were in a parking lot, she had to check anyway. Several times. Looking his way. She'd never taken him for the scholarly type, but oh there was nothing like a goose pimple-inducing badass nerd.

So this is his focused face, eh?

Quick as lightening, her thoughts flashed to that deep well of sexual frustration she was determined to pretend wasn't there. And her danged mind decided to walk through a number of yummy scenarios.

What was it like to be the sole focus of a man like this? Whether they were in conversation or in bed, certainly it would be just this side of overwhelming.

In conversation, would he watch her mouth as she spoke as if anticipating the sound and flavor of the next syllable? Would he listen intently, then jump in and give her a healthy challenge? In bed, would he dedicate his full attention to where his fingers touched her skin? Or would he be more intent on where his tongue tasted and teased? Or was he a talented multi-tasker who could do all of the above?

And when he'd kissed her on her forehead with that combination of soft lips and blade sharp stance? Just *gah!*

The breath thickened in her lungs. The thermostat read forty-five degrees outside. *Still too hot in here. Too hot.*

She flipped on the air system and went still as the light scent of Larien's earthy cologne blasted through the car. Oh my. She squeezed her thighs together.

Don't you dare close your eyes and moan. Stop basking in his sexiness already.

"Stop it, Jayla."

Braking at the parking lot exit, she looked his way.

"Stop what?" she challenged. It didn't matter she'd been telling herself the same thing.

"You are letting your imagination wander into territory that you really don't want me to follow you into." She snatched her shades off her face and gave him the stink eye. His gaze was plastered on a gray-looking page of a big leather bound book. He was definitely reading if the tracking of his eyes was any indication. So how…?

"I smell you, is how. And you smell really, really good."

Shit.

She squeezed her legs together tighter then decided, screw it. If she could suffer, then so could he. She spread her legs like a tomboy sitting in the bleachers at a football game. Looking over her shoulder, Jayla eased her Hello Kitty shades back onto her face, stomped on the gas and merged Larien's oversized ride into the afternoon's typically ridiculous traffic and headed for the freeway on-ramp.

At the last minute, she maneuvered to the opposite lane.

"On second thought, I think I'll take the street rather than the freeway." The ride would take three times as long.

Slowly, so very slowly, he raised his gaze from the book in his lap and slid it over to her. "Woman, you are a menace. Are you sure you are not a Fallen demon?"

She didn't answer...but she did catch his smile out of her periphery.

* * * * *

Larien absolutely refused to adjust his cock in his pants, though the woman had deliberately filled the cab of the car with her mouthwatering scent as she took the long way home. Oh she was aroused and annoyed, which just made her more aroused. God, it was the most intoxicating scent ever. And he refused to give a clue how much he wanted to slip his hand past the console, across her jean-clad thigh to the center of heat that sizzled at him from the other seat. Grrrr.

Forcing himself not to squirm, Larien concentrated on the words of the book in his hands.

"I had a hunch angels might be involved. I believe I was right."

"What do angels have to do with this?" she asked distractedly.

"Did you know that your last name is derived from the word 'protector'?"

Ah. There was the "who-gives-a-shit" face she'd no doubt spent years perfecting.

"Okaay?" he said. "Never mind then. How much do you know about the Watchers?"

She cocked her head sideways and appeared to drop deep in thought while merging across lanes. Her forehead was all scrunched up as if she tried to recall something that wouldn't cooperate. Finally she spoke.

"Not much. Just that they were angels that were kicked out of the heavens."

"Not really. Watchers, or Nophelim, are Fallen angels. But they were part of the second fall."

"Second fall? There was more than one? And I thought Nephilim were the children of Fallen and humans?"

"Nope. It's a mistranslation. Nophelim are of the second Fall and the word truly means 'fallen'. Nephilim, however, means 'cast out ones'. Those are the angels of the first Fall. And for the record, angels are no one's offspring. Period."

Jayla's mouth hung open. Literally.

"Your grandmother left you all this information but didn't explain any of it to you?"

"I told you that my mom used to get upset when Grams spoke of this kind of stuff. It freaked her out. Scared her. It wasn't Grams' fault. She told me what she could, you know? She tried but mom…well. Never mind."

A flash of pain was quickly snuffed out by her will alone. Instead of pushing, he said, "The Watchers were Nophelim who fell because of their own lust. They were more concerned with chasing ass than they were with Watching over our human charges."

"*Our* human charges?"

Larien ignored the question and said, "Long before that time, those angels who refused to bow before the image and likeness of the creative Source were kicked out of the heavenlies. Forcibly. *That* was the first Fall."

"Lucifer and his guys? Wait, I don't get it."

Larien dropped the book in his hands, and then grabbed another one from the pile at his feet. It hurt to bend over. His cock was still hard as a Roman brick and that woman sat there with her shapely legs in the most unladylike position.

He liked unladylike positions.

Wait. That wasn't right. Okay, back to work.

"Listen to this. A conversation between the former Son of the Morning and Adam. It explains why those of the first Fall have no love of humans. It's from the Book of Adam. "

"There's no such book," she declared resolutely.

"You mean like there's no Seal?"

"Touché. Read it."

Larien braced himself and began to speak. God, he remembered this as if it were yesterday. Could almost hear Luc's voice as he said…

The very day when you were created, I fell from before the face of the Creator. Because He breathed a spirit onto your face, you had the image and likeness of the divinity. And then Michael came and he presented you and made you bend down before the Creator. And the Creator told Michael, "I have created Adam according to my image and my divinity." Then Michael summoned all the troops of angels and told them, "Bow down before the likeness and the image of the divinity." And then, when Michael summoned them and all had bowed down to you, he summoned me also. And I told him, "I shall not bow down to him who is younger than me, indeed, I am master prior to him and it is proper for him to bow down to me." The six classes of other angels heard that and my speech pleased them and they did not bow down to you. Then God became angry with us and commanded us, them and me, to be cast down from our dwellings to the earth. As for you, he commanded you to dwell in paradise.

"Oooh, well I can see how that would piss him off. So Lucifer blames Adam, and by extension, all of mankind for his Fall. Not good."

"Yes. Those are the true Nephilim. And I can guarantee they aren't going to be keen on you finding the Seal."

"I don't have anything against any Fallen, good, bad or ugly. Why would they care if I find the damn Seal? I want to keep the demons from getting it. I'm not concerned about angels. Some of my best friends are angels, right?"

"The Seal is a lot more powerful than you can imagine. You're thinking like a human, Jayla."

"Well, duh."

"I mean free will is something that has always been yours. Angels weren't created to exercise free will. They were created to obey and to serve. They do it gladly. Protect their charges with all their hearts. However, the ones who decided they'd rather have free will down here than obey up there won't want anyone, particularly someone like you with your natural abilities, to have the Seal."

"But why? I still don't understand."

"Angels come when you call because that's their job. However—"

"So what. That still doesn't explain why the not-so-nice angels care if I have the Seal or not."

Larien pulled out more sheaves of ancient looking papers from her Grandma's stash.

"Part of the Book of Solomon."

"There's no such thing as—"

"Haven't we been there already, sweetheart?"

Jayla was annoyed but she didn't miss the slip of endearment that sent a little shock into her toes. She definitely liked the way it sounded on his tongue.

"Go ahead," she sighed dramatically, though there was a seriously big grin on her face that she didn't bother to try and hide as Larien started to read.

Grace was given to me from the Lord by Michael his Archangel—a little ring having a seal consisting of an engraved stone. Michael said, 'Take this gift. With it you shall lock up all demons of the earth, male and female, and with their help build up your lands.

"That says demons, not angels," Jayla said.

"There's more. The account says that Solomon asked a demon who she was. She claimed to be the offspring of the Archangel Uriel. The demon didn't want to cooperate with what Solomon asked her to do."

"So?"

"So Solomon called Uriel to come and *make* the demon obey."

"Are you serious?"

"Get it now? They don't want you to find it because you'll be able to control them, Jay. Plain and simple. If you call them, they must come, whether they want to or not."

"Just like the demons that Solomon enslaved to build the temple? Angels and demons? Fallen or not?"

"Yes."

"Holy shit."

After a silence that seemed to suck the air out of the car, Jayla found her voice again.

"Where do you fit into all of this, Larien? What are you?"

The silence reminded her of Saturday morning cartoons where someone asked a dumb question and the sound of crickets and much-too-loud quiet was the response. *Chirp, chirp, chirp.*

"You may as well spill. I know you're a supernatural being. Figured that out the night you walked past my guardians, popped into my bedroom and showed me your hall pass, so to speak."

"I'm Fallen."

"Really? You don't look like a Fallen."

"Well, what does one look like, Jay?"

"I don't know. Mean or evil, maybe?" Larien was neither of those things. Then the light bulb went on in her head. "You're one that fell because of a woman rather than kicked out for pride."

She was caught totally off guard at the shame and pain that froze and shattered the warm brown of his eyes for barely a moment. Her big, bad supernatural was embarrassed.

And that made him vulnerable, which he couldn't possibly appreciate.

She smiled. Couldn't help it, the man was so damn sexy, even when pissed off.

The second he realized where her thoughts had gone, his expression hardened. He snarled at her. Oh. Fangs. She hadn't noticed those before.

With a bright blue flash he was gone, leaving nothing behind but a flurry of papers where his body had been and the outline of his body against the inside of her eyelids.

And even *that* was hot.

* * * * *

"You should know that Jabon is hunting the human woman you've set on the trail of Solomon's Seal," Abaddon said. He uttered not another word to his commander as he touched the story-high bronze gates that would take them out of the sprawling city. The gates swung open on silent hinges secured with bolts made of fire.

"You're ratting out Jabon, Abaddon? I thought you and that traitor were thick as thieves."

Disgust rolled off Gabriel in sludge-like waves. Abaddon understood completely. He had no love for Jabon either. There were various classes of Fallen, some demon, some daemon. Abaddon, however, was neither. Abaddon was eudaemon, ascended and in the service of the Host since the beginning of his days. Yet for some reason Jabon believed that simply because Abaddon had been created to oversee the most vile and dangerous of all the realms that he was as evil as those he policed, or worse, a traitor like Jabon himself.

"Not as thick as many think. Jabon is after the Seal of Solomon and the idiot has pulled Luc into the search. It was bad enough we had to take part in enforcing the first Fall because of Luc, but then Jabon decides to be responsible for the second Fall. Between the two of them, we lost a lot of our kin, including my cousin. One day, those two need to get what's coming to them. And I'd love to be the one to give it to them."

And just like that, he was back at that terrible sad day. The events unfolded in his mind like a bad movie. Abaddon recalled watching Luc, an Archangel that he'd loved like a brother, get hit so hard that part of his face had caved in. Remembered watching the feathers of family and friends burned away, majestic wings broken and hacked off. All because of pride, all because Luc chose to see himself above his purpose, above what he was created for. And then he convinced others to rally to his losing cause. Later the awareness of loss had come when the Watchers separated themselves by choosing to walk away from their first home. God, it had caused a flash of emotion so painful it was almost physical.

Amazing how he could feel sorry for someone, miss them, and still want to kick their ass for choosing something as vile and unspeakable as rebellion.

Through those events he'd learned there was no such thing as right and wrong, black and white. On the contrary, there were plenty of levels of wrong with just as many shades of gray, and both Jabon and Luc had managed to navigate themselves through them all while dragging their kin along.

But Luc was smart enough not to come anywhere near Abaddon.

Jabon? Not so much.

Abaddon and Gabriel reached Achrom Forest, a seemingly endless grove that separated this part of She'ol's main city of Aegypto from the borders of the other zones. The blood-red rays of the rising sun reflected off of the white-leaves and trunks of each tree until the entire stand looked aflame from the bases to the highest branches. On the other side of the grove they stopped in the Ebon Plains and its acres of deepest-black grass, lush, soft and perfectly bladed as any on the earth realm.

This was Abaddon's domain, and as such he had residences in all three zones of She'ol—here in Aegypto, in Gehenna's Hall of Tortured Souls to the east and the Ravus, or Gray Court, to the north.

The Ravus was the main hang out of Luc and some of the more twisted Fallen. Needless to say, Abaddon ventured there as little as possible except to make sure the locals were behaving as much as demons, minions and the dead could behave. The more space he kept between himself, Luc, Jabon and the rest of their ilk, the better.

"You really should just let me end Jabon, Gabriel. Seriously."

The commander seemed to ignore him, but Abaddon knew better. Gabriel hadn't missed a single word, including the depth of sadness he still carried for his brethren along with the rage.

With a thought, four practice targets appeared perfectly placed down the meadow just as the clouds started rolling in.

"Interesting. The cause of the first Fall teaming up with the instigator of the second Fall. Who'da thought?" The words were delivered deadpan as Gabriel sighted the first target.

"I don't think it's interesting," Abaddon grouched. "I think it's stupid. And I also think I'm tired of Jabon waltzing his skinny ass in and out of Aegypto like he owns the place."

"You could always revoke his permission into this zone, Abaddon. It's not like you aren't in charge of the place."

Abaddon answered with a chilling smile. "If he weren't such a good, though unwitting, informant, I would. In fact, if I weren't so keen on not Falling myself, I'd break the law and toss his ass through the Abyss gate. You really should give me the order to toss him through the Abyss gate, Gabe."

"Yes, I could, but I think I will leave Jabon's demise to Larien."

Understanding dawned, but Abaddon didn't trust it. There was no way in hell he was going to assume what Gabriel meant by suggesting that one Fallen would end another. Even after the Host had decimated Luc and his followers, none of the judged had been *un*made. Beaten all to hell? Yes. Destroyed? Not so much.

There was no other being in heaven or earth that played games as strategically or diabolically as Archangels. Especially the warring ones. It would be totally Gabriel's style to have Abaddon think one thing while orchestrating another.

"It feels like someone is walking around the mortal realm with a piece of me, using the Abyss gate from up there. I feel it every time he, she or it calls on the power that has always been uniquely mine. So is it Larien? Is that why you brought him up, Gabe?"

Instead of answering, The Messenger raised his bow with preternatural speed and let fly. The entire motion was barely a blur but the target was hit with a muted *thunk*, dead center at two hundred paces. No surprise there.

Abaddon lifted his own weapon, a heavy pistol that sat comfortably in his hand, and aimed at the same target as Gabriel. Bull's-eye.

After winning the best fifteen out of twenty Gabriel finally said, "Do not worry. It is under control. As soon as the mission is done, Larien loses his ability to banish any celestial through the Abyss gate."

"So Larien's ability is temporary? Good to know." Abaddon cleaned and repacked his weapon. "But there is another that has been given my gift. Is his temporary, too?"

Gabriel flashed an amused grin, turned and picked up his bow kit off the ground. Abaddon grimaced at the rush of energy that spiced the air, stinging his skin and nose like raw pepper. It felt different on this realm when the creative Source was tapped.

The surge of power in the midst of silence made it clear that Gabe was about to vanish without answering the question. Pompous sneaky bastard.

"Who is it, Gabe?" Abaddon pressed.

With nothing more than a wink over his shoulder, Gabriel's eyes lit neon blue as he vanished right out of She'ol.

CHAPTER EIGHT

After almost running over a still-brooding Larien in her driveway, they'd unloaded the stash from her Gram's storage unit in silence. He'd worn his blank-as-a-piece-of-sheetrock face the whole time they ferried boxes into the house. She'd dropped the last bit on the living room floor and then turned on him.

"Your brooding is getting on my nerves. I'm sorry if I hurt your feelings by pointing out the obvious earlier, but I refuse to be responsible for your emotions, dude."

He'd pinned her with a glare and gave her a mirthless, tightlipped grin. "I don't expect such a thing from you, human."

"Oh, so I'm human now rather than Jayla?" Her fists had found her hips but surprisingly she'd been intrigued rather than pissed off. "And no fangs this time?"

"No. I can conceal them if I wish," he'd ground out. "And don't change the subject."

"So do all Fallen have fangs?" she'd asked, ignoring his command to stay on task.

"All celestials have them, Fallen or not. It is normal for us, not something associated with, as you say, bad guys. That is a human television thing."

"Really? You can tell me all about it while we drive."

He'd looked at her sideways then. "Drive where? I have work to do."

"So do I," she'd replied as she'd changed her shoes and

grabbed her gear bag from the front door. "And Seal or no Seal, I have responsibilities. Since we, as you said, are glued at the hip then you can spend the day lugging me around."

Other than a bit of growling he'd maintained his air of coolness almost to the point of being aloof until he'd decided to put his protective hat on. In no time flat she'd wanted to ditch him somewhere. It was bad enough he'd blown into her life like a testosterone hurricane, but then he'd drill-sergeanted his way around her gym to the point that the trainers would surely run the other way the next time they saw him escorting her into the building.

Then he'd tagged along to the newspaper and scared the shit out of all the staff. Posing as her cameraman, he waved a Nikon around while looking every inch the badass he was. No one could get to her without him first doing his angel x-ray thing, checking their auras and such. He'd been a veritable nightmare. Too bad he couldn't be killed, otherwise she would have done it herself at least thrice over by now.

By the time they returned home and made dinner she was more than ready to throttle him, protective hunk of hotness or not.

The doorbell rang and before Larien could react, Jayla ran to the front door and snatched it open.

"I haven't been able to reach you since this morning. How do you always know what time to show up for dinner?"

With a grin as genuinely bright as the mid-day sun, Talan shed his coat as he walked through the door. Toeing off his shoes, he tossed the jacket to Jayla, who snatched it out of the air and hung it up in the closet.

"I haven't missed the food yet, have I?" Talan asked.

She so loved his Irish lilt, even with the hint of New York upbringing that laced his words. Talan was ginger to the bone—red mop of wavy hair, neat red beard and mustache and eyes as green as a meadow in springtime. Just his presence made her smile. An image of Talan in the middle of a Lucky Charms commercial had her biting back a giggle.

"And don't think I don't know what you're thinking. I'm much better looking than any leprechaun. Mmm, what's that smell?"

"I'm not answering any questions until you bring your greedy self over here and give me a hug."

"Yes, ma'am."

After the last couple of days of having a bulldozer named Larien to contend with, it was nice to have a bit of familiar calm, non-pushy goings-on, such as dinner in her own house, along with comforting hugs from Talan.

"Why is it you always smell like a science experiment, though thankfully not an unpleasant one?" she asked.

It warmed Jayla to know that her friend enjoyed spending time with her and eating her food as much as she enjoyed cooking it for him. They cared genuinely for each other, and that would make it easier to say what she needed to. She hoped their long years of friendship would keep him from thinking she was bonkers.

The only thing missing from this comfortably common exchange was Chel, who wasn't due back in town until tomorrow night.

Talan dipped his finger in the strawberry cream cheese icing she'd just whipped and then laid a doozy on her.

"Guess what happened to me?"

"You know I'm not going to guess, so spill it already."

"I got jumped in my apartment by a couple of total goons."

Alarm sent her gut into a wild tumble as the breath caught in her chest. The pan of scratch rolls dropped from nerveless fingers back onto the oven rack with a loud clang. "Oh my god, are you hurt? What the hell happened?"

"Jay, I'm fine. Not a single scratch on me."

Her skin seemed to wriggle around on the bone from the rush of adrenaline and sheer panic at the thought of anything happening to her oldest, dearest friend. A friend who was special like her…though he believed she was none the wiser. But special could still be killed, damn it. She gritted her teeth and tried to keep from tearing his head off for something that wasn't his fault.

Hands braced on the counter, Jayla took in a few calming breaths.

"I didn't mean to scare the hell out of you." Talan's eyes widened then dimmed with sadness. He hadn't meant to alarm her. He was simply too sweet to pull such a stunt. But dread remained in her periphery like a looming specter hiding around a corner waiting for her to walk by. Determined to enjoy his company, Jayla sent the unease a mental one-fingered salute and forced away the remnants of fear and anger.

She snatched up her oven mitt and smacked Talan in the head with it.

"Ow!" But he was smiling, so she immediately felt better. The man's grin could brighten the cloudiest day, and that was really saying something considering they lived in the land of perpetual fog.

"I keep telling you to move out of the Tenderloin, Talan," Jayla fussed, as she set the rolls on the counter, slathered them with butter and a sprinkle of sea salt, and left them to cool while she checked on the rest of their meal. Talan stood at the breakfast nook near the backdoor that led out to the small patio in the backyard.

"And why didn't you call me after it happened? Chel's out of town, but I was here."

"So what are we eating with those rolls, Jay?"

"Don't think I didn't notice you changed the subject. Roast chicken with rosemary and stop drooling and get on with the story before I strangle you."

"Anyway, this guy comes out of nowhere and helps me kick ass. It was amazing. The perps came at me with big ass blades—"

"Blades? Holy shit!"

"Yes, blades. This guy helped me out, pulled out this gleaming piece of...of whatever it was and, along with my special skills, we totally kicked ass."

"Special skills? Eating counts as a special skill in a fight?" Jayla dipped the tip of her finger in the bubbling pot on the stove and moaned with pleasure. "God, that's good if I may say so myself."

"Well, I—" Talan's gaze swung a hard left. "Hey, that's the guy!"

Jayla whirled around, went dead still with her mouth half-way to the floor. Larien stood there...in nothing but a towel.

Gulp.

If was now official—she'd never get tired of looking at him in his clothing of choice. Larien was *so* not a pretty boy. This man could grace the cover of one of those sporting and bodybuilding magazines. Jesus, he was sleek yet sturdy like a running back that could switch up his strategy and play linebacker any day he chose. His pecs flexed as he rubbed a cloth over his scalp. Surely he could just whoosh the water away or something, but Jayla stood dry-mouthed and happy that he chose to use that towel...which now moved down across his chest and over the ridges of his stomach where dark swirls of the finest-looking down arrowed to a narrow strip.

There the jewel blue fabric wrapped around his trim waist and contrasted beautifully with his deeply tanned skin. Power crackled off of that flesh, coloring the air around him until it almost rippled like heat waves on a blazing summer day.

My goodness. This man had the whole "dark angel" thing down pat. And he'd helped save Talan's life?

Whoa, backtrack.

Talan. In trouble. And Larien had known?

Jayla's hands fisted on her hips and the toe of her fluffy Stewie slipper tapped lightly on the tile of the kitchen floor. Her friend had been in danger and neither of these blockheads bothered to mention it.

"Uh oh," Talan grumbled under his breath.

Larien's eyes took on a "huh?" expression while Talan began backing up. Yep, she'd always known he was a smart man.

Looking around for something to throw at their heads, Jayla growled "So you fellas want to explain why I'm just now hearing about this fight from either of you?"

* * * * *

"I don't think Larien knew we were friends, Jay. He just happened to be having lunch near my place when I got jumped. And I've only been here for five minutes and I'm already telling you, right?"

In the next instant, Talan's expression frosted over as he looked at Larien. "And now that I think about it, what are you doing here? And uh, what's with the towel?" Talan's spine stiffened into what could only be considered subtly hostile and not-so-subtly protective as he took a step in front of Jayla.

The towel bunched in Larien's fist as an image of Jayla and Talan kissing flashed into his head. The strong urge to "poof"—as Jayla called it—the little man somewhere and peel his skin from his body surged in Larien's gut. Was Talan laying claim to Jayla?

The question answered itself when he shifted his focus to the woman in question and caught her gaze as it ate him up. A bolt of intense need shot straight to his cock at the feeling of being explored from head to toe by her. And he liked it.

Besides, Jayla had shown no signs of doing the little man, so Larien ignored Talan's posturing.

Rather than explaining why he'd stepped out of Jayla's bathroom in nothing but his skin and a towel, Larien simply said, "Jayla and I have been tasked with something extremely important. Because you're important to her she asked me to explain it to you."

He turned to Jayla and said, "When you said you wanted to include your friend I didn't know you were talking about Talan." The lie lay like ashes on the back of his tongue, acrid and charred.

Jayla huffed her annoyance. "Can we get back to the attempted Talan jacking, please?"

Talan winked at Larien and proceeded to *not* tell Jayla exactly what happened. He kept Larien's ability to vanish into thin air quiet, as well as his own ability to see and use magick against beings that shouldn't be spoken of in sane company. Talan was a smart man—he wasn't ratting out either of them. The why's of him keeping his mouth shut would have to wait until later.

Jayla grabbed Talan's cheek like she would a small child. "Okay, you're off the hook this time, mister, but next time you have trouble you'd better let me know faster, 'hear?"

Talan playfully slapped her hands away. "I'm the oldest, so why do you get to be the bossy one?"

"Because I'm better at it, that's why. Now, on with the show."

* * * * *

"Set the table, Red." Order given, Talan quickly got the place settings ready for their dinner.

Jayla looked up and stilled. Larien winked and couldn't have held back his smile if he'd tried. She'd been ogling his manly parts. Boldly. Jayla caught her bottom lip between her teeth and looked down at her toes. If he wasn't mistaken the woman was collecting herself, though blushing like crazy.

One moment Larien stood across the room wrapped in practically nothing as he dripped all over Jayla's hardwood floors, and the next he was at her side completely dry in a pair of comfy sweats and a plain white t-shirt.

Jayla squeaked. Talan grinned.

"So what are you doing here?" Talan asked.

"Jayla has agreed to help me find something important, and we must get our hands on it before others do."

"You're sure you aren't the bad guy?" Talan's frosty said he'd pull his wand and do his best to fry Larien on the spot if he meant Jayla any ill. Larien could respect that.

"Jayla's family line is from that of the great king, Solomon."

"Solomon? Huh?" Talan wondered aloud. "No offense, Jay, but you're a sistah from New York."

Jayla laughed out loud and pushed a glass of cold strawberry lemonade at both of them. "True, but my dad is, or was, Semitic, sweetie."

The underlying sadness was hard to miss. Not just in word, but her aura faltered and faded, the color infused with bone-deep loss before it was restored to her typical bubbly hue. Just as it had when they'd first stepped into her grandmother's storage space. Obviously, this woman deeply loved those who'd passed on. He only wished he could wipe the sorrow away.

"Jewish?" Talan asked.

"No, Semitic," Larien answered. "It doesn't mean Jewish, but a subfamily of Afro-asiatic languages, like old Akkadian, Arabic, Aramaic, Ethiopic, Hebrew, and Phoenician."

"Sexy beast and book worm, too?" Jayla chided with a smile that warmed Larien to his toes and melted the chill that had been rolling off of Talan. No surprise at the puzzled look on Talan's face. It wasn't the first time he'd been mistaken for all brawn and no brains, which typically worked to his advantage. Yet Jayla proved herself above the pale, set herself above others in his mind. With six little words she made it clear that she saw more in him than just his physique and ability to stomp his enemies into the ground. His gut squeezed tight at the admiration in her eyes. And as such, he admired his human right back for seeing what others typically did not.

"I hate that I never got to meet your dad," Talan said. "My family came to the states right after he passed, right?"

"Yes. He was an extraordinary man," she said. "I think his

passing is what set mom on edge. She tolerated Grams while Dad was alive, but after he died she treated Grams like a leper, as if my dad's passing was her fault or something. Mom didn't want me to spend time with her, didn't like me calling her. It was just weird. It got to the point where I would sneak a flight to Grams' house during school breaks instead of going home. I'd just claim that I couldn't make it home because I had class projects to work on. I hated lying to my mom, but I needed that time with Grams. I wouldn't be who I am today if I had allowed myself to be deprived of it."

"Your mom would have killed you if she'd known you were really just an hour away in Pulaski."

"No doubt. And if you're thinking that's blackmail material, my friend, prepare to get your ass kicked." She turned to Larien and flashed a wicked grin. "And that goes for you, too, you sexy beast, you."

Amazing. Both Jayla and Talan knew what he was yet Larien couldn't deny the comfortable atmosphere. They laughed, talked and told on each other as if he truly belonged.

Jayla had them all grab a dish from the table or the stovetop and bring it into the family room. In spite of Talan's grumbling about setting the table for nothing, they all enjoyed eating around the coffee table and filling the small space with good-natured ribbing.

Talan rubbed his full belly, slid off the couch and laid flat on the floor with a smile and a sigh. Larien had never seen a human eat so much. Especially one as reed-thin as Talan. Jayla called the man wiry, but whatever. The scent of homemade cinnamon rolls baking in the oven tickled Larien's nose and he almost groaned. He'd put away as much food as Talan but his mouth still watered to taste Jayla's baking. Almost as much as his mouth watered to taste the woman herself.

Time to accept it—he wanted her. Period. By choice, feelings weren't something he'd had to deal with in quite some time. The occasional wayward erection in reaction to a beautiful woman, sure. But there hadn't been any feelings, *emotions*, tied up in it. It had simply been a normal biological reaction, one he had no urge to follow up on.

But Jayla? Jesus, she had him all tied up in knots since the night he'd waltzed into her room with the intention of simply getting a look at the person, the woman, that he would partner with for this job. God, he wanted to strangle Gabriel. Or strangle whoever ordered Gabriel to get Larien to take this mission.

Why? Because with Jayla this was more than a hormone eruption. He was struggling to keep his feelings disengaged, to keep the empty chambers of his heart from longing to be filled with her.

And he had no fucking idea why. He hadn't slept with her. He hadn't even touched her, not really. Yet she called to him. Pushed all his buttons. And it pissed him off considering this woman could force him to obey her. Now *that* was something he'd never in his life experienced.

Anger kicked him in the head, filled him with brick-hard determination to finish his task and get the hell out of here. Thoughts of losing himself in Jayla vanished like a puff of smoke, but like smoke, it lingered and teased the edges of his mind.

"We have to find the Seal of Solomon," Larien blurted. Jayla knew something was wrong. She hadn't said a word, yet he *knew* that she was aware of his inner struggle. Fuck.

"Man, I'm so full I almost forgot you said we had to find something. So what is it you're asking Jayla to do?"

"The Seal of Solomon," he repeated.

"Well, I don't know what that is," Talan said as he motioned to the piles of boxes they'd hauled out of storage. "But I'm guessing this has something to do with it?"

"Smart man," Larien drawled.

Talan winked, scooted across the floor and dove right into the nearest box. While Talan muttered, picked up this piece, muttered some more and put that piece down, Larien's arm decided—all by itself—to wrap around the back of the couch. He almost pulled Jayla close, but stopped himself just before his fingers wrapped around her shoulder.

Distraction. He needed one. Now.

"Talan, I understand that you're a mythology and history major." And a Shadow priest that is something *other*. "What do you think about these things?"

"This is amazing. Where did you—?"

"Not important. Can you make out any of it?"

"Absolutely. I can read some of it. Seems to be a mix of

Cuneiform, Aramaic and something else." Talan held up one of the scrolls that Larien had translated earlier. "I can't read this one at all." The hair stood up all over Larien's body at the thought of what that scroll contained. According to that piece of parchment, written by the hand of the Archangel Michael himself, Jayla's family was highly favored with all kinds of celestial perks that he was sure the woman was unaware of. And he would go on keeping it to himself for now.

"This is going to be an all-nighter, dude." Talan sighed tiredly but his aura sparkled with brilliant yellow, the color of inner joy and contentment.

"I'm game. Jayla, you mind putting on some coffee?" Larien asked.

"Sure. Coming right up. Any other way I can help, handsome?" That last word was drawn out and infused with so much delicious innuendo, it was as if she'd taken a piece of taffy between her fingers and pulled until it was a taut string of sweetness…right before she took a bite out of the center.

Before he could squash it, the lust brewing beneath the surface shot forth and showed itself. No filter, no dampening, no subtlety. Earlier she'd called him a sexy beast. The woman had no idea how close she was to the truth in regard to the beast part. A lone fingertip touched the bare skin of her shoulder. Though barely a whisper, the catch in her throat whooshed into his eardrums like the evening wind blowing across the sand of the ocean across the street. He couldn't blame her. He'd felt that simple contact clear down to his soul. The touch brought a little bit of her essence with it, as if his finger had sucked some of her into himself. And the woman was potent.

Her eyes met his then fell to half-mast. God, another punch in the gut that had him grunting under the blow.

"Uh. Coffee. Yeah." Jayla jumped up and was gone.

Talan looked after her, perplexed. "Well, that was interesting. Did she just run away?" Confusion cleared as Talan turned his gaze on Larien.

Larien knew exactly what the other man saw, knew the gears turning in his head were practically visible to the naked eye as he considered how to get what he wanted. The tight set of his jaw belied his body's relaxed position on the couch.

Talan stilled, but not in fear.

"Uh, I think that was the wrong thing for her to do," Talan said quietly, knowingly.

"You know what they say," Larien unfolded himself off the couch and stood. "Never run from a predator." The words were little more than a growl.

"Warn me never to do that, eh, Larien?"

"Consider yourself warned." He stalked out of the room in pursuit of the prey that every bit of common sense he possessed told him he should leave alone.

CHAPTER NINE

Oh now *this* felt good. Larien had followed her into the kitchen. He hadn't touched her, yet she felt the warmth radiating from the front of his body. *All* of his front, from neck to knees. If he leaned in just a hair he'd be flush against her ass. Instead, he backed up a bit and leaned one hip against the counter next to her.

Trying her best to ignore the affect the big jerk had on her, she scooped her best fine-ground coffee into a small bowl.

Okay, so he wasn't really a jerk, just gruff and grumbly and so Larien.

Adding a pinch of clove, a dash of cayenne and some cocoa, she used a single finger to mix it before wrapping her lips around that finger. The action drew his gaze...just like she wanted it to.

So after her initial burst of panic a few moments ago, she was fully back to baiting him?

Bad. Bad Jayla.

She dumped the blend into the coffee maker and flipped the switch. Immediately the scent of fresh brewed heaven began to fill the space.

"Here." She handed him two oven mitts. "Get the cinnamon rolls out of the oven will you? They'll have to cool a bit before we can ice them, though."

Larien bent his sexy ass down and eased the pans out of the oven. And *gah* he was scrumptious to look at. She'd been looking forward to cinnamon rolls slathered with her special strawberry cream cheese icing all day. But now all she wanted was a bite of a man she should be wary of. After all, everyone knew that Fallen weren't to be trusted. Then again, she'd just learned that Solomon had a magic ring and controlled demons, which was nowhere in any history she'd ever heard. So just maybe she'd heard wrong. Right?

He chose that moment to look up. She didn't bother playing shy or looking away. It was her turn to leave her guard down, to let him see what burned beneath her skin—him. She let it show in her eyes, her slightly parted lips and the words that followed.

"So, how do you take your coffee? I like mine overflowing...with cream."

His throat worked up and down as he swallowed hard. She almost smiled when it took him a second to answer her question. She hadn't meant for a simple offer—aw, hell, who was she trying to fool? She certainly *had* meant it. But damn if she could help it when he looked so damn...*dayum*.

Bottom line—she wanted to eat him up in small, savored bites. All night.

* * * * *

"This is going to be a long night," Larien mumbled to himself, raking those long fingers across the barely there stubble on his scalp.

Jayla whispered, "Are you okay? You feel funny."

He cocked his brow in question.

"I can feel you, your energy I mean. It's...different. Just enough for me to know you're doing something."

"I just dropped my cloak. I'd been holding it since I walked out of the bathroom fresh from the shower. It uses some of my stored energy. I sometimes forget to drop it, though you'd be able to see me anyway."

"Wait, what?" She turned mid-pour, spilling coffee on the counter.

"Be careful." He snatched a towel from the nearest kitchen rack and sopped up the mess while simultaneously checking her over for visible signs of injury. "I would be unhappy with you if you burned yourself, Jayla."

"I've been making coffee and tying my shoes all by myself for a while now. I think I can handle it, thank you verra much."

"Smartass," Larien grumbled.

"That's right. And smart everything else."

It was her favorite comeback. "So, back to the 'Talan can see you while cloaked' thing."

"All I can say is Talan has a part to play or he wouldn't be able to see me at all. What Talan didn't tell you was that the goons who jumped him were Fallen demons. Interrogators, no less. They were looking for the Seal, too."

"What?" she yelled.

"Keep your voice down. He doesn't need to know."

"What?" she said again, this time the words were hissed through clenched teeth.

"You guys okay in there?" Talan called from the family room. The faint click-hum of the surround system coming on was quickly followed by the boom of explosives, fighting and fast paced music.

"Yep, fine," Jayla called back sweetly though her gaze crackled with anger.

"I don't know what they wanted with him, but I think it makes sense to keep our guard up. What are the odds that those particular demons went after your friend around the same time you and I started working together?"

"I agree. And if anything happens to him I'm kicking everyone's ass. Yours. The one that sent you. The demons. Everybody. Got it?"

She was a bloodthirsty little thing. Larien almost smiled at her vehemence but decided he liked his cock where it was. "I'm less concerned about Talan and more concerned about you staying out of trouble."

"Me? What'd I do?" Ah, such wide-eyed innocence. But Larien was no fool. He knew trouble when he saw it. In fact, he was neck deep in it.

So, idiot, is it sink or swim?

* * * * *

Jayla was passed out on the sofa when a bang, bang, bang had her jumping out of her skin. Up and headed to the door, she had to elbow Talan out of the way just to stiff-arm Larien out of the way. She might be annoyed that they acted as if she needed a personal bodyguard but she wasn't stupid enough to be unappreciative that they were ready to charge whoever the hell was at her door at this time of night.

A quick glance through the peep hole had her jerking the door open.

"Chel? What the hell are you doing here at this hour banging on my door like the police?" she snapped.

"You sounded weird on the phone the last time we talked, like something was up. So I came home early. Now what the fuck…?"

Chel's eyes widened for the briefest moment. Eyes hard and suspicious, yet not quite giving away why, she stared past Jayla's shoulder. Jayla looked back and forth between the man behind her and the woman standing at her front. She'd barely caught it, but Jayla knew the "what the hell are you doing here" look on a woman's face when she saw it.

The "nice to meet you" Chel pushed through her perfectly painted lips was barely a growl, and not the sexy kind. And while Chel glowered at Larien, he took her measure in mere seconds, and then wiped the slate of his face clean. If he didn't like what he saw, he made sure nobody else in the room knew what he was thinking.

Huh.

"Come on in. It's cold," Jayla said, not bothering to hide her confusion. Besides, her friends knew her well enough to know when she was faking it anyway.

Chel kicked off her shoes and tossed her coat over the nearest chair then turned around like she was ready to fight. Then Talan was there to wrap her up in a hug. Chel's aggressive posture melted like snow beneath a clear sun-filled sky.

Now *here* was the Chel she knew—the one who smiled as she allowed herself to be rocked back and forth in the arms of a friend because she'd been so missed.

"How's my favorite leprechaun?" Chel's words were muffled in Talan's thick fiery waves. Funny, the two were practically the same height, but somehow Chel always seemed larger than life, as if her very presence took up more space than her body.

"How are you, gorgeous?" Talan asked.

Chel just kept right on smiling, though she didn't answer the question.

Jayla spoke into the awkward silence. "Hungry, Chel?"

"No. Fine."

"Okaay? Uh, Chel this is my friend Larien. Larien, Chel."

Larien gave a cordial dip of his head and even a hint of a friendly smile. But he didn't extend his hand or move toward Chel in any way. Instead he gave the most subtle of motions to Talan and the two of them returned to the floor and got back to work.

But there was no missing the spike in the energy that now buzzed through the room. Strange.

"So what are you guys up to?" Chel glided into the family room and took to the couch, leaning in to get a look at all the papers, trinkets, scrolls, books and boxes spread about the floor.

Jayla didn't immediately answer. Supernatural stuff was a topic she and Talan discussed frequently but Chel typically kept her mouth shut during those talks. In fact, Talan had been one of Jayla's first teachers, after her dad and her Grams had passed on. He'd been the one to explain what her third eye was and had helped her find and meditate on it. He was a skilled holistic with his herbs and stuff, but there was a dark side to him that he didn't share, which was okay. She certainly kept certain things about herself private.

But God, how she wanted to give all of herself to someone. Trust someone enough to tell them all her wild and crazy beliefs. Share her talents and dreams. Her desires. Her body.

Sigh.

Part of her believed Larien could be that person. Only one small problem—he was an angel. He would live forever while she had perhaps a good fifty or sixty years left. Then again, what about that whole "better to have loved and lost" thing?

With her thoughts tumbling around in her head, Jayla almost missed when Chel replied.

"Well?" Chel pressed. "What's going on? What are they doing with all those books and things?"

"Well, Larien is, uh, well, he—" Jayla faltered. She'd intended to include Chel in their treasure hunting, but she hadn't counted on the woman popping up tonight.

"Larien is…what?" Chel asked with more than a little menace as she turned toward the man in question. Jayla wondered if she stuck her finger out in front of her face, would she be able to feel the tension in the air. Just then Larien looked up. His eyes glowed an otherworldly blue for the barest of moments. And just as quickly he'd dismissed Chel and picked up a black dust-covered tome as if nothing had happened.

Jayla rolled her eyes and headed toward the kitchen with a grumbled, "Well, now that *that's* out of the way."

Chel was on her heels.

Jayla gathered snacks and put them on the tray with two large mugs of fresh steaming coffee with an assortment of flavored creams, sugar, and plain milk. She took it out to the living room and set it on the floor off to the side of the two men.

"Aah, this is good. Thanks Jay. You know, this is quite a cache your Grams left you." Talan blew steam away from the surface of the hot brew then took another sip. "Mmm." He set the cup down and passed Larien a sheaf of papers to sort into yet another pile.

Larien looked up from where all six-foot-something of him was folded Indian-style on her area rug in front of the fireplace. What a nice view he made.

"I bet we'll be at this all night," Larien mumbled to Talan.

"Then I'm staying too!"

Chel's announcement sent Jayla's brows flying upward. What the hell was wrong with this woman? She never stayed over. Even if they ate popcorn, watched movies and talked until four in the morning, Chel always went home. Talan, on the other hand practically lived in the room that Larien had claimed as his temporary sleeping place.

Larien broke yet another layer of ice and said, "It's okay, Jayla. Talan and I will be up most of the night researching anyway."

"No worries. I'll sleep with Jayla," Chel declared.

"Oh, no you won't. I love you girlfriend, but my bed is just that—mine."

"Then I'll sleep in Talan's room."

Larien's dark brown gaze snapped up and pinned Talan to the spot. "Talan's room?"

Some kind of manly silent communication must have taken place because Talan tilted his head, smiled and lifted both hands in the universal "I surrender" gesture known by every male throughout the galaxy.

"Whoa. Jay is like a sister to me. She feeds me, lets me crash here when I'm too tired to head home."

"You mean when it's too damn dangerous for you to be walking around in the Tenderloin at night," Chel snapped.

"Damn, Chel, chill out. You're acting like you've got a hornet up your ass. If you want to stay, that's fine, but Larien is already holed up in Talan's room, so unless you can help with all that crap they're wading through, get a good night sleep. At home. Besides, you must have come straight here after your long flight. I know you're tired, so stop weirding out."

"Jayla, can I speak with you a moment?"

With a sigh, she said, "Sure, Chel. Let me put on another pot of coffee for the boys and I'll be right there."

Chel stormed from the room. No gliding gait. No classy air. All piss, no priss.

* * * * *

"Jay, you don't know anything about this guy. How do we know he's on the level?"

"I know you love me, chicklet, but I've already agreed to help him. Because you're my best friend I want you to know what's up. Larien is a good guy. I promise."

As they sat on Jayla's bed facing each other, Chel launched into what would surely become a thirty minute rant to tick off a list of reasons why Larien wasn't to be trusted whether she knew him or not.

"Okay, okay, just hush a moment, Chel. You're going to think I'm crazy but—" She paused, took a deep breath then blurted. "Larien is an angel, Chel. Fallen. I know it sounds crazy, but remember the times I talked to you about things I used to see as a child. Well, those things were real, Chel. And Larien is…not human."

To Jayla's shock, but immeasurable relief, Chel just sat there with her mouth open. But that was better than being told she was crazy.

Oh yeah, 'cause having a person just think *you're crazy is just so much better.*

"He's here on a mission. Actually, *we're* on a mission. It's related to my family legacy, believe it or not. "

After what felt like an eon, Chel's hand shot to her hip as she stood.

"So he's an angel?" Chel pressed. "Jayla, if the man could abandon his duty as an angel to become Fallen, what could possibly make you believe he'll be there when or if you need him?"

"Point taken." But she still wasn't shaken from her current path. Larien Fell, yes. But this was a man who made no apologies for what he was. He'd "done his time", accepted responsibility for the choice a long time ago.

He called to her on a level she hadn't known existed. And being drop-dead gorgeous with an indescribably delicious-looking body and a voice like liquid sin didn't hurt none either.

Chel scrunched up her face with a deep frown. "I swear, Jayla, if he does you dirty I'll kick his gorgeous ass the length of Ocean Beach. And you know that's a nice long stretch of sand."

She wrapped Chel in what she hoped was a reassuring hug and pressed a kiss to her cheek. "Go home, already, sweetpea. Talan told me earlier that you have another modeling job and will be out of here tomorrow anyway. Go get some sleep. I'll let you know what the plans are as soon as we have any."

"Fine. But don't go anywhere without me. Love you."

"Love you back."

"You're my girl, Jayla. I won't let you be hurt by his kind."

Jayla hugged her friend again and shooed her out the door. Ready for bed, she headed to the bathroom for a wash up. Two steps into the shower she stilled.

Jayla was worried she hadn't told Chel enough. Sure, she'd shared the facts of the mission with Chel in that few moments after she'd barreled into the house, but she hadn't had time to get into the specifics about who or what they were up against.

On the other hand, Chel was totally serious in the threat she'd made against Larien even though she knew what he was. No fear. No surprise. She wasn't sure what kind of reaction she'd expected, but *that* certainly hadn't been it.

The thought slipped away as the events of the day caught up with her. Being surrounded by her Grandma's things had done a number of her. Then having to drag a grumpy Larien around with her afterward had been less than fun. Then he'd turned on the sex appeal and she'd practically melted while fleeing from her own living room. Then Chel showing up? Just too damn much. Tired and emotionally wrung out, she'd deal with the rest of it in the morning.

Snuggling under the comfy blankets, she punched her pillow and settled in on a yawn. Almost immediately came dreams of a dark, rough-cut angel doing all kinds of naughtiness to her person...with her enthusiastic encouragement, of course.

CHAPTER TEN

Thick, comfy layers of slumber fell away and thoughts of Larien had a smile tugging at the corner of her mouth. It was still fully dark out. The glow of the bedside clock revealed it was two thirty-five in the morning.

It had only been a few hours since she'd hit the sheets after walking Chel to the sidewalk with Larien at her back. Her long-time *Seraphs* had insisted on continuing to camp around her home, Larien insisted that they go to hell. Literally. The man had relished flipping Ambriel and crew the bird...again.

A deep breath brought with it a tantalizing scent and her stomach dropped through the mattress and hit the floor. This wasn't worry. No, this nervous roll of her gut had everything to do with the potent male standing next to her bed. He'd silently poofed into her room.

"Everything okay?" she asked.

"Don't scrunch up your face like that," Larien murmured tiredly. Amazing how he could see in the dark like that. Then a single finger slid across the skin between her brows, smoothing the frown there. The contact left the faintest zing behind, warming the spot he'd touched.

"What's going on?" she asked around a yawn.

"We found something. Discuss it over breakfast in the morning?"

"You woke me up for that?"

"You slept for a couple of hours and then started flipping around in the bed. Definitely not truly sleeping, Jayla."

Note to self—don't try to fool an angel that has super hearing.

"We think we have a lead. I knew you were half-awake and thought perhaps you could get some deeper sleep if I informed you of our progress."

And he was right, but she'd keep that bit to herself. "Thanks. I, uh, I really appreciate that."

She'd forgotten to close the blinds and the moonlight cast his face in shadows and harsh planes of stone. Then, for just a moment, the expression he kept so carefully guarded slipped and her head tilted in wonder. What made him look at her like she was the most precious thing on earth—a puzzle, but precious none the less. Then his gaze chilled and he turned to leave.

Jayla's hand shot out and grabbed his and he froze, turned slowly, shoulders stiff enough to break from his body.

"Larien, I just want you to know that I don't see this partnership in helping you find what you need as doing you a favor."

"Oh?"

"No. It's as much for my good as it is for yours, no matter your reasons for accepting the task. So, we're in this together. We're partners. Friends." She wasn't sure where the hell all this was coming from, but it felt right so she went with it.

Silence.

"Right?" she prodded gently. Still nothing so Jayla sat up and pulled him toward her by the easy grip she had on his hand. He allowed it as if he were in a trance and unaware that his feet moved without his permission.

Then she was up on her knees in the bed, hands pressed to his chest with a need to ease his obvious perplexity. His confusion was tangible, as if it were alive and searching for understanding.

She wanted to kiss him, soothe the warring factions inside into one cohesive team, one man, and one goal. But just as it was obvious he was attracted to her, it was just as clear that he didn't *want* to be. For now, she contented herself to wrap her arms around him, press her ear to his heart and listen to the solid tha-thump of his heart, to the air moving in and out of his lungs in long steady rushes. She could almost imagine the oxygen soaking into the blood vessels on each breath, nourishing the cells in his body, giving him life.

"Hug me back already. You're not going to die if you give me this. It's what friends do, by the way. We hug. Often," she murmured into his t-shirt.

She tightened her hold and waited.

Slowly, almost as if he were resigned to the inevitable, Larien returned her embrace. Jayla inhaled with pleasure at being surrounded by hard, warm man. His arms moved tentatively at first, barely around her, as if he was afraid to touch her. Jayla snuggled in closer, encouraged him without demanding, until he had completely wrapped her up within himself.

She felt his biceps flex as he held her tighter. So much strength, yet so much tenderness.

She wasn't sure how long they stayed like that, only that it was comfortable, like snuggling into her favorite faux fur that she curled up in whenever she sat next to the fireplace on a gray rainy day. Next thing she knew, there was a gentle tap, tap, tap against her cheek.

"Jayla?"

"Hmmm—"

"Jay."

"Wha?"

"You're dozing."

"No'um not."

"Jayla, you're on your knees asleep. Go to bed. I'll see you in the morning."

"Don't wanna sleep by myself. I'm always by myself."

"I'm just in the other room, sweetheart."

"Doesn't count."

Arms that had been warm and heavy against her back dropped away. She almost groaned in protest but the gesture of the kiss he dropped on top of her head was so sweet she couldn't make herself complain. Strong but gentle fingers wrapped around her biceps, untangled her from around his body and eased her back under the covers.

He tucked her in and in seconds she felt herself drift away as he said something about...lemon waffles for breakfast?

* * * * *

The warmth of Jayla's body faded from his skin as Larien headed back to his temporary bedroom in her office. He dropped onto the futon but refused to let loose the deep sigh that sat just behind his lips. It was killing him. Times like this he wished he had no supernatural abilities, no special sight, hearing or smell. The woman was everywhere. One side of his mouth tipped up into a short-lived smile as he took in the various scents. Fickle, this woman. She loved everything from apple and vanilla to orange and musk. The overtones of sandalwood overlaid all the others.

He glanced up at the typical office chair across the small space and pictured Jayla's curvy frame settling down into it to piece together her thoughts in front of the computer.

Even through the closed door he heard her deep breathing. Though he was strangely comforted by the thought of her resting—something she didn't do nearly enough of—he wasn't the least bit happy about why he was in her home.

How would Jayla feel once she knew the entire truth of why he needed her, rather than the two-thirds of honesty he'd surrendered?

She wanted him. The knowledge that she was attracted to him as much as he was to her had his conscience pricking. And if he let himself have her would he be the one to jade this woman? Be the one to break her heart so completely that the willingness to love another was choked into non-existence because of his lies?

Would he, himself, be destroyed? Correction, destroyed *again*? How many times had he met rejection after revealing what he was? And when he'd hidden his true nature, how many times had a woman fallen for him only to scorn him later? Or slept with him in hopes of getting some kind of fairytale favor, like immortality or some dumb shit like that?

He'd been loved for himself once…but by none of the women he'd Fallen for. After all, he'd Fallen for sex. Love had come much, much later…

Dark curls were plastered against their foreheads, skin dampened from the cool compresses that kept the fevers from raging out of control. They had their mother's startling green eyes but Larien's thick black hair. But after this, he would never again show that side of himself to the world. No, from now on he would shave his head in honor of them, in remembrance of the loss...

"Father, will you be here if we wake tomorrow?" his firstborn, Deni, had whispered. It took all his strength just to form the words.

"I will always be here, son," Larien promised as he silently demanded his tears to remain at bay. He had to be strong for them in their final moments. He absolutely must.

His third born, Dalos, tried to reassure him even though his young body was practically hacked into pieces. "Please do not be sad, Father. You taught us to make our own choices, and chosen we have. Please do not be angry that we choose to die—"

They'd been so brave, his boys. All three had been taken from him on the same day on the same battlefield. He'd raised them alone and those had been the most treasured years of his life. Larien had razed kingdoms, counseled kings and torn apart all manner of creatures before his Fall. Because of those three boys, Larien had come to see his Fall as the chance to have something that he otherwise would have never experienced. He'd taught his boys to be ruthless in battle and faithful to none but each other. Yet that day, Larien, Angel of the Art of War could do nothing but watch those who meant more to him than his own life, leave him forever.

Yes, he'd finally found love on this earth...in his sons. And he'd endured endless pain ever since. Those three young warriors had chosen to die together though they'd known that if they were ever injured to the point of death they could, by rights, call on Rafael, the Healer, and become eudaemon. Yet they'd chosen to defend their people and accept the consequences of war rather than embrace immortality. Larien's heart had gone with them when they'd taken their final breaths. And that day he'd resigned himself to the fact that it was simply impossible to have a love like that twice in a lifetime.

Lights doused, Larien set away his memories, shucked his clothes with a thought and climbed into bed. As a man that liked to see what was headed his way, he left the blinds up. According to his sources word had gotten out that a human Descendant was on the hunt for the Seal of Solomon, yet there'd been no flurry of activity in the underworld realms, no hordes of bad guys sent after Jayla. Nothing. But intuition said this was the quiet before the storm.

With nothing but a sheet draped over his waist Larien dropped his human skin and let his battle form come forward. Heavy wings hung off either side of the bed to the floor, darker than the rest of the blackness of the room. He smiled at the thought of showing them to Jayla someday knowing her eyes would widen in wonder and she'd have a million questions. Many humans had their myths mixed up in this regard. The judgment rendered on the Watchers of the second Fall was a cakewalk compared to what had been done to those of the first.

As part of the latter, Larien couldn't go home, but he was still whole in body and spirit, including his wings. As for the former, Larien had been part of the Host who'd executed their judgment. A whisper of memory brought with it the gore that had covered his boots, the vibration that had traveled up his blade as he'd sliced through joints and bone and sinew to take their wings.

A shiver passed through the nerves at Larien's back at the spot where his wing's humerus bones, layered with dense toned muscle, protruded from his back—it was the spot where he'd aimed his blade and hacked over and over again until his brethren's silken feathers flew or their wings simply plopped to the ground whole.

Yanking his thoughts away from the memory of that carnage Larien's mind skipped partly to the activity in the yard where Ambriel and some of his sidekicks still quietly patrolled, and partly to the woman in the other room. Jayla hadn't balked in the face of anything he'd presented her with so far. Hadn't looked at him with distaste. Hadn't had a calculating gleam in her eye after learning his origins.

A soft snuffle sounded from down the hall. Even in her sleep she had the ability to make him smile, and that was something he hadn't had a reason to do in quite some time.

* * * * *

The following morning, Jayla stretched awake. She'd slept hard but her dreams were far from peaceful. They'd been sensual, dark, lingering about the edges of her mind as her body tried to remember the delicious sensations it had experienced in sleep.

Noooooo, come back! Come back, damn it.

She lay on her stomach, pillow jammed over her head trying to block out the daylight and recapture the feeling of strong, slightly roughened fingers gliding along the skin on the back of her knees. Short fingernails scraping sensuously up her thighs, over her butt cheeks and along her sides.

But the more she awakened, the less she remembered.

Damn it, damn it, damn it, she snapped at herself in frustration.

Then she picked up a scent. There was no mistaking it.

Coffee! Oh thank god!

Blankets pooled around her waist and bared her sweaty skin to the cool morning air as she jackknifed to a sitting position. She hopped up, shoved her feet into her favorite gold and red 49'ers slippers with matching robe, dipped into the bathroom for a quick wash-up and then headed toward the kitchen.

Larien had promised her breakfast. She wasn't sure whether she was looking more forward to the food, or just the opportunity to ogle him. Judging by the smells greeting her as she moved down the hallway, she may just get a bit of both.

She barged into the kitchen and skidded to a halt just inside the doorway. A shirtless Larien effortlessly flipped the waffle iron. He hadn't turned toward her but Jayla didn't miss the subtle shifting of muscle, the almost imperceptible jolt that rippled through him the moment she'd stepped into the room. Yes, he was very much aware of her presence.

Chel stood scowling in the corner dressed in a green polka-dot sundress and low strappy sandals. One arm was crossed over her breasts as she sipped a glass of orange juice and watched her two companions out of the corner of her eye.

Talan spilled words out at a mile a minute to no one in particular as he pointed to a piece of yellowed curled paper in his hands. The second he spotted Jayla, he stopped mid-sentence, hopped out of his chair and motioned for her to sit.

"Good morning, sleepyhead," Talan said and then set a steaming mug of coffee in front of her. "I believe this is just the way you like it. Vanilla creamer and no sugar, am I right?"

Oh boy was he ever. "Talan you are my new best friend."

The confusion on his face had her laughing into her mug. "I've been your best friend for years? How—"

"Good grief, she's just kidding, Talan. It's just a saying." Chel slammed the empty orange juice glass down on the counter with a bit too much force. Jayla didn't bother hiding her surprise.

"Uh, Chel…?"

"Sorry, Jay. Didn't mean to bang the glass. I know it's one of your favorites."

"Thank you for the apology because I really don't feel like kicking your ass this early in the morning." Then she blew Chel a very heartfelt kiss.

The heart stopping smile Larien laid on Jayla just then shattered the funk emanating from Chel. For that one moment the hardness disappeared and in its place was a man that looked boyish and free. She realized that this was the first time he'd ever truly smiled quite like that. Was she the reason? If not, then whatever he and Talan had discovered last night must be a doozy. Her now favorite Fallen delivered a plate full of steaming, crispy on the outside, tender on the inside, Belgian waffles smothered in butter and drizzled with some kind of white syrup.

She stuck out a finger and sampled a bit.

"Oh my god, that's good!"

Larien snorted and said, "I promised you lemon waffles, didn't I?"

"So I didn't dream that bit?"

"No."

Just the bit about licking lemon syrup off his chest. Good lord.

Shaking the thoughts away, she said, "Mmm mmm mmm! Lemon is my favorite flavor in the world, followed by dark chocolate and cinnamon." Not only had the man delivered, but he upped the ante and sprinkled shaved chocolate and a dash of cinnamon in her coffee.

"Goodness gracious, Larien, I think you're a keeper," she mumbled around a mouthful of griddled perfection made by a specimen of male perfection.

Yep, she had lots of perfection going on this morning. Jayla was a happy woman.

"Wow, I can't say I've seen that look on your face at this hour before," Talan said with a smirk. He turned to Larien. "I think you may have converted our girl to a morning person. Usually she's not this awake for another hour or two."

"Hush and let me enjoy my breakfast." But Jayla's words were filled with a smile.

Several appreciative culinary-related moans later, she shuffled into the living room and sprawled on the couch. "Tal, I think I need another cup of coffee before I slip into a lemon syrup-induced coma. Yes, I'm definitely close to overdosing."

Moments later, cup in hand, she eyed the piles of books and papers stacked on and around the coffee table with an expectant air, though with all the food she'd just eaten, she was surprised she could breathe, let alone think.

"My god, woman, should we help you up so you can waddle back to your room and lay down for a bit? We can do this later." Talan jumped out of kicking distance.

"Smart ass." Chel and Jayla said at the exact same time. Only, Jayla's words were infused with laughter. Chel, not so much.

"Obviously the UMS you left with last night has returned full-force this morning, Chel," Jayla mumbled and sat up. "Okay, what do we have?"

"Wait, what is UMS?" Larien asked, brow drawn in question.

"Ugly mood swings. You get used to it with Chel," Jayla answered. Talan snorted while Larien looked at Chel as if she might bite at any moment. At her friend's scowl, Jayla reached out and patted Chel's hand. "Stop looking like that. You know it's true, but we love you anyway. Now—" Jayla curled up in a ball with a sleepy grin, tucked a pillow under her head and blew out a sated sigh. "I swear I'm not dozing. Go ahead, I'm listening."

"I know just where to go. Isthus."

"Is this? Is this, what?" Chel snapped.

Talan replied patiently, "Isthus is a person, not a thing. He's a bit unconventional, but I'd bet my left nut that he'll see something we're missing. Larien can read the celestial bits but it's all riddles and clues. I feel like one of the gang from Scooby Doo."

"Your left nut?" Jayla snorted. "Uh, don't you need that? Just kidding. So, can you call Isthus up, have him come over?"

"Not likely. He's in Nevada."

"Nevada?" Larien stood, hands on hips and looking like he wanted to take off right this instant. "No problem. I can have Jayla and myself there and back in no time."

Chel shot to her feet. "Oh hell no! You're not taking Jayla anywhere. I don't trust you."

Larien ignored the jab. "It's the fastest way. I can't take all of us at once, and I'm not willing to take Jayla and leave her there to wait while I come back for Talan. She's not out of my sight. Period."

"Nevada, huh? Well, you guys figure it out. I'm going to work. And Chel, don't miss your plane. I don't want to hear it if you're late for your photo shoot."

With that, Jayla headed to her bedroom, the fluffy slippers making a *swish-slide* sound against the hardwood floor. In barely five minutes, she strode back into the kitchen for a last sip of coffee, then through the family room to the coat closet.

It was drizzling outside. Thick gray clouds hugged the horizon and turned the ocean across the street to a deep churning green. Jayla put the light shawl she'd grabbed back into the closet and grabbed a classy-looking belted leather jacket instead.

"Why are you dressed like that?"

Jayla's spine stiffened at the growl in Larien's words. "And just who the hell are you talking to like that?"

The violet scarf around her neck complimented the knitted sweater that showed off the curve of her breasts. The suede skirt fell to just above the knee and hugged her hips. The entire ensemble was a shade of deep purple that made her think of a bunch of grapes ready to be plucked from the vine. In short, the color alone made her happy, and the way the clothes fit was wholly feminine.

"It is..." he paused, looked her up and down like she was dressed in a Bozo The Clown Suit. "Cold out today."

"This is San Francisco. Normal. Fog will burn off by ten and be back by six."

She slid her feet into a pair of low-heeled sandals that were totally inappropriate for the damp chilly weather, but they were sexy and matched her outfit. The second her hand closed around the door knob, Larien was on her.

"Move already. I've got to go to the newspaper and turn in a story to my editor, and then I'm headed to my gym. I'll change there."

"Didn't you hear me? You're not out of my sight." Had he really snapped at her like that? And when she was looking so cute, too? Her hair was up in a soft ponytail, baring the smooth skin of her neck and Larien was so near, the warmth of his breath fanned over that skin. So, so close. If she turned around and tipped up her chin just a bit she could kiss him—something she instinctively fought though she could practically taste him. She could privately moon over him all she wanted, but kissing was a no-no. Was Larien a bad guy? She didn't think so. But there was more to this story than he'd shared so far, and that knowledge cast just enough of a shadow to help her rein in her horniness.

In a flash, she'd turned, pushed him back a step and had the door open.

"You are too damn bossy, Larien. Last I checked, my daddy had passed on and he didn't need a replacement."

"You are not leaving without me, woman. End of story."

Interesting. A mix of angered heat and amusement danced in his eyes. "Fine. My bus hits the corner in five minutes so unless you're driving you'd better hurry up because I don't intend to miss it." She grabbed her gym bag from its spot next to the shoe basket by the front door and was gone.

"You have a car, why don't you just drive?" he called after her.

The only answer he got was the clicking of her heels on the steps as she headed for the street.

CHAPTER ELEVEN

After reminding her of the Fallen who had attacked Talan looking for the Seal, mean ole' Larien had stomped over to the bookshelf in the corner of her office, told her to stay put with a big scowl marring his oh-so-gorgeous face, then did the diapha-whatever-the-hell he called it and was gone. Interesting. If she weren't so annoyed with him, she would have allowed herself to think about how cool it was that he got that faint translucent bluish glow around him right before he did the poofy thing and disappeared. Did all angels have that? She'd have to pay closer attention.

"Asshole," Jayla grumbled. "How dare he imply that he can't leave me alone for five minutes and then look at me as if I was a clueless four-year-old searching for shiny rocks at the edge of a crocodile-infested swamp."

She might not know all there was to know about the stupid Seal they were after, but she knew enough to trust her intuition—and it said that she was on someone's radar. She had no idea who was watching, there were so many possibilities—friend, foe, human, angel, Fallen angel, Fallen demon, daemon or born demon. Geesh! But she sure as hell knew better than to go romping around while her Spidey senses were tingling.

In the meantime, she had paperwork to do. Her office was certainly conducive to such boring tasks. Organized and contemporary, it boasted a large white maple glass-topped desk with matching file cabinets and credenza all arranged for efficiency. A whiteboard was attached to one entire wall and was covered with plans for upcoming events, ideas for the remodel of the inside of this facility as well as next year's budget. Yep, definitely a work-inducing atmosphere. She'd get her work done as quickly as possible, and then get out to the sparring ring to play.

Talan should be on his way home from her Grams' storage room with some new clue or another, and then he'd be off to get ready for his first date with a woman he'd recently met. Mandy or Candy or something like that. She'd have to ask him about this woman. Maybe she'd call him to come over and have lunch with her so he could give her the skinny on the chick.

Her personal trainers were in the weight lifting area making their clients produce the sweat for which they paid so handsomely. Jayla started to call Chel to have someone to commiserate her bitchy mood with, then remembered that her friend was on a plane to New York headed for some handsome photographer's den where they would blow through a few dozen memory cards of pictures for one magazine or another. She'd check in sooner or later, as was her way.

The thought brought a strange trickle of weirdness with it. Chel. She'd been acting strange, well more strange than normal, since meeting Larien last night. If she wasn't pissed off and butt-hurt over one thing, she was annoyed about another. The woman could give Larien a run for his money in the snarly-growly department.

And what did she really know about Chel? Sure she knew what made the woman tick—attention, good food and a lazy popcorn-fest with Jayla and Talan in pajamas over a good movie. But where was her family? Chel didn't talk about her growing-up years much, and Jayla didn't believe in prying. But the thought of walking into a possible life-and-death situation while not really knowing much about one of her best friends left a bit of a bitter aspirin-like taste on the back of her tongue. Red-flags regarding Chel? Nah. Not really. Just some healthy curiosity now that she knew there were more beings out there than her own personal angel brigade.

This shade-of-gray brand of supernatural of the Fallen kind painted things in a whole new light, though a dim one. She'd never run into anything that was hell bent on harming her, like the duo that Larien and Talan had battled together. Truth be told, she had no idea what to do if she found herself in that kind of danger. She didn't even know if she could feel or see them like she could with Larien.

"Well, two guesses what we'll be talking about when he gets back here to pick me up," she grumbled, abusing the computer's keyboard as she banged data into the accounting software.

Whoa. What the hell was that?

She hadn't actually heard anything. It was more of a strange *pop-hum* that shimmied around in her belly yet seemed to come from somewhere far away. Her gaze snapped up from the pages that lay open in front of her. Pushing away from the computer, Jayla moved out from behind the desk and eased toward the locked door.

Relax, relax. It was probably nothing.

Besides, she'd spoken the protections around this place and...

"Jayla?"

Shit! She scrambled three feet back from the still-closed door and rammed her backside into the sharp corner of the desk.

"Ouch!"

"Jay, you okay? Can I come in?"

Okay, she was entirely too jumpy. Damn Larien. Having her scared of her shadow with all the talk about demons of the Fallen variety and other such nonsense. Well, not nonsense, but that wasn't the point. Flipping the deadbolt, she twisted the knob.

Marv, one of her personal trainers, ducked his head in. She'd known him for years, but he could still make her draw in a breath. He was all sunlight and cream with a honed, hard and totally drool-worthy body. Jade green eyes sparkled with a mix of determination and "damn I'm sexy". Gah! They made a woman want to sidle up, smile and then roll around on the mat with him. Even when sweating like a pig and his naturally blonde hair spiked with sweat the man was über hot.

"You know, Marv, it's totally unfair that you're just so damn pretty."

"Always willing to add another gorgeous person to the mix, Jay."

"Yeah," she grinned, "but I don't share."

Marv was already in a relationship—a ménage, actually. Even

if she were the sharing type it was a brooding, grumpy, drop-dead handsome Fallen that her mind conjured. And he was playing as hard to get as she was. Bastard.

"So what's up, handsome?"

"Nothing much. Two-thirty walk-in is here."

"Walk-in?"

"Yes, can you take it?" Marv asked.

"Why? Where's Carlo?"

Her brain swirled with what-if's. What if it was a bad guy? What if something got past her guardians? What if...?

Oh girl, stop it. Over reacting much? Jayla mentally smacked herself in the forehead.

"I'd take it myself but I'm already booked. Lan is covering at the other gym across the Bay and Carlo called in sick. Was hoping you could step in since you don't have anything booked this afternoon."

"Sure, Marv. I'll take care of it. Personal training or consultation?"

"Consultation."

"Who is it?" she asked, reaching for the clipboard in Marv's hands.

"Some guy named Winters. He's prepping for the Nor Cal natural bodybuilding contest. Guess he's having trouble getting his body fat down that last half-percentage point and was hoping we could recommend a plateau buster. Maybe some supplements or something?"

"Sure. Take him into conference room two. Tell him I'll be right there."

"You've got it boss," Marvin said with a wink and a smile. God, she was surrounded by capable gorgeous men and couldn't get laid. What was the world coming to?

* * * * *

Footsteps dragged along the carpet and the hall seemed to grow longer the closer she got to conference room two. She saw nothing, heard nothing. But God, she just *knew* something wasn't quite right.

Okay, stop wigging out. There is nothing wrong here.

Everything is normal. If something was wrong Ambriel and the crew would be here kicking ass while Larien is doing whatever the hell he's doing. Right? Right.

Several steps away from the door and Jayla's spine felt like it wanted to run away from her body.

With a deep breath, she put her hand to the knob, turned it and stepped through. Her feet rooted themselves to the floor. On the other side of the large conference table in the center of the room was one of the most handsome men she'd ever seen in her life. And she'd seen plenty of lookers given her business was the art of perfecting bodies.

Yet, this man was...God, she wasn't sure how to even put it into words. It was like his face had been fashioned with every wet dream she'd ever had in mind. And that's how she knew something was four kinds of wrong.

Too damn perfect. Too sexy. And way too fuckable.

"Ah, Miss Protegenu, it's so nice to meet you."

Her senses screamed "non-human" loud and clear, like one of those horns people blew at football games. This wasn't a man. This was a...actually she didn't know what it was, but the mix of lust and menace that rolled off of it slithered up her body and punched her gut from the inside out. Flesh felt stretched too tight. Perhaps if he touched her in the proper spot, she'd simply zip her skin off and leave it behind, freeing her spirit to float about the room in a gloriously horny haze. Her hair was on fire, blood boiled beneath the scalp. Her mind tore off into two directions. It screamed "Run", or was that "Stay"...actually she couldn't remember now.

Oh, he's so verra verra pretteh. Seductive. Gloriously hot.

He stepped closer.

No wait. He hadn't actually moved his feet. Yet here he stood, barely an arm's length away. Too damn close.

"Who are you?" It was all she could manage to croak out.

"I'm Winters. I came for," he drawled as he looked down at her—oooh, so tall—with a satisfied gleam in his black eyes and a half-smirk that flashed a bit of...fang? Oh, that couldn't be good. "My consultation."

The longer she met his gaze, the faster he seemed to morph back and forth from beatific hottie to scary-as-hell, taller, larger, muscle bound fang boy until his entire presence was one big flickering blur.

An instant, pounding, nausea-inducing headache slammed into the back of her skull and she began to slip—not physically, but more of a mental fade. Even her peripheral vision was a slithering gray fuzz. She should go with him.

No!

But why not?

And why the hell was she having a conversation with herself?

Her lips were beginning to numb with cold, but the rest of her body was ablaze, like a mix of fierce longing and attack of the killer bees. She screamed at herself in her head to back up a measly twelve inches and get out of the room.

No, I want to stay here.

Obviously she was seeing things that weren't real, right?

But it felt real. Smelled real. Then Winters was all around her, covering her as surely as if she'd fallen into a hole and someone was bulldozing it over with a substance made purely of this man. Yet, his feet remained in the same spot they'd been when she'd walked into this daymare. Wait, maybe it was a nightmare. Was it night yet? She couldn't tell. Couldn't reason. Stuck. Couldn't get out. Frozen with terror.

She almost cocked her head in wonder—so this was what true fear felt like? It wasn't a feeling she'd drowned in before. Strange gully-wash of emotion, this.

Then Mr. Winters let the façade dissolve completely and she saw him for what he was. No more illusion. Yet he was just as visually seductive. Certainly no less potent. He called to her, asked her to submit to him of her own free will. Her mouth opened to answer even as her common sense bit down on her tongue to quiet it.

Several inches added themselves to his already ginormous frame as his skin changed from perfectly tanned to a pearly gray. He was large and muscular, so built his chest and legs could hold up the Golden Gate Bridge. And he had wings. Red ones. The gold tips called to her fingers to stroke them. Were the little talons on the ends sharp? Even if they were, she could still play with them anyway, right?

The so-called Mr. Winters lifted a now tree-sized arm and stretched his hand out to her again. His eyes began to glow that otherworldly blue, like Larien's did right before he did the flashy thing. Was he leaving? Or was something far worse on its way?

"Come, stroke my wings. Stroke me. Come away with me."

That voice, those eyes. His wings. It all beckoned. God, she wanted him.

"Are you...?" The words were slurred as if she'd been on a three day alcohol binge.

"Fallen?" he sang. Or at least it sounded like a song, but the key was off. Warped. Wrong. "I was Fallen, but now I am more. You want me, don't you, Descendant."

It wasn't a question. The thought had been shoved into her brain and left to expand as if it were truth. Planted firmly, like a fist to her face. He'd been toying with her, manipulating her. His mistake was letting her *know* it. If there was one thing Jayla hated, it was being handled. Now *that* pissed her off. Self-righteous bastard. That's probably why he'd Fallen in the first place.

Anger cleared her mind with a sharpness she was thankful for.

"No, I don't want you, asshat."

Then she was fading again, knew she had time for a single word.

Better make it good.

"Larien!"

* * * * *

Larien tightened the muscle in his legs, refusing to shift his weight in annoyance. Standing in Gabriel's presence up on the First Tier after all this time was a bit...uncomfortable. It was like having the sun stuffed behind his eyeballs and blown up a thousand times. God, he was going to be blind and useless after this. It was glorious. Brilliant. And not for him. Not anymore.

"Mind dialing back all that glory for a moment, Gabe? I will do you no good if I can't see."

"As if you could really go blind," Gabriel snorted.

"*So* not the point."

Larien held on to his temper, unsure of why he was pissed off in the first place. Gabriel had given him the opportunity of a lifetime by choosing him for this task. He'd also put him in much too close a proximity to a woman that called to him, body and soul.

Speaking of said woman, he wondered what she was doing just now.

"So, she is on board and all the arrangements are made?" Gabriel asked.

"All ready. We're heading out at the end of the week to meet with an expert in antiquity. Her friends are coming with us. It makes her more comfortable."

"So, why do you look uncomfortable?"

Larien hadn't bothered to put on any pretense of being happy about exactly how the search for the Seal was going, but there was an old saying—keep your friends close and your enemies closer.

He shoved his hands into the pocket of his leather bomber jacket and answered the question put to him. A question he still hadn't gotten to the bottom of. "Chelriad is in the picture."

The storm cloud that passed over Gabriel's brow mirrored the one on Larien's. The Messenger's eyes blazed with anger as his fabled sword flamed into existence at the ready, comfortable in his hand.

"Chelriad? What the hell is she doing involved in this?"

"Good question. Unfortunately, I have no answer. I just learned last night that the best friend Jayla has been speaking of is our own dear Chelriad, now calling herself Arlisa Chelton. Chel for short. They became friends some years ago, supposedly by chance. And believe it or not, she's a high fashion model."

Gabriel snarled. Larien's fist tightened, ready to land a blow if needed. Gabriel was an Archangel of the Host. Nothing about them equaled fluffy bunnies and sunshine. He could be a real dick when the situation called for it. And with a rumored bed partner of Lucifer hanging around Jayla, the Messenger might feel that this did indeed call for a bit of hard wall-to-wall counseling, mainly Larien's head against the nearest wall.

But regardless of Larien's Fall, Gabriel was his peer, not his master. Not bothering to keep the tension from his shoulders nor hide the hand planted firmly on the hilt of his own blade—though he had sense enough not to draw it—Larien said, "There are many things you didn't bother to brief me on. I did not appreciate learning of Jayla's ability to call our kind through Ambriel."

Gabriel's sharp gaze raked him over. It was like having his naked skin scraped with a sharp garden tool while being soothed with oil and honey at the same time. He wasn't sure whether he should feel abused or rubbed down like a turkey.

Gabriel seemed to pull himself together and looked out over the terrain. "Ambriel, eh? I am sure he rubbed that in as much as possible." His words were filled with mirth, but his smile would have chilled a human. Literally.

Larien relaxed and leaned against a tree. The bark was warm under his back though it looked of bronze with leaves of pearl. "He's lucky you didn't give me permission to toss him through the Abyss gate."

"Details. Now," Gabriel demanded.

"I can't give you any. But I can say that Jayla has no idea that one of her best friends if a Fallen of the first Fall. She also has very little knowledge of her birthright. I don't feel quite so bad at being in the dark about all this considering she has even less of an idea of what's going on than I do."

"Stop your whining, Larien. I gave you the information that I could. We are not omnipresent, omniscient, or omni-anything-else. We are simply tools that do what we must."

"Bullshit. No one plays games like you, Gabriel. Luckily this Jayla is quite resilient. Even when I poofed, she didn't—"

"Poofed?"

"Yes, that's what Jayla calls diaphaneity. What? Is there a problem?"

Gabriel had *that* look on his face. Larien ignored both Gabriel and the warmth that settled in his chest at the thought of Jayla. Damn woman.

"Get to the bottom of it Larien. We have to find that Seal. Chelriad is a complication we do not need."

"Yes, and the more time I spend here giving you book reports the less time I have to figure out what's going on." Gabriel scowled. So the sanctimonious bastard didn't appreciate his tone of voice? Tough shit.

"Did you tell her about our agreement? Does she know what you get out of the bargain?"

Gabriel might not be his boss any longer, but The Messenger had him in chains with this assignment none the less. And Larien had no problem voicing his displeasure.

"Gabe, I may have Fallen but I am far from stupid." Even if he,

Gabriel and all the celestial tiers were indeed using Jayla, it was important to Larien that she not *feel* used. "We need to understand what we are dealing with here. We've acquired both Talan and Jayla, and now have a lead to help us decipher the first clues about the lost artifact. You'll have to be satisfied with that for now. And why the hell are you looking at me like that?"

"You are falling for her, this human. Or should I say *another* human. How much more misery do you—"

"Remember, Gabriel, I am not looking for redemption. Only freedom."

Gabriel shook him head. "I just do not understand. Of all the angels of your class, you could have had it all. You were a counselor to kings and governors. Advisor to—"

"I was a fucking babysitter, Gabriel. And I will never be sorry to have been loved. I became something unexpected to those who made us, and I get that. But believe it or not, I'm at peace with what I became."

Suddenly the back of his skull vibrated as if a twenty pound weight had been thrown against it and vibrated like a thick steel gong.

"Fuck!"

Larien had never transformed so fast and was sure he'd left a few pieces of skin behind in Gabriel's presence as he was literally snatched away.

CHAPTER TWELVE

Larien's head filled with an audible buzz as he landed hard on one knee in the corner of one of Jayla's conference rooms in her gym. He looked up and snarled.

A Fallen demon was trying to leave with her.

The moment she'd caught sight of Larien her eyes brightened, her expression changed from one twisted with absolute suffering to one of hope.

She opened her mouth. "You c-cannot la-leave," she pushed through lips blue with cold even as her aura flared. Fingers that had been trying to push the Fallen demon away now dug into his tough flesh to hold him. Smoky white wisps of power bled from around her body to encompass both herself and the Fallen demon. She'd trapped him. Bound him. How the hell had she done that?

But this wasn't a puzzle to solve just now. Now, he needed to help Jayla. She was fading fast. Whatever the Fallen had done to her was slipping into her very soul, touching her in the deepest part of her being. Corrupting. Destroying.

This *so* was not going to happen.

It wouldn't be smart to fight all out, then not have enough power to get Jayla the hell out of here. Destroying this creature wasn't an option right now, but he could certainly hurt it good and proper. Larien pulled his sword with practiced ease. The blade, comfortable and welcome in his left hand, was encompassed in black flame that set a hum into the very air. A specially crafted semi-automatic pistol cleared its holster and was at the ready in his other hand.

Like all the other miscreant cast-outs in this realm, this one didn't have a connection to the Source. No endless energy to draw on meant wounds from either of his weapons would hurt like a son of a bitch and take the bastard out of commission for a while.

Larien would have grinned at the damage his specialized gear could do if he weren't so pissed off.

With Jayla still in his arms, the intruder let his skin slip completely, shot up to his full height and snarled. This one wasn't an interrogator of demon-kind, like the bastards that had accosted Talan. No, this one's specialty was twisted into casting imagination and seduction. In short, he'd scramble Jayla's very spirit until she didn't know up from down.

A glance at the woman who'd gone entirely too still filled him with relief and dread—she was drifting in and out of consciousness, which meant she wouldn't see the violence he was capable of. On the other hand, it could mean she was hurt. Bad.

Damn, he wanted to kick ass, but this woman was his first priority. Period. Her aura flared again, this time fainter, grayer. "Put me down," she rasped and power pushed at the Fallen demon. The fine hair on Larien's forearms stirred under the strength infused in each syllable. Not much, but just enough. The Fallen demon obeyed, gritting his teeth yet doing what she asked all the same.

Her feet touched the carpet without a sound. A second later Jayla crumpled to the floor and Larien let his battle form burst through, felt his body stretch to accommodate his true height. The familiar sting of parting skin signaled the emergence of his wings at the same time he raised his bad-assed gun and unloaded round after round of angelized ammo into his foe before the thing could raise a hand to defend itself.

It went down under a barrage of bullets and flopped to the floor as nothing but a mound of wriggling flesh.

God, why did they always smell like rotten cow ass when they were damaged?

The dimming essence of the creature, it's very life energy, glowed through the holes in its skin. Energy could not actually be destroyed, so soon this one would slink off somewhere to regenerate.

Larien grabbed Jayla, powered up his diaphaneity and got them the hell out of there.

* * * * *

Chel's eyes flew open but the dream continued to play in her head like a bad movie.

Sadness. Those she'd always known, had always felt down to the marrow of her bones now turned on her with such a vengeance it was unfathomable. Such ferocity had never been focused on her. Had never been directed at her.

Even when learning to fight, as every angel must, her body had never experienced such pain. It was as if a layer of herself had been skinned away leaving her raw and exposed to feel the full impact of each blow. The blows reverberated down through her body, through skin, muscle and bone, down to the cellular level they vibrated through her.

She felt them—some brimming with righteous indignation, disgusted and appalled at the thought of rebellion, others full of sorrow at what they were doing even as she was filled with the anguish of betrayal. Her people had turned on her.

Then the rending began. Not just the tearing of flesh, but also the decimation of spirit as she was ripped away from the consciousness of the family that she had felt from the moment of her first breath.

And with the rending came crippling loneliness and despair. It felt like she'd been marooned, closed off. The pain of being alone came in waves of absolute crushing agony.

She'd never been alone before. Even if she'd sat in one of the training halls with no one around, she'd never truly been by herself. Had never called out to her brothers, sisters, and cousins only to have the sound of her own voice bounce around in her head and then echo into nothingness.

The last she'd seen of her home was the bottom of an Archangel's boot. And then she Fell. The stars flew past until they appeared to be one long streak of light. A second before she understood what waited, she turned her head toward the earth. It rose up fast to meet her.

This was no graceful floating down to the ground. No, it was as if she'd been blasted through time and space until even the very air passed over her skin so quickly it burned, left rifts and welts behind.

She'd slammed into the earth. Lay there barely drawing breath. Each shallow pant sent new agony streaking through every limb. Her organs felt flattened in her body. Her wings had been snapped off before she'd been kicked down here, so this current cracking of bone was something else—likely every other bone in her body.

If she'd ever wished to be a human, it was now. At least she could have died to escape the hell of her new existence, the desolation of her plight.

Instead, she lay there, healing slowly even as a simmer began in her soul. Hatred. Pure burning hatred, but not for man. No, her anger was at the asshole that had talked her into rebelling. As the sun rose and set in what seemed like endless days, Chel lay in the middle of the desert, thoughts focused on the angel who had held the highest office in their world. One who walked with the creative Source themselves. So handsome, perfectly formed, with a voice that brought one to ones knees in reverence as he sang to those that had made him. He'd been called the Son of the Morning because the glory of his being had been like the rising of the sun whenever he walked into a room.

Lucifer.

And that fucker had been the cause of her worst nightmare— Chelriad, Angel of the Second Tier, Virtue and commander of the elements, had Fallen.

Shivering under the sheet that was stuck to her body by nothing but sweat, Chel sat up and swung her legs over the side of the bed. God she hated that memory. Hated that there was nothing she could do about it when it chose to surface as she slept. She was so cold, as if she'd just come in out of a freezing rain, drenched to the skin. But she didn't strip off the soaked nightgown or move off of the wet sheets. She needed to feel. Needed to let this wash through her. Again.

It had been quite a while since she'd been a shivering mess in her bed at night and Chel knew exactly what had triggered the nightmare—Larien. Even with all the supernaturals in her city, she hadn't expected to come face to face with someone who had witnessed her utter humiliation. The result of that little childhood rebellion had ended up costing her everything. Literally.

And Larien had been there. Had seen it happen. Participated side-by-side with the others of the Host tasked with meeting out their special brand of brutal justice.

Finally she rose and padded over to the floor-to-ceiling windows of her hotel room. The moon reflected off the Hudson and light rippled across the black surface of the water as Chel sank to the carpet and wrapped her arms around herself.

She hung her head and winced at the pull of tense muscle in her neck but she didn't attempt to soothe the pain.

Larien had been there when she Fell. It had been beyond a surprise to learn he'd Fallen himself several millennia after that great disaster. But now, to find him in her friend's home helping with a quest to find the one artifact that gave demons pause? Chel didn't know what to think. Why had he, of all beings, been sent? And why had he accepted?

Chel shook her head with a snort remembering that unexpected meeting in Jayla's living room. Larien had powered up his diaphaneity. He hadn't used it, but he knew she would feel the push against her insides. He'd wanted to shake her and he'd been quite successful. In fact, Chel had been speechless, but not for the reason Larien probably thought.

Larien hadn't exposed what Chel really was. The more she thought on it, the more "why's" popped into her head.

A shiver stole down her spine. Shower. She needed a hot shower.

She moved into the bathroom and set the water to scalding. As it sprayed over her skin, Chel realized that she'd always known this day would come. If not with Larien, then another of her kind. Or former kind.

Sigh.

Jayla and Talan had been the only lights in her life in a very long time. There was no way she would survive being abandoned again, driven away from the two people that had shown her love and care after so much loneliness and despair.

She tried to push back the lump that always clogged her throat at thoughts of home. This time she was unsuccessful. Tears streamed down her face and blended with the droplets from the shower as sobs that hadn't wracked her body in ages tore through her. Behind closed lids she saw wide bright avenues, tall white-stoned buildings where she'd trained in combat, physics and celestial healing. Saw her house, built to her specifications by her own powers soaring upward, all elegant lines, arches and light. Most heart wrenching was remembering the spots she used to hang out with her cousins, Abaddon and Azrael. A faint smile tugged at the corner of her lips as memories of their expression flitted through her mind as they'd joked, ribbed each other, laughed and loved. The camaraderie—*that*, she missed most of all.

She slid down to the shower floor and let the sorrow wash through her. Let herself reel with the emotions usually kept checked and locked deep inside. Pushing her thick dark brown hair back and out of her face she sniffled and squared her shoulders as she realized something Larien's unexpected presence forced her to acknowledge.

Home was her friends, Jayla and Talan. She loved them, though they were human. She still loved her family and didn't blame them for her Fall—it had been her dumb choice to follow Luc and she accepted that. And while she still loved her kin she could never go to that particular home again.

Thanks to Talan and Jay, she now had a new home. And she would do whatever was necessary to protect it. Protect them.

She knew one day she would have to reveal what she was, and Larien's arrival simply made that day sooner rather than later. The last thing Chel wanted was for either Jayla or Talan to believe she'd lied to them. At the thought of the 'b' word—betrayal—anger sat on the back of her tongue, bitter and acrid, like crushed aspirin left to dissolve slowly with nothing but saliva to wash it down. And that anger was directed at one person.

The person who'd chosen this very moment to call her.

Luc.

It was a long-standing rumor that she'd taken him as a lover. But Chel had never shared his bed. She'd only shared his moment of temporary insanity.

Resisting the summons Chel stepped from the shower, dried off and dressed in a warm cotton gown. A quick call down to the front desk and clean linens quickly replaced the soaked ones. She climbed back into bed, her resolve rock solid. She'd be getting home just in time to accompany her family to Nevada to see the Isthus guy. As soon as she arrived she'd come clean, tell them everything, and trust them to forgive her.

The summons came again.

She rolled over, fluffed her pillow and lay down with a smile.

Kiss my ass, Luc.

CHAPTER THIRTEEN

In Jayla's bedroom, Larien removed her clothes with a thought, tucked her shivering body beneath the covers and flashed out again. In seconds he'd grabbed Talan and was back in Jayla's home.

"What the hell?" Talan stuttered and dry heaved on his knees.

"Jayla was attacked at the gym moments ago. Fix it."

"Who? How?"

Now this was a man Larien could work with. Talan focused on the big picture rather than the fact he kneeled naked and dripping from the shower Larien had snatched him out of.

Talan rose, laid one hand gently over Jayla's heart, the other over her stomach. Talan's eyes closed and Larien felt every hair on his body stand at attention. Whatever the man did, the energy he put off was potent.

"She hasn't sustained any physical wounds. This is magical," he murmured.

Larien tossed a robe from the foot of the bed and stepped back and out of the way. Talan slipped into the very girly clothing without batting an eye.

"What got to her?"

"Improbael," Larien replied.

A fiery red brow lifted. "A what?"

"Improbael. A Fallen demon. His specialty is perversion and illusion."

Talan laid his hands on Jayla's head and stilled.

"Her skin is like ice, but her internal temperature is burning off the charts. She's definitely got a fever of sorts."

"Well, he's also the former angel of winter. And currently on my shit list."

"Fine." The words were a bite, urgent and determined. "Larien, come over here. Hold her hand. She needs the warmth, the contact."

Larien hesitated. The last thing Jayla needed was someone like him to…

"Larien, now. I need you to touch her while I change."

"Change? Into what?" It came out a menacing growl.

"I told you when I'm not a Shadow Priest, I'm something else. I need to change to that something else if we're going to save her. Now get your ass over here so I can help my friend."

Larien grabbed Jayla's hand and forced himself to hold on. She was freezing to the touch with a strange energy that murmured just beneath the skin, foreign and pulsing, as if something wiggled through her veins. He'd never felt anything like it. It made him want to throw up.

Talan's body dimmed then flared like a bulb as if the Shadow magic had been drained right out of him and replaced by brilliance. Seconds later he grunted and fell to his knees with a thud. Larien tensed, ready to grab the guy if he keeled over. Damn, he was tired of surprises today.

"Hey, you alright?" he asked.

"Yeah. Fine. Just—" Gasp. Pant. "Give me a second to get my mana up."

"Mana?"

"Tell you later. I should have a potion in my… Ah, there it is." Out of thin air, appeared a clear vial of candy-red liquid. Talan gulped it down and winced. Larien watched impatiently as color filled the human's cheeks again.

Though the house was toasty and warm, Jayla began to tremble, her breathing grew labored and her face paled to the color of ashes. When Larien realized her exhalations emerged in puffs of frosty condensation, his concern bloomed into an emotion buried so deeply in his past he'd almost forgotten what it was—terror.

Holding Jayla's hand tighter, as if he could somehow keep her from slipping away by sheer force of will alone, he ground out, "If you do not move faster, I swear I will kill you where you stand, Talan. She's shaking like a fucking leaf!"

To his credit, Talan didn't so much as blink at the threat. Jayla was obviously his only concern. There was probably nothing Larien could threaten him with that would affect him more than the thought of losing this woman.

"Okay, let's do this." Talan jumped up off his knees and rushed to the bed. He closed his eyes and gently laid one hand on Jayla's forehead. With the other he conjured a wand. It smelled of eucalyptus and something else Larien couldn't place. The magick of the thing buzzed and hummed in his ears.

"What is that?"

"Willow wand. Good for healing. Move." With that, Talan pointed it at Jayla's chest. Magick flowed freely in tendrils of warm-colored energies. The scent of rich earth filled the air. It energized and brought clarity of mind, just as it had during that fight against the two Fallen demons in Talan's apartment.

A faint bronze glow visible to the naked eye flowed from Talan into Jayla. Whatever it was, Talan seemed to be pulling it from the very air around them. After a few minutes, Jayla's erratic breathing began to settle though she was still deathly cold and breathing icy puffs of fog. Talan opened his eyes and conjured a vial of milky-white sweet smelling fluid.

"Sit her up just a bit. Just enough to get this into her. After that I'll need you out of the way, but don't go far. Jay will need you before the night is done."

Larien backed up and prepared to flash out, with one thing on his mind. Finding what was left of Improbael and ending him for good. Just as he gathered his gift to him, Talan looked up with a gaze so cold, calculating and intent, Larien was glad it wasn't directed at him.

The ferocity of Talan's voice, though barely a whisper, slashed through the quietness of the room.

"And don't leave to find the asshole without me. Give me your word."

Smart man. Very smart man.

"You have it," Larien promised.

Hiding a smile at the ferocity of Talan's demand, Larien

vanished, glad Jayla had this man at his back, human or not.

* * * * *

Behind Jayla's house Larien pulled a bit of charmed parchment from his pocket, spoke the summoning spell in a rush and tossed it up into the air. An instant breeze kicked up and carried it away. Leaning against the fence near the small area that Jayla used as a garden, he waited impatiently.

"What?"

Whipping around, gun drawn, Larien glared at the person who currently owned his ass—Gabriel.

"Took you long enough."

"And you have not answered my question. What?" Gabriel demanded.

Larien glared at the Messenger and thought about shooting him. Too bad he was the only one that could get him what he needed just now. Fuck.

"Jayla was attacked today. It's why I was pulled away from my little meeting with you earlier. Fallen demon walked right into her gym and almost made away with her. If she weren't so damn stubborn she'd be lost to us. Somehow Jayla kept herself from being taken God-knows-where. She actually held Improbael to this plane until I could get to her and wound the son of a bitch."

"How did he get inside? Where were her guardians?" Gabriel's words were stiff with what Larien thought was anger, but with this particular Archangel, one never could tell. Gabriel played his secrets close to the vest always, the bastard.

"How the fuck am I supposed to know, Gabe? I know you know what the hell is going on. I can't protect her if I'm in the dark. This is pissing me the fuck off."

Gabriel shot him a warning glare. Larien didn't give a rat's ass. He didn't have time to accommodate the Messenger's delicate sensibilities, or anyone else's just now. Jayla was his main concern. Period.

"I will look into it," Gabriel said grudgingly. "How is she, the Protegenu Descendant?"

"Her friend, Talan, is working on her now. Thanks to him it looks like she will recover. I fucking know more about Talan and his Shadow Priest abilities than I do about Jayla at this point, Gabriel. This is un-fucking-acceptable."

"I do not think I have heard you use that many f-words in so short a time in all your existence."

"Then that should tell you how fucking angry I am about these unknowns popping up in the middle of my mission. By the way, we need to get her guardians in place. You know I don't have the authority to call them. Other than you, only Jayla can do that, which she is in no shape to do just now."

"Of course." Without another word, Gabriel faded from sight even as Ambriel, Barchiel and at least twenty others stalked into the little yard.

"What the hell happened to her?" Ambriel yelled as he stormed across the grass, so angry he left charred footprints in his wake.

Ambriel stopped short when the nose of Larien's modified gun pressed flush against his chest just as Larien's sword cleared the sheath beneath his arm with a loud *schwing*.

"Do not fuck with me, Ambriel. I will fill your ass so full of bullets you will give the word 'holy' a new meaning. Jayla is hurt and I am *not* in the mood for your bullshit."

With that, he turned his back on the lot of them and made a beeline for the one woman who managed to wiggle her way into his head even when she was unconscious.

* * * * *

Just because she had a high pain tolerance didn't mean she was big on feeling it. She would be sure to remember to tell that to the asshole that'd managed to turn her body into one big breathing unhappy bruise. Hopefully she'd be kicking his ass during that particular conversation.

Bone deep soreness—this must be what it felt like to get electrocuted to the point where your body seized up until you bruised the muscle beneath the skin.

Well, at least I'm breathing.

She thought back on the moments just before she'd croaked out a plea for Larien. Had she really wanted to strip off her clothes and spread her legs for a creature that seemed to sweat sensuality and malice? One who'd had her so confused she wasn't sure whether she was coming or going even while her feet were rooted to the floor? Had she truly seen her breath form a thick frosty fog in front of her face while standing in her seventy-degree office? The lingering chill in her blood declared that it had indeed happened. And that chill seeped into her flesh and bones with mind-numbing agony.

Okay, lay here and just breathe. Ow. Okay, breathe shallow.

The earthiness of her favorite Nag Champa incense immediately soothed. Another scent, otherworldly, subtle and pleasantly familiar, told her Larien was close. With a slow drag of air the last bit of haze cleared from her head, and then she wished she'd remained passed out. Along with clarity of thinking came a flare of pain intense enough to seize her lungs yet again. God, she thought she hurt just a few seconds ago, but this was beyond pain. She hoped she didn't look as awful as she felt.

And now the chill dissipated from her insides and it was boiling hot in here. Not bothering to open her eyes, she scooted to the edge of the bed to go open the window. Or she tried to scoot. Her limbs decided they weren't making the trip across the bed, let alone a trip across the room, especially with a large, very heavy arm draped over her body and a hand splayed about her stomach.

"What do you need?"

Oooh.

Larien's words, deep with the remnants of sleep, sent a gentle waft of air over the skin on the back of her neck. Turning slowly, because that's as fast as she could go no matter how much energy she expended, Jayla smiled when the bulge of muscle beneath her cheek flexed. Amazing the man's arm was big enough to pillow her head. When she finally made it all the way over, the edge of her forehead brushed against a slightly scratchy jaw. She'd wondered what his five o'clock shadow felt like against her skin and her new-found knowledge brought with it a delicious shiver that had nothing to do with the residual cold left behind by her ordeal.

"You're injured, Jay. Where were you trying to go?"

"How do you know I was going anywhere? I barely moved." Just the thought of lifting a finger after the eternity it took to roll over and face Larien literally made her break out in a nervous sweat.

If not for the soothing *something* that poured off of Larien, she'd be beyond miserable instead of just plain ole' miserable.

"You stiffened up in my arms. Felt like you were trying to move."

"It's hot in here and I was going to open the window. But I don't need to now."

"You sure?"

"Yes."

Larien was the source of the warmth. Now that she was aware of where all the heat came from, she decided it was quite lovely and would rather have it than not.

"This is nice."

"Mmm?" he asked.

"Waking up with you."

"Well, I'm flattered, considering you could have been killed on my watch."

"But I thought there was a rule that celestials, no matter what kind, can't kill humans."

"But some can use the elements against you. Make you wish you were dead. Or they can affect your body to the point where your mind just can't cope. At that point, you'd beg for Death. Manage to call that particular angel, and he will indeed arrive."

"Wow. The angel of Death is real? Man, the time I snuck away and spent with Grams obviously wasn't enough. I missed that particular lesson."

His arms tightened around her and she found her head on his chest. Her head rose and fell as he breathed. "So what are you doing in my bed?" she asked. "Don't get me wrong, I quite like it."

"Talan did some magickal healing on you, and then insisted you needed the warmth and physical contact to help you heal. Kind of like drawing from my celestial energy, my Source, to boost your own."

Well that explained the bare skin beneath her cheek and the slight tickle of hair from the long legs rubbing ever so slightly against hers. And the delicious weight of the sizeable erection pressed into her hip. The temperature of the room shot up some more, but it had nothing to do with her illness and everything to do with the fact that, even in her wonky physical state, she wanted this man. The flight of butterflies in her stomach and the heat between her thighs said as much, considering they seemed to agree with her head. What fucked up timing.

But wait, had he said…

"Talan…magickal? What…?"

"And you have to take some medicine now that you're awake," Larien said.

"What is it?"

"I couldn't possibly pronounce it, but Talan made it. It's for the pain."

Pain medicine? Yeah, she could get with that. But she hadn't missed the fact that he hadn't answered the magickal Talan question. God, she was tired now. Later. Yes, she'd ask later.

"Can you move on your own at all?" he asked.

"Hardly," she replied with a bit more snark than she intended. It cost her. Pounding lit off just behind her lids.

Larien sat up and gently repositioned her body until her back was to his front. Reaching past her, he grabbed something off of her nightstand. The quiet pop of a cork sounded just before he pressed a small cool vial to her lips. She stiffened, expecting to gag, but the stuff was somewhat fruity even with the unmistakable twang of medicinal bitters that hit her on the back end. In seconds, the effects kicked in.

Jayla felt her lips tilt up into a goofy smile as Larien dropped a kiss on top of her head. She didn't think he was even aware of the gentle gesture, or that a single finger traced a short path across the skin on her arms.

Oooh, tingly.

"So what attacked me?"

"Fallen."

"Doesn't make sense," she drawled as the medicine sped through her system. "He didn't look anything like you. You're pretty."

* * * * *

Larien sighed with relief as Jayla's eyes drifted shut. Just like that she was out as if someone had switched off a light.

God bless Talan's pain herbs.

He lay with her in his arms and thought on the question she'd

126

asked just before she'd passed out.

What had attacked her?

Fallen. But this one was no daemon, like himself. No, Improbael had fully turned. And going rogue came with its share of interesting side-effects, apart from the whole evil-man-walking thing. While all of his kind had fangs that could be kept hidden, along with their true forms, only those that had embraced the dark side had the tell-tale cement-gray skin and grunge-filled auras that stank with ill intent.

Note to self—teach Jayla to see auras so she knows what she's dealing with. Damn Gabriel's game playing and secrets.

Done with his mental to-do list, Larien braced himself for the truly hard questions he knew this woman would have when she finally woke. She was no slacker and was as bright as they came.

Mumbling in her sleep, Jayla rolled over, dragged herself on top of him and draped her arms and legs over his body. Naked as the day she was born, the woman pushed at his chest like he was her favorite pillow, nuzzled her face into his skin and promptly fell asleep again with a sigh of his name. He smiled and grimaced at the same time. This was as close to torture as he ever wanted to get—to feel her against him and not have her the way his flesh screamed to.

Was hell anything like this?

Jayla lay right on top of his now painfully hard cock. God, the pictures his mind conjured —her stark naked, the moist lips of her pussy warm against the base of his sex. He imagined her wet and slick for him begging for him to lift her just a bit and ease inside.

Obviously your cock wants her, but what of your heart?

No. Not going there.

He rolled his eyes at his line of thinking, knowing good and well that even if his little fantasy came to life, Jayla was in no shape for lovemaking. Talan had said it could be a week or three before she fully recovered. And he had yet to tell her she'd been out for three days already.

With a thought, he re-clothed them both—her in a silky pair of long pajamas instead of the cute little camisole, and himself in a thick pair of sweatpants instead of his sleeping shorts. Hell, if he could sleep in armor, he would.

She shifted, turned her head and snored.

Larien grimaced. Well, at least one of them was comfortable.

He lay there through the night thinking on the woman wrapped around his body. Larien shook his head at himself. Here he was, an angel, a celestial being created to teach all of humanity to protect itself against its enemies, and yet he wished for nothing more than to be as carefree as this mere human. Jayla was an open book—unafraid to expose her heart, to show her vulnerabilities and hurts, or to haul off and deck him while telling him what a jerk he was being.

But Larien didn't deserve a woman as vibrantly alive as Jayla. No way in hell…or any other realm.

The parade of women he'd plowed through played like a slideshow through his mind, one after the other, an endless stream of nameless, faceless dolls. He'd been insatiable after Jabon had introduced him to his first bed partner. That first taste of sex had set him off like a wildfire consuming a grove of dead trees—he'd succumbed to the heat and burned alive.

When he'd finally pulled his head out and learned there was more to human women than simply sinking his cock into them, he'd already hurt so many he knew he would never live it down.

Then had come the hollowness in his soul, the bottomless pit of despair when he'd finally realized that life on Earth meant witnessing an endless stream of deaths, watching the light fade from the eyes of friends, lovers and finally his only sons.

Though shredded from the inside out, he'd survived all of that. Yet here he was. Again. Wanting something he shouldn't. Not because he felt guilty about his past—no, he had accepted that, or accepted it as much as he was able. But he shouldn't want Jayla because he had no plans to stick around. And a gem such as this woman deserved more than a one-night stand. Period.

Fuck.

Larien eased out from underneath Jayla's body and scooted to the edge of the bed. Immediately, she began to tremble. Her breathing became shallow as her teeth chattered. In seconds she'd gone from practically normal to wintry chilled. She needed him, needed the physical contact just as Talan said.

Self-centered much?

A wave of guilt rode him hard. He scooted back to her side,

wrapped her in his arms and breathed a sigh of relief as she quieted almost instantly.

Damn. He couldn't win for losing.

Yeah? Well, what else is new?

CHAPTER FOURTEEN

Death turned in a slow circle, checking out the surroundings. He'd been called to any number of rough and depressing locations before, but it had been awhile since he visited this one. He could taste the despair wriggling through the gloom of the room.

He moved to the broken window and wrinkled his nose at the faint whiff of smoke from a recent house fire. In the distance came the tat-tat-tat of gunfire, the squeal of tires and barking of dogs. A woman screamed into the night. The sound resonated off of the dank walls of the abandoned building Death stood in. He had a feeling that after his current business was done, he'd be right back here to conduct another transaction.

Even with a clear night sky, the entire neighborhood sat in a dreary soup-like fog. The perfect place for demons of all kinds.

He crossed the room and stood before the one who had summoned him.

"You called, Improbael? Not sure why since you can't die, though you look like you wish you could."

The Fallen demon groaned, then threw up a bucketful of black, syrupy liquid laced with strange golden flecks that popped and sizzled in the sludge. His body was covered with holes ringed by the same gold metal-looking material. Whatever had been done to the demon was impressive. It was as if the residue left behind by whatever weapon had done this, continued to inflict damage long after the initial wound was made.

With dull wings bent at an odd angle, Improbael leaned over as much as his slumped form and deep wounds would allow, and hurled.

Death jumped back a few feet to spare his polished knee-high black biker boots—after all, they were brand new—as Improbael heaved again, then lay against the cracked plaster of the wall panting.

Must be excruciating. Poor baby. Pfft.

Finally, Improbael spoke.

"I have a message for Abaddon."

"Then you should have called Abaddon. I have deaths to oversee. I am no errand boy."

"This is important. I need you to get this message to him. I have. Little. Time."

Gasp. Heave.

Death's lip curled. "Well that's obvious." In fact, the idiot— because only an idiot would allow himself to be injured so gravely—should have been unconscious already to regenerate the energy he needed to heal from whatever had been done to him.

"But sorry, can't help you," Death said.

"You are his brother. Of course you can help me." The words were a pain-filled hiss.

"What would he want with the likes of you? If you were merely a Fallen I might have considered helping you for about two seconds, but you've transgressed to a Fallen demon. You don't even get the two secs."

"Listen, you eudaemon pussy, if I do not get this message to Abaddon or Jabon, it is your ass, not mine."

Death gave a supercilious smile. "Do you really think so?"

Death rolled his eyes. If Jabon was involved, it was yet another reason to ignore the imbecile heaving on the floor. Jabon was one of the reasons he'd lost part of his kin. That ass, along with Simjela, had talked friends and family alike into chasing after humans for bed sport. Sure, some of his angel brethren— correction, *former* angel brethren—loved their mates. But that wasn't their purpose, wasn't why they'd been created. What damage those two hadn't managed to do in the second Fall, Lucifer had accomplished with the first Fall. They'd driven their own kind to corruption at laser speed. All of them had paid the price. Dearly.

Death's mind sought out the presence of his most beloved cousin, Chelriad. She'd been created as a Second Tier angel, one of the *Virtues*. He hadn't been able to feel her since she was caught up in the fever of rebellion millennia ago. He closed his eyes against the pain and anger that he knew would never fade and, as always, Chel's image was fresh in his mind. He should despise her for even having the ability to *think* on rebellion. Yet, he couldn't and felt shame for being so damn soft where she was concerned.

Death remembered when she was first learning the difference between using her magick at the Source and using it on Earth. He'd taken her and some of her friends on a field trip to the sub-Saharan desert to practice. She'd been clothed in swirling robes of gold and white. When she'd created her first rainbow, the magick had gotten away from her. Color had latched onto her and she looked like a candy coated *Virtue* for hours as the colors swirled across her skin and through her garments. She'd actually pouted when it had begun to fade.

Chel and all the others were responsible for their own choices, yet he couldn't help holding those who'd riled up the less experienced angels into rebellion.

Fuckers.

From the latest reports he'd received from those who owed him favors, Chel was now somewhat of a rock star. The former innocent was now an object of desire. Her job—to give the illusion of perfection. Thankfully, she was usually clothed when on the cover of some ridiculously overpriced magazine when she did it. In fact, the label he favored when he was in human form was all Chel's fault. He'd spotted her that first time in an odd looking get up and then researched the designer—Ralph Lauren. He hadn't expected to find a male line that was totally to his liking.

When she'd first Fallen she was nothing more than a shadow of her former self. Now, Chelriad was doing well here on Earth, though she would never live up to the potential for which she'd been made.

Chel. She'd been a loving positive entity who'd enlightened and led others towards harmony, though when it was necessary she'd protected them as well. In fact she'd been a formidable fighter and would have been a skilled healer by now, able to use elemental energies like fire and water to bind wounds of the flesh and soul. In her original state, she'd have been able to help the idiot rolling on the floor at Death's feet. But in her lesser state she could wield no healing abilities and would probably be able to do nothing more than burn Improbael to a writhing cinder.

The thought brought him back to the present. Whatever Improbael was mixed up in couldn't possibly be good. If it were, he wouldn't be leaking nasty black shit with metal-looking pieces in it that seemed to burn through all it came in contact with, including the concrete slab of the floor.

The last thing Death wanted was to bring whatever had kicked Improbael's ass to his brother's doorstep. Abaddon was a bad boy in his own right, but that didn't mean he was invincible.

Death hadn't protected Chel. But he would absolutely protect his brother.

"What's the message, demon?" Death asked.

"I found the Descendant they have been looking for. Had...in my grasp, but. But got—" Rattling cough with more black ooze. "Got. Away."

"And this Descendant, he did this to you?"

"It is a she, and no, s-she didn't do...to me. It, it was La—"

Death held his hand to his ear and said, "What's that?"

No response.

"So is that the extent of the message?" Death asked with a toothy smile and the words infused with four kinds of sarcasm. Aw, too bad. Improbael passed out.

"Got it. I'll get right on that, asshole."

With a huff of annoyance Death disappeared, leaving the body of the idiot that had summoned him on the floor of a condemned building in the projects of San Francisco, coming apart at the seams. Literally.

* * * * *

After making sure Jayla was comfortably sleeping and well protected, Talan followed Larien out the front door and braced himself for wherever they were going tonight. They'd been hunting for days and finally had gotten a lead on their bad guy. A daemon over in the Bayview-Hunter's Point neighborhood had passed on a tip that a Fallen demon matching Improbael's description had been seen over in Double Rock.

They flashed to a shadowed part of the parking lot of the city's football stadium. Too bad Talan's totally unsettled stomach didn't resemble their current quiet and seemingly calm location. He clenched his teeth. The salty precursor to vomit filled his mouth the second his flesh had solidified.

Gross.

"You claim one gets used to this popping in and out of places, eh?" Talan could barely get the words out. It seemed every other syllable stuck on his tongue as he tried not to toss up his dinner.

"Jayla calls it poofing, but yes, you get used to it," Larien replied absently, already in seek-and-destroy mode, muscles loose and weapons at the ready.

"Not that I don't trust you, mate, but I'm not sure I believe that." Talan gasped as he sucked in a gulp of cool air. "Don't think a body can ever learn to accept being deconstructed then pulled back together miles from where it had been standing moments ago. Not a mere human body, anyway." He spit into the nearest shrub and grumbled, "Gross."

When he felt well enough, they left the shadow of the stadium, crossed the street and headed into the Double Rock neighborhood in search of their prey. Talan was in full Shadow Priest mode. He couldn't wait to wrap a Mind Control spell around the asshole that had attacked Jayla. He had a feeling that tonight they'd find him.

"So did you tell her where we were going?" Larien asked.

Interesting how the man could make the simplest question sound like an interrogation.

"Yep, and she was pissed we're out hunting for the Fallen demon without her," Talan whispered as they moved quietly into the night.

Larien's response was his typical *humph*.

Talan filled in the silence. "Yep, she was hot, all right. Wanted to come with us, but she's far from being well. I've never seen anything like her condition before. I'm just thankful that the treatment seems to be working."

"She hates your potions, by the way."

"Big surprise there," Talan chuckled. He didn't care if she loathed them as long as she kept drinking them. "Perhaps another few days and she won't need you to sleep with her anymore. But don't hold me to that. Could be shorter, could be more. I just don't know."

"I shouldn't be sleeping with her at all," Larien growled, though Talan wasn't fooled. There was heat in his voice, all right, but not all of it was because the man was angry. Larien might deny it, but he was head over heels about Jayla. And who could blame him? The woman was simply fabulous, yet Larien fought the attraction with all his Fallen might.

"Well, she needs you sleeping with her, whether you like it or not. Skin on skin is important for her right now. Even as a celestial being you have the same creative Source as we humans. She needs that energy to recharge her inner battery. Haven't you noticed that you feel a pull on your reserves when you're near her? Right now, she's a big sponge and she needs you. I just don't have the big pool of energy like you do or I'd sleep with her myself. After all, Jayla is a beautiful woman."

A storm cloud of anger darkened Larien's features.

You should probably stop baiting the Fallen, Talan. Nah. Too much fun.

"Does Jayla know what you are, Shadow Priest?"

"Does she know what *you* are, Fallen?" Talan retorted smoothly. It was a silly question. They *all* knew what Larien was.

And the glare was back.

Talan was no punk but Larien could level a building with that mean-assed glare. Since they'd been hunting for the asshole that had attacked Jayla, he'd learned that the iridescent blue glow of Larien's eyes signaled one of two things—he was getting ready to vanish, or there was an oncoming transformation. The first one he could learn to handle and was already to the point of not puking each time they flashed from one spot to another. It was nasty but tolerable.

But that second thing? Watching Larien transform into his battle form, stretch to his true height and width, brandishing an arm's-length black blade while flashing those pitch-colored eyes and deadly looking fangs? No thank you. And those wings, when he chose to display them, were black as the blade he carried, with taloned tips edged in shimmering gold. The menace that rolled off the man shouted what he was made for—war.

It was gloriously frightening.

Talan shuddered. It wasn't something he wanted to see again anytime soon. He preferred his pants clean rather than pissed in, thank you very much.

Speaking of piss, they turned down a dank alley that smelled of the stuff as they moved toward the heart of the neighborhood. It was eerily quiet for a Saturday night in this part of town.

"Tell me again what your job as a Watcher, er, former Watcher was?"

Larien's eyes constantly moved. His steps made no sound and his body was honed for serious damage. The man was a hulking walking weapon.

"I was to teach men the Arts of War so they could protect themselves against their enemies."

"Gotcha. So did you ever meet Goliath? I hear he was angel spawn," Talan asked.

Larien rolled his eyes and said, "Not."

"Really? So what was he, seriously? I could learn a thing or two from you. I mean, how often does a man like me get to meet someone who was around during the fall of Rome?"

Larien stopped, closed his eyes and Talan felt a rush of something brush over his skin. He looked down at his bare forearms expecting to see welts just as Larien's lids snapped open.

"We go that way."

Then Larien pursued his own line of questioning like he did whenever he didn't want to talk about something. Talan didn't mind since the other man always got around to answering his questions in his own good time anyway. For a kill-'em-as-dead-as-you-can Fallen, Larien was remarkably cooperative.

"Did you put wards on Jayla's gym?"

"When she opened the place I helped finance it. I warded it fully against all kinds of nasty threats, even wrote the spells into the walls before they put up the sheetrock, though I never told Jayla about that. That was years ago. Never had a problem until now."

"I haven't found a ward for these Fallen demons yet, but I'm working on it. Maybe Isthus can help me with it when we finally get there."

Too bad he hadn't known that angels walked the earth and were so *not* the cute, chubby cheeked, baby doll-like beings often seen in pictures and paintings.

Larien stared off in the distance. Talan followed his line of sight, but didn't see anything. But something was there. The dark side of Talan's magick responded to it, readied to tear it apart.

"How long does it take you to change from Shadow spec to Holy?"

Changing specs didn't take long, but while his Shadow form could deliver serious damage to his enemies, his Holy form was no good for fighting at all. "A few seconds," Talan responded. "Why?"

"You have any of that smelly potion that replenishes your magick stores?"

"Yeah, mana potion. I have a few right here, plus the necessary herbs in my bag to make more if I run out. What's up?"

"I think this would be a good time to put your Holy Priest hat on. I think I'm going to need you to use it on me."

"What?" Okay, the big bad Fallen was scaring Talan now.

"I'm sensing something ahead. A whole lot of something. I want you to be ready to heal me if we hit a big mob."

The air rolled and shimmered like the ripples of rings on a pond as Larien cloaked them just before he took off at a dead run toward God-knew-what. They rounded a corner and came upon a small group of beings huddled in a doorway. "See them, Talan?" It was little more than a whisper, yet rang like a bell in his head.

Talan hated to admit it, but he nodded in the affirmative anyway. They were all sizes and shapes in varying degrees of "bad" but they all scattered at Larien's approach.

Larien eased through the door. Talan was on his heels, ivy-wood wand at the ready. The room was bare, long abandoned except for whatever had been here recently.

"What the hell is that smell?"

Cement walls boasted cracked plaster. The floor, also of cement, had had its carpet stripped away ages ago. The place reeked of despair and something Talan couldn't quite place, as if the very air was infused with death itself.

They passed into a rear room.

"Improbael," Larien said.

Or what was left of him. A swirl of gray dust shimmered in the air with just a bit of recognizable energy that was quickly dissipating. And it was too familiar to be a coincidence. The Fallen demon was simply gone with no true evidence of what happened to him other than a single burgundy feather pushed across the floor by the wind whipping through the empty pane. Just like the two Fallen demons that he and Larien had fought off that day in Talan's apartment.

Larien had told him that while he could slaughter demons to his heart's content, the Fallen variety were a different story. They could be wounded but not killed. For them to be truly destroyed, Abaddon, guardian of the Abyss, must receive a warrant for their destruction. Only then could he summon them to the Abyss gate where he called up his power to to *un*make them.

But the guy who'd been here was destroyed in this very spot, on this plane. Yet *no one* had that power but Abaddon, who had no need to come up here.

"What the fuck is going on?" Talan's words broke the strange, still quiet as Larien's words echoed in his ears. The same exact words, actually.

* * * * *

The unseen meddler grinned shamelessly. Oh, the look on Improbael's face when he'd popped in for a visit—classic Fallen idiocy at its best.

"What the hell are you doing here? If you are looking for Death, he's long gone," Improbael had said.

"Oh, I'm not looking for Death, my dear Improbael. I'm here just for you."

"Why? What do you want?"

The words had rattled in what was left of Improbael's chest. Larien had really done a number on him with that gun and angelized ammo. It must have been made by the Host's Master Weaponsmith himself. Must be nice to call in favors through Gabriel every once in a while. Maybe he should look into that? But that would mean he'd have to *earn* a favor first. Damn. He didn't see that happening anytime soon. Oh well.

"I want the exact opposite of what you want, Improb, my friend."

"You're not making any fucking sense, you crazy eudaemon.

But that's not unusual. You're so bass ackwards there's a bet among demon-kind that you're on crack."

On crack? That had been funny. In fact, it had been so funny he'd almost forgotten to take his time tearing Improbael apart. In fact, he'd reduced the Fallen demon to little more than a bit of dust and a blip on the energy signature scale. Gabriel would probably be mad that he'd done it...again.

A few curious lesser demons had made their way toward the door to peer inside. No doubt they'd wondered if they'd seen what they thought they had as he'd belted out kick ass sixties music. "Get back, get back, get back to where you once belonged!" Certainly he was almost as good as Billy Preston now...wait, perhaps even as good as the Beatles. Oh yeah!

The lessers' mouths gaped as they'd stared at him as if he were nuts. Fingers to his lips, he'd flashed what he knew was a malevolent smile that conveyed all his thoughts without fail. How he'd managed to deconstruct a celestial being was, and would remain, his own little secret. At least for now.

"Shhh..." he'd whispered to the onlookers.

They'd all nodded and backed away fast. Obviously smarter than Improbael. Correction, the *former* Improbael.

And now from his perch in the tree across the street, he watched his favorite to-fuck-with Fallen enter the very door that Death, and then he himself, had strolled out of not long ago.

This was just so much fun. Wasn't every day he got to fuck with Larien while looking after a charge at the same time. What more could he ask for?

Actually, that confused, pissy-looking expression on Larien's face as he left the building might just do.

CHAPTER FIFTEEN

Jayla jerked awake with the dark sensuality of a dream fading from the edges of her mind. She'd never had particularly sexy dreams. Now it seemed to be all she thought about. Why? Because all that was on her mind these day was a dark, brooding, sexy-assin Fallen who called her little office home these days.

A quick peek at the clock on the nightstand told her it was entirely too early in the morning to be awake. Talan had accompanied Larien on their little hunting expeditions every night for the past week.

Being confined to the house meant she couldn't help them track down the one who'd done this to her. And worse, they couldn't leave for Nevada to begin unraveling the mystery of the location of the Seal until she was well enough to travel.

Nothing like being useless. Bleh. It was getting old fast. If Talan wasn't thrusting soup at her along with some smelly concoction or another—she'd have to ask him where he got such nasty medicine—then Larien was making her do muscle exercises and practice seeing auras, and all while in bed. The only thing she got to do by herself was go to the bathroom and fantasize about Larien doing more under the covers than simply sharing energy with her.

Neither Larien nor Talan would talk about whatever they were or weren't finding on their nightly outings. It was obvious the bossy bastards were keeping something from her.

And what was Talan doing to help Larien anyway? He was good-looking, sweet as pie and adept with a bit of magick, but he was still just human, right?

Yeah, her attitude was all kinds of surly but so what. She felt like crossing her arms over her chest, huffing loudly and stomping her toe in frustration. She might have done it, too, if she thought she'd remain standing afterward. Wobbly knees and the relentless chill beneath her skin reminded her that if she hoped to accomplish what she'd climbed out of bed to do just now, then she'd better get moving before she found herself face down on the very hard floor.

The house sounded empty but the low hum of energy at the base of her spine told her she wasn't alone. The sensation was one her body recognized as the presence of one man—Larien.

She eased down the hallway, holding onto the wall, wood cool against her bare feet even as her insides heated with anticipation. In moments she stood outside the door of her office and raised her hand to knock. But if he was resting she didn't really want to disturb him. Maybe she should go back to bed.

Closing her eyes, Jayla shored up her determination. She'd never pursued a man before and wasn't sure how to go about it. She knew Larien wanted her but he fought the attraction with all his Fallen little heart. Her being sick just made it that much easier for him to run.

She wanted to touch him. Hold him. Take all he had to give and give him all of herself in turn. But damn, what jacked up timing. She was useless, and she was sure whatever he'd been doing with Talan was dangerous. And what if something happened to him? Could angels be destroyed? What if...? Okay now she was rambling to herself.

"Jayla, if you are coming in, do it already." The words were gruff and muffled from the other side of the door. Said door proceeded to open on its own to reveal the wide back of a deliciously shirtless Larien as he stood in the dark and stared intently out at the darkness outside the window. He tilted his head just a bit, as if he were trying to see more deeply out into the black.

"What's wrong?"

"Nothing. Why are you out of bed?"

"Wanted to see if you and Talan were back." She wasn't sure why she lied. They were both well aware of her ability to sense him clear across the house as well as see him whether he was cloaked or not. To his credit he didn't say anything.

She plopped down on the futon that was surely too small for his huge frame and let out a loud huff. She hated this weakness.

"So is Tal still here?" she asked.

"He's on the couch. Probably snoring by now."

He turned away from the window and pinned her with a glare. "Back to bed, Jayla."

She huffed a bit but didn't fuss when he took her by the elbow and steered her back to her room. Besides, she was tiring fast, and if she didn't watch it he'd insist on carrying her. She simply didn't have the energy to be aroused by iron-hard forearms flexing beneath her knees, or the feel of mountainous pecs, so warm and tight as they pressed against the side of her breast as he cradled her in his arms.

"Are you sleeping with me tonight?"

"Would you like me to?" The words were almost a whisper.

"That's a really stupid question, Larien. What woman wouldn't want a luscious hunk of man to share her bed?"

He snorted. Actually snorted. It sounded somewhat flustered and flattered at the same time.

"What? What'd I say?" she questioned, lashes fluttering outrageously. Damn, where had that bit of sass come from? She hadn't gotten out of bed all day except to go to the bathroom and felt wiped out afterward. Yet she had enough stamina to flirt?

"I don't think I've ever met anyone quite like you before. You're all kinds of sassy, woman."

"Perhaps you simply have amazing restorative powers."

"Hush," he grumbled, but the sound wasn't quite as stern as he would have liked, she could tell.

"Did you really just shush me?"

He glared. "I did."

She smiled. "Bossy."

With a wave of his hand, the blankets were pulled back and the pillows fluffed.

"You learn how to make beds in Warring Angel School?"

"In you go and no fussing."

With one knee on the mattress and a foot on the floor, a good whiff of her own personal essence hit her in the face. She wrinkled her nose.

"Ewww. Can you…you know, give me a bath?"

In a blink she was freshly cleaned from head to toe and sporting a sexy cream-colored satin pajama short outfit.

When he hesitated to join her beneath the covers she blew out an exasperated breath. "Come on already. Just watching you stand there is making me tired."

"Don't you think I'm evil, Jayla? You know big bad Fallen and all."

The question kept to his typical sarcasm, yet there was an underlying worry she'd caught in his tone. Did he really think she would judge him? She'd have to fix that.

He slid under the covers on the other side of the big bed and folded his arms behind his head. She poked out her bottom lip in an exaggerated pout.

He held open his arms to her. "Oh come on, you big baby."

Jayla grinned, scooted across the cool sheets and arranged herself to her liking—with her head on his shoulder, and her cheek pressed just left of a flat, darkly tanned male nipple.

"So?" he asked, reminding her that he'd asked her a question. She closed her eyes, took in a deep breath of sexy bed partner, relaxed and answered truthfully.

"I don't think one choice makes you evil, Larien. It may change your life's path, but it's not like you can flip a bad guy switch and poof, you're a non-horned, eight-foot tall, terror inducing, nasty, cold, gray-skinned fucked up demon, right?" She curled her lip and shivered. "With blood-colored wings. Just…ewww already."

Larien's stomach tightened as a laugh burst from his diaphragm. Jayla was making him do that a lot lately. It was refreshing to know that the person he was talking to knew exactly who he was, *what* he was, and still didn't hesitate to poke fun at him, or tell jokes. Jokes about his own kind, at that.

"Okay, you didn't answer about the bad guy switch," she said.

And she didn't miss much, either.

Larien propped one arm behind his head. She pushed up on her elbow, scrunched her brows together with a serious frown. "Oh, come on. You're kidding right? There *is* a bad guy switch?" She looked like she'd had absolutely enough. "You may as well spill it. Not like I'm going to tell anyone. Nobody outside of this house would believe me anyway."

"This is a closely guarded secret, Jay."

She pinned him with a "don't test me" glare. The woman could be really scary at times, even when recuperating from near death.

"There is no switch that makes one evil. It's simply a choice, Jayla."

"Geez, big secret, that."

Larien bit back a delighted smile before it could slide across his lips.

"We're creatures of constants. We're created do to a thing and we expect to do it forever unless we make a different choice. Don't look so bored, this is important."

"The evil switch seemed more interesting," she said on a yawn.

"Smart ass."

"Yep. And smart everything else, too." She grinned, followed closely by yet another yawn, this one louder.

"You're tired. Back to sleep."

"And miss this? Not a chance." She snuggled back in and waited for him to continue. His arms automatically closed over her and pulled her close. Rather than examine why she felt as if she belonged exactly where she was, Larien began to answer her question. Besides, Jayla might be tired from healing from her ordeal, but there was absolutely nothing wrong with her mind. It wasn't tired, slow, or otherwise.

"Talk faster, Larien."

"If we pledge ourselves to something contrary to natural or spiritual law, and rebel against the true Source, we Fall and our true natures come out."

"That's just common sense. It's the same with humans," she said. "Some of us are just bad eggs and it eventually shows. Not like it takes an event of nature for a true asshole's colors to shine through."

"Well, when we allow ours to shine through we become Fallen demons. And there very unpleasant places created just for us."

"You mean for them," she rebutted. "I don't care what you say, you're Fallen, but you're not a bad guy, or even your garden variety demon. Certainly not like that seducing slash winter thingy that tried to make me want to screw him blind, then turned me into a human popsicle."

He paused. He'd never been known for an abundance of tact or ability to spout bullshit. Hell, he didn't have the patience for it. So how to say this without revealing something that was a danger to him and all his kind. If she ever repeated it he'd have to end her. There weren't many things he regretted in life, but the thought of taking Jayla from this world set a lump in his gut that made him sick. Strange sensation given he'd never been sick before. Ever.

He opened his mouth, but hesitated.

"You can trust me, Larien."

"Reading my mind?" he asked.

"Nope. But you went all stiff for a second, and your jaw tightened. Don't forget if I can sense you across the house I can certainly feel you if you're right next to me. Gah!"

But there was a tinkle in her voice that reminded him of bells at Christmas time, a sound of joy that belied her protest.

"If a celestial passes through the Abyss gate, or whatever humans choose to call it, they're…finished."

"Are you talking about Hell?"

"No. Not Hell. Hell is a place created by religion. The Abyss is a place far worse, and guarded by Abaddon."

"So Abaddon isn't a bad guy?"

"Oh he's plenty bad, but he was created to guard a place that is home to some of the most dangerous creatures ever known. He's not Fallen because he has never forsaken what he was created to do."

"Well that sucks. So the Abyss is a real place? I always thought it was bullshit. Ever been there?"

"My dear Jayla, there isn't anything or anyone, anywhere, that I want badly enough that I would willingly go to the Abyss. Not even a piece of ass and you're talking to a man who Fell for it. Literally."

"Okaay? Though I don't think you made the decision to Fall as lightly as you try to make it. Jerk." She huffed, turned out of his arms, gave him her back and yawned again. "So what's down there?"

"You're still talking to me?" he asked, genuinely perplexed.

"I just asked you a question, didn't I?"

"I'm sure you know as well as I do that when most women get mad at a man, he is given the silent treatment for more than ten

How refreshing. A woman who was as straightforward as she said she was.

"I'll take that grunt you just gave me as your understanding, Larien. So, what's down there?"

"Nothing. Absolutely nothing."

"If the Abyss is nothing, what happens if you go there?"

"I end."

He felt her shudder though she didn't say a word and he could relate on every level. Very few places made him apprehensive and none of them could cause him to tremble at the mere mention of it. However, the Abyss gate was such a place. It was the only place in the known Universe where his kind could be completely and utterly *un*made.

"You mean you die?" she asked.

"No. I am *un*made. No body. No soul. No spirit. Simply...nothing." Like Improbael, whom they'd found tonight. No one had power over the Abyss gate except for its Keeper, Abaddon, and Larien, though only for a season.

So the question was, if neither himself nor Abaddon utterly destroyed three Fallen demons in San Francisco, who had?

CHAPTER SIXTEEN

She awoke with a start in what was quickly becoming her favorite position—with her arm draped over Larien and her head pillowed by his thick shoulder muscles. Though it was still dark out, Jayla took the time to look at him rather than drop immediately back into sleep. His face, usually lined with seriousness, was relaxed in sleep. Thick brows showed off their sexy arch rather than gracing the deep frown Larien usually sported.

It was in her nature to give without hesitation and with no expectations— no expectations meant no disappointments, right? It still didn't change the fact that she should have been freaking out considering she lay next to a man she barely knew while quietly discerning secrets he didn't want to reveal.

And then there was the comfort, the ease she felt in his presence. Not normal. But so very, very good. Her fingers itched to touch him so she snuggled in, followed her gut and left her head out of the equation altogether.

The curve of his thick neck sloped down to meet well-defined pecs. Larien's broad chest beckoned, tempted her fingers to circle tight male nipples and then trace the lines along the ridges of his rib cage. The planes of his stomach lay flat, with little hills and valleys where the bundles of muscle lay beneath the skin. The man was large, lean and long. Pure brawny yumminess.

Her gaze walked down his body as far as the bunched sheets

147

would allow. Then Jayla looked up at his face once more and started in surprise. Wide awake, he hadn't moved an inch, just lay there watching her watch him.

She reached up and caressed his cheek. The quality of the stubble there sent a shiver of sensation from her palm clear up her arm. The texture reminded her of the man himself—gorgeous with just the right amount of "rough" around the edges. A rough that had tucked her in, brought her soup and shared energy with her. A rough that had cared enough for her well-being to sleep with her though she knew he didn't really want to. A rough that hadn't managed to keep the expression of raw longing out of those dark eyes before it morphed into a mix of want and...fear?

The need, the *requirement* to declare that he was worthy of happiness was a living, tangible thing inside of Jayla. He deserved love, deserved to be wanted. Accepted.

Her palm hovered just above his skin. "May I touch you?" she asked quietly.

After a deep huff that carried just a hint of shakiness, he grumbled, "Go ahead." She almost chuckled at the long drawn out syllables of each word. Instead, she went to work. The hand closest to him eased beneath the curve of Larien's back while the other skated over his chest, top to bottom, side to side. When she dragged her nails over the nerve-laden areola, strong fingers clamped down over hers to still the action. She shook him off and almost smiled when he simply grunted his annoyance, tucked his arms behind his head and let her play a bit more.

Lost in the feelings that came with touching him, Jayla simply couldn't get close enough. She draped her leg over Larien's thigh and sighed happily. The warmth of his sac seeped into the skin over her knee, even through the stupid sweatpants he insisted on wearing to bed. Shifting her leg she felt the man's spine go stiff as a board when she gently nudged his goods.

But certainly not on purpose, mind you.

"Jayla." The warning growl was blatantly ignored.

His breathing deepened and she swore she caught a quickly stifled hiss or two when she plucked at his now diamond-hard nipples. The sound of his attempt to hide the pleasure he received from her touch made her determined to have what she now realized she'd truly wanted all along—him.

"I think we should get up now," he suggested quickly, the words tripping over each other as they rushed from his mouth.

Right. It was one o'clock in the morning.

"It's time to practice your *othersight*," he stuttered.

"Nah." Practicing seeing auras was *so* not what she had on her mind just now. The muscles in his thighs tightened as if he were trying not to squirm. She leaned in and inhaled the scent of his skin and exhaled. He smelled *charged*, like the wicked electricity of ozone laced with the clean yet dangerous wind of a hard oncoming storm.

He jackknifed in the bed, swung his legs over the side. With his elbows braced on his knees, he hung his head as he sucked in a wild breath.

"Larien, stop running from me."

"Run? Are you insane?"

"I know a retreat when I see one."

"Jayla, look, you couldn't possibly want to be involved with a man like me."

"Why? What's wrong with you?"

"You just want me because of the energy I give off. It's seductive to most humans. I don't fault you for it."

"Now it's my turn to ask, are you insane?"

He turned to glance over his shoulder, his expression thoroughly confused. She smiled. Her big warring angel really didn't get it.

"Look, Larien, I've been around your kind for as long as I can remember. I've never been attracted by any of them, angelfied aura, funky energy or not. Not until you."

"It doesn't matter. After this mission is done, I am leaving."

"Then I guess we'd better make the best use of the time we have."

With that she took him by the shoulders, forced his rigid body back down to the mattress and climbed up until her legs settled on either side of his rib cage. Jayla ran her fingers along the almost-bare nape of his neck and lowered her lips until she was just out of reach.

* * * * *

Larien marveled at this woman. She'd made her intentions quite clear but he knew she wouldn't truly take anything from him against his will, not even a kiss. The next step would have to be his.

"You are simply too much," he breathed.

"Do tell?"

"In my manwhoring days it had been the females that had to be concerned about me controlling my base urges. Yet here I am sprawled beneath a woman who makes no secret about wanting me, yet you hold yourself back to give me time to make up my mind? Too much."

My how time changes a man.

She was a Descendent of one of the greatest kings to ever walk the earth. She'd walked in that knowledge long before she was ever aware of it. At the same time she cared for her friends, her family. This woman was one he absolutely did not deserve.

Wiggling backwards until her luscious ass pressed against the ridge of his now marble-hard cock, Jayla sat on top of him and grinned as wickedly as he'd ever seen. It made him smile and shake his head in turn. She had no shame and he liked it. A lot.

And it was the last thing he'd expected. Would it be so wrong to allow her to indulge her curiosity about his body? About him as a person? To end his self-imposed loneliness for just a little while?

Larien had been propositioned by starlets, women of power, young and old, both before and after he Fell. But truth was, he'd become jaded, numb, until resisting took little to no effort. But with Jayla, he found he didn't want to be at arm's length. It seemed so cliché, but there was simply something about the woman, something uniquely *her* that not only called to him, but shored him up, strengthened him. Made him feel wanted—so much more important than being needed. After so much life and death, loving a woman, any woman, meant more than sex to Larien. The need to be connected, rather than have sex for sex's sake, was imperative.

"Jayla, if you kiss me, you need to understand what it means. This isn't just a meeting of mouths to me."

"So tell me what's what." Her fingers sank into the muscle near his neck and kneaded as she waited and listened.

"God, that feels good," he moaned. Her mouth formed more of an unspoken "yes, I know it does" grin than a smile. Sassy and sweet. God, he was addicted to the very thought of her.

He opened his mouth to spill his secrets. Nothing happened. The words stuck like balls of dough in his throat that were unsure how to move themselves past the lump lodged there. This was not a subject he enjoyed. In fact, hadn't taken the time to explain to a woman since he'd made a commitment to give up being a manwhore. Goodness, how long ago was that, anyway?

But that didn't matter now. All that mattered was being honest with the woman trying to sooth and comfort him by easing her fingers across his skin even as she drove him crazy with the core of her heat as she sat on his chest.

Deep breathe in. He watched her whole body rise and fall with his chest.

Fall. Just the thought was enough to bring him to his senses.

"Jayla, look, after my Fall I...moved around a lot." He groaned when she hit a particularly tight spot. "Finally, I married and remained faithful until she passed on. I grieved for I don't know how long and I'm not really sure why."

"Didn't you love her?"

"No."

"Then why did you get married?"

"I had fucked her, became addicted to it. She was only one of many that I'd used as an excuse to leave my true home. When, I finally came to my senses, though much too late, wedding her seemed the right thing to do." He sucked in a ragged breath. "After her death, I remained alone for centuries. I met my next wife. Watched her live, watched her die birthing my precious sons. My boys. I watched them die as well."

"Children? Oh, Larien, I'm so sorry." Warmed by her care and concern, Larien marveled at the strength wrapped in feminine softness as she laid her head on his chest, held him tight and tried to comfort him. He deserved no comfort, not after what he'd done. It didn't matter that it happened a lifetime ago—wrong was wrong then, and it was wrong now.

"Yes, children. Contrary to popular belief, angels and humans do not make bad-assed earth-stomping giants. The children are born fully human and can ascend any time after they come of age, if they wish."

"Ascend?" she asked.

"Yes, they can transform, shed their humanity, become angels and begin training as such on the celestial plane. My line would have become warring angels or protectors, such as *Seraphs, Cherubs* or even *Principalities*, like myself...or like I was. Others are *Virtues, Powers*, or wherever they fit in the angel hierarchy."

"I had no idea there were so many kinds of angels. But what about your children? What happened to them?"

"My children did not ascend." At her obvious confusion he paused, but he couldn't deal with that just now. So instead of answering the question etched across her lovely features, he said, "As for angel and demon spawn, that is another story and typically not a good one. Anyway, after so much death and—" He paused, breathed into her hair. "I know it is hard to believe that I have been alive so long and have never shared this, but it was simply easier to be alone."

She pushed up a bit, looked down at him and spoke softly into the silence. "Tell me? Please??"

"I lost my sons, all of them. All on the same day. They had a choice. They chose death."

"Oh my God."

"When their mother died I held them in my arms, so small and vulnerable, and vowed to be the best father to them that I could. I thought that if I taught them well, instilled in them a sense of honor, taught them who they were, their birthright, that I could make a difference. Make up for my Falling by doing something right for a change.

I couldn't have been more mistaken. When they died it was like Falling all over again. Such loneliness without their presence, their laughter. And the pain, to watch them suffer as they took their last breaths...God. Indescribable."

"How?" she whispered. "How did they pass?"

"In battle, or rather as the result of one. Several families on the outskirts of Kish had been attacked. It was a time of incessant warfare, each township trying to assert rule over the other. My sons joined in the fight to help protect the city. I was, *am*, proud of them."

"It sounds like they were valiant boys who did what they felt was right. Isn't that what you taught them?"

"It is, but it doesn't change the fact that if I had not fucked around and Fallen in the first place, they would never have come into being. Would never have had to endure so much suffering. Or have the light of their lives snuffed out at such young ages. Barely twenty-two when they left me. Triplets. That day I decided no more families, no more children. Ever. To do that meant no more serious relationships."

"But think of it this way. If you'd never Fallen, you never would have known such love either," Jayla said.

What could he say to that? It wasn't as if he'd never considered such a thing, but it did nothing to quell the hurt or erase the agony on his sons' faces forever silk-screened in his mind.

Yet the burden seemed lighter just from having shared with this woman. He shook the realization away.

"So what did you do next?"

"I simply walked the earth, watched civilizations come and go. I took the occasional mission from 'the powers that be' to hunt down certain demons that were harassing this king or that monarch, but they were few and far between. Other than that I had no purpose. Nothing and no one to live for, yet I would live forever or until I chose to end myself."

"By yourself? With no one to look after, or to look after you?"

"Look after me? I don't need anyone to look after me."

"Of course you do. You're more of a trouble magnet than I am." Her smile was watery. Eyes glossy with tears. "So why did you tell me all that? I appreciate you sharing, but why?"

"Because I promised myself that I would be alone before I ever walked into another relationship. The woman I took would have to be worth the pain I would suffer when it was time to watch her die. I know it seems selfish."

"No it doesn't. Not selfish at all. I can't imagine watching my family and friends die like that? It's just...wow."

"I didn't mean to make you cry, sweetheart." His arms wrapped around her shivering body, held her close as she sniffled and wiped the tears away. Her emotions punched through his chest. He felt it, felt *her*, beneath the skin, clear down through the cells of his blood. He tried to mentally step away but his resolve slipped and he knew there was no going back.

But if she wasn't ready to have him, fully have him and only him then he would have to find a way to cut off this rebirth of emotion and need. She would probably think he was crazy considering they'd never even shared a kiss.

"So, you think I'm worth the pain, Larien?"

"I can't believe I'm saying this, feeling this, but yes. I do. You are…something special."

She cocked her head as if she didn't understand.

"Jayla, you may not see yourself as special but I do. I've lived among your kind for millennia and the majority of women are simply not like you, especially in this generation. Think about it. You fought off a Fallen demon while severely injured, yet you are ready to go forward as if nothing happened. Your resolve to see to yourself and your friends is unquestionable."

She reached up and placed her very sweet-smelling hands on either side of his face. "Do you like the cocoa butter soap I've been using on your skin?" He didn't tell her that he'd slipped out one morning while she slept and taken a quick trip to Brazil just to get it for her. It contained clays specific to the region, was hand stirred, hand cut and hand wrapped, every bar.

"Yes, I love it by the way. It makes me smell like chocolate." Then with a sniffle, she said, "Not quite the first kiss I envisioned, all snotty and stuff. But I want it all the same."

He snatched a big hankie out of the air and pressed it into her hand. After she'd cleaned up her face a bit, she spoke. The words were barely a whisper, but no less profound.

"Larien, one thing my Grams taught me was we all tend to forget that when everything was made, it was all good. Not just some of it, all of it. That includes sex. The only thing that makes sex perverse is the intent of the heart."

And she was right. He'd learned that the hard way.

CHAPTER SEVENTEEN

Larien realized a long time ago that the act hadn't caused his Fall. He'd Fallen because he'd forsaken the purpose for which he'd been made. Abandoning his home as well as those he'd sworn to protect, he'd allowed himself to be led by his cock rather than his heart. That was the reason he was banished to the earth.

It seemed he'd spent an eternity without love, but now this woman who'd brought a spark of *something* into his life felt natural and right. Not evil or forbidden. Sure, she'd only asked for a kiss, but he knew one would never be enough. And if he came to love her and then walked away, forsaking his promise to help and protect her…God, he couldn't even complete the thought.

"Larien? Where did you go just now?"

He turned his head away but couldn't bring himself to push her away. "I can't. I don't think we should do this." Thankful his voice was steady and firm considering his inside were as firm as room temperature gelatin.

"Why not?"

"I'm supposed to be helping you find the Seal, not taking advantage of you."

"Larien, do I look like a woman being taken advantage of to you?"

Her question swirled around in his brain, alive and vibrant as the woman herself. Jayla, taken advantage of? He couldn't even picture it.

"You know, Larien, I seem to be developing some kind of connection to you. Beyond being able to see past your cloak, more than being able to sense you. And I sense what you're not saying. No manwhoring for you, I get that. But no love? Ever? I can't imagine a more lonely existence. Kiss me. Let me fill that space in your heart that you've closed off for so long. Even if for just a little while."

Just as a smile began to tickle the corners of his mouth, he slammed his eyes shut against memories buried in the deepest pit of what was left of his soul. They swarmed his mind, bright swirls of color that devolved into grays and blacks overlaid with despair.

Flesh tore as his blade rent through bone. Screams of those thrown down to the earth filled his ears. Feathers flew as he'd hacked through majestic wings at the joint.

"Larien? Oh my God, breathe! Breathe, damn it."

He couldn't answer. Couldn't breathe. Literally.

Blood made squishing sounds beneath the soles of his boots as he tread through ankle deep puddles of it. He lost his balance as he slipped on a piece of intestines.

The scene switched.

"Larien, listen to me." The voice was muffled, far away. He almost recognized it then he slipped away again.

Deni, Dalos and Darius lay pale from blood loss, skin hacked away, gaping wounds clear down to the bone. The entire left half of Darius face was black with blood pooled beneath the skin. The other side was simply...gone. Dalos, unconscious as he took his final fifteen breaths. Deni lay between his brothers, holding their hands as he left this plane.

He was supposed to have protected them. Failed.

Lost. His home. His sons. His life. Himself. Everything. Lost.

"Larien!"

Larien felt Jayla sitting there on his chest trying her best to shake him out of the dark, but he couldn't see her. The fear of losing her was all encompassing. Magnified. Paralyzing. He tried to tune in to her words but he couldn't pull himself back from the maw of endless deep that loomed on the edge of his consciousness. It was a pit of his own making. One filled with regret and endless darkness.

What if he failed her? What if she was harmed because he

couldn't control his need for her? What if she called him and he didn't make it in time to take care of her?

"Larien! Remember the Speedo-looking thing Ambriel wore when he brought you into my gym that first time?" Her power flared and the authority of her birthright forced the image into his head, forced his mind to go where she wanted it to. He wondered briefly if she had any idea just how much she was in control. "I bought him a lemon yellow one for his birthday and he's promised to wear it on his head the next time he goes back to the First Tier. Imagine it. Now."

Ambriel, with a pair of sun-bright Speedos covering his long brown hair popped into Larien's mind. Little tufts poked out of the leg holes and the crotch stretched from Ambriel's nose clear to the back of his head. He wore that damn Speedo and nothing else but twelve foot wide cream white wings. And the idiot smiled as if he sported the height of fashion.

Larien's lungs relaxed enough for him to laugh. Once he started he couldn't stop. The image of Ambriel and those yellow racing briefs faded as Jayla laughed along with him, bouncing up and down on his chest as he chuckled.

"This is fucking embarrassing. I do not believe I have ever felt more like a little boy than at this moment."

"Those were some strong emotions, Hoss," she drawled with a ridiculously fake southern twang. It made him want to smile. "I could practically feel them trying to pull me in with you." Then she straightened. "That's not healthy, Larien."

But it was his penalty and his alone. And he'd vowed to himself to carry it until the end.

"So do you?" she asked.

Sobering, he remembered her question and answered truthfully even as he braced for the pang of guilt. "Yes, Jayla, I care about you."

Without another word she lowered her mouth to his and his arms tightened of their own accord, as if his body knew what to do even if his mind was all messed up.

Lips met, nipped and sampled. And then Jayla got serious.

The woman poured herself into that kiss until her emotions colored the very air of her room. Oooh, now *this* was a kiss. Hot. Hungry. Brutally honest. It was bold with a sharp bite that testified to her nature. When mixed with his own longing it became as potent as aged brandy, as heady as the scent of expensive perfume.

Her nails scraped over the fuzz on his scalp. A rushing current streaked from his head to his knees and Larien snapped like a rubber band pulled too tight.

Her squeal at suddenly finding herself on her back was followed by a breathy acceptance of his mouth, and of his weight on her as he tasted her thoroughly.

God, he must be crazy, but the heels pressed into his ass told him that at least he hadn't gone insane alone. Warm arousal scented the air as she arched to keep contact with the ridge of his now-aching cock. With a grimace he stilled and eased back, separated his moist lips from her kiss-swollen ones.

"You're smiling," she said.

Larien cocked his head.

"Not with your mouth but I can see it in your eyes, Larien. It makes me happy, especially after what you've shared with me."

But he didn't want to go back there just now. That thought brought others, all of them dark. He didn't want to think about whether he would ever be able to leave the past behind him. Or whether he could start over, live his life without throwing up the walls that kept everyone out...but kept him in as well.

Jayla looked up into his eyes, her hazel gaze speaking where words did not. And he was lost, yet whole. For the first time since his world had been shattered by the loss of the only good to come of his Fall—his sons—Larien, Angel of the Art of War, former Principality of the First Tier, had met his match. And knew it.

"Now, since you're so conveniently in *this* spot—" Her hips lifted with a sharp pump. Larien hissed. God, Jayla felt so good against him, her skin warm and smooth to the touch, her body welcoming and demanding all at the same time. And she had no problem telling him what she wanted.

"I'd like—" she started.

"No sex," he blurted.

"...some more kisses, please."

Oh. Okay, so when was the last time he'd blushed?

The thought formed and flitted away as she pulled him back to her mouth and teased him with licks, nips and sucks both tender and naughty. She pushed against his chest. Thinking she wanted up, Larien scooted back, only to find himself returned to his back with a delicious Jayla straddled over his stomach.

"Hands here." She took his hands, placed them around the back of her legs where knee met thigh. She'd begun to sweat there and his fingers eased back and forth over the slick skin.

So she wanted to be in charge, eh? He raised a single brow. His naturally dominant instinct had him ready to balk, but for pulling him back from the brink, he'd give her this. This time.

Jayla lifted her ass in the air, lay chest to chest, and laid a kiss on him that sucked all the rest of the common sense out of his head.

"God woman, what are you trying—?"

"I am not trying, I'm succeeding," she said between kisses.

"Succeeding," he gasped as she sucked at the skin on his neck. "In what?"

"In making you the most moaning, groaning, writhing, lusting, falling-for-me celestial creature on this plane."

Disagreement was simply impossible.

The following morning Larien awoke to a sleep-warmed, delicious smelling woman tucked against his body. He nuzzled Jayla's neck as he whispered against her skin. "God, I could kiss you all night."

He felt her smile against his skin where she nibbled him right back. "You did kiss me all night. Time to get up already?" She yawned, but looked bright and ready for the day.

They should both be tired as dogs who'd been hunting for two days without a break. But Larien noticed that Jayla charged him up somehow. He mentally added the whole "energy thing" to his list of questions for Gabriel when he delivered his next status report.

"Speaking of getting up in the morning," he said as he rolled her beneath him yet again, "I forgot to tell you that Talan said you're all healed now and it's okay for you to travel. I went ahead and updated our train reservations. We leave day after tomorrow."

"What? When did this happen?"

"He told me last night."

"Where is Talan?"

"Sleeping on the couch."

"Wait. Did you say day after tomorrow?" She was out of bed so fast he tumbled off to the side, caught completely off guard. She stood, fists jammed into her hips. The skimpy spaghetti-strapped camisole left nothing to the imagination. And he could imagine quite a bit now that she'd had those pretty breasts pressed against his body. They were a little more than a handful, soft with puffy nipples that became stiff cocoa buds and...

"Larien! Stop ogling my boobs already. I can't be ready in two days. I haven't done laundry in forever, more accurately, since the unhealthy incident at the hands of a no good winter Fallen demon. And given you haven't let me lift a finger since I was injured I don't even want to know what my house looks like with you and Talan taking care of everything. Oh my God, I have a news piece due to my editor. Shit!"

"Are you insinuating that I'm messy?"

"Out of all that, all you got was that I think you're messy? Hey, I'm the one that's been out of commission for weeks." A sharp index finger pinned him in the chest. Damn. That almost hurt. "You don't get to make this about you. Then again, it *is* about you and *you* not bothering to *ask* me if I can be ready to go in barely forty eight hours."

"Ask? For what? Anything you need, I can get or fashion for you."

"Ask for what? *For what?*"

Was she turning colors?

He rose and gently stroked his hand down her spine to calm her. That earned him her back and an elbow in the ribs as she walked away, grabbed a robe off the little bench at the end of her bed and practically ripped a sleeve off as she jammed her arm through it.

"Can you clean my house with a sweep of your hand, too, then?"

Larien was at a loss. Sure he'd had plenty of experience with women but nothing like the spitfire glaring daggers at him just now.

"Jayla, are you angry?"

"Answer my question, damn it," she snapped.

"No, I cannot clean your house with a wave of my hand. I am a warring angel, not Harry Potter."

"Didn't think so. And for the record, making decisions for me when I'm perfectly capable of making them myself falls firmly into the assholery department, damn it. And Talan told me that you two have been sharing dinner duty. I don't know about you, but I can guarantee Talan hasn't washed a dish since he's been here! Goddamn men! Think you know every damn thing in the whole damn world and—"

He should have pretended to miss out on the rest as she stomped out of the room and down the hall. Soon her words were accompanied by various banging and slamming of pots, pans, and what sounded like the stove and dishwasher.

So much for spending the morning kissing in bed.

"Talan, get in here and help me," she yelled from the kitchen, and then grumbled, "Before I break something…like a plate over your bonehead. Talan! Wake up." Followed by a splash, a yowl and a sputter in what sounded like old Gaelic. But it didn't keep Larien from laughing as he fashioned some clothes and moved toward the racket with a shake of his head.

* * * * *

Cloaked from human sight, Gabriel found himself yet again in the realm of humans. There were Fallen here. The thought of breathing their air made his lips twist in disgust. The lot of them should have been disintegrated on the spot when they'd rebelled but it was not his call so he just had to deal with it.

He had angels stationed on this plane that did a good job carrying out their assigned tasks. Then…there were the crazy celestials under his command.

A faint rush of air blew against the breeze and alerted him to a new arrival. The other man didn't speak. The two seconds of silence that passed were two too many.

"You are late, so move it already," Gabriel snapped, not bothering to look up from the fashion magazine in his hands. Chelriad was featured on the center page. What would the world do if they knew a Fallen was one of their favorite runway models? Thankfully she stuck to the fashion scene and otherwise stayed off the radar. From what he could tell, there had not been a single celebrity scandal pinned on Chel. No human knew where she lived, who she hung out with or where she went on vacation, thank God. If not for Larien bringing her to Gabriel's attention, he would have had no idea that the former *Virtue* was now best friends with a Descendant—the very Descendant he'd sent Larien to recruit, and that his current visitor must betray.

Gabriel's flesh crawled with revulsion at having to be this close to this...this bizarre excuse for a celestial. He might not be Fallen, but he was so close to the fence that Gabriel was sure it was just a matter of time before he hopped over it.

I hope he skins his sac on the way over.

His visitor leaned over his shoulder and whistled at the picture of Chelriad spread decadently over the glossy pages. Her hair was a riot of long curls all over her head. Dark smoky eye makeup contrasted against flawless skin. The vibrant royal colors of the outfit she wore complimented the entire package. She had been wonderfully and perfectly created. Now she was nothing.

What a waste.

"I had no idea she looked so lovely in that shade of purple," the visitor said. "But I've only seen her with all her clothes on. Victoria Secret or Frederick's of Hollywood?"

Without bothering to answer, Gabriel snapped the magazine shut, rolled it up and slapped it into the palm of his guest. "Here. Enjoy," he said flatly. "Now, have you introduced yourself to your new charge?"

"Not a chance. I'm having too much fun tormenting Larien. He's going crazy trying to figure out who is zapping the Fallen demons before he can get to them."

"That is not your job." Gabriel wanted to choke the pompous idiot, but it wouldn't get rid of him so it didn't make sense to waste the energy.

"Are you saying I'm not allowed to have any fun?"

"Have as much fun as you want as long as you are looking after the one you are supposed to be looking after. And if I learn that you have been using your borrowed power for anything other than saving the life of your charge I will escort you to the Abyss gate myself."

"Wound tight much?" the angel asked.

Gabriel hissed back. "Tell me what is going on with Jabon?"

With a dramatic flourish that set Gabriel's temper on a low simmer, the angel bowed and then replied, "He is planning to use Chelriad to get to the Descendant. In the meantime he's stirring up the local riffraff, trying to get them to rally to the cause, so to speak."

"And what cause is that?"

"It's all over the 'verse that we oh-so-lily-white-pure eudaemon, the Fallen and the demons are all after the Seal of Solomon. So Jabon wants Abaddon to influence those in his realm of She'ol to give up some of their skin to get to the Seal first. On the other side of the fence, Jabon is tapping Lucifer, too. I don't think that needs any explanation, do you?"

Gabriel glared at the angel who'd brought the news. It all lined up with what Abaddon himself had already shared, but he wasn't about to reveal that bit of news to this spastic Elvis wannabe eudaemon.

With an over-bright smile, Gabriel's guest said, "That's all I have right now, boss. I shall report more when I have it."

With yet another flourish, he bowed and was gone.

God, why did he get all the nutcases to do the heavy lifting? What was a shame was that the weirdo angels delivered. Every damn time.

CHAPTER EIGHTEEN

Larien looked up as an exhausted Jayla walked into her office and fell onto the futon next to him.

"Jeebers, I'm tired," she said, snuggling in to his side automatically. They had only shared a few kisses yet it felt like she was supposed to lean into him this way.

"You should be. You've been going non-stop since this morning, woman."

"Your fault."

He wasn't about to bring up the fact that not only had she completed everything she needed to in order to be ready to get on a train day after tomorrow, but she had time to spare.

"I am not going to win that fight, so I won't walk into it." He dropped a kiss into the soft curls on the top of her head.

"Smart man," she chuckled, and then pecked him on the jaw.

"I'm impressed that you didn't blow up your computer while writing your article. You almost killed my mp3 player the last time you were in my car, which is quite a feat considering it's voice activated."

"Oh, shut up," she snorted.

Of course he did the complete opposite. "Talan was the smart one. He went home."

"How does the make him smart considering he had to pack for our trip?"

"Sure, that's what he told you. But he was really running from you."

Laughter was followed by a few minutes of companionable silence as he simply held her to him. The warmth of her body, as well as the warmth of her spirit, seeped into Larien, and filled him with a fresh contentment. The level of peace achieved in Jayla's presence should have been unnerving, yet he found himself reveling in it like a big dog rolling around in knee-high sweet grass during Summer. It was almost enough to block out the low level hum of danger that sat at the edge of his senses. Almost.

Out of the blue, she asked, "So you can change your form, right? Like the asshat that jumped me? He looked human one minute and a freaking giant the next."

"Of course. All Fallen can take human form or revert to their working form."

"Working form? What's a working form?"

"I am a warring angel, so my working form is for battle. It is the form I take most often, or would take often if I still had my old job. We can also transform to celestial bodies, unless we go demon."

"What happens if you choose Fallen demonhood rather than Fallen angelhood?"

"We lose the ability to take our celestial forms ever again."

"Can I see? Your celestial form, I mean." Her honey brown eyes sparkled, full of mischief. What was she up to? He tilted his head and tried to read between whatever lines he was sure were there. "Well, can I?"

I can refuse her nothing.

Without another word, Larien rose and padded to the living room with Jayla on his heels.

"Why the living room instead of the office?"

"You'll see."

The moment she settled on the couch he let the change explode from his very cells. His body stretched and expanded. The familiar burn of the emergence of his wings was followed by an awed gasp from Jayla.

"Wow. You have wings?! And you're so big, uh, bigg*er*."

But even at eight feet ten inches this body was still restricted by flesh.

"This is my battle form." His voice, deepened by the

165

transformation, caused her eyes to widen even more, yet the stink of fear was absent. Humans usually pissed themselves if they managed to glimpse an angel's battle form, Fallen or not. "But I want you to see my true form though it is dimmer than when I was eudaemon."

Nodding enthusiastically, Jayla simply sat with her eyes aglow with wonder. The eager acceptance in her gaze never ceased to make him feel special. Proud, even, of what he was. Or rather, what was left of him.

* * * * *

Jayla was fully along for the ride. Energy crackled in the air, rode along the ridges of her spine and then sank into her blood. It pumped through her heart, infused her cells and then burst forth like an explosion of moonlight and starlight behind her eyes. It was peaceful yet so beautifully vibrant she could almost hear the hum of electricity in the room. The tips of Larien's beautiful wings trailed the floor and then snapped out to fill the room. A variation of black she'd never seen before, the color seemed alive and swirled with luminescence. Lethal-looking talons on the end of perfectly sculpted feathers were a-glow with shimmering gold.

Wow, how did he ever walk away from such power, she wondered. Larien outshone anything her mind could even possibly conceive. When Improbael had morphed from his human form he'd grown at least a good two feet, just like Larien, but where Larien's skin was an almost-glowing dove gray, Improbael's Fallen demon skin had become as dank as cement—lifeless and cold like the dirty ash that remained in the bottom of a grill long after the charcoal had burned itself out.

As Larien continued to morph, his skin dropped away to reveal a burnished being of sunlit gold. He had hair of flame in this form, infused with light like the rest of him. And he was just as sexy with those long glowing locks as he was with the barest of stubble on his scalp in his human form.

At his true height he was so tall, so wide, no wonder he wanted to do this in the living room—it had vaulted ceilings.

"And this," he said with a voice that seemed miles away yet

right in her ear at the same time, "is my celestial form, my true form." And then Larien was pure light. Not blinding, yet still beautiful, radiant. Wow. When the light winked out, a somewhat pale, very *naked* Fallen stumbled to the couch.

The muscular chest she'd explored just last night beckoned to her hands to come and stroke it. And the cock she'd only had a clue of before was revealed. Even when not aroused Larien was impressive. Thick, heavily veined flesh was as perfectly tanned as the rest of him and looked as if it were made just for her. It brought to mind an old geometry equation—length times width times height equaled 'oh my'. Her mouth watered.

"So why aren't you wearing any clothes? Not that I'm complaining, mind you," she asked.

"It takes a lot of energy to transform. I don't have the reserves to make anything more than a pair of briefs. On second thought—" He flopped back onto the cushions. "This will have to do," he said and pulled a thick cushion over his sex. "I hope there is no need to pummel anyone or any*thing* anytime soon."

"You need time to recover?" she asked.

"Yes. I can't tap into the Source like the ascended eudaemon can, so when I transform the energy I use must regenerate on its own. It won't take long, and with you close by the recovery time should be even shorter than usual."

She wondered at the last part, unsure of what her presence had to do with anything, but let it go for now. There were other things she was more curious about.

"So right now you're what? Weak?" she asked.

"A little, yes. Not completely helpless, but close."

She jumped him. Literally.

"Holy…! Jayla, wait."

"Not a chance." The pillow he'd been holding flew across the room. Her legging-clad core settled over his naked one as she leaned in for an open-mouthed kiss that lit him up from the inside out. His head spun and it had nothing to do with being depleted. She'd simply wrapped a maelstrom around him and sent his senses whirling.

The little moan from her throat when he enfolded her in his embrace sent a shiver up his spine. But there was no way in hell he could let this go any further without an understanding between them. He'd let her have her way to a point last night, but in the end, the buck stopped with him. It was his responsibility to make sure this was done right.

"Jayla, if you want more than a kiss from me you have to give me what I want."

"And that is?" she asked, nibbling his ear. God, he felt that bit of a caress with her tongue clear to his toes. Larien sucked in a deep breath and pushed on.

"I want... God, that feels good. I want a commitment. I vowed to myself that I would never again have sex for sex's sake. You've become important to me. I didn't expect this when I took this mission but it's the truth. I want you. And if you want me, then you'll have only me. Period."

"Is that supposed to scare me away when you're what I want in the first place?"

Oh. Well then.

Then suddenly—Bam!—there it was, the energy inherent to his kind ignited like an open flame to gun powder. It was Jayla. Somehow she replenished him, refilled him, just as he'd done for her when she'd been injured. God, she was like having his own personal Source—one so potent his body sizzled as if he'd flown through an exploding star!

She sat up, her expression baffled as her hand flew up to cover her lips with trembling fingers.

"What the hell was that?"

He had an idea but couldn't quite corral the words into a coherent sentence. Shoulders lifted in a shrug while his brain reeled at the realization of what this woman was to him.

"My God, Larien, it was like kissing a car battery while the engine revved. Do it again," she demanded, then dove back in for more.

When they were both breathless and panting, Larien sank his fingers into her soft tresses and gently maneuvered her head where he wanted it.

"Are you sure this is what you want?" The words were gritted through clenched teeth as Larien tried to stay in his skin as his energy level flew up and off the scale. "You and I. A couple at the getting-to-know-you-with-every-intention-of-keeping-you   stage?

Be sure because I won't ask again."

"Yes, already. Are you waiting for me to change my mind? I've only wanted you since the moment I saw you skulking around in my room that first time."

"Skulking? I do not skulk, woman."

His heart sank as she pushed away. He let his arms fall away from her luscious body and prepared himself, ready to walk away if that was what she wanted

Hands on hips, she asked, "Are you going to make me take what I want?"

Profound relief.

"That, woman, is my role."

He stripped her in record time and then made her squeal. Loudly.

"I thought you didn't have any energy!" Her now-naked sex slid flush against his equally naked cock.

"I usually would have none, especially after a change like that, but you replenish me." He took her hand, pressed it to his throbbing erection. "In more ways than one. You are a woman after her own pleasure and it is fucking hot. And now, I can call you mine."

Jayla reveled in the flash of sensation, of nerves sizzling just beneath the skin as Larien's short fingernails gently trailed over her skin. Her hips squirmed and breath was drawn in on a hiss between clenched teeth. His fingers skated beneath the swell of her breasts, down her side to tickle her ribs. A giggle she couldn't suppress bubbled up and out.

Larien continued his exploration down to her waist, over hips and around to slide beneath her backside. His reward—a delicious mix of deep moans and delighted laughter.

"Damn, woman, you feel so good in my arms. Your skin, so soft and warm. Especially here. It's been, well, a very long time since—"

"Shhh—" she whispered. A soft touch to his lips silenced his concern. She was well aware of the grief he'd been carrying for literal ages, and the last thing she wanted was for him to recall it now. "Just enjoy this."

With a lopsided grin and a nod, Larien went to work. Fingertips eased through the slick folds of her sex—a sex that was now throbbing and oh-so-ready to be filled.

Indescribably yummy warmth rushed through her body like the waters of a river overflowing its banks. The touch of a man, this man, was too much, yet not enough. Her breasts grew heavy with arousal. They needed attention. Before she could finish the thought, Larien sat up and curled his tongue around a ready nipple while a large, strong hand wrapped around the other breast. He lapped, sucked and nipped until her hips rolled with need and her dew soaked the hard ridge of flesh that she shamelessly ground down upon.

He pulled the entire crown of one aching breast deeply inside, let his teeth rasp over the skin as he eased back to the nipple, then bit down. Oh, yes. Just this side of pleasure, yet just enough on that side of pain.

Her need was raw, rough. Desperate. There was no tenderness in his touch. And Jayla didn't want any.

"Ah, God," she groaned.

"Do you like that?" Larien asked, nipping the underside of a breast.

"Oh, yes. That feels so good. Bite me again."

He did. The breath caught in her throat as the dam of their shared passion spilled over. Lifting her hands, she let her fingers glide over his scalp to hold him to her. Her skin was so sensitized, so attuned to him, that even the rasp of stubble beneath her nails sent a shiver through her body.

And the sounds he made? God, they sent tremors up the backs of her legs. A deep growly-rumbly hum that made it clear he enjoyed every move he made over her body.

And the kisses were like…she couldn't even think of a word to describe them. Addictive wasn't strong enough. Sweet wasn't decadent enough. And though she loved the way he sucked her nipples, drawing them into his mouth with deep pulls that shot clear through her blood, the skin of her throat already anticipated the trail he blazed toward it. He was going to kiss her neck. She simply *knew* it and almost let out a 'squeee' in anticipation of his lips sucking her in that certain spot near her shoulder, marking her just as the heavy length of his cock pressed against her core, burning and branding the impression of its veined thickness on her skin forever.

A hand raced down her back to land on her ass and pulled her body tight to his as he rolled his hips.

"Please. God, give it to me," she begged.

"Condom?" he croaked.

"No. I'm clean."

"Jay, I can't catch human diseases. But I can get you pregnant."

"On the pill. Hurry."

She gasped when the flared head breached the tight ring of muscles at her entrance and he began the press in. He lifted her hips, shifted slightly and began the long, slow slide inside. God, it was exquisite. The stretch, the burn, the heat of it. The fullness as he worked himself deeper sent her spine into a deep arch.

"More. Oh please, more."

Once fully seated, he rose from the couch with her impaled on his cock and moved with preternatural speed back to the bedroom.

The moment her back hit the cool sheets Larien gave her everything she asked for. Dove into her flesh as if he wanted to live there forever.

Beneath him, Jayla drowned in sensation. The slip and slide of flesh. The mingling of breath and of sweat. The flex of the muscle of Larien's ass where her heels pressed. The sweet friction of him moving in and out, slicing through the clenching walls of her sex.

Orgasm hovered just out of reach. So close, so very close.

"Larien, please." She could barely breathe now. Too indescribably good.

He pushed back, knelt and dragged her hips along with him without missing a beat. Holding onto her, he said, "Touch yourself. Make yourself come around my cock, Jay."

Her fingers zeroed in on the swollen bundle of nerves and stroked. Fast.

Five breaths later she exploded, felt herself tighten like a vice around him as his gaze captured hers. Teeth clenched, the man gasped and went perfectly still as the throb of her sex pulled around him.

Moments later his deep breathy yell rang out. His head fell back, the tendons in his neck pulled tight. He clenched his jaw and held her even more tightly.

His cock flexed as he came. Her eyes went wide on a silent

scream as the splash of his seed set off an unexpected second orgasm. God, she'd never come twice. Ever.

And twenty minutes later, Larien set yet another record when he rolled Jayla beneath him and had her coming in record time. Again.

* * * * *

Larien turned from the window and shook his head at himself. The silly grin spread across his mouth disappeared. Thoughts moved from the giving, succulent, feisty female in the bed back to the task at hand—finding the Seal of Solomon.

Surprises—this mission had been full of too many of them. So far he'd discovered Chelriad in the mix, and a human Shadow Priest that could see Fallen, cloaked or not, yet was unaware of his own ability to do so. And some unknown supernatural was running around *un*making angels as if he'd paid a personal visit to the Abyss gate and snagged a bit of Abaddon's banishing powers.

And Jayla, a human woman with the ability to control demons, call angels, as well as replenish his energy stores? And she wanted him with a fervor that he'd never experienced with anyone. Hell, what was next?

The voice he already loved broke into his thoughts from across the room.

"Why is it every time I go to sleep with you, I wake up and you're off somewhere else?"

"I'm not off somewhere else. I'm right here."

"Not the point. You're not in the bed, Larien." Then she sighed. The sound brought to mind a stretching, sated kitty. And she should be sated. "What time is it anyway?"

"Almost four a.m.," he replied.

He'd made love to her practically around the world and back. The woman awoke all his hungers and set them loose in such a frenzy of need it had been all he could do to let her sleep at all. But it wasn't just her body that drew him, though she was a sexy, curvy, gorgeous thing. So what was it? Her stubborn streak or her morning grouchy side?

Larien smiled into the darkness of the room.

Her inner strength? Her willingness to run into the unknown?

A rustle of silk was followed by soft padding across the floor. Jayla's natural scent mixed with his reached him before her arms wrapped around him from the back. "I like the way I smell on you," he murmured as the warmth of her body sank into his skin. She placed a kiss at the middle of his spine, and then moved to his side, taking his arm and draping it over her shoulder. He pulled her closer, leaned over and met her upturned face to plant a soft kiss over kiss-swollen lips. He pulled his gaze away from the woman in his arms and back to the source of what had pulled him from the bed in the first place.

"What are you staring at? Your eyes haven't left that window since I rolled over."

"What do you see?" Larien asked.

"Nothing."

"Don't you think that's a problem?"

She frowned and looked from the darkness beyond the window and back up at him. "I don't follow, Larien."

"You called your guardians, right?"

"Yes, while I was in the shower earlier," she said.

He had let her up long enough to wash up...then taken her again. God, he was a greedy bastard and he knew it. Then, feeling guilty, he'd backed off to let her rest, and the woman had attacked him. Again.

Back to the problem at hand.

"Did you release the *Seraphs* or *Cherubim*?" he asked.

"No, I didn't release—" She tilted her head at an angle and paused. After a few seconds she said, "Wait, actually I only called Ambriel. He brings the others with him on his own."

But he sensed no eudaemon at all. And if his cousin was gone, it made sense for the others to leave. They weren't beholden to Jayla because she hadn't actually called them. But that didn't explain why Ambriel would or *could* leave his post?

He scanned the darkness around her house again, pushed his senses further just in time to catch a shadow of movement just out of his periphery to the left. Or was that the waves of the Pacific in the distance? Even with his exceptional eyesight he couldn't tell from this far away.

"So did you release Ambriel?"

"No. Did you?" she asked on a yawn.

"I can't release any angel called by a Descendant." He had at least learned that much through their research into leads on the Seal. Off in the distance a purple-black ripple stretched across the sky just beneath the low hanging clouds and fog. At the same time, faint otherworldly blue blended and swirled in Larien's dark eyes as he powered up.

Jayla squinted into the darkness. "Oh, there they are. Hmmm. There are more of them than usual. Do you see Ambriel?"

"Jayla, call your guardians."

"But they're right there."

"Call them. Now!"

At Larien's snapped demand, he saw terror flash in her pretty hazel eyes, then heard her heart rate kick up with a spike of adrenaline. Larien burst into his battle form just as a loud boom rocked the house. Moments later her bedroom door blew in and the wood rained down around them in pieces so fine they may as well have been toothpicks.

Arms wrapped around a wide-eyed Jayla, Larien flashed out.

Moments later, Larien held a trembling Jayla tightly against his chest. She took in a deep breath and went stiff as a board with one hand over her mouth.

Her wrap was soaked through with sweat, skin clammy and her cinnamon complexion was under laid with a ghastly green.

"You alright?" Larien asked quietly, beyond angry that he'd had to snatch her away from her home with little to no warning. Jayla absolutely hated traveling this way but there'd been no help for it. A series of gurgled pants sounded in her throat as her body adjusted. Larien buried his hand in her hair while the other continued to stroke the tense muscles on either side of her spine. His fingers stilled, chest tightened as realization dawned. He had to get back to her house and fast.

"Stay put. Be right back."

"Where are you going?"

"Going back."

"No!" The words were a horrified gasp in Jayla's throat. Her panic and fear hit him in the gut like a bat. "Please. Don't go, Larien. Don't—"

"I won't be long," he heard himself promise, even as her misery wrapped around him and pulled at the protective strings of his heart. It was in his nature to protect and it almost killed him to leave her behind. But he couldn't shirk his duty. He had to find out how their enemies had gotten past her guardians. More importantly, *who* was their enemy?

"If you get hurt," she growled through clenched teeth, "I am going to kick your ass." So fierce, his woman.

In a blink he was back at Jayla's house just outside the back door, peeking through the glass into the moonlit kitchen and on into her living room. It looked like a warzone. The place was filled with smoke though he could see nothing burning. The furniture lay shredded and toppled, and ribbons of what probably used to be books floated to the now-scorched and scratched wood floors.

But more interesting was the mix of Fallen and full-fledged right-out-of-human-nightmares demons milling about with confused looks.

"Where is she?" he heard a particularly thick-headed demon ask a scaly looking short-tailed creature. "We had better report back."

Now that couldn't be allowed, could it?

Larien smiled, pulled his gun and sword, and then charged right into the midst of the bad guys standing around scratching their heads.

CHAPTER NINETEEN

Six Fallen and two demons lay in various states of existence around Jayla's house, including her bedroom, den and another in her office. Hell, he'd even caught one in the bathroom who was now unconscious with one leg hanging out of the tub. And what that one had oh-so-cooperatively shared with Larien had him beyond pissed.

Jabon. Jabon was behind the search for Jayla.

Unfortunately, the pawn in the tub had no idea how they were finding her given that demons were no more omniscient than angels. The woman could be anywhere in the world yet they managed to home in on her. Nor had he learned why Jayla's guardians weren't where they were supposed to be.

This was becoming a clusterfuck of epic proportions. There was no choice but to summon Gabriel. This was the second attack on Jayla. Larien needed to pass on the details of this new development and fast. Perhaps Gabriel could find out who Jabon was getting his intelligence from before Jayla ended up in heaven several years ahead of schedule.

Making his way through streams of blood and torn flesh, Larien side-stepped the oozing bodies and parts. Bodies that had been full of sizzling and popping wounds from his special ammunition were beginning to fade away now. He wished he could keep the grayish balls of energy—all that was left of his enemies—from escaping knowing they were only going to regenerate elsewhere.

Larien's feet hit the grass path just on the other side of Jayla's small patio mere steps from the back door. A familiar energy washed over him, a signature that was unforgettable...and unforgiveable.

Jabon.

"Ah, so you're the one they've gotten to protect the human?" Jabon called out from the darkness. A *schwing* filled the silence between them as Jabon pulled his weapon. "Where's the Descendant, Larien?"

Oh, now that was just dumb. Did he really think Larien would just tell him where Jayla was after he'd just gotten her to safety? Larien couldn't believe this was the same asshole that had gotten him to give up his purpose in exchange for life here on Earth.

And for this particular Fallen demon, an ass kicking was long overdue.

* * * * *

As soon as the nausea began to ease, Jayla dragged herself up off the cool tiled floor and wandered to a thankfully close bathroom. If she hadn't been so keen on splashing her face with cold water and dry heaving up her guts, she would have taken the time to be impressed. She wondered whose home it was. Then common sense intruded—obviously it was Larien's place. The man was a total control freak and wouldn't leave her anywhere unprotected.

Finally the shivering faded and Jayla's legs steadied a bit. She rummaged around for a towel and moved toward the shower.

Now she was impressed.

The glass steam shower was built for two...or three or four. Tiles done in warm wheats and golden yellows mixed with sea blue were splashed in sunbursts across the walls. Nozzles for steam, rain and massage were strategically placed in the semi-circular space to allow all parties access to the various sprays.

She dropped her robe and set the temperature of the water. Stepping in, she sat on one of the benches with a sigh. The back of her head met the wall as she thought on the events that had brought her here.

With it came an anger that rivaled Larien on a good day. She was tired of being a target. Tired of having a big red bulls-eye blazing on her forehead. The bad guys wouldn't be after her if she didn't have something valuable to them. On the other hand, it made sense that they would want to take her out before she found that damn Seal before someone of Solomon's line could control them with it.

Wrapped in a plush blue towel and her mind full of questions, Jayla left the bathroom and ambled through the house while her mind tried to work through the dilemma of how to not get whacked. Her bare feet met wood then creamy tile as she moved into what was obviously a relaxing area. The space was big and open, yet cozy. The couches faced a wall of glass that let in the still-rising sun so the entire area was bathed in comfy warmth. As she moved toward the glass, the panes automatically slid apart to allow her through. Not sure if they would close behind her and lock her out, Jayla stood between them and looked out past a sparkling pool towards a stretch of wild grass that ended at a wall of tall lush trees.

The sharp musical chirp sounded to her left. A fountain set into one of the pristine walls hosted a pair of royal blue birds with black beaks and black tipped feathers. They cooed and sang as they dipped their heads and enjoyed sips of crystal clear water.

The property sat on a steep incline surrounded by the dips and hollows of green rolling hills. Off in the distance were mountain peaks with the slightest bit of white at the very tip tops.

What in the world is that?

A quiet hum filled the air. It was a low-grade swirl of energy that made the back of her teeth vibrate and reminded her of the faint buzz of the third-rail of a subway train—not truly audible, but felt down in her gut.

Hmmm. Maybe it was some kind of ward or something to keep Larien's enemies out.

With a sigh and a shrug, she eased back into the open living space where she and Larien had literally landed. A quick look around drew her gaze to the kitchen. If she were able to ask her fairy godmother for the perfect kitchen with every chef's gadget, the result would be Larien's place.

So the big growly Fallen hadn't put in a one-time performance when he made me breakfast.

Stainless steel everything surrounded by some kind of smooth white stone. All the neat gadgets and Swedish cookware would have normally made her *squeee* in delight.

Not today. The knowledge that he was out there in danger sat in her stomach like a rock. A very big jagged rock.

After backing out of the chef's wet dream, she explored both stories of the pristine house, admired the sleek contemporary lines and complementing furniture, and ended up right back in the kitchen. No surprise there. She'd always been a foodie. She cooked when she was happy, sad, worried or mad. And right now she was all of those.

A clock made of what looked like a blend of thinly sliced bamboo, brass and glass read six o'clock which, if including the puke and shower time, put her about four hours ahead of San Francisco. Hell she could be anywhere in the Northern hemisphere.

If she were home it would be way too early for breakfast but there was no way in hell she was going to sleep without knowing whether Larien was okay.

Alright, let's figure this out.

With a flip of a switch the stereo pounded hardcore grunge out of the wall-mounted speakers as Jayla dove into the fridge and pantry. Bending her mind to the task of mixing dough for scratch rolls she recalled every story Larien and Talan had read her out of the clues her Grams had left.

The Book of Solomon claimed that the Seal allowed her ancestor to control demons and summon angels. Even if she'd found the damn thing she wasn't interested in controlling anyone.

Why can't they just leave me the hell alone already?

On the other hand, there was no ignoring the truth that even though the Seal wasn't in her possession she could still call angels, good, bad and otherwise. In fact, Larien had told her that when she'd been attacked by Improbael, he'd been in a meeting with the Archangel Gabriel and she'd *forced* him to her side. Larien had literally been snatched away from the First Tier by her plea for help. And if he'd been a few minutes later she would have been crispy burnt bacon instead.

So other than yanking Larien to her when there was trouble, what else could she do? And did she really want to experiment by trying to call things that she knew very little about? Uh, not really.

179

But on the other hand, how was she to learn what she was truly capable of?

Why was she important to the Fallen demons that were after her? And did they want to capture her...or kill her? No, wait. Larien said that killing humans was against the rules...but these guys didn't play by the rules, so hell. What a mess. God, she really needed soothing right about now. Time to hit the grill.

Several trips across the kitchen later, Jayla stood back and surveyed the damage. Everything was made with Larien in mind.

She'd made scratch rolls, sliced them down the middle and stuffed them with butter and honey. It was shaping up to be a warm humid day so gazpacho—a cold soup made with fresh tomatoes, cucumber, bell peppers and such, sprinkled with diced green onions—would cool them off. Yummies out of the freezer had become spicy seafood pasta, three different chicken dishes with an Asian flair, several beef and pork deals, smoked, braised, roasted and whatever else she could think of. Dessert—lemon mousse drizzled with chocolate...or cherry apple pie, peach burst cinnamon rolls with strawberry cream cheese icing or ice cream.

A glance at the clock set her stomach churning all over again. Five hours. He'd been gone for five whole hours.

"Hold it together, Jayla. He'll be back." Surely there'd be some sign if he were hurt or gone...right?

I have no goddamn idea. And it fucking SUCKS!

Crap, she'd forgotten the lobster. Grabbing a pan, Jayla dashed through a side door that let out to the huge stainless steel monster grill. She popped open the top, waved away the smoke, tossed the lobster onto the platter, and hustled back inside.

Right into Larien's arms.

"Oh thank God!"

She dropped the seafood on the nearest counter, launched herself at him and hung on for dear life. Feast and everything else forgotten, she pressed kisses across his face, only pulling back at his hiss of pain. Relief was too calm a word to describe her emotional state at seeing him whole. Well, almost whole. But it was good enough.

"Are you crying?" he mumbled into her hair.

Oh lord, she was but hadn't noticed the tears flowed until he'd said something. Fine. All she wore was a towel anyway. They were good for wiping tears, right?

"I'm just relieved is all. And you look like you kicked someone's ass. Tell me about it over lunch?"

"Lunch? How many people are coming to join us? Forty-seven?" He seriously, truly laughed while totally ignoring the encrusted blood on the side of his head and down along his jaw. A bad case of road rash, complete with patches of yellow and purple, decorated his left arm.

He dropped a dust-covered bag at her feet. Things must have gone okay if he remembered to grab the luggage they'd packed for their trip to see Isthus, even if it did look like he'd dragged it through an old fire pit and tossed it down a flight of stairs.

"Let me wash up, then we'll talk." He pressed a quick kiss to her forehead then hissed. Damn, his bottom lip was split. "Oh, thought you might want this."

He winked as he slipped her cellphone out of his back pocket and into her hand with the speed dial already engaged. Moments later, Talan's rich New York-n-Irish brogue filled the line.

"Talan, oh my God!"

"What?! What's wrong?"

"They, I don't know who, broke into my house."

"What happened? Where are you? Where's Larien?"

"Hold on, dude. Stop asking questions so I can tell you what hap… Wait, did you just yell at me?"

Okay, she couldn't really blame him. This was a disaster and it didn't make sense to pretend Talan shouldn't be upset when she was angry and terrified herself.

"But you're safe?" Talan asked, sounding as if he'd ride to her rescue if he could.

"Yes, we're…uh, hold on a second." She put the phone to her chest. "Larien, where are we exactly?"

"Rio Grande do Sul."

"Uh, okay, and where is that, exactly?"

"Brazil. Up in the mountains. No roads in or out," he said as his perfectly-formed self moved away from her and toward the stairs. Immediately her mind swerved to the right at the thought of the bachelor's bedroom she'd discovered up there earlier. With the huge bed. And a decadent bathroom that made the one downstairs that she'd showered in look like an outhouse. A bathroom where

Larien would be naked in just a few moments.

Sigh.

"Jay, you okay?" Talan asked through the phone.

"Uh, yeah. Just, uh, sighing with relief that Larien is back."

What's wrong, Jayla, don't want your best friend to know you're ogling Larien's butt?

As she poured two glasses of chilled wine, Talan grilled her for details as thoroughly as the lobster she'd just taken off the coals moments ago.

By the time she was finished with her phone call Jayla was a bucket full of emotions so diverse she wasn't sure how to sort them. Should she be terrified of what was out there gunning for her? Be pissed at whatever, *whoever* dared break into her house and run her out of town? Love a broken angel? Be horny for the most fabulous lover she'd ever had? All of the above?

She wished she had a clue.

* * * * *

Back downstairs, hair still wet from a shower, Larien paced like a caged tiger. Adrenaline rode him hard and shaking it off wasn't happening. He should be bone tired. He'd vanished twice, fought at least a half dozen foes at Jayla's house and was currently healing a nice number of cuts and bruises. But despite the energy he'd up, Larien was soaring. Then he remembered why—Jayla was here. Being near her filled him with Source energy so pure, so potent that it sent his amped-up-meter soaring. And he didn't even want to think about what her scent was doing to him. God.

She must have noticed him wearing a path into the hardwood, back and forth in front of the glass walls.

"Look," he heard her say into the phone. "I need to go. I need to talk to Larien and find out what the hell happened at my house. Huh? What? No, he's fine. A few cuts that are already healing. Yep, we'll meet you at the train station on time tomorrow afternoon."

Outside, she tucked a glass of red wine into Larien's hand and sat down next to him at the beautifully set dining table on the veranda.

"Okay, spill."

She was wearing nothing but a towel. He could barely think with all that skin calling to him.

Larien almost smiled at her gasp when sunglasses, sandals and a sundress suddenly covered her. He'd almost fashioned a spacesuit to dress her in, something that hid her whole delicious body from him, damn it.

"Thank you," she said as she watched him take a long drink and then set his glass down. What he didn't do...was talk.

"Dude, I just know you're going to tell me what the hell happened back at my place."

Instead of answering he stuffed a large forkful of lobster into his mouth followed by a scratch roll so good it melted in his mouth. The food was fabulous but he was still amazed he was able to push it past the glacier-sized lump in his throat.

Jayla was in more danger than ever and the last thing he wanted to do was tell her so.

CHAPTER TWENTY

"Larien, what's...?"

"Nothing's wrong." But the man clamped his lips shut and gave her the most mutinous glare she'd seen yet. And the man was an expert in the glare department. Fine. She obviously needed to use some honey to draw this particular bee if she didn't want to get stung.

Good thing she wore sunglasses now, otherwise the equally hard stare aimed right back at him would undo the sweetness getting ready to come out of her mouth.

"Well, handsome, I think you're being less than honest with me, but I'm not going to push."

Jayla leaned back, kicked off her sandals and put her feet into Larien's lap. She relaxed when he automatically took a swollen foot in hand and worked out the soreness from standing on her feet cooking.

"Mmm, that's really nice. Larien I need to understand, really understand, my part in all this. I mean, at first I was just going to help find the Seal, or the ring, or whatever we want to call it. But now I'm a spot on the radar of somebody who isn't playing nice. I need to get why that is. I've thought about it over and over since that first attack and I still feel like I'm missing pieces."

"I want you to practice using your gift on me."

His response rocked her back in the chair. Good thing she was already sitting down.

Practice? Practice what?

The very thing you were thinking about earlier—calling and controlling his *kind. Remember?*

God, she didn't even know where to start. He must have seen the indecision in her eyes because in true bowl-you-over fashion, Larien was out of the chair and dragging her behind him.

"Follow me."

He led her to a chaise beside the pool. "Sit here. In about thirty seconds I want you to close your eyes, quiet your mind and imagine that you're the most powerful woman in the world. Whatever you say goes."

"Okaay? Then what?"

"Call me. Call me as if you expect me to come to you no matter what."

"But how will I know if I did it right?"

"You'll know you did it right if I'm standing here rather than over there." He pointed to the edge of the trees way off in the distance." He seemed to know what he was doing but that didn't keep her from worrying.

"What about other things?"

"It doesn't work that way. You get who you call. Besides, this place is mine and mine alone."

"So."

"So, it's almost like the energy of another plane. I can't go to the creative Source because it's on a plane forbidden to me. Similarly, no angel or demon can walk into my private space without my express invitation. It's not the same as your house or any other human's. You are sensitive enough that if you still yourself you can probably feel my energy humming about the place."

Now that was the truth. She'd wondered earlier if that particular hum she felt down in her gut was some kind of warding. But the longer she'd been here, the more she realized that what she'd felt was *him*. As if Larien had poured himself into the very foundations of this place.

"Ready?" he asked.

Hell no, she wasn't ready. But she sat, looking into those beautiful dark eyes of his, and said, "Yep. Let's do it."

That now-familiar otherworldly glow lit behind his whisky-brown irises. One moment he was a gorgeous hunk of human-looking Fallen, and the next he was gone with little more than a *whoosh-pop* that she felt more than heard.

Looking past the edge of the pool where he'd told her to sit, Jayla caught a blur of movement at the tree line. The faraway glint of gold must be the sun reflecting off the talons of his wings.

Without hesitation, she reached inside herself for every ounce of power she possessed. Warmth spread across the inside of her belly as something began to rise inside of her. She recognized it for what it was—power. Undeniably potent, raw power.

She spoke to the empty space beside her. "Larien, come to me."

Nothing.

Determination sent the pool of energy in her belly boiling over.

"Larien, come to me. Now."

A rush of wind blew her hair away from her face. Larien hovered above her, wings blocking out the sunlight above.

"Why are you up there?"

"Because you didn't call me beside you."

"But when you rescued me from Improbael, I hadn't called you beside me either."

"Jayla, you called me to your side all right. You just didn't know you had."

Yeah, but that had been pure desperation. Her life had been literally slipping away.

"Again. Call me as if it's your birthright, which it is."

He powered up and was gone again.

She called him six, eight, ten more times. With each summons she added a bit more complexity as he directed her. She'd even made him stand on his head!

With each call the well of power she'd been drawing on filled and replenished itself quickly and flowed more easily. But it sure took a toll on her human body.

By the time they were done her sundress was stuck to her back and her limbs trembled as if she'd run a marathon without the proper training. She flopped back on the chaise, thankful for the breeze that cooled her sweat-soaked skin. The pool beckoned but she wasn't sure she could make it to the edge barely two feet away, let alone haul herself out of it again.

Larien eased behind her and arranged her in his lap. The next moment she wore a clean, dry, bright yellow sarong. Her sandals were gone and she rubbed her bare toes along Larien's calves. That bit of skin-on-skin contact was exquisite.

She sighed.

"That was pretty good for your first time," he said quietly, then dropped a kiss on her forehead. She loved when he did that.

"Thanks. Is it always so tiring?"

"It's like exercising. As you use it, you get stronger and able to do more. You know, same as increasing your stamina."

"Mmm," she said, rubbing her hands over his perfectly sculpted chest. "Stamina. You definitely know a thing or two about that."

"Stop it, woman. You know I'm a greedy pig and who knows when I'll let you up for air if we get started now. Besides, you need to eat to replenish."

A plate loaded with leftovers appeared in her hand, and icy drinks on the tray table next to the chaise. She pigged out while Larien reminded her of a few of the passages from some of the lost books—well, books labeled as lost anyway.

He started with the Books of Adam.

"Bottom line is, Jayla, you have access that I don't."

"I don't see how—"

"You can command what others can't, including me. You can call on powers that I can't."

"But you're an angel."

"And you're something greater. Think about it. Think about everything you've learned, everything you've seen. You can command demons. You can call angels, Jayla. Not just me, but the good, the bad and the worst." She wanted to argue, but instead she inclined her head and simply said, "Meh."

"Just the fact that you're human means there are agreements in place."

"Excuse me?"

"Agreements. Covenants, if you will. Woman, you can demand things from the Universe, from the creative Source, that I can't get close to imagining."

"Why?" she asked.

"Because humans were favored above all. Even above the angels. The Source gave man dominion over the earth along with

187

everything in it, under it and above it. What was given to them is theirs to keep and theirs alone. Regardless of man's decline, the Source is honor bound by covenant to hold up their end of the bargain even if it meant harming themselves to do it.

Bottom line, it was this fact, in and of itself, that brought about the rebellion that led to the First Fall. Man, above all, was esteemed in the eyes of the Source. Period. Man has been easily corrupted and practically destroyed on more than one occasion."

She sat up and cocked her head sideways. "You resent us?"

"Not 'us' because that would include you, but certainly some. With many of your kind ignorance is, unfortunately, king. How many humans bother to learn about the relationships between angels, demons and gods? How many bother to determine what exists out there, and just how unchanging it is? Nothing new under the sun...it simply changes hats.

Even with all of man's knowledge very few today realize that when the ancient Romans called on the god, Neptune, the Archangel Asariel showed up. Oh, and the Greek's Zeus, also known as the Roman's Jupiter? That was Sachiel. Egotistical *Cherub* ate up all the attention. Bastard."

She realized that if he'd wanted to, Larien could have responded to any human that had called out to any of the gods of war then proceeded to pretend to be that god. But what would have been the point? He was only truly obligated to come when called by someone who walked in their authority.

"Jayla your father and grandmother were exceptional in that they at least taught you not to fear things that most parents would have written off as an overactive child's imagination. Because of them you've had an idea of how to play in my world. But having a clue is not enough. I need you to push harder, farther, than you've ever thought possible. You truly are part of a legacy."

"So what happened when you went back to my place?"

"I kicked ass like the bad man that I am," Larien replied with a straight face.

Jayla laughed and said, "Yes, that you are. What else?"

"I captured and interrogated one of the lesser demons. They'd been trying to kill you." She knew she had a horrified expression on her face as her hands flew to cover her mouth on a gasp, but she just couldn't help. Her gut churned and everything she'd eaten that day threatened to make a reappearance.

"Jayla, I swear I'll keep you safe. And I will get to the bottom of this. Humans are off limits, even to demons. They may torment and influence, yes. But kill? Not allowed. Obviously rebellion knows no bounds when it comes to the Seal and you. And I'm curious to know where the hell Abaddon is hiding. It's his job to keep order down there in demon land. How are they just roaming about unchecked?"

An hour later, after calming an understandably upset Jayla, Larien looked down at the woman asleep in his arms. Not wanting to wake her, he held his anger in check, kissed the top of her head, and tightened his embrace.

Larien hadn't spared a thought before grabbing Jayla and vanishing to his home up in these mountains. He'd thought about bringing her here before but there was no way she'd agree to leaving Talan or Chel behind. And God knew he wasn't bringing the two of *them* into his private space. Away from any and every one, this place was as close to home as he'd ever be again. There was no way to undo the past, and he wasn't looking to try. Just wanted a bit of peace was all. And this place was it.

He'd continually updated it as times and trends changed and building materials and methods improved.

As much of a manwhore as he'd been, he'd never brought a woman here before in all the time since he'd built this place. And now Jayla was here, stretched out on a chaise on his deck, enjoying the same sky he'd looked up at so many nights, eating off of his dishes. There was a certain contentment in seeing her in his space, using his things. He only wished the circumstances didn't suck so much ass.

Jayla. Sass and spice. A beautiful soul wrapped in smooth beautiful cocoa skin. Funny, he'd taken this job so he could be immune to the power of the Seal, but now that he knew what it was like to have a woman like Jayla, he wanted nothing else. Only her.

"God, I must be crazy."

Jayla grumbled in her sleep and snuggled in, mumbling something about big goofy eyes. Emotion tightened in his chest even as his arms wrapped more surely around her body.

He needed to have a talk with Gabriel. This was out of hand and the bad guys after his charge really didn't want Larien to take issue with them.

* * * * *

"Daddy? Daddy are you awake?"

"Of course I'm not awake, sweetpea. It's the middle of the night." But there was a smile in his voice that told her no matter what she needed, no matter when, her daddy would be there for her. *"What's wrong, baby?"*

"I-I saw something in my room."

He held his arms out to her and she quietly climbed up onto his side of the bed and carefully snuggled in.

"Tell me about it, but quietly. We don't want to wake your mother."

Boy wasn't that the truth. She'd learned at only seven years old that her daddy was the go-to for scary stuff. Mom never believed she saw anything. And she wasn't a child. Daddy said so.

"I saw something on my wall. It came out of my closet."

"What does it look like?"

"It doesn't look like anything, Daddy. It's like a big black circle on the wall that blends with the dark. But the dark isn't supposed to have big goofy eyes, is it, Daddy?"

"Big goofy eyes?"

"Yeah. Big goofy eyes, like off one of the cartoons from Saturday morning. Only they're not funny, Daddy. They're kinda purplely-green or something."

"Are the eyes trying to talk to you?"

"No, not really. But it doesn't feel friendly. Like it's not 'posed to be in my room."

"Well, then if it doesn't feel like it's supposed to be there, tell it to go away."

She knew he'd say that, but a girl had to check with her daddy about certain things, didn't she?

"What do I say, Daddy?"

"You know what to say, sweetie. You're special and you are not subject to anything you don't want to be subject to."

"Subject? You mean like in school?"

"No. I mean subject like you don't have to subject yourself to it. You don't have to listen to them or it or whatever and you don't

have to just accept it when it feels like it wants to visit but you don't want it to. You have the say-so, right? It has no authority over you. So you know what that means?"

"Yeah. Grams told me that I can tell 'em what to do."

"That's right. Now go ahead. If you don't want them in your room or in our house, tell them to go away and not to come back, just like your Grams and I have taught you, okay?"

"M'kay, Daddy. Love you."

Jayla kissed her daddy on the cheek and beamed with a smile so big she felt her jaws creak with joy.

"I love you, too, sweetpea. Scoot now and don't forget to close my door."

"G'night Daddy. Sleep good."

"Sleep well, you mean."

"Yeah. That's what I said. Sleep good."

He smiled and rolled over as Jayla closed the door. Her nervous tummy settled and she skipped back to her room. Besides, if Daddy thought something really bad was happening, he would have jumped up and run to kick the bad guy's butt. But she wasn't scared because he wasn't scared. Her daddy trusted her to do what she was supposed to. To behave the way she'd been taught.

Back in her own room, Jayla spoke the words her Grams had taught her and then sat there just long enough for her invited guest to arrive. She greeted him with a wave.

"Good night, Mr. Guardian Angel. Thanks for coming."

"You may call me Ambriel, little one."

"G'night Mr. Ambriel." Jayla fluffed her pillows and passed right on out without a second thought other than that Mr. Ambriel had brought a lot of friends. Yep, any other goofy-eyed things would get their butts handed to 'em and she wouldn't have to bother with them at all. Yay!

CHAPTER TWENTY-ONE

Jayla rolled her eyes as Larien pushed past her and boarded the train first, ever alert for any sign of danger. Talan wasn't much better, taking up the rear as if he expected a demon to fly out of the ass of the people boarding around them.

"Okay, you two are getting on my goddamn nerves," she hissed, not wanting the other passengers to overhear. "If you don't sense any bad guys then calm the hell down already."

Larien snorted and kept right on patrolling the immediate area. His sharp gaze took in every nook and cranny as he led her toward the private berth they would share for the next thirteen hours. In spite of Larien's broody overprotectiveness, Jayla found herself distracted and then awed at the interior of the train.

The walkways were wide, well lit and laid with cream and blue patterned carpet. How in the world did they keep it so clean with people constantly getting on and off? The common area was lined with huge windows next to comfortable looking tables and booths. Everything was awash in light from the bright sun shining against the warm brownish red of the stained wood panels.

The steward welcomed them aboard with a smile and a playful wink of crystal green eyes. Just a bit taller than Jayla, he stretched out his hand for a friendly shake and offered to take her bag. His skin was warm, his grip strong and competent rather than overpowering or posturing.

"Stop mean-mugging at the purser." But Larien wasn't

listening. Instead, he'd stopped dead in his tracks to scowl at the man being so nice to her. And that competent man paled as Larien seemed to grow before her eyes. A wicked smile spread across her Fallen's lips when the purser's eyes widened until she was sure they would fall from the sockets. Chel boarded behind them, took in the scene with a quiet, though snorty-sounding "heh." The woman stalked off down the hall, rolling her eyes at Larien as she passed. Talan took up the rear. What was it about men that made them behave like they were part of a S.W.A.T. surveillance team that needed to protect her from her luggage or something?

"Your, uh, berth is that...way?" the purser stammered, gaze locked on Larien's as if he expected to be struck dead at any moment. Poor guy.

"Oh good grief. Let's go already," Jayla said as she snagged Larien by the elbow, grateful that he let her pull him away, knowing that if he didn't wish to be moved, he wouldn't be.

After he'd cased their cube of a room Jayla shoved their door closed. Bags hit the floor with a *thunk*. She turned toward her tormentor and opened her mouth to tell him all about himself in no uncertain terms. Instead a breath soughed into her lungs and stuck there.

The almost-black of Larien's eyes crackled with his *other*ness. Without thought Jayla let her natural sight drop away and used her *othersight*.

The real him flared a bright, power-filled blue and flickered wildly.

In spite of the surge, she wasn't afraid. He might flatten anyone else, but with her he was gentle, giving. And dead sexy. The next inhale brought his natural scent deep into her body. Her skin hummed, blazed beneath his stare.

When her gaze crashed into his, the man's energy buzzed through the room and bounced off the walls. Hunger. Longing. And hers reached up to meet it.

She should be beyond pissed that he'd done his He-man knuckle-dragger thing. But rather than do her own Tarzan act, courtesy of her overnight bag upside his head, instinct took over, responded to and understood his need to protect. She wasn't just his charge anymore. She was his woman. His lover. Simply *his*. Period.

Her stomach tightened. Skin warmed in a way that had nothing to do with the sunshine that filled the small room. In two steps he towered over her, jaw clenched and hands fisted at his sides.

"Oh God, kiss me," she demanded. Her feet left the floor and her legs automatically went where they wanted to be the most—wrapped around his waist.

His mouth came down on hers, seeking—no, demanding. His touch, urgent. His kisses, rough and untamed. He was relentless in the pursuit of her mouth, nipping her bottom lip in the spot she tended to drag through her own teeth when he looked at her. When she returned the gesture with equal fervor, he went wild, laying a fire trail of wet, carnal kisses from her lips to her cheeks to the sensitive spot behind her ear.

Sharp teeth bit down on the cords in her neck and her gasp was of pure pleasure. Oh yes, he knew what she liked. And she knew he would give it to her until she couldn't take anymore.

His finger hooked into the front of her dress, then yanked away as if he'd been burned. Larien set her down on shaky feet, dropped to his knees and croaked, "You do it. If I...I'll rip it."

Her fingers flew over the buttons of her short flippy dress, eased it off over her shoulders and let it float to the floor. The silky swish of the fabric as it pooled around her feet was followed closely by the sound of shredding cotton—her underwear. The *riiip* of the fibers sent her hips into a whirl and then...

"Ah yes!"

God, he was *so* there—his rough against her smooth, her semi-sweet tones sliding against his fairer ones. Her kitten purr against his raspy growls. God, it was all so fucking sexy.

"Oh God!" she cried as he filled his hands with her breasts as his mouth blazed down her rib cage. There was nothing soft or slow about any of this. It was all flame and heat as he rubbed his face back and forth across her chest and the rippling flesh of her stomach. Suddenly he halted, his frenzied motions replaced by the sensation of him breathing her in, then the rush of air over her skin as he exhaled. Mmm. It seemed so...primal.

"Tell me what you want, Jay," he breathed raggedly.

"You want me to talk now?"

He gazed up at her through those thick black lashes. When one side of his mouth quirked up into the evilest grin she'd ever seen the voltage amped up beyond anything close to managcable.

Somehow she managed to croak, "I want...oh, yes. I want you to touch me. Please."

No problem there. She knew he loved to touch her, loved the scent of her arousal, the aroma of her skin. He planted a kiss on her belly and Jayla felt him smile against her skin at her swift intake of breath.

Already on his knees he moved closer to her slickening center. Shivered as she slipped her fingers across his scalp. Anticipation was killing her.

And he knew it.

"Taste me, Larien. I need you to." She let out an unsteady moan as the stubble on his scalp rasped against her inner thigh. And when long fingers parted her slick folds followed by a long, open-mouthed lick Jayla was so close to coming it was all she could do to stand there. Her feet wanted to run. Her flesh wanted to fly away on its own. And her brain was a completely lost cause. Yes, she'd become pure feeling, abandoned to sensation, a woman that wanted nothing more than to give up her orgasm to the man kneeling before her.

"Yes." Arms raised over her head, Jayla became one long undulating line of needy flesh. "Yes, taste me." Her skin seemed to fever from the inside out as Larien continued his sweet assault. He made her fly until she was flush against the hot summer sun. And just when she couldn't take anymore, he hummed against her swollen clit and she exploded in a spectacular show of brilliant sparkling lights.

There was no time to recover from her first orgasm when his clothes melted away as if they'd never been.

Then he was on her, and the man was magnificent. Every part of his body, including his silken cock, was hard and taut, corded with sinew and muscle. And when he entered her, he was so big, so warm. And so *there*!

They both let out a cry of urgency as he pushed deep. Jayla's legs wrapped around his waist, urged him deeper. Her release came swift. Hard. One stroke, two. On three she burst, yelled and then chanted. A litany of praise and awe on her lips as wave after wave of sensual pleasure washed over and through.

Larien followed her over that cliff. When they opened their

eyes they were both bare-assed on the floor, his legs crossed and her sitting on top of him like a carved piece of sensual art.

Beautiful.

* * * * *

A familiar, uncomfortable tug drew Chel's gaze to the screened window of her berth. She rose and peered through the dusty glass, but night had fallen and all she could see was the reflection of the small desk lamp glaring back at her against the pane.

Her stomach knotted against the compulsion pulling at her gut. It was dark and seductively potent. Tempting and forbidden. But she was not required to give in to it. The ass could call her all he wanted but she did not have to obey. Had never had to obey. Chel lay back on her bunk. The scent of freshly laundered sheets and red roses, courtesy of the small vase of flowers on the nightstand, soothed and relaxed her.

The novel she'd picked up in preparation for this trip was a welcome distraction as she cracked it open. Lovingly, she passed her fingers over the stiff spine of the hardback book and released a comfortable sigh. She loved books. Always a new place to go, a new adventure to experience, or a new love to have. Something new to learn or old to forget. Whether between the pages of a book or in front of a photographer's lens, Chel escaped the grayness of the life she'd chosen, her true existence hidden behind a mask of glamour and beauty.

Chelriad.

Fuck. Maybe he'd just go away. She almost snorted at herself. Go away? Not bloody likely, the bastard.

Chel looked down at the half-empty can of Poppycock then the book in her hands. Not only had the can of toffee sweetened popcorn and nutty goodness been full when she'd sat down to read, but she was still on the same page as an hour ago—page six.

And the call still came.

Grrrr!

Annoyed, she rose, donned a warm jacket and slipped out of her berth. The deserted halls were comfortably dimmed and the stream of travelers that had been moving about the train earlier seemed all buttoned up for the night. Eyes closed, Chel reached out with her senses until she found what she was looking for. Direction clear, she homed in on the thrum of celestial magic. Something she hadn't allowed herself to feel in millennia flowed through and around her. Chel sank into the vibration that hid her from human eyes, turned to the right and flew unseen through the long line of train cars until she reached the very last one.

Ignoring the caution signs and thick locks, Chel snapped the sliding door open and hissed as a blast of cold wind lashed her hair against her face. Nothing like sticking your head out of a moving train traveling at eighty miles per hour. Well, at least she was in the back of the long train rather than up front riding into the wind.

At least the idiot has gained some semblance of common sense by now. Pfft.

Looking left and right, she saw no one, and then remembered to adjust her *othersight*. Immediately the auras of the beings standing right in front of her flared in her peripheral vision, one a calming yellow and the other a black so deep it was amazing that it still managed to glow and outline his body.

"What the hell are you doing here?" Chel hissed into the darkness.

"I'm here to deliver a message from Jabon."

"Why didn't he come himself? I don't recall you being the errand boy type," Chel retorted.

With a flash of fang, Luc said, "He's...indisposed. We can't come in, so you'll need to come out."

"You can't come in? Why?"

"Your human has the place locked down tight."

"How come I'm in?"

"Because she trusts you. You're exempt from those she believes would do her harm."

Seeing no hope for it, Chel stepped out to the small platform just short of the edge of the speeding car. She crinkled her nose in distaste and stared at her company. Lucifer himself, the idiot responsible for the first fall. And behind him stood...no way. She had to be seeing things.

"Ascended angels, eudaemon working with and Fallen demons? You're kidding," she said in true astonishment.

Luc smiled. It sent a chill up her spine. "We do what we must in order to protect what's important to us, yes?"

197

Chel didn't bother hiding the blank look that made it clear she didn't know what the hell he was talking about. And judging from the apprehension that danced in her gut, she wasn't sure she wanted to know.

"Ah, sweet Chelriad, you never were much of a history buff."

Chel rolled her eyes and turned to leave. No way was she going to stand here and be insulted by the biggest idiot of all time.

Her fingers wrapped around the door handle just as Luc's heavy hand landed on her shoulder. Her body went taut a she locked her knees and resisted the ridiculous slam of lust that smacked her between her shoulder blades. There was no denying, Luc was one of the most handsome beings ever created. Just his presence was prone to make a woman cream her jeans. But he was no longer the Son of the Morning. He was the most black-hearted, egotistical, self-centered, conniving creature imaginable. And she hated him with everything within her.

Turning slowly back to her unwelcome company, Chel pinned Luc and his guest with a vicious glare. She grit her teeth and snarled quietly.

"Take. Your. Hand. Off. Of. Me."

Taking an easy step back, Luc straightened the already-perfect lapels of his custom gray pinstripe suit, and flashed a beguiling smile. Chel caught a glimpse of fang and knew he barely held his temper in check. And she cared as much about his gentle sensibilities as she did for a boil on her ass.

"Speak fast or I'm out of here, Luc."

"Fine." He snapped then loosened his tie. A tie, for cripes sake?

"Vain much?" She looked him up and down with all the contempt she could muster.

"Here's the deal, Chel. We've got a little problem with your human, or rather your human's ancestry."

"Why?" She already knew the answer but if Luc wanted something he was going to work for it. End of story.

"She's a Descendant of Solomon. I hear she's been asked by The Powers That Be to find the Seal of Solomon."

This was nothing new. The moment Larien had barged into Jayla's life and declared that Jayla had been chosen to seek the Seal, Chel had been grateful to have been included at all, given her unfortunate history. So far, Larien hadn't revealed her secret to

Jayla, a secret that she should have shared with her friend a long time ago. But Luc didn't know that and there was no way Chel would tip her hand even if she wasn't quite sure what that hand was yet.

"Solomon not only forced born demons into servitude with his Seal, but he was able to call turned demon and even eudaemon to do his bidding," Luc said.

"That doesn't make any sense, Luc. We're Fallen—"

"You're Fallen. However, I, with my oh-so-special self, am a Fallen demon. Which brings to mind something I've never quite understood, my dear Chelriad?"

Here it comes.

"All of our previous acquaintances—"

"You mean all of those who were dumb enough to get caught up in your stupid rebellion?" she interrupted.

"...were changed. They all became Fallen demons. All except you and a handful of others. Any idea why?"

"Nope," she lied. "Not a clue. And what does that have to do with my friend?"

"Oh, nothing." His smile was as beautiful and oily as ever. "Just curious."

"Finish it up already. I have a romance novel waiting for me back in my berth, Luc."

"Still prefer a book to me, Chelriad?"

"If you have to ask, I think you know the answer."

"Are you familiar with the demon Ornial?"

She wasn't, but he didn't really want her to answer anyway. He kept going before she'd had the chance to open her mouth.

"Well, this Ornial is the offspring of Uriel, the Archangel."

Chel's mouth fell open. Uriel was *not* Fallen so how the hell did he have demon offspring?

"Before your imagination takes off, just remember that Uriel may have fucked a demon to beget Ornial, but Uriel never forsook his purpose."

"But those of the second Fall had sex and—"

"And they left home of their own accord. However Uriel, my dear Chel, did return home and fulfills his purpose to this day."

Shock still resonated through her. She'd had no idea such a thing was possible. How could she possibly have been alive for so

long and not know this? So for those of the second Fall, it wasn't
the sex? It was the forsaking of one's purpose? Bottom line, it was
the intent of the heart. This was huge. She wondered if Larien
knew.

"Solomon captured the demon, Ornial, by binding him with the
Seal. Ornial was the one that revealed that his father was an
Archangel. And when Ornial refused to obey Solomon's wishes,
Solomon summoned Uriel to *make* Ornial obey."

Holy shit. A human summoned an *Archangel?* And then sent
him on an errand to enforce the human's will? No wonder the
Book of Solomon had been left out of the traditional human bible.
Calling supernatural beings had nothing to do with religion and
everything to do with the dominion given to men by the creative
Source from the beginning. But *commanding* them? Well that was
a different story.

"So in the end," Luc continued, "Solomon had the ability to call
both Archangel and demon alike. And once Solomon's spawn
learns the extent of the Seal's power and exactly what *you* are, it's
just a matter of time before she brings you to heel."

"So, again, what the hell do you want?"

"Get her to give you the Seal."

"What?"

"It can't be taken or stolen, Chel. She has to give it to you, and
not just for you to borrow, but to have."

"I don't get that, Luc." And even if she did, Chel wasn't stupid.
Not anymore. "What's to keep me from using it against you
myself?"

"You can't use it. No one but the Descendants of Solomon can
use the thing except under specific circumstances. For example, if
she gives you the Seal to compel one of our, excuse me, *my* kind to
do her bidding, then you can exorcise power over us but only long
enough to carry out *her* wishes. In the end you have to return the
Seal. However, if she gives it to you for safekeeping? Well—"

Right. You mean gives it to me to hand over to you, asshole.

He stared as if expecting a response. Well, that was just too
bad. There was no way she would commit to this or anything else
for Luc. For herself, perhaps. But for him? No way in hell.

With a sigh, he once again straightened his already straight suit
jacket and stepped back.

"Think on it. I can't force you to do anything but if your human finds the Seal and learns what you are—"

"What's in it for me?" Chel demanded.

"You? If you get your hands on the Seal, you can keep it."

Really? He must think I'm beyond stupid.

"But you already said I can't use it," she said with a yawn.

"Well, if you happen to keep her from finding it, I'll welcome you into my world where you can join me at the top of the food chain. You know I've always had a thing for you, beautiful Chelriad." His true form flickered like a ghost over his human skin. Beautiful, yet so cruel it made her break out in goose bumps.

Chel knew that if she set her heart against her friend it would be the end for her. Her Fall would be complete and she would no longer be Fallen, no longer daemon. No, she would make the final leap to Fallen demon. Chel would have to hurt Jayla to pull off Luc's plan, not to mention seriously hurt Larien to keep them from finding the Seal at all. Just the thought of anything happening to Jayla set her gut churning and filled her ear with a roar that had nothing to do with the turning of the train's wheels on the metal tracks.

"I followed you before, Luc. That didn't turn out so well."

Luc grinned. Then with a dull-sounding poof of stale air, Luc and his eudaemon friend were gone. Interesting. The angel that accompanied Luc hadn't committed or affirmed anything, nor had he said a single word.

A sound just on the other sound of the closed door startled her. Someone was coming. She couldn't be caught out here.

Closing her eyes, she imagined her room, let her diaphaneity fire up and flashed out. Yanking off her coat, she shoved it in the closet and dove for the bunk and the novel she'd set aside earlier.

Larien appeared just seconds later. Right next to her bed.

"Don't you know how to knock? I could have been changing or something."

"Don't flatter yourself, Chelriad."

"Don't call me that, damn it. It's just plain Chel now."

He said nothing, just looked at her as if he didn't want to be in her presence any more than she wanted him there.

"What do you want, *Larry*?"

He ignored the barb, and then rocked her world.

"I've been authorized to offer you a deal from Gabriel himself."

Wait. First Luc shows up with an angel, and now Larien says he's working with one? And another deal? Geesh, this was the second offer in less than fifteen minutes. What, she'd lapsed into a celestial version of "Let's Make a Deal"?

Chel, shall we guess what's behind door number two—the Seal of Solomon, friendship with Jayla or Fallen demonhood?

Fuck.

* * * * *

Larien hoped Jayla never found out that he'd known who Chel was the second he'd sensed her outside Jayla's front door weeks ago. The fact that she was one of Jayla's best friends made no difference. He had every intention of blackmailing this particular Fallen. By any means necessary.

So far she didn't seem impressed by his offer. Instead of a yes or no, she did exactly what he expected—she balked, and with plenty of snark.

"Amazing. You're offering me a deal? You of all people? Remember why you Fell in the first place, Larien. Making deals with the wrong sort."

Oh, he remembered, all right. It was an act he'd regretted for ages; not because he could never return, but because of those he'd hurt by his selfishness.

The faces of his sons, his beautiful boys, flashed into his mind. Strong and courageous, they'd died as they'd lived—with bravery. But now when he thought on them, instead of a haunting sorrow, he remembered the love they'd shared, the time they'd spent laying out under the sky as Larien pointed out the stars to them, their acceptance of what he was, how proud they were of how he'd loved and cared for them, trained them, honed them. And it was true—they'd been the most skilled warriors of their time. Larien thought on how full his earthly days were with them rather than how bereft he'd been without them.

He had Jayla to thank for that. And if Jayla didn't lord his old misdeeds over him, a bitch like Chelriad certainly didn't get to own him through it.

Larien let his thoughts form in his mind and then pushed it

outward in all its vicious glory until he knew the woman in front of him could do nothing but catch them. He knew the very moment she'd picked up his vibration. It gave a whole new meaning to the term 'you feel me?'

"And if I say what's on my mind rather than just think it, what will you do, Chelriad? Try to kick my ass the way the Host kicked yours as we tossed your sorry ass down here by the seat of your once-pristine white pants?"

The corners of her eyes tightened just as her jaw did. Yet he pressed on, knowing exactly how far he would have to push her to get what he wanted.

"So why are you here, Chel? Why are you serving Jayla? You and your fellow Fallen were booted for refusing to bow before humans, the image and likeness of the creative Source. Some of you have even gone totally demon because of your dark ambition. You believed that humans were nothing, just weak flesh that deserved no homage from you. Yet you freely serve one now? And in secret? Tsk, tsk, tsk."

A curl formed on her perfectly painted lips, revealing the fangs she kept hidden from the world. Her powerful but graceful form uncurled from her bunk and took on a shape he hadn't seen since the beginning of time—Chelriad, former *Virtue*, an angel of the elements. In her true form, the agony of her Fall was evident, but it made her no less powerful. Her skin rippled to accommodate her true height until it settled around her body.

Stubs of white jagged bone poked holes in her shirt where her wings should have been. Scarred and pitted, the flesh looked as though it had only partially healed though it had been ages uncountable since she'd been tossed. And the woman was pissed. Her head touched the ceiling as all eight feet of her became encircled in a glow as bright as the orbs of starfire that floated just above her outstretched hands.

"Are you really stupid enough to attack me in this small space on a train full of humans, one of which is your best friend?"

Chel stalled. A knock sounded.

"Chel? Hey, you okay in there?" The familiar voice came from the other side of the door. After a few seconds, the knock came again.

Quietly, so only Chel's supersensory hearing could pick up the words, Larien pulled his ace.

"She knows what I am, Chelriad. Shall we let her see what you are? Or, as you were thinking earlier, would you like to see what's behind door number two?"

In a blink, the room was returned to its shaded hues of blues and cream with a very human-looking Chel chewing Poppycock like she was mad at it. Larien disappeared just as Jayla pushed open the door.

CHAPTER TWENTY-TWO

"Larien, I'm telling you, you should have taken a left turn at Albuquerque," Talan said.

The resulting growl at his Bugs Bunny impersonations set Jayla off into peals of infectious laughter. Jayla was holding her stomach by the time they settled down, and Talan was holding his breath trying to keep the chuckles to a minimum since Larien threatened to put him out on the side of the road minus a good bit of skin.

It should have been a short trek from the train station in Elko, Nevada out to Isthus' place of business but Larien, control freak extraordinaire who didn't trust anyone to drive his ever-precious Jayla anywhere, wouldn't admit he'd taken a wrong off-ramp.

In spite of the obvious humor the good friends got at Larien's expense, Chel hadn't made a sound. Big surprise there.

About midday, Talan pulled his shirt away from his sweaty skin. About forty miles ago, the temperate warmth of spring had given way to what felt like blazing summer as the sun beat down on them through the sunroof. God, was it supposed to be this hot so early in the season? The answer was obviously a resounding "yes" as they pushed farther into the desert minus air conditioning.

Finally their oversized rental pulled off the main road and onto a rough gravel trail that ended at what looked like a wall of nothing but brown sunbaked rock. As they got closer, wooden clapboard and shuttered windows became apparent, but were so covered with dust you could barely tell the building from the rock it was built next to.

Talan hopped out and took a quick look around while Larien went around to the other side of the vehicle for Jayla.

He let his magick flare up and out of his gut and engaged his *othersight*. There was nothing out here. Absolutely nothing. No insects. No birds. No signs of life other than theirs.

Interesting it hadn't seemed as desolate as they'd pulled up to the place.

"I thought you said he owns a record store," Larien said. Larien turned slow circles and took in the barren landscape around them.

"He does," Talan said peering up toward the clear blue sky as he relaxed. It might be desolate here, but there was no danger. No surprise there. Isthus would have seen to it. "I've never visited him here before."

"And what the fuck is going on with all the warding or whatever the hell is around the place?"

The familiar electric-like charge straightened the hair along Talan's arms. Gifts fully engaged his eyes went wide. "Holy shit. You're right. He's got some serious spells in place. If I were in my Shadow spec, I'm not sure *I* could even get in and I'm always welcome here. Strange. He knew we were coming."

"Yeah, well if I get any closer we're going to have a problem. This shit stings, hitting me from every angle. Pushing at my control, like it's trying to strip me of the ability to—"

"Hide."

They all turned in a different direction in reaction to the voice that echoed from everywhere all at once.

"What the...?" Jayla's eyes were glued to a spot off to Larien's right.

Following her line of sight, they found the man standing near the side of the building.

Huh. Seeing Isthus was always a shock to the retinas but this outfit took it to a whole new level. Today there were enough buckles and chains on Isthus' clothes to supply a local rock concert. The eyebrow piercing was typical, but the snake bite piercing on his lower lip, now *that* was new. Isthus' punk style was usually more downplayed than this. Perhaps it was his way of dressing for new company or something?

Isthus straightened his impeccable red and black short sleeved leather suit jacket, and dusted off the matching red and black tartan patterned pants. Who wore a red leather suit out in the middle of the desert? And we weren't talking Santa Clause red suit, but New York red carpet couture punk rock duds, complete with coordinated jet black dress shirt with strategic rips and holes. To top it all off—a red leather tie draped with thick dog-collar-like links. And around his neck...jeweler's glass?

Oh, and let's not forget the shoes. Jesus. Yes, they matched— blood red Doc Marten's patent leather loafers without a single speck of dust to be seen though dust seemed to permeate the dry air. Talan hoped his eyes didn't start bleeding.

Talan shook his head in wonder at his longtime friend. Isthus really was a fascinating combination of light and dark in both body and spirit, a blend of bad and sort of bad. Not truly committed to either side but just kind of hanging around in the middle somewhere. And even if he was gruff and almost as grumbly as Larien, it was still impossible to miss the mischief in his eyes. And mischief was something Isthus was very, very good at.

"I am Isthus. Welcome to Fantasy Island." A tight, absolutely *not* genuine smile accompanied the almost-snarled words, which only served to thicken the brogue laced through them.

Chel sucked in a swift but quiet breath and whispered, "Talan, he's not human?"

"Nope. And whatever you do, don't touch any of his stuff once we get inside. He's...particular."

"You could have told us that before we got here," Chel hissed.

Just then the wind picked up. Isthus tucked an errant wisp of hair behind his ear, exposing the pointed tips.

Talan could see when Chel put two and two together. "He's fae. Oh my God, is he a leper...?"

"Don't say it. Trust me. Just...don't." Talan whispered back, then strode toward his friend raising outstretched arms, which was quite funny given Isthus was at least a foot shorter than Talan's five-foot-ten inches. "Isthus, you trouble maker."

Isthus hand shot out in front of him. "No! Wait. Don't come any closer. I was expecting you at—" He looked down at his watch—a metal-banded heavy-looking piece that was decorated with spikes and dripped with jewels. "At exactly twelve-thirty. You're three minutes early."

"So what," Talan said but stopped short anyway. One thing he'd learned—if Isthus said to stop walking, stop and do it fast.

"The spell won't drop until the three minutes are up. Stay there and I'll come to you."

"I don't recognize this spell. Not sure I've ever felt anything quite like it, Issy."

His friend's answering grin was filled with naughtiness. As usual. Talan smiled right back when Isthus said, "Remember that revelation spell we used to play with when you were a kid? Well I perfected it."

"To the point that you can put it on a timer?" Talan snorted.

"Yep."

"Seriously?" Talan knew his eyes were bugging out of the sockets now but, hell, he was impressed. Actually, there was some amazement and more than a bit of awe there, too, for his friend's command of magick. He felt his brain expand with the possibilities of how he could put this particular warding to use back home.

"Yep. It's like programming my TiVo, man. I am truly the shit."

"So you're a...what are you?" Jayla asked with a friendly smile. Talan braced himself as Isthus turned an assessing eye on her.

"Uh, I'm sorry. Jayla, this is Isthus. Isthus this is Jayla. She's the one I've been telling you about for years." To Talan's surprise, Isthus' head tilted as if he'd suddenly met a puzzle he couldn't quite figure out though he said nothing. "The big grumpy one over there with the ginormous biceps is Larien. And the lady version of the grumpy one staring daggers at the one with the biceps is Chel."

Larien nodded. "Fae."

With a return of the gesture, he simply said, "Fallen," then turned and headed back toward the rickety looking front door. And with a muted *'plick'* that was felt more than heard, Isthus said, "Ah, it's all clear now. Let's get you all inside and settled. That spell will pop back into place in exactly three minutes, enough time to grab a bag or two and make it past the first checkpoint. I'll show you around, maybe grab a bite to eat, and then you can come back and get the rest later."

"No problem. So, what's going on, Isthus? Anything new," Talan asked as they moved quickly through the front door.

The clapboard, frontier-styled façade was effectively deceptive. Rather than a dusty room on the other side of the door, there was a wide tunnel that led deep into the mountain. There were no lights yet they could see perfectly, as if there were skylights built into the low rock ceiling overhead. The walkway was remarkably clean, the walls smooth and dust-free, almost as if they'd been carved and then polished to a high sheen.

Talan was beginning to wonder where in the world they were going when after about two minutes of walking, Isthus stopped short. Then with a wave of his hand, a door slid open and disappeared into the wall. It was like walking into the secret underground base of the X-men, and definitely swankier than the Batcave by quite a stretch.

Isthus clicked on all the lights with a little remote he'd dug out of his pocket. Inside, was a huge room that reminded him of Jayla's family room at home, complete with comfy couches, a roaring fire in a huge stone hearth and the biggest TV he'd ever seen. Orderly shelves with case after case of…stuff—paintings, sculptures, items of stone and some of gold—lined every visible wall. Talan even spotted some framed artifacts that looked like ancient hieroglyphs. The place was a veritable museum. Looked like a few new pieces had been added since his last visit.

Talan took his best friend's hand and led her to the nearest glass shelf filled with rare colored Faberge eggs. "My first visit to this place was as a child in Kinsale, Ireland. Another time, it was in a little town in Switzerland. One time after that, in the Paris catacombs. Neat how Isthus can move the entrance to his stash at will."

"It can move? Really?" Jayla grinned with delight. "How did all this stuff come to be here? Just what are we dealing with? A pointy-eared obviously not human hoarder? And by the way, we're safe here, right?"

Talan couldn't blame her for asking the question. After all, the unknown had been creeping up on her lately in ways none of them appreciated. Jayla turned to Isthus. "So are we? Safe, I mean."

"*I'm* safe here. My friend and my things are safe here. You? Well, I think that's up to him." The little man tossed his purposely half-messy, half-perfectly-spiky-haired head Larien's direction. Larien's answer was his typical grunt.

"Your friend and your things?" Jayla wondered aloud.

"Yep, my buddy, the skinny redheaded Irish guy drooling all over *my* record collection. Key word, *my*," Isthus said.

Talan winked but kept his mouth shut. Isthus' secrets were for Isthus to tell. The man was this way for a very good reason, as was all of his kind. Their purpose in life was to guard their treasures and their secrets. It could be a tricky proposition. As a result, Talan had learned to be exceptionally good at explaining to humans all the freaky shit they were seeing.

Especially since at times Isthus *was* the freaky shit—a magickal creature that could be your worst nightmare on a good day. Thankfully, Talan had garnered favor, something unheard of for a human to get from a fae.

Chel moved closer and looked him up and down with a wry grin. "Can I touch your ears? The little points look so soft," she said. After a few seconds of intense stare-down with Isthus' mouth set in a tight line, Chel moved away with a broad grin to explore the racks of rare photos along one of the fake windows.

"If she makes one fucking Lucky Charms joke, Tal, I'm gonna have to fry her." Whispered, but purposely not quietly enough. Across the room Chel laughed for the first time since, well, Talan wasn't sure. Certainly for as long as Larien had been around.

"Jay, I need to talk to you. Alone."

Talan turned at the growled words to see Chel looking at the arm that Larien had draped around Jayla's shoulder.

He wished she would get over it already…whatever *it* was. This would not end well if Chel kept pushing like this. What in the wide world was her problem with Larien anyway?

"Sure, sweetie, but after that ride I seriously need to go to the bathroom. Isthus, do you have a restroom I can use, please?"

"Yes, just don't touch anything," Isthus said.

"Does that include allowing her ass to touch the seat?"

"Sarcasm," Jayla said, "thy name is Chel. Good grief, woman." But even with the tension in the air so thick it seemed to coat the walls, it was impossible not to laugh at Chel's zero calorie tone of voice—plenty sweet but nothing to it.

Then his attention was snagged for an altogether different reason. "Whoa, Issy! Is this an original Ray Charles album?

'Modern Sounds in Country and Western Music' with 'I Can't Stop Loving You'? Are you serious?"

Isthus shooed Jayla toward the hallway that led to the bathroom. "Down the hall, first door on the left. And don't forget to wash your hands." He turned to Talan with a smirk. "Well, this *is* a record shop."

"But do they even make record players that spin vinyl anymore? I mean, certainly not for a record cut in 1962?"

"Says who?" Isthus grinned.

Talan turned to Larien. "Come on, Larien, even you have to admit this is a thing of beauty." At that Isthus' smile lit up his whole face, reflected the pride he had in his collection. Isthus motioned with a subtle tilt of his head and Talan followed his line of vision to a long lacquered shelf of pristine phonographs. "Were these here last time?" Certainly not. He would have noticed. Each was carefully labeled and dust-free like everything else.

Isthus moved a little ways down the line of record players, from an old hand-crank model to a ridiculously expensive newer platinum-plated one. He singled out a bronze and black machine in perfect condition. No surprise there. It was the only way Isthus would claim anything as part of his treasure trove of collectibles. Priceless. Pristine. Like the original Mona Lisa—which the rest of the world believed sat in The Louvre—stashed in here somewhere, along with an original Michelangelo that had never been seen by the public because Isthus had stolen it before it could be presented.

"I give you, my skeptical friend, a 1960's Magnavox Micromatic turntable. And while I appreciate the blues of the 1960's..." Isthus turned, snatched an LP out of one of the storage boxes and fanned it in Talan's face as he said, "This is a bit more to my liking just now."

A funky beat filled the room and Isthus danced around as if he were the only one home. He stomped his feet and bobbed his head, singing, "We will, we will rock you. Yeah!" A picture of a hobbit, minus hairy feet, decked out in red leather punk gear popped into Talan's head and he almost burst out laughing.

God he loved times like this, when he could just let the stress flow out of his body while enjoying some good music with even better friends. Amazing what a little music and an uncoordinated friend could do for one's mood.

* * * * *

When Talan burst into song in a perfect imitation of Freddy Mercury with Isthus backing him up on the chorus, Larien tried not to be surprised. It proved impossible.

Exactly four minutes and fifteen seconds later—yes, he counted—Larien brought them back to the reason they were here. He simply didn't have the patience to hang about any longer than necessary. It was time to get the information they needed and get the hell out of here for one simple reason—Isthus was a fae of the dark variety and they played by a different set of rules. Isthus' protection didn't extend to Jayla. Nothing personal. It was just the way it worked.

But Larien wasn't a total asshole. He even let them finish the song.

Then he said, "Isthus, you know why we're here. So let's get started, shall we?"

Isthus' answer was a single raised brow.

Hand over his heart, Larien pledged, "You tell me what I need to know and I give you my word; as one beholden to the Messenger, I will procure something worthy to be added to your collection."

Isthus laughed, eyes wide with mock disbelief. "Really, Fallen? How very special of you. Tell you what you want to know? You know what I am so you, of all people, know I can't do that. So here's the deal, you read between the lines and I still get a boon. Deal?"

Fuck. He'd have to do some serious negotiating to get what he needed without trying to kill the bastard...which would be counterproductive. Besides, Larien respected the fae. They were what they were and made no attempts to be anything but. And leprechauns like Isthus were ruthless to the core, and even less inclined to care what anyone thought of them. The most cunning and manipulative creatures breathing, they cared about one thing—protecting their treasures.

How in the world had Talan managed to make a friend of Isthus? Carefully was the only word that came to Larien given how rare it was for a fae of this type to trust a human. But there was one thing that was not in question—Isthus' loyalty. If he truly called Talan friend, he would not betray that trust for any reason, which meant Larien had no problem trusting him with the details of their mission. The leprechaun would keep his word no matter what.

Isthus might be Hobbit-sized but Larien sensed his magick was potent, powerful. Very old. Thankfully, Gabriel had foreseen this little complication, which should have surprised Larien but with all the other bombshells along the way, this one just seemed par for the course.

"In a show of good faith, let's start with this." Larien dug into his pocket, keeping his fingers closed around the object until he'd put it in Isthus' hand. The little bastard's eyes lit up as he realized what he held—a pristine white nephrite jade pendant in the form of a flawless lily blossom. "Compliments of the Messenger himself. You'll find its age somewhere around the ninth century."

Isthus fished out the jeweler's glass that hung on one of the many chains around his neck and examined the trinket. "Ninth century?" he murmured quizzically.

"Yes," Larien answered patiently. "As in BC."

Peals of laughter bubbled up out of Isthus chest. "Woohoo! Iron deposits. Perfectly carved white jade." Isthus looked up and asked, "About 1050 BC?" The little bounder was dead on. As for a deal, Isthus simply said, "Done."

Getting down to business, Larien said, "I need clues on the whereabouts of the Seal of Solomon."

Holding Larien's gaze Isthus went completely still as if in shock. What was going on here? A leprechaun's specialty was keeping and hiding secrets, so why would he be surprised that Larien searched for one? Isthus shook it off and turned to Talan with a simple, "I'll need something to work with."

"Had a feeling." Talan snatched his gear bag up off the floor, took it over to a cleared space on the nearest table and simply upended it. Out spilled several items taken from the clues left by Jayla's grandmother. Larien wanted to kiss him. Good man.

Isthus snatched up a small clay tablet carefully mounted in a plastic case. "Hmmm. This is interesting. Based on the formation of the symbols this looks to be Sumerian. Very, very old. I've not seen anything like this in a long time. But I do know what it is. It's a poem that speaks of fine cloth. Silk to be exact. If you want more than what I just told you, you'll have to give me something else."

"Fine," Larien said. "For every question you answer or every clue you give, you can have one of the items Talan just dumped on the table. They're all unique. Treasure, as it were."

Again, Isthus replied with a simple, "Done." And then set the clay artifact aside and picked up a parchment, turned it face out for them all to see and looked Talan dead in the eye. Larien watched the unspoken communication and wondered if they could actually hear one another's thoughts. When Talan's brows dropped into a frown, Isthus sighed dramatically and said, "Oh come on. Look at the symbols, the colors. You know what this means."

"Uh…I do?" Talan replied quizzically. It made Larien nervous. He'd never seen Talan genuinely confused. Not good.

"Good grief, Tal, you specialized in mythology and legends of ancient cultures in school."

"Yeah, but—"

"Aw shut up and listen." Then Isthus translated and read the scroll aloud. "The Yellow River runs up to the white sky, a lonely tower stands in a thousand mountains, spring never reaches the Jade Gate."

"Again," Talan demanded and then closed his eyes and concentrated on Isthus' words. Isthus repeated the bit of poetry and Talan's green eyes popped wide. "The Silk Road. Holy crap, the Silk Road."

"Silk Road? But it's all covered by concrete now," Jayla said as she returned from the bathroom and put her chilled, freshly-washed hands on the bare skin of Larien's forearm. Cool to the touch, her skin was soft and smooth, and brought to mind all the places those fingers had touched him since they'd become lovers. Forcing his mind back to the task at hand, Larien wrapped his fingers around her chilled ones.

"But it was more than just a single road. It was a number of different routes that the ancient dynasties used to get their goods across the continent. The towns, villages, and in some case, cities are still there. Bigger, but there all the same. The beginning of the route system is Xi'an, China," Talan said.

"Xi'an? Why does that sound familiar?" Jayla wondered aloud.

"It's where they discovered the big cache of terra cotta warriors," Isthus said, lifting a sweeping hand toward a corner off to the right where one of those very same statues stood proudly. "So far, these docs mention several places where your ancestors may have hidden the Seal. There's mention of Byzantium, Alexandria—"

"Alexandria? As in Egypt?" Jayla asked.

"Yes. Also Baghdad, the Taklimakan Desert, everywhere from Rome to the Gobi Desert. The Silk Road was the merchant highway as far back as...well, ancient times. Even the Egyptians traded on the Silk Road somewhere between 4000 BC and 5000 BC. Solomon was king at around 940 BC, meaning the road was already well established."

"Sorry, Jay. I don't think there's a train that crosses the Pacific to China." Talan smiled but there was no missing the concern in his eyes.

With a flourish, Isthus gathered his goodies, moved to the far side of the room and opened a huge wooden chest with so many padlocks, there were almost more locks than wood. With a wave of his hand, it popped open and Isthus placed the items he'd chosen inside and then walked away as the chest resealed itself.

Jayla's mouth dropped open. "I know what you are! You're a fairy!"

"Fairy?" Smoothing the lapels of his jacket again Isthus looked down his nose at her, which should have been impossible given she was quite a stretch taller than he was even at her modest five-foot-six inches. "Do I look like a tight-wearing, pantywaist, milquetoast, wing-flapping...?"

Whoa. The man went from pale to strawberry to beet read and beyond with each word that made it past his clenched teeth. Surely his head was going to pop off at any moment. The tension in the room rose along with Isthus' deepening voice.

"Sorry, Issy. She's human." Talan eased in between them. "He's a leprechaun, Jay. He's fae, but definitely not a fairy." The words were spoken out of the side of his mouth as if Isthus couldn't hear them.

"Oh. Sorry. No disrespect intended. But I don't give a shit what you are, don't ever holler at me again."

Isthus' mouth snapped shut in shock. It was obvious he was used to holding all the cards. The thing about Jayla was that she didn't recognize the deck. Larien could almost empathize with

Isthus. Almost. Instead he bit back a smile. His woman took shit
from no one. God, he loved it.

Pulling Jayla into his arms, Larien said, "Okay, let's get back to
it. So, China means we would have to fly, and I don't want Jayla in
the air," Larien said.

"Why not?" Jayla's hand left his and made its way as a fist to
the dip of her hip.

He turned and pinned her with a 'duh' glare. "Because one, you
hate flying. And two, my kind aren't called the princes and powers
of the air for nothing. That's their domain, not yours."

"Why can't you flash her?" Talan asked.

"I can. But even I have rules to follow, which means I'm
restricted to moving that way with one person and one person only.
And there's no way I'm going to take her all the way to fucking
China and leave her there while I return for you."

"Okay," said Talan. "So flash her there, stay there with her and
we'll follow."

"Eighteen hours later? Really, dude?" Chel rolled his eyes even
as the words left her mouth.

"Stop it, you guys. I refuse to allow anyone or anything to
make me cower," Jayla snapped. "We need to find this damn Seal
and whatever way we have to do it is simply what has to be done. I
may be stubborn but I'm not stupid. I agree with Larien. I don't
want him to diapha-whatever me to China, then leave me there
while he plays taxi. So if we have to fly to China—" She visibly
shuddered. "Then I'm packed and ready, like, yesterday."

Chel tapped Jayla on her shoulder. "Jay, I really need to talk to
you. Perhaps they can work on the transportation issue while we
step out for a moment."

"Whoa, step out where?" Larien demanded.

"Oh good grief, Larien. We have to get our stuff out of the car.
I've gotten pretty good at sensing bad guys so unless you're
picking up something on your demon GPS, Chel and I can grab
our stuff and have our girl talk on the way back through the
tunnel."

His senses said it was all clear. Picked up nothing. Nothing at
all.

"Talan, are you sensing anything?"

Though invisible to the naked eye, Talan's magick charged the air. "Nope. All clear."

"It's okay. I can drop the warding for them." Isthus said absently, his focus on a gold coin he'd plucked out of a small wooden box.

"Jayla, don't be a horror film casualty," Talan said. Of course she looked at him like he'd lost his mind. "I mean it. Isn't this the part of every horror movie where the women go off by themselves and get attacked? Oh, and then they fall down as they're running away or something?"

Isthus cut in and surely saved him from a Jayla-sized tongue lashing.

"Look, it's a ten minute walk up the tunnel and back. Certainly two women can talk enough from here to there and back again and stay out of trouble."

Larien rolled his eyes. Talan bit his lip. Jayla smiled at Isthus before turning to glower at Larien. And Chel simply turned and called over her shoulder. "Come on, Jayla. Who needs a snarky-assed faery to help with the bags? My suitcase is probably taller than he is anyway."

Jayla whacked her friend playfully on the back of her neck as they strolled away.

Larien waited all of three minutes, signaled to Talan and they headed out after them.

CHAPTER TWENTY-THREE

"So, what's up, sweetpea?"

"Jay, I need to tell you something." Chel's voice actually wavered? Whatever it was must be serious.

"Chel, you know I'm not going to push, so whatever it is just take your time. But I'm getting the impression it must be a doozy." God, she hoped it wasn't a Larien discussion. Again.

They were all the way up the tunnel and exiting the clapboard façade and her friend still hadn't said a word. Back at the vehicle, they yanked the rest of their bags out of the trunk and turned back to the building.

"Come on, Chel. You can tell me. I'm sure what I'm imagining is worse than whatever is really going on."

"Well...it's just that...uh, I. Shit."

"Chel! I think that's the first time I've ever heard you swear in all the years I've known you. Yep. Definitely a doozy."

Chel opened her mouth again, and then snapped it shut with an audible click as if she'd been sucker punched in the face. Jayla followed Chel's line of sight towards the desolate stretch of dunes. The sky was clear, though strangely dim. There was nothing out here. No cars. No homes. Hell, there was barely a road onto Isthus' property.

And then she felt it.

A flash of black energy so strong it blazed over her skin like a swarm of bees, stinging until it seemed as if each pore held its own individual stinger.

Jayla looked down at her arms just to be sure. No bees. No stingers. Yet the pain was incredible. Almost debilitating. And it came from inside of herself as if someone, something was trying to suck out her very essence.

"Jayla run!"

The first clawed hand appeared out of nowhere and Chel was swiped aside like a Lego character.

There was nothing visible in the failing light, yet spiky boned fingers dug between her ribs, stretched them apart and proceeded to dig out the power pooled in her core. Jayla's blood ran cold but the chill didn't last beneath the flash of anger that gave her the courage to fight. Goddamit, she was beyond tired of feeling as if her ass was one big painted target. Without another thought she clamped down within herself, cut off the siphon of power from whatever invisible force tried to steal it from her and yanked it back. Chel was back up on her feet and together they looked up to the darkening sky to see a swarm of Fallen and demons.

These had no weapons that she could see, but their armor was unmistakable—black as night with glowing gray-tinged ooze that seeped out of the joints like supercharged pus. Their faces were what she expected, having seen them since she was a child—some were gorgeous with an unmistakable menace, perfectly formed and beyond beautiful. Others were as ghastly and malformed as something right out of a horror movie, complete with fangs and brittle cracked skin or enormous leather wings sporting wicked flesh-ripping talons or both.

Power flared from Jayla's gut, strong and ready to do her bidding. She commanded it to form a hedge of protection around her and Chel.

One creature dove from directly above and two from the sides. Jayla commanded them to turn and fight their comrades. The chaos was most welcome, but didn't last long enough. They tore each other apart, the defectors quickly subdued as several others readied to take their place and do damage.

She forced another group to freeze and they were quickly trampled underfoot by the horde as they stood like statues, unable to attack anyone or defend themselves. And there were more. Always more.

She cold cocked one and then winced as her fist made contact with the razor sharp scales of his face, splitting her knuckles open.

Fuck. She could neither compel them all nor fight them all. There was no way they were going to get out of this alive without help.

Her mind screamed, "Larien!" as she turned a tight circle to see...

Whoa. What the hell? Chel?

Chel was a moving work of art. The full moon had just begun its climb over a mountain off to the East like a large piece of perfect china. Chel's equally flawless complexion was set aglow by the growing light of it. Jaw set and brows narrowed, Chel met their enemies with a ferocity that boggled Jayla's mind even as the creatures whooshed up, down and all around them. Even in the dust kicked up by the movement of the battle that clogged her nose and throat, Jayla caught every movement her friend made as she earnestly defended them.

And where the hell had those blades come from? They hummed with celestial energy as she wielded them, gold and blue blurs that whipped through the air so fast they were like something off the Lord of the Rings in the hands of an elf.

The ice pick-like talons of a mean-looking purple-gray demon slid between Jayla's ribs at the same time she realized that she was the only one being attacked. Chel was fighting the demons but they weren't fighting her back. They simply bypassed her or tried to swipe her aside. Well, as much as she allowed them to swipe, anyway.

There was no doubt who they were gunning for.

Jayla shifted slightly and the breath caught in her lungs at the flash of agony tearing through her side. The pain stripped away the desire to try to make heads or tails of what the hell Chel was as a dense fog crowded into her field of vision. She tried to look down at the source of the ache, but it felt as if a tether were attached to the back of her head, keeping her from moving it. Jayla felt her mouth open on a silent scream. The more she tried to call out, the tighter the tether became until it felt like her brain was being pulled from the stem at the base of her neck.

Too hard. To. Breathe.

Her head dropped to her chest with a gasp. Blood. So much

blood. It bubbled up through the fingers pressed to her ribs, soaked her shirt and pooled in the top of her pants before running down her clothes to splatter in the desert sand.

But there was no fear. Chel was with her and Larien was on the way. She'd called him and he would come without fail. Wait! He was here already. Even though her eyesight dimmed but there was no mistaking that crackle and hum of very specific energy—Larien's energy.

He was a beautiful, avenging, furious angel.

The tails of his long duster coat flapped wildly in a wind that wasn't there. Without preamble his battle form burst forth. Larien disappeared and the Angel of the Art of War stood in his place. Demons were no match for angels of any sort, but in his battle form he would be unstoppable. Pride bloomed in her bruised and battered chest. With it came a mixture of fear and peace. Peace that Larien would never fail her…yet fear that something might happen to him in his bid to save her life.

She watched in awe, wondering if she were conscious when the sword he carried transformed along with his flesh. Instead of polished tempered steel, a living black flame blazed from pommel to tip in his left hand. In the right hand was the biggest, baddest gun she'd ever seen.

Wings snapped out to an impressive span from either side of his spine, shredding his clothing as they burst through. The play of muscle as he pulled them in tight to his back was inspiring even in her muddled half-conscious state. Black as night, the tips edged in shimmering gold and adorned with wicked looking talons, they rippled and flexed with power as a roar left his mouth that promised unholy retribution to the thinning swarm.

"Fuck!" She couldn't' hold back the scream as a new set of talons joined the game of connect-the-dots on her body. Jayla felt herself, the very essence of her spirit, finally begin to slip. Terror was a gripping monster, literally. One that had her head between what felt like scaled palms with fingers of spiny-edged bone.

"Talan!" Larien yelled.

"Ready."

And with that Larien became a blur of unimaginable speed to engage their enemies. Talan, though not inhumanly fast, was right behind him, throwing laser-like beams of various colors from a...wand? At Larien rather than their foes?

A cut appeared across Larien's cheek. It was gone instantly. What was left of his shirt was ripped from his body and a pattern of bloody hash-like marks appeared across his back. Talan motioned and instantly they were gone. Holy shit! Talan was healing Larien as they tore through the horde together. Where teeth and claws made deep furrows, Talan's power sank beneath the skin and immediately the flesh knitted together.

Then Talan was no longer healing Larien, but had instead become a dusky shadow of himself. A shadow with the power to blast blackish waves of whatever-it-was at his enemies, pushing them back and sometimes tearing them apart altogether.

Then again, maybe it was her imagination. Word had it that hallucinations were a common side effect of bleeding out. Her head fell back. She flopped onto the ground and wondered why there was no pain when her head bonked against something. A sharp dig suggested the edge of a rock dug into her scalp. Still, no pain.

Then arms came around her, trying to move her away from Larien and Talan.

"Jayla, stop squirming. I have to get you out of here."

"Isthus?"

"Yes, let's go."

"No, wait. Have to. Help." She managed to push her power at a nasty multi-armed slimy thing poised at Talan's back. It froze just as she commanded it to, but the energy it took to enforce the command sent a hammer of pounding agony directly to her head, her gut, her heart. God, everywhere.

"You're about to pass out. You're hurt. I have to get you to safety, Jayla."

"Pass? Never passed." Ah, God. Ow. "Out. In...life."

"Well, there's a first time for everything."

* * * * *

"Holy shit!"

They'd come out of the tunnel right behind the girls and right into the middle of demon central. Talan didn't have time to do anything but take in the swarm of Fallen demons and their cohorts at the same time he and Larien fought their way toward Jayla.

A pitch-black golem that looked as if its parts had been randomly glued together prepared to hurl a chunk of earth the size of a small car at Larien's back. Talan cursed as his binding spell almost missed his target when Chel came into view. Stunned was an understatement for what he felt at the sight. She was beautiful yet horribly scarred. Her body stretched and then stretched some more until she was as tall and broad as Larien himself.

Smooth creamy skin was gone, replaced by what looked like a full body road rash. On her back was nothing but jagged spikes of bone, as if whatever had been there was literally hacked away. She was absolutely fierce, her expression hard and filled with a fury so potent it rolled off of her in waves and rippled the very air around her. The sight of her turned Talan's guts to water. What the hell was she?

Just then she spoke—if you could call her deadly vibrating growl speech—to one of the creatures advancing on Jayla as Isthus tried to shelter her from harm.

"You shall not harm my friend!" Chel's hair blew wildly around her face and her voice rose like the thunder during a storm. One of the blades she'd been skinning demons with disappeared and in its place was a shimmering orb. He had no idea what it was made of, but it undulated, whirled and glowed like a mix of molten rock, glass and colorful sand. The underlying power of the thing made Talan's skin want to crawl away and hide.

After beheading a demon with the remaining blade, Chel turned to the next enemy, swung her arm as if she pitched a baseball and sent the orb flying across the distance between her and the demon. The creature landed in the dirt with a splat, nothing but a mess of flesh, bones and blackish-blue blood. A small glowing ball, what Talan now knew was all that was left of the thing's lifesource, rose from the carnage, flared and then disappeared.

"Isthus, get her the hell out of here! Crazy woman is still trying to shield me." Larien yelled and motioned to a crumpled Jayla and an uncharacteristically ruffled Isthus who had his hands full trying to get her to safety.

As a unit they turned back to the horde. God, they were everywhere. Some Fallen. Some demon. All bad. Larien's "Fuck this!" reverberated above the din in a snarled bass so deep Talan felt it in his bones.

"Incoming!" Talan yelled and braced himself for the next wave.

Guts and dirt formed a muddy, bloody cake along Larien's blade. Then the crazy man dropped his weapon.

Hands raised in the air, a burst of blinding light flared from within his body and punched outward like a solar flare. Suddenly, all was still.

When the spots cleared from behind Talan's eyes, he stood rooted in disbelief—every single entity in the swarm determined to end them was...gone.

Larien stumbled, barely righted himself then wobbled his way to Jayla. She gasped, clearly in horrendous pain when he snatched her away from Isthus and held her gently against his chest.

"Chel. Follow. Now!" Chel gave a terse nod, grabbed Talan and the world fell away.

* * * * *

"Jayla? Jay?"

Warmth surrounded her, kept the fear clawing at her gut from erupting and overtaking what little sense she had left. But something else pulled in the opposite direction, told her it was time to go.

Forcing her eyes open she battled to remain topside.

Larien was calling to her. Oh! There he was. He was so handsome. Moving only her eyes, she was able to recognize his beauty in her blurry surroundings. Hmmm. It seemed out of place given the lash of agony that made breathing almost impossible. The sun shone down on her somehow. Had Larien taken her to heaven? No, he couldn't go there anymore. Besides there was no anguish in heaven and the grief-stricken lines carved into his face as he leaned over her said he was definitely upset.

"Jay, speak to me."

She tried. She really did. But all she could manage was a gurgle, and with the foreign sound came a bubble of blood. Ew. She tried to spit it out, but her lips felt like so much raw meat, thick and swollen, she couldn't purse them properly. Instead, it ran down her chin and throat to pool warm and sticky around the collar of what was left of her shirt. She raised her hand to wipe it away.

Her arm wouldn't work. And whatever she was laying on was uncomfortable.

"Be still," Larien said at the same time someone else said, "You are injured."

Really?

She tried to see the genius who spoke while amazing herself that she could still obtain this level of snark, even if only in her mind. She closed her eyes and began to drift again. The voice wasn't familiar, but it was definitely male, deep and rolled over her frayed senses like warm buttered rum. Soothing. Calming. Lulling her back from the brink of unconsciousness. She knew pain awaited her if she managed to surface completely but the need to reach her friends, to make sure they were safe, set her heart racing in urgency.

"Stop trying to move," the deep voice commanded.

"Don't tell me what to do." The intended snap came out a slur and it sounded like her ears were stuffed with cotton. Had they given her some pain meds or something? Her brain was fuzzy, foggy. But the pain was fading quickly, decreasing with each beat of her heart, each gush of blood from her throat.

"She's almost beyond my aid, though she's putting up quite a fight."

Who was that?

"She's fading. It's now or never, Larien," the voice said. "What do you want?"

"Do it."

Do what? What were they talking about? And what did the deep-voiced guy mean by now or never? Then she slipped away to where Death awaited. And boy was he handsome.

CHAPTER TWENTY-FOUR

Climbing her way up through layers of gauzy thoughts was becoming more of a habit than Jayla cared for. In fact, that whole adage about some habits should be broken? Yeah, she agreed this habit could totally go away.

Eyes closed, Jayla lay still. Her skin was warm, as if she were wrapped in sunshine. Lungs expanded with ease rather than pain. The air was humid, ripe with the scent of blooming wildflowers. A wash of memories told her that she should be having tea in the ever after with her Grams by now. So where was she? What happened? Was Death around the corner just waiting to finish checking her into her new afterlife?

Goodness, Death was a gorgeous devil, uh, angel. Whatever.

Hmmm. Her arms seemed to work just fine too. A super-soft blanket tickled her skin as she pulled it up over her bare shoulders.

It was way too quiet. If her crew was near they'd be making plenty of raspy, hurting sounds right? Then again, if she was in okay shape, maybe they were, too? God, she'd never seen so many bad guys in one place. And they'd all been after her. The thought made her literally shiver. She couldn't remember ever being so scared in all of her adult life. Hell, in all of her entire life, actually.

Jayla settled more deeply into the comforter and let thoughts of her new best friend settle into that little space in her heart that was distinctly his. And then she felt him. Keenly.

Larien.

SILK ROAD

Her eyes were gummy and tired, but she forced them open then squinted against the bright light from the…floor-to-ceiling windows? Wait, she'd been here before, knew exactly where she was. The familiar vivid green of the forest was visible from this high, vibrant and alive with a variation of jade and dark greens. She lay on the couch in the open space of Larien's family room. The plush cushions under her body brought to mind other thoughts. Thoughts of Larien easing her down, arranging her to his liking before he loved her fiercely, leaving no doubt that he was indeed the badass he appeared to be, both in and out of bed.

Yet silence still reigned. There should have been the quiet hum of the air conditioner, the swish of the dishwasher, the wind blowing lightly through the trees outside. Perhaps the trickle of the fountain she knew was to the left of the open glass doors. Something.

She kicked the blanket away, rolled carefully from her back over to her side and took a good look around. Relief flooded her heart that all of her family was present, including their new friend, Isthus. They'd been much too quiet, but now that she could focus, the silence was understandable.

"Okay," she said sitting up, thankful that whoever had put her to bed had slipped a soft cotton gown over her body. "So what happened? How come I don't feel like total crap?"

"Raphael was here," Larien said tiredly.

And that was the end of the explanation? Like hell.

"And?" she pressed.

But Larien didn't seem inclined to say another word. Those dark eyes of his bored right through her as if he sought the source of some nonexistent discomfort. Then the dim light bulb of her mind brightened. "Wait, Raphael who?"

Larien gave her that 'duh' look that never ceased to pluck her nerves, but she was too happy to be alive to care.

"You mean the Raphael? As in the Archangel? The Healer, Raphael?! Here? So that wasn't Death I saw?"

"Oh Death was here all right," Larien said quietly. "But he wasn't an option."

Jayla felt her eyebrows climb up her face. The relief that she'd come so close to never drawing another breathe yet was still on this plane was impossible to describe. Grateful just didn't seem

227

adequate.

Then she took a second look at Larien. "Why do you look like hell?"

And he did. The typically warm tan of his skin was as pale as a piece of notebook paper. A crumpled, worn and tatty piece of notebook paper. He sat on the floor in nothing but a pair of shorts, so there was no hiding the cuts, bruises and scratches painted across his skin in a rainbow of colors. Wounds that should have healed by now.

Jayla looked toward Chel. Her longtime friend lowered her gaze to the floor and left it there, looking two steps past miserable and just as beat up as Larien. The perfect up-do she'd sported into Isthus camp was now a tangled mess of glossy brown curls, though freshly washed. Various shades of blue and purple marred fair skin.

Larien took a gulp from a big mug on the floor at his side. The nasty gagging noise and grimace told the entire story better than words ever could—whatever he was drinking had been cooked up by Talan for sure. Larien leaned back against the foot of the couch with a tired sigh.

"It's good for you. Just shut up and drink it," Talan groused. Jayla laughed and Talan turned her way. "And here's some for you."

An oversized mug was pressed into Jayla's hands and the laughter she'd directed at Larien was cut short. Bleh.

Finally, Larien said, "I banished that horde that came after us. Sent them through the Abyss gate. I only had enough energy to get you back here, call Rafael and pass out for a little while."

"How long was I out?" Jayla asked.

Isthus walked out of the bathroom, and said, "Just a little over twelve hours. Glad you're all right." Huh. Compared to the other two, Talan and Isthus looked like they'd been picnicking at the beach, black eyes and all.

"Thanks, Isthus. That makes two of us," Jayla replied between sips of what must surely be hot tar rather than some healing tonic. Sitting the cup down on the side table, she lay back down. She might not feel any pain but it was obvious by the swimming in her head that she still needed some rest. "Larien, why didn't he heal you, too? And Chel?" Who still hadn't managed to fully meet her eyes.

"He isn't allowed. It's against the rules."

She tried to roll her eyes at the stupidity of all these rules but was so tired her eyeballs only made it halfway around.

"Yes. And between Talan and that fucking—" Larien took a deep, frustrated, teeth-clenched breath, calmed and then continued. "That ever-helpful Rafael, we were able to save you."

"But why would he come help me? I wasn't in any shape to call out for help from anyone, let alone an angel of Raphael's caliber."

"Of Raphael's caliber? What are you saying?" Larien's dark brows crashed together in a fierce yet tired frown.

"Oh good grief," Chel jumped in from her spot on the other side of the plush space. "Don't let your ego get your drawers in a twist. No one was inferring that you're not as strong or helpful as Raphael. Geesh."

Talan dropped into the nearest chair and said, "Even with all my skill in healing I was way out of my element with the injuries you sustained, Jay. If Raphael hadn't come when Larien called for him, you wouldn't be here. And that's the truth of it, Jay. That's why Death was here. We weren't sure you were going to make it."

"Well, me getting attacked is getting old." She tested her limbs, still amazed that there was no pain. No soreness. She was wiped out and fatigued, yes, but she'd take that over stab wounds and frozen innards any day.

So the bottom line was that Larien had saved her life. Sure, Raphael had mended her, but Larien had called to him for help. Knowing how her man felt about his fellow eudaemon kin, for Larien to call any of them for anything, well, that told her plenty. Yet still, she had to ask.

"Larien, you called him? For me?"

"Jayla, I'd call the devil himself for you if he had something you needed. And he'd help you, I swear."

"Or what? You'd kick his ass?"

"Actually I'd kick his ass whether he helped you or not, but he'd give you what you needed or I'd kick his ass twice."

She smiled. "Aw, you're such a romantic."

* * * * *

229

Larien carried Jayla into the guest room and tucked in next to her. Her skin was warm, her spirit vibrant, alive. And he wanted nothing more than to wrap himself around her and never let her leave his side again.

She turned in his arms and boldly wrapped her hand around his cock. He stilled her hand.

"What? Why are you looking at me like that?" she asked.

"Weren't you recently injured? I mean, practically skewered-like-a-kabob injured?" Yes, he was griping, but there was simply no ability to temper the words. The woman was acting as if she hadn't just almost died. Again. On his watch.

"For such a smart guy, you sure ask dumb questions." The twinkle in her eye doused the sting of the words.

"And...?"

"Of course I've been hurt. But that was yesterday."

He stared with what was surely a stupefied expression. And it described his wonder pretty accurately. "I have never encountered anyone quite so open. Or so willing to forgive and move on."

"You mean willing to overlook having claws sunk into my back? Or willing to give it a go with you?"

"Well, both. No, wait. There have been many willing to 'give it a go' as you say. But they did not really want me. They wanted what they thought I could give them. You, on the other hand, just kind of throw yourself headlong into everything. No walls or fear of falling."

"Everyone has walls, Larien. Mine are just a bit lower than most."

"But why?"

"My Grams taught me that if I erect walls after every letdown not only do I keep everyone out, but I keep myself in as well. I can't give. And I can't receive."

"Profound woman, your Grandmother. I wish I could have known her."

"Me, too," she continued. "Because of her if I get hurt in a relationship or friendship, I consider it a lesson learned and try not to repeat the same mistake. But I can do that without cutting off everyone. I live freely, as we were all meant to. I'm not stupid by any means, but I'm not so fearful of getting hurt that I shut myself away. Besides, fear is a tormentor. I'd rather be a lover."

He laughed. Couldn't help it. "Oh you are definitely a lover. More than that."

"Really?" she teased. "How much more are we talking?"

"So much more that you are the only one I will ever back down from a fight for. Lay down my pride for. Kick ass for. The rest of the world can go to hell for all I care."

She smiled, pulled him down to meet her lips and gave him one of the sweetest kisses he'd ever known. It was a kiss of promise, of long walks in the evening under the stars, of breakfast in bed on Sunday mornings. Of love. And life.

The truth of Jayla's inevitable death pushed to the forefront of his mind, bringing with it the old memories of loss that had plagued him through the centuries. But instead of the expected grief and agony, he pictured her old and gray-haired with the same sharp, quick wit and wicked sense of humor. She sat on a couch surrounded by beaming children, all grown up and holding children of their own. She was exactly as she was today with a soul so vivid it rivaled the brightest star. And a piece of her thrived within each of her Descendants.

When he pictured this woman growing old, there was no sadness. No regret. Only love, endless and all encompassing.

And once this "find the Seal" madness was over and done with, Larien would begin to walk the same path as Jayla. He would throw himself into life with her and not look back.

Some hours later Larien awoke to find himself almost completely healed.

And my woman has plastered her backside against my groin. He bit his lip to keep from moaning aloud. He even managed to hold his composure until she started a slow winding of her hips that sent his temperature soaring clear up to the vaulted ceilings.

"Awake?" she whispered.

Imp.

She knew good and well he was awake. The tree branch of a cock poking her in the ass certainly wasn't of the olive variety. And where had her clothes gone?

Jayla's strong fingers dug into his thigh as she pressed herself back more surely. Eyes closed, Larien let himself sink into the sensation of her skin sliding against his. It was like being rolled over by a deep soulful wave as he lay naked on a warm Caribbean beach. He eased his hips forward simply unable to keep still a second longer.

Her breathing hitched. A longing-filled "Mmm" worked its way up through her body. The deep rumble penetrated his thoughts even as the ridge of his already-filled cock nestled perfectly against her.

"Jay? You really awake or you having one hell of a dream?"

"Oh God, don't talk. Just fuck me."

He was stupefied just long enough for both his brain and his cock to catch up with what she'd just said. The words echoed in his head, bouncing off the inside of his skull until his thoughts rang with them. Fuck me. Fuck me. Fuck me.

And he asked a question he'd never thought would pass his lips at a time like this.

"Why? Why should I fuck you, Jayla?" Okay, he was definitely crazy.

"Because I want you. All of you. All the time. Just the sight of you makes me hot."

"The sight of me?" He was almost disappointed. He'd been created to be perfect so of course she would enjoy his looks. But hadn't every woman he'd ever met enjoyed that…at first?

"Yes. And I love the way you touch me. You're created for the sole purpose of teaching us mere mortals how to destroy enemies, to decimate whatever is in your way, yet you touch me with something so close to reverence it almost makes me speechless. Almost."

He smiled. Yeah, almost was right. Larien didn't think there was anything that would quiet this woman if she didn't want to be. And he wouldn't change a single thing about her.

"You look at me with such longing, Larien. Like you want me with everything within you, yet you hold yourself back. It's so damn sexy watching you exercise such restraint. But—" She ground particularly hard against his growing erection. "Watching you lose it turns me on even more."

His arms had come around her body.

"I want you inside me, Larien. "

He buried his nose in her hair and inhaled deeply to try to get some control just as she said, "I want you out of control. To take me like you really want to."

Larien stilled as his mind began to dredge up the movie of his memories of just how wrong things could go. But Jayla was strong enough for the both of them.

"No, Larien. Don't you dare wander on me. I can't see your eyes but I know that you were just about to start thinking of some depressing event of your past to keep you from enjoying the present you have with me."

Larien had no idea why he was surprised with her intuition and couldn't suppress a chuckle. His arms tightened around her, held her closer.

"Mmm, I like that. I like when you hold me so tight." His now-scalding erection slid through her drenched folds and then nudged her clit as his hips involuntarily rolled forward. Her breath hissed through her teeth on a deep inhale as she lifted a leg and draped it back over his hip.

"Ooh, yes. Again."

Instead, Larien turned her over to her back, slid down her body and peppered her overheated skin with kisses along the way. He teased, nipped and nibbled from her belly, around to her side and up to the swell of her breasts.

* * * * *

God, she ached for him. Everywhere. It was such a delicious pain, one that sent her head a-whirl. She couldn't decide if she wanted him to make the ache go away, or if she wanted him to continue torturing her, amping up the pleasure until she practically hummed with it.

A firm hand wrapped around her breast from underneath, weighing and kneading it until she writhed with need.

He teased her. It wasn't enough, and he knew it. If she hadn't been so turned on, Jayla would have smiled at the evil thoroughness with which he explored her. Her nipples were drawn tight. Puckered and hard. She needed a mouth on them. Now.

"Larien. Please."

"Please what, sweetheart?" His words were muffled, his dark head tucked beneath her arm as he kissed a tender spot just to the left of her breast. The fingers of one hand played with the plumping nipple while the other hand held her arm up in the air so he could get at her skin more thoroughly.

"Please taste me," she begged without shame.

"I thought I was already doing that."

"Suck my nipples already before I go bananas."

"Mmm, bananas. I could picture some dirty things to do with one of those just about now. I have whipped cream in the fridge."

"Oh dear God, Larien."

With that, the teasing ended and he dove in for the kill. His lips wrapped around a nipple, tongue pressed underneath and pulled the entire crown into his mouth. Hard.

It felt so good, sent her hips into a tailspin. She couldn't stop writhing. Squirming. Needing. As he worked his way down her body, tension pulled at her spine in anticipation of his destination.

Her sex bloomed as he took his time tasting the tender folds, intensifying the pleasure by swiping up along the seam then dipping inside. He hadn't even touched the bundle of nerves that would trigger her release yet she spiraled toward orgasm at record pace anyway.

"I need it. Oh God, I need it. Please."

He raised his head. His chin glistened with her honey. And she knew just how much he loved honey.

"I love it when you beg for it," he whispered against her soaked flesh.

"If you keep making me beg, I'm going hurt you. God, yes!"

He sat back on his heels, cock in hand. He was so pretty there. Flushed, full of life, throbbing. For her.

"I love when you watch me, love knowing that you crave my cock. Oh, yes, that's it. When you slide your tongue across your lips like that, it just makes me harder."

"Inside. Now. Need it."

"Yes, ma'am."

The scalding heat of his sex set her core to pulsing. The thick flare of his head parted her soaked folds. Jayla gasped in pleasure as he worked himself inside. Out just a bit. Then in a tad. Out. In a bit more. Until he was buried to the hilt, panting as his breath mingled with hers.

He tried to ease his weight off of her, but that wasn't what she wanted.

"No," she pleaded as she wrapped her legs around him to hold him close. Larien tried to protect her in every way. Even in this, he kept himself from crushing her. "I love your weight on me. Love feeling safe. Encircled by you. Surroun...oh yes! Surrounded by you. Protected. Always."

"There is nothing in this world quite like fucking you."

Easing a hand underneath her body so he could hold her closer, plumb deeper. And it was good. So good.

She had to taste him, had to have those addictive kisses. So good, like sweet, smoky, spice-filled liqueur, a heady blend of their combined flavors. When she came up for air her orgasm shimmered like a gossamer curtain of pearlescent light.

"Yes, more." Each word was a gasp of pure need, deep longing. Desire.

"Say it again."

"Give it to me. More!"

"Always, baby. Always."

The waters of her orgasm broke over her head and took her under. And she wanted nothing more than to drown in it. In him. Always.

CHAPTER TWENTY-FIVE

"Is she still sleeping?" Talan asked Larien as he stepped out of the bedroom.

"No, she's not," Jayla said groggily as she shuffled right behind him. "And she doesn't want to be cooped up in the bedroom by herself when all her friends are out here planning how to save her ass."

Cooped up? Hardly. Larien didn't bother reminding the woman that the master bedroom had the same wall of glass windows as this room had, but with a better view of the plush vivid green forest off in the distance. It was so open she may as well be outside. Was he going to tell her that? Hell no. He preferred his balls exactly where they were, thank you very much.

Instead he tucked her up on the same couch she'd come awake on earlier and dropped a soft kiss on her forehead. Moments after Talan got her to drink yet another cup full of tea she nodded off. Larien hadn't mentioned to her that the man had added a vitamin fluid and a bit of sleeping extract to it.

Now that Jayla was sufficiently passed out, he chugged down his own nasty-assed potion, dropped onto the loveseat across from her sleeping form and leveled his gaze on an annoyed-looking Isthus.

"So what aren't you telling us, Isthus?"

"If I could answer that question you wouldn't be asking."

Damn, he really hated leprechauns. Actually, that wasn't quite accurate. He just hated this one just now.

"Look, if you want to know where the Seal is, begin at the beginning," Isthus said moving away into the kitchen, his expression as exasperated as the one Larien knew was pulled across his own face. It was obvious Isthus really wanted to help here, but Larien knew the man's options were limited. Pushing away the temptation to pull his blade from its sheath and start carving off pieces of punk rock fae, he took a deep cleansing breath and counted to ten. Then twenty. Thirty.

"All right, let me think about this," Larien said aloud to no one in particular. The words bordered on silly considering he'd thought of nothing else…but that was before Isthus' clues. The fae couldn't come right out and reveal the secret so he wouldn't say anything unless it was significant. Begin at the beginning. Begin at the beginning? "So what happened at the beginning? The beginning of what? Solomon received a Seal millennia ago, but was that really the start of all this?"

Perhaps. But on the other hand the hunt for Jayla started after she'd been dragged into searching for the Seal. So the beginning was…Jayla?

But why?

"Is it because she's a Descendant of Solomon? Even if we find the Seal, if there are no Descendants to use it, then what good is it? Perhaps that's why the bad guys hadn't cared about the Seal for thousands of years. Not until someone who could use it was sent to follow it," Talan reasoned aloud.

But at the same time, did Jayla truly need it?

"True," Larien said. "Add to that the fact that we all saw what she did out there. She repelled a good number of Fallen demon and full-fledged demons alike." She'd had them walking around looking as confused as two blindfolded drunks and had bought herself precious time. He thought back a bit further to the night she'd commanded him before she knew she was able. The image of Ambriel in a yellow Speedo was forever branded in his brain.

Seriously, he was still trying to scrub that image away, but it didn't change the fact that Larien had had no control over his own mind at the moment. Jayla had told him to see a certain thing, and he had. She'd gone well beyond exercising her birthright, and she hadn't needed the Seal to do it.

So what was the fucking answer?

Jayla rolled over on the couch and snuffled in her sleep. Larien stood and looked her way, then noticed they were all looking at her.

Larien said, "Oh my God, Jayla—"

"—is the key." This from Talan.

"To all of this?" asked Chel.

Isthus sat down at the barstool sipping something fruity-looking from a frosted glass. He said nothing. Simply raised his drink in a silent toast and gave a tight-lipped smile.

"Are you sure you should be drinking, Issy?" Talan asked. "You know how you get when you're—" Isthus scowled. "Uh, never mind. So does this mean that the ring itself with the Seal carved into the top of it was simply a representation of the power given to Solomon? If so, then Jayla is the Seal." Talan paced the floor, his bare feet silent on the pale cream tiles. His hair looked like a portrait of the burning bush—flaming red and all over his head. He turned to Larien and asked, "So what's the next move, big guy?"

"We still need to get to the Silk Road. And now that Chel's outted herself, she can help with transportation. Isthus?"

"I'll go if Talan wants me to go." It was a simple, straightforward reply.

Talan nodded and put his hand over his heart, expressing gratefulness to his friend that didn't require words.

"Where on the Silk Road? It's a long stretch of highway. Multiple stretches, actually," Talan said, rubbing the bit of skin between his eyes. Larien could relate. Hell, even he had a headache.

"We'll do exactly what Isthus said. Begin at the beginning. Xi'an. It's where the original trade route began."

Isthus' easy smile now spread over his fine-boned face. Yes, they must definitely be on the right track.

"Let's hurry up and find this damn Seal thing so we can tell these guys to go fuck themselves and then enjoy watching them be unable to resist doing it," Talan said.

"As soon as Jayla gets her energy back?" Chel asked, pulling another blanket up over Jayla though the house was plenty warm enough.

"Talan, Isthus and I will go now. Chel, you watch over Jayla."

"What if they track us down again with the same numbers they did last time? We'd be toast," Chel asked even as her eyes glinted hard with anger at just the thought.

"Not possible here. This is my domain and mine alone. Even if Jayla spoke protections over the place the closest her guardians could get is the edge of my property several miles from this spot."

"Well, why the hell didn't you just bring her here in the first place to keep her safe?" Chel's teeth were bared, each word bitten off at the end.

"Are you serious? Can you imagine Jayla allowing herself to be whisked away somewhere when she'd rather be at home?" Talan didn't bother hiding his incredulousness. They all knew Jayla better than that.

"So back to the point," Larien declared. "We will go scout it out and get back here as fast as possible."

"But—"

"Look Chelriad, I am absolutely not taking Jayla to China without a fucking plan. Besides, I believe you two have some talking to do. No doubt you prefer to do it in private. No matter what, promise you'll keep her in bed. I do not want her out of bed except to pee. I need you to take care of her while we scout Xi'an. We must know what or who is there."

Talan snorted, "Well, no arguing with that one."

To Larien's relief, Chel snapped her mouth shut. Across from Jayla, she sat down slowly as if she had to think through the movement. But there was no doubt where her thoughts were. What was she going to tell Jayla? How the hell would she explain why she'd hidden who and what she was for so many years?

He would have paid to be a fly on the wall for that conversation but he didn't have time to deal with it now. As he padded from the room to pack a gear bag, Larien couldn't decide whether to be thankful or pissed off. If not for Chel, Jayla wouldn't have been outside of Isthus' place to get skewered. But without Chel there was no way Jayla would have survived long enough for the rest of them to join the fight.

A thought went 'round and 'round in his head until it bugged him like a mosquito at a barbeque—was Chel for them or against them? How was it that their little group was constantly being located by the bad guys? It just didn't make any sense. Once you were separated from the creative Source, it was impossible to zero in on daemon, eudaemon, demon or human from a great distance. A target either had to be fairly close or you had to expend a good deal of energy and concentration locating them...unless someone tipped you off.

At the same time, Larien had to admit that nothing they'd run up against was as it seemed. Perhaps they were all being played. Maybe someone or something wanted them to believe Chel was working both sides. But that didn't make sense either. Chel had been Jayla and Talan's friend for years. If she wanted to betray Jayla she could have done it long before now. And the first time Jayla had been attacked in her gym in San Francisco, Chel had been clear across the country in New York.

Secrets and lies. Lies and secrets.

Keeping something like being Fallen from your friends was huge. And an angel of the first Fall at that. On the other hand, it wasn't all on Chel—Talan hadn't shared his Shadow Priest half with anyone except him, and only because they were in the middle of trying not to die at the time.

Now, all bets were off. It was time to go on the offensive. To do that, they had to have each other's back. Period.

* * * * *

Jayla opened her eyes and silently stretched, thankful for such comfy furniture in Larien's house. She looked toward the windows and smiled. The sun was setting here and the wispy clouds reflected the purple and orange of the waning day. Chel stood at that window looking out toward the mountains. Jayla's smile faded. The day just didn't seem as beautiful when she beheld the dread etched across her friend's brow. A friend in pain was not something Jayla could tolerate.

"Chel? You okay?"

Chel whipped around from where she'd been standing looking out of the windows that led to the patio. In a few strides she was at Jayla's side.

"Jayla, I'm sorry. I'm so, so sorry I didn't tell you who...what I am."

"Well, I can see why you'd keep something like this a secret." Quietly, gently, she took her friend by the hand. After spending time with her new lover, it was easy to forgive Chel for the deceit.

Chel jerked her head back, clearly baffled. "Huh?"

"Larien explained what it was like to reveal what he was to humans, then be rejected for it, or used as a year-round Santa Claus."

"After I saw Larien that first time at your house I went to New York for a job. I swear that before I'd even gotten off the plane that I was going to tell you and Talan. You two mean everything to me and I—" Chel sucked in a ragged, pain-filled breath. "Damn it, I was just so ashamed."

"Ashamed? Come on, woman, you're awesome. You've been a good friend to me and Talan for years. You've had my back up until this very second, including fighting like a maniac when we were attacked at Isthus' place. If not for you, I wouldn't have lived long enough for Larien to get me out of there. We all have one secret or another. And given the events of the last few weeks, regardless of what you did or didn't reveal about yourself until recently, you've proven your loyalty to me and Talan."

"I don't understand, Jay."

"I've pretty much put the pieces together in my head. I am a Seal of Solomon, Chel. A true Descendant. You could easily hate me because I could control you if I want to. But instead you've helped look after me while I stumbled along not knowing what I was."

"But I'm Fallen. I can't be redeemed. I can't go home. I can't be forgi—"

"Girlfriend, you are home," Jayla interrupted as she sat up and gathered Chel in her arms. "I love you. All of you. And so does Talan. Do you understand? And speaking of Talan," Jayla chided. "He's got his wands in the closet, too. You can bet we'll be having a little chat about his special magickal abilities. I'd love to know why he can't make potions that don't taste like ass."

Chel stiffened, and then let the damn of her emotions burst. Jayla practically felt the bitterness of exile flow out as she allowed the affection of her friend to warm her cold and splintered soul. After a few deep breaths and what sounded suspiciously like slurpy sniffles, Chel raised her head from Jayla's shoulder and gave a relieved, million dollar smile.

Now this was the Chel she knew. Almost.

"So let me see."

"See? See what?"

Jayla pinned her with an expectant stare and she watched understanding dawn in her friend's eyes. Chel shook her head hard and fast enough to send the curls that framed her face flying.

"No," she said. "I can't, Jayla. It's…it's not pretty. Not anymore."

"Oh come on. I made Larien do it, too."

"Really? He must really love you. It takes a lot of energy to transform. He must have passed out right afterward."

"Well, almost right afterward. Maybe…sort of." Jayla didn't bother hiding the wicked grin that tilted the sides of her mouth.

Chel gave one that matched it and said, "Oh my God, what did you do?" Her eyes went wider. Jayla's smile got bigger. "You jumped him didn't you?!"

"Perhaps—"

"Jayla!"

"What?!"

Chel's mouth dropped open and the astonishment on her friend's face was a true reward. Through a hearty round of laughter she confessed. "Well, he was sprawled on my couch all naked and studly and stuff, so…uh, I—"

"Oh my God! Really?"

Chel's surprised "squeee!" filled the formerly somber space. The carefree sound pulled Jayla's own peals of laughter out to fly about the room until the sound rivaled a different kind of light.

"Jay, you're awake! I—" Talan stopped short.

Jayla and Chel's gazed whipped toward the sound.

Jayla's skin flushed so furiously she was sure she looked like a caramel apple. And Chel? Well, she could pass for a sugar beet just now.

"Do I even want to know what you two are laughing about?" Larien asked.

Isthus just shook his head.

The two women laughed even harder when Larien turned on his heel and got the hell out of there mumbling something about troublemaking Virtues. Talan and Isthus were smart—they backed out of the room.

* * * * *

The observer couldn't believe he was here inside the Ravus Court. Translated, Ravus meant Gray Court and he could see why. It had nothing to do with the color of the place, but the nature of it—not quite black, but definitely not white. The screams of tortured souls still awaiting their final judgment could be heard all the way from the Halls of Torment across the square. Oppression hung in the air and rubbed against his spirit like fine sandpaper. Enough to remind him of why he didn't belong here, but not enough to tempt him to abandon his task.

From the window he saw demons of all ranks flying in and out of the many buildings. Those without wings simply walked, ambled, shuffled or flashed where they needed to go. Some of the generals had their troops out in the practice yards drilling them into oblivion. Literally.

On the way into this particularly massive black stone building they'd passed several open rooms along the hallway, almost like passing through a luxury hotel with massive archways cut into each space rather than doors. How the hell did they pull off posh and pernicious? Designer and demonic?

A lesser demon delivered a surprisingly fragrant meal on several trays. As it turned to leave he suppressed a revolted shudder when it almost brushed against him on the way out the door. God he hated this place and those who made it their abode, didn't matter whether they were at home here or trapped here.

He turned to where the others had begun to dig into the sumptuous fare across the room. No way would he touch one morsel of it. Disgust danced in his gut, but he bit the inside of his jaw to keep a curl of distaste from appearing on his lips.

Getting this job done would be worth it.

Not to mention, watching the back-and-forth between Luc and Jabon almost made up for the discomfort of sucking in the faint miasma that floated about the place like an imagined fog.

The entire Ravus Court was under the control of the most bad-assed good guy ever created—Abaddon. Just the name undid his typical calm, even if only for a few uncomfortable seconds.

Careful did not begin to describe his movements while on this plane as there was no way he could allow himself to be seen by that particular angel. Could not afford any questions to come up about what the hell he was doing here.

Forcing his limbs to appear relaxed and at ease, he rose from his seat and walked over to a nook tucked into a corner and pretended to study the gruesome painting on the wall there. Neither Luc nor Jabon seemed to notice. Idiots.

"You said Chel was willing to play nice," Jabon snarled.

"I said no such thing. We simply gave her an offer." Luc lit a short thick cigar and then blew on the end to extinguish a bit of flame.

Jabon stood rigid with anger. His face pulled so tight as he spoke that the healing cuts around his mouth opened again to bleed freely down his chin. The observer held onto his glee at the thought of what had caused Jabon to be in such bad shape—an ass kicking by Larien twice in one week couldn't have been fun. Well, fun for Larien, perhaps.

"Are you telling me that you sent a horde of our best men up against a war angel—correction, the war angel—and you didn't bother to get a fucking commitment from Chel to turn to our side first?" Jabon was practically snarling by the time he finished his rant.

Luc stood, the movement controlled and deliberate. It was like watching smoke uncurl, dark and thick as he slowly eased to his full height. Everyone knows that smoke looks unsubstantial, but if you breathe in too much of it you're dead.

The observer almost smiled when Luc took that first easy-looking step toward the practically-foaming Jabon.

"Careful Jabon. I may not have dominion over mankind, but you I can squash like a bug," Luc said. The words were a lulling mix of a purr and the sweetest, darkest music imaginable.

"Fuck you, Luc! You don't own me!"

"Wrong, asshole." Luc raised a flat palm at Jabon. A wave of dusky shadow rippled like heat waves in the air and smashed into Jabon's chest. Luc hadn't touched him, yet Jabon flew across the room and landed hard against the blindingly-white stone wall. A trail of stark red followed him down the wall to the floor. "Not only are you my bitch, but you keep up the insolence and you'll be my whore, too."

Like the idiot he'd shown himself to be just within the last few minutes, Jabon opened his mouth with a snarl. "You dare touch me?" He rose and charged Luc only to slam into a wall that wasn't there.

"This is my domain, Jabon. My Court."

"You do not rule me. I'm a demon. Abaddon has—"

"Correction, bitch, you're a Fallen demon, and therein lies the difference. Abaddon doesn't own your ass. I do."

Jabon's expensive gray silk shirt ripped away from his body of its own accord. The sound of tearing fabric was lost beneath Jabon's screams as another grim wave slammed into him. The silent observer felt no heat and the temperature in the room remained quite comfortable, yet Jabon's flesh blistered and singed as if someone held an old-fashioned pitch torch to it.

"You never did understand hierarchy, Jabon. And shut up already." Luc sounded absolutely bored as yet another blast hit Jabon. Suddenly the screaming stopped.

"Abaddon keeps order in She'ol. May even call you once in a while to Aegypto. But your leash is, and always has been mine to pull from the second you submitted to me and went from Fallen to Fallen demon, Jabon."

Jabon gagged, pleaded with his eyes. But he was just a little too late to appeal to Luc's gracious side. The former Archangel was pissed. In fact, as the bystander watched the two former eudaemon, he thought back to when Luc was still the Son of the Morning. He had been created as a force to be reckoned with. Even in his diminished state, he would always be hell on wheels. It was simply a matter of displacement. While Luc had stood by the side of the creative Source, he'd been top dog in beauty, strength and skill. Today he might not have any place within the Host, but he was still powerful.

The observer stood off to the side of the room and quietly watched Luc sit back down in one of the many comfy chairs provided for guests. He extended a single finger, twirled it in the air and the skin from Jabon's torso came away from Jabon's body in long elastic-like strips. The Fallen demon's mouth was open in silent agony as the blood pooled thick at his feet. Luc had been right—Jabon had never understood hierarchy.

The observer remained silent, careful not to shake his head in pity or curl his lip in disgust. It was a fucking shame, really. The only thing that kept others from taking Luc's top-dog status…was knowledge. What Jabon didn't understand was that no matter how much shit Luc talked, even a human could wipe the floor with him. And Luc knew it. But he sure wasn't about to give anyone the details of that particular secret.

If a Fallen demon found the will or way to talk an uninitiated Descendant into exercising their authority over Luc…well, one could imagine how Luc would take that bit of comeuppance. Why? Because Luc had power. Had it in scads. But only over those that freely gave themselves to him—whether by choice or sheer ignorance made no difference.

Luc finally released the grip on Jabon's vocal chords and the Fallen demon's vibrato soprano notes rang through the room and ended on an oomph as he collapsed to the floor.

"And you'd better be healed in enough time to find that fucking human Descendant and bring her to me. When I tell you where Chel is, you'd better be ready or I'll peel your hide again. Only next time it'll be your dick that gets stripped. Understand me, underling?"

Oh ho ho! Luc played a good game here. When I tell you where Chel is? Dabwahaha! What a hoot considering Luc didn't know where Chel was half the time. He could summon her, but she didn't have to answer. In fact he couldn't track or compel her because she hadn't made the choice to go completely rogue. Chel was Fallen, not a Fallen demon. She could only be compelled by a Descendant or an angel of high enough caliber. There was only one reason Luc was able to find Chel, and it was a secret the visitor wouldn't be sharing anytime soon.

The observer crossed his arms over his chest and said not a word. It wasn't his job to school Jabon. Let him learn the hard way. Hopefully, the really really hard way. Bastard.

And then Abaddon strolled in. The observer backed deeper into the dim corner, breath stuck in his chest.

Even in human form Abaddon was a dark haired, tank wide, muscled tower of perpetually pissed off eudaemon. And while Luc's power was really a sham, Abaddon's authority over everyone and everything in this realm was not. The mighty

Guardian of the Abyss took in the scene between Luc and Jabon in mere seconds. Booming laughter rocked the room as he laughed and walked right back out the way he'd come.

CHAPTER TWENTY-SIX

It had taken a few days for Jayla to fully recover all her energy and now they were finally ready to head to China.

While drinking yet another cup of Talan's potion-de-la-ass, Jayla was ready to tackle a question they'd all been dancing around since Rafael had come to heal her from the last nasty battle.

So to no one in particular, she said, "What do I do with the Seal if we find it?"

Silence.

"Okay, if this were a cartoon this would be the part where everything goes quiet and all I can hear are crickets."

Finally Larien said, "I am supposed to turn it over to Gabriel, but this isn't the first time I'm going to defy orders." His laugh was full of self-deprecation even as he stroked his hands lovingly up and down her back. It broke her heart that her Fallen was still just a little bit broken. "Jayla, you make the call."

This decision was huge, big enough to endanger not just humans like her, but eudaemon, daemon and even nasty-assed demons. Yet he'd given her his trust when he could have simply bulldozed his way through.

Jayla's heart bloomed with love.

She let her feelings shine in her eyes as she looked at him and then said, "Isthus has kept the Seal's secret for millennia and did such a good job that no one figured out until a few days ago that Solomon's Descendants are the Seals. The Seal of Solomon

But Jayla knew they were missing something. This was the spot, she could feel it. But she just didn't see anything.

Wait…I don't see anything. That's it, Jayla, you nutball.

She closed her eyes a moment, centered herself and invoked her othersight. Immediately the area was alive with color. The aura of everything around her lit up her vision.

Okay, it's an artifact. It'll have an aura just like the things Grams left you.

So she looked for something that had the same hue.

"There," she said, tugging on Larien's shirtsleeve. "Try over there." Jayla pointed off to a spot Isthus had sifted through only moments before. Isthus raised a single black brow.

"Not the exact spot, Isthus. Try just a bit to the right." Moments later the earth quietly churned as if an army of ants were beneath the dirt, sifting the sand. Moments later a small square badly battered object floated into the still air. Isthus' magic surrounded it and cleared away God-knew-how-many years of dirt to reveal a gold unmarked box.

Jayla held out her palm. The moment it touched her skin it sent a shudder of energy clear through to her bones. Warmth. Comfort. And power.

Finally, they had it—the artifact of fable and myth, the one thing that had allowed a mere human to control creatures that should have been untouchable by flesh and blood.

No flash, glitz or bling—just a single solid precious stone of midnight blue lapis lazuli. The cabochon was veined with silver, etched with sacred symbols all rimmed in a setting of gold. Beautiful and untarnished, this piece of history looked as if it had been fashioned just yesterday. The famed six-sided star was set firmly into the top and there was no mistaking what it was—the Seal of Solomon.

Jayla slipped the ring that had once graced the hand of her predecessor onto her finger. She smiled, imagining what it must have looked like on the hand of Solomon himself. It was several sizes too big.

Jayla held it out to Isthus and said, "Take this. Include it in your treasures. If anyone can keep this thing hidden from now until forever, it's you, Is."

Isthus turned to Talan and rolled his eyes. "Did she really just call me Is?" Not waiting for an answer, he focused on Jayla. "What are the terms?"

"Terms? None, other than what we already agreed on. It remains a secret. And…I have a question."

"You know the rules now, Jayla."

"Yes, I do, but I'm still going to ask. So—" She braced herself against the answer because if he actually gave her one it would mean she was the only one of her kind.

"Are there others like me? Other Descendants?"

Isthus' lids slid closed. Jayla thought he was simply ignoring her until his brow wrinkled as if he were in pain. Then she knew exactly what was going on. He wanted to answer her question, was trying to give her what she wanted against whatever compulsion or rules that were in place to keep him from doing so. Now that was uncharacteristic for one of his kind. Had he come to count her as a friend? Nah. It was too much to hope for.

After a few minutes of internal struggle so intense she could practically feel it, she touched Isthus on the shoulder.

"Stop. Stop fighting it. Just the fact that you can't answer me is answer enough."

Whether there were other Descendants or not really didn't matter anyway. The Seal was safe now because there was no way in hell this particular fae would allow a celestial or any other entity to steal what belonged to him.

Jayla turned to her friends, happy that they'd gotten what they came for. It was over. "Alright, let's get the hell out of here."

"You are a most irreverent human."

"I know, Isthus. And you like me for it."

"True. But don't tell anyone."

They turned as a unit, Larien taking point followed by Talan, Isthus and Jayla with Chel bringing up the rear. A solid stone wall on one side, a tight line of sculpted soldiers on the other and Chel's reassuring presence behind her left very little room to maneuver. But she didn't mind given there was no room for anyone to sneak up on her either. Soon a glimpse of midnight sky became visible as they made their way out of the tomb and Jayla felt the tension at the sides of her mouth fade away as she loosed the first true smile in days.

* * * * *

Talan got up off the ground from a blow he never saw coming. "Somebody want to tell me what the hell just happened?" he demanded.

"They were obviously waiting for us," Isthus said. "We were almost out of the tomb."

Talan turned to his friend and said, "Chel?"

But Larien was in her face so fast the female Fallen didn't have time to move out of the way let alone avoid the thick fingers that suddenly wrapped around her neck.

"Take your fucking hands off of me. She's my friend and if anyone has the right to be upset that she's yet again in danger, it's me and Talan." Chel's voice was like thunder on the wind—the words carried on a barely-there but clearly lethal whisper.

Talan had a second of momentary awe as Chel's battle form erupted, her neck so thick Larien's hand barely collared her. But Larien didn't release her. If anything his fingers dug in further, nowhere near intimidated by the fact that Chel now stood more than a foot over him.

Fury snuffed out his amazement. "We don't have time for this bullshit, you two."

With that Larien eased back, but only enough to allow Chel more air to speak. But she didn't talk. She glared daggers as her fingers began to crackle with that otherworldly energy that meant she was preparing to kick some ass.

"Damn it, it's obvious they knew exactly where we were and why. Chel, what happened?"

"Jayla stopped for a moment and turned back as if she'd forgotten something. She looked right at me and smiled. Then her smile faded and she looked past me. But I didn't see or sense anything until it was too late. Next thing I know I was slammed up against the wall just steps from the tomb entrance. We were literally steps behind you."

Talan wanted to kick himself in the ass. He knew they all did.

"They grabbed her and were gone? Just like that?" Isthus snapped his fingers.

Talan shook his head in wonder. "With all the power between us there is no way in hell anyone should have been able to get close to Jayla. One of us would have felt them coming. Hell, all of us!" His voice vibrated with anger.

"Which means," Larien cut across him, "more powerful beings have stepped into the game."

"They must think she has the Seal. What will they do to her when they find she doesn't have it at all? We all saw Jayla give it to Isthus." Chel said as her visage morphed from anger to worry to pissed off again.

Isthus opened his palm and the gleaming gold ring shimmered out of existence as he spoke. "But Jayla is the manifestation of the power of this artifact just as you guessed before. She can manifest the power of the Seal. She's a treasure in and of herself. It's not something I can touch or hide away, but it is precious and rare just the same. I was supposed to guard that knowledge. I can't think of how anyone else, other than this group, would know the true nature of the Seal and that Jayla is one, but obviously the news got out somehow."

Anxiety for Jayla swirled in Talan's belly but at the same time he was relieved. The Jayla taken from them tonight was a far different woman than she'd been when this whole madness had begun. She was stronger, owned what she was, and would no doubt give her abductors a hell of a time trying to keep her.

* * * * *

Larien checked his weapons. "I'm going to get her."

"What? How?" Talan snapped. "We don't even know where she is."

"There's only one place they could go from here. The Hall of Tortured Souls in Gehenna."

"What the fuck are you talking about? Jayla is alive. She can't be down there. Isn't that against the rules or something?"

"Talan, she doesn't belong there, but she has a soul and can be taken there. The Hall of Tortured Souls is the only place of the three domains in She'ol that's suitable because Aegypto and The Gray Court can only be walked by celestials and demons. They know not to keep her on this plane. Our enemies have to be somewhat close for me to sense them but because Jayla is my charge I can find her anywhere on this planet. Now, Chel, take this."

Chel jumped back a step as if she'd been physically stabbed. Eyes wide, she looked at the thing in Larien's hand as if it held certain death. "No way. I can't. That's…that's the Messenger's sigil. I'd know it anywhere."

"Yes, and you are going to use it to tell Gabriel what the hell is going on. I do not have time to summon him and wait. I must get to Jayla. Now."

Larien knew what Chel was thinking. She was Fallen. Exiled. Forbidden to even be in the presence of one such as Gabriel without the Archangel's express permission…which meant he summoned you, not the other way around.

But the urgency of the moment was lost on none of them.

Chel's chin shot up even as her spine straightened. Blood had dried along the underside of her jaw and her split lip was mending. Her hand shook as she held it out for the sigil, but she didn't flinch when Larien dropped it into her palm. She simply said, "For Jay, anything."

"Wait. How are you going to get in?" Talan asked.

"The same way they took her. I didn't feel them arrive, but the trail is fairly fresh. The signature of their aura is faint, but it is definitely there."

Larien and Isthus both looked off in the direction of the fading trail. Isthus spoke what Larien was thinking. And the thought wasn't comforting at all.

"They probably headed toward the mystical gate at Huashan Mountain," Isthus said.

"How do you know?" Chel whirled and took a few steps out from under the cover of a cluster of trees at the base of the city wall—the very spot Jayla should be standing right now. She tossed the sigil into the wind even as dark orbs of elemental energy floated above her free hand ready to fry anything that headed their way.

Good girl, Larien thought.

"Because," Isthus said angrily, "Huashan is one of the five sacred mountains of China. The energy around such a place would be ideal for dragging a living, breathing human down into a realm where they don't belong. It's close and they would need to get her off our radar fast. It just makes sense."

"But that place is well-known for its sheer cliffs and ravines. It's the most dangerous mountain in China for climbers." Talan paced as he ground out the words.

"Then I guess I'd better not climb down into the ravines then," Larien said, not bothering to mute his power as he let fragile skin slip. Senses were freed from the confinement of human flesh. Sight, hearing, sense of smell rocketed as his limbs lengthened, skin toughened and wings erupted silently from his back.

The next second he was streaking through the air after Jayla's aura trail like a bloodhound on the hunt. And he was going to bite every ass he came across until he got what he wanted.

* * * * *

Jayla didn't bother playing coy. Whatever the assholes had done to knock her out had worn off. She was fully conscious and had no problem making her current mood known.

The spike of adrenaline that sent her heart pounding wasn't just a sign of imminent danger. It was a sign that she was close to seriously losing her cool and even closer to not giving a damn. Was she afraid? Hell yes. But her pissed-off meter indicated that her temper had overtaken her fear by a measure of five to one.

It wasn't the swelling welts on her cheek where they'd knocked her out that made her testy. Nor the strap that scraped against her jaw and held a gag in place. It was being snatched away from the only people in this world that meant anything to her. The image of Chel crumpling against the stone wall of the tomb was stamped behind her eye lids. They'd hurt her friend. And worse, just knowing her family worried and wondered after her made her mad.

Jayla knew exactly where she was. Not that she recognized the place, but deep in her gut she simply knew—She'ol.

The energy of this realm sent her skin on a crawl for its life. Her insides cringed as if a thousand nails scraped across every chalkboard in the world all at the same time, yet all was quiet and uncommonly still.

Swallowing against the bile rising in her throat, Jayla turned her focus on her surroundings instead. Forcing her breathing to remain deep and even, she took in the smell of the place. Most importantly, she did not call out to the one person that absolutely must not come to her rescue.

Larien.

Just the thought of that man brought a moment of calm. Though they'd been lovers for only a short time, she felt him in every bit of her being—body, mind and soul. Almost down to the very molecules that shaded her. He'd face the hounds of hell for her without blinking. Protect her. Cherish her. Amazing how such a bristly, bumpy, broken man could be so caring with her, could let her into a heart that had known so much pain and give her his trust. And she would not betray that trust by calling him here.

Why? Because somewhere down here...was the Abyss gate. And she knew exactly what that meant—she was bait this time around.

Not gonna happen.

So...back to the smell. There was no rotten stench or disgusting whiff of decaying flesh as most people would think existed down here. No, it was more of a feeling than a scent. An impression of mineral rich earth and thick smoke, mixed with torment until it was just short of cloying. A blend of despair and otherworldly not-quite-right buzz of energy that she was sure she noticed simply because she didn't belong here. The one thing amazingly missing was the feeling of death. No, whatever lived here might not be human, but it, they, were very much alive.

Jayla looked around the empty room and was surprised to find smooth walls done in an equally surprising palate—royal purple that bled into a lighter, more lavender purple to end in a creamy hue with just the slightest hint of color.

Two doorless arches off to the left and right led to curved hallways well-lit by greenish-blue sconces set high up on the walls. There were no shadows except those cast by the guards she barely glimpsed.

Directly in front of her across the room, Jayla took in the strange color of the setting sun through a huge bay window—an orange-red ball in an indescribable sky. Fluffy bluish-black clouds floated by on a warm wind she could feel all the way from where she sat tied to an unexpectedly comfortable chair.

If the place weren't so oppressive, it could have doubled for a mansion off the Southern California coast. Minus the traffic.

A wail of agony pierced the silence and shattered the illusion of peacefulness. The sound echoed all around her, as if the very walls were acoustic perfection. That vibration was so full of pain her ears rebelled as if they could keep it out. Whatever or whoever made that sound was terrified. The pitch sent a fresh wave of adrenaline spiking through her body. She slammed her eyes shut against bone deep shivers so potent she had to force herself back from the keen edge of a fear so sharp she'd almost called for Larien out of pure gut reaction.

But she would not call him.

Besides, she could take care of herself. He'd made sure of it while working her backside off at his home until she was comfortable with wielding her gift. And for that she would always be grateful no matter how this turned out.

The energy in the room developed a deep bass-like buzz. Jayla's lids snapped open.

"Oh, she looks mad. Matters not. She cannot talk, speak protections around herself or call for help." The new addition spoke to the guards that had accompanied him into the room but his gaze clashed with Jayla's. His eyes were absolutely black, so dark they seemed to suck the very color from the room. Dressed in an immaculate white shirt and a pair of very expensive looking black trousers, the man with the face of an angel looked as if he had recently taken a serious beating.

Bruises in a myriad of colors covered the skin where his collar was open, the flesh painted in colors she was hard-pressed to describe.

"I am Jabon."

Okay, now that was a name she knew and knew well. And now she understood the bruises. Larien had kicked this one's ass recently for bringing his minions to her home and blowing her door in. Good.

"You may narrow your eyes at me all you want," he said. "But it changes nothing. You have no dominion here, fleshling."

Now see, that's where you Fallen demon types are wrong, she thought. Maybe you should read more.

Eyes closed again, she whimpered. Jayla allowed the fear for her lover to push at her being until real tears ran and her nose stuffed up. Her now stuffy nose made breathing impossible with the gag in place.

"She can't choke, idiots," he snapped at the guards. "Not before he gets here."

With a snap the gag was gone. She coughed quite deliberately and hoped she was convincing. After all, the discomfort of this place was close enough to the surface that it really wasn't too hard to fake feeling ill.

"What do you want with me? Where am I?" she whispered.

Bruised Jabon looked her up and down. "You're in She'ol, human."

"Please, please don't hurt me."

He turned to the guard and said, "One of you go get Luc. Tell him she's awake...and a bit of a disappointment." Then he spat at her feet, put the gag right back. Jayla let the flame of anger show in her eyes as he swaggered away in the opposite direction of the guard.

The moment the hallways were clear, Jayla went to work, pushed her gift at the one guard that remained at the door.

Her hold on him wasn't strong, but it was there all the same. She sent silent commands to him, concentrating fiercely until sweat formed on her brow and then dripped into her eye. Damn, that stung.

Then the second guard returned, which meant the message that she was coherent had been delivered to the head creep in charge. Time was running out.

Jayla expanded her sphere of influence until both guards took a few steps away from their post while wondering aloud what the hell was going on. Not the brightest bulbs in She'ol.

Jayla kept her head down as if she were whipped, beaten and out for the count. One of the demons put down his weapon. Yes, she was doing it. It was working. She was working. The Seal of Solomon in the flesh.

Right then she owned her gift— not just in her head, but in her heart. And her birthright, the knowledge of who and what she was brought with it a burst of power that spilled out of her belly like Old Faithful.

She could practically hear Larien's voice in her head as he'd drilled her ruthlessly at his home. Control it, Jayla. Control your gift.

And she would. For the sake of the man she loved, for all those she loved, she would, damn it.

CHAPTER TWENTY-SEVEN

Down at the bottom of the ravine Larien stared at the unmovable rock all around him. No cave entrances. No cracks in the walls. No visible path down to She'ol. Yet, the hum of power was unmistakable. So where the hell was the entry point?

Then out of his periphery, in the very face of the rock, something…shimmered. Then it came clearly into focus, as clear as the brilliant hunter's moon overhead—the entrance to She'ol.

Once in the cave, darkness and shadows filled the tunnel. Brown walls glowed—how brown stone could glow so that even a human could have been guided by it remained a mystery.

Less than a quarter mile in, a gate of fire loomed before him and filled the entire cavern from top to bottom and side to side. There was no way around. And it was shut tight.

How was he supposed to get through?

The fierce anger that simmered in his gut churned up. The gate vibrated and hummed then opened just a crack with a loud cringe-inducing screech as if the fire had rusted the hinges. He wondered…and the gate abruptly stopped moving.

Rage flared at the lack of momentum…and then it moved again.

"Anger," he whispered to himself. "It moved in response to my anger." So he did something he hadn't in a long time—he gave all his anger, grief, resentment for any and everything he could think of free rein. He thought of Jayla dying before her time, destroyed for something that came to her by birth through no fault of her own, thought of her being ripped apart by those with no conscience or remorse. Thought on the endless wars and battles that had taken those he cared for. Thought on the endless loneliness that he would be forced to return to if anything happened to his little miss sunshine.

The gates flew open and crashed against the stone walls.

As he passed down the hall, the hands of the tormented wriggled up out of the slippery ground and from the jagged rock walls to grab at his flesh. Though they couldn't physically hurt him, their pain was a tangible thing, their cries both pitiful and terrifying. Even moving with preternatural speed the journey seemed to take days though it had been only minutes.

Finally he was through and the tunnel opened onto a ledge guarded by two giants. Warriors, damned for eternity, still dressed in their armor with shields and swords, yet unable to move. Man-sized links of chain attached to their chests, wrapped around their necks and locked them to the floor. Then Larien understood. Their punishment was that they couldn't do what they longed to do—fight. They were useless, unable to save anyone, including themselves. Incapable of protecting anything. Unable to keep anyone in…or out.

Part of their punishment was that from this very spot they could see the place where men of valor and renown took their rest after leaving the plane of the living, but could not join them there. It was an illusion, of course. There were no men of valor down here beneath the world.

Beyond the warrior's ledge was a steep drop of several stories, straight down. It was the entrance into Aegypto, Abaddon's main place of residence where the old war gods, or those that humans thought were gods, were held until the end of days.

Though Aegypto was Abaddon's main haunt, the Ravus Court was a close second, even if only because he made it a point to give Luc hell in, well, hell.

Either Luc or Jabon had his woman and neither was stupid enough to keep her anywhere near Abaddon. He'd fry their asses for pissing wrong, let alone bringing a living soul to She'ol. They hadn't taken Jayla to the Ravus Court for the same reason she couldn't stay in Aegypto—Abaddon, and the fact that a human soul couldn't pass through to those sub-realms.

There was no choice but to pass through Aegypto and out the other side to the only place in She'ol that was suitable—Gehenna and its Hall of Tortured Souls.

Wings spread, Larien stepped off the ledge and glided toward the rolling black terrain and the grove of pearl white trees beyond. As he passed through the city there appeared to be myriad of creatures in and about the place. The closer he got to the other side, the thicker the thieves became.

Strange. No one paid him any attention.

Huh. Times like this, being Fallen had its advantages.

Like now as he flew in a realm where evil attempted to reign, kept in check by the will of Abaddon alone.

His wings pumped through the air as hard and as fast as he could go. He had to get to…

"Shit!"

Suddenly Larien was on the ground in a heap. It was as if he'd flown headlong into a brick wall that scraped at his skin as he slid down it. Blood oozed from the welts and cuts, stinging like nettles as he pushed to his feet. One glance up and his question was answered.

He'd reached the edge of his destination—the border between Aegypto and Gehenna. There was no easy way through here. No shortcuts. No skipping the horror scenes. He had to walk.

It was like trudging through a canal minus the water—deep with high walls on each side, wide enough for the largest ship and no other way out. People, or former people, ran around everywhere, yet got nowhere. Gray and orange flames left no heat or soot behind on the walls or floor, yet rolled through like thick sentient mist, over and through the tormented souls, leaving nothing but ash behind.

Moments later the people reappeared and tried to run from the flames only to be destroyed, disintegrated, demolished…over and over.

Had Jayla been forced to walk through here? Had she been subjected to horrors never meant for human eyes? He quickened his pace down yet another stretch of black road.

Story-high alcoves in the walls held bodies of huge rock-hewn men. Were these the titans of myth and legend? It was possible given all those old stories were based on variations of his history anyway. As he eased down the hall he passed by flameless torches set into the walls that glowed an eerie green between each gigantic form.

A rumble beneath his feet and a whoosh of air sent Larien ducking off to the side as a huge stone fist flew past the spot where his head had been only moments before. The stone statues had moved. No amount of hacking or shooting would kill these guys. But beneath the rock he sensed something. Life...or what little of it could be maintained here. He couldn't physically hurt them, but anything with a celestial spark was fair game. Without a second of hesitation, Larien blasted them into oblivion and mentally sent them through the Abyss gate.

He hoped Abaddon hadn't noticed even as he prayed he would regain the spent energy by the time he reached Jayla.

* * * * *

She'd just powered up to send the command to get the idiot guards to untie and escort her out of here when someone yelled, "What the hell are you two doing?"

Busted!

The discovery of the two guards waltzing together up and down the left hallway meant she'd run out of time. A gang of very unhappy looking Fallen demons and full-fledged demons headed her way. They filled the hallways from wall to wall, six or eight wide and God-knew how many deep. And at the lead was an exquisitely beautiful Fallen that could only be one man—Luc himself.

At the exact same time, a bruised and furious Larien wore his battle form as he tore toward her from the right with sword and gun at the ready.

No! Oh, God, Larien! You as SO not supposed to be here!

But there was no fear. Only power. And the determination to keep the man she knew would be determined to head to her rescue from harm.

And that power burst loose deep in her belly, set her insides aflame until it overflowed. Reaching down into that brimming well, Jayla opened up and let it rip.

It wasn't enough to send them all stepping backward, but it was enough to give Larien a fighting chance as half the bad guys backed up and milled around in confusion as they began to fight each other...except for the squat hairy dwarf-looking demon she'd compelled to untie her before running back into the fight against his own kind.

But there were more, always more. And they joined the fray, swarmed into the thankfully large space to dog pile Larien.

Jayla was yanked from behind just as she'd lifted a blade off of one of the downed demons. She struggled to get loose, but the bands around her arms just got tighter as a voice growled in her ear.

"Stay still woman! Let me get you out of the thick of this or Larien will be so worried about keeping you safe he won't be able to concentrate on the fight."

Holy shit. Isthus? A surprisingly strong Isthus...in She'ol? How the hell?

"Questions later. Haul ass now," Isthus growled into her ear.

She scooted aside just as a body fell unconscious and twitched in the very spot that Isthus had yanked her from.

And that's when she saw it—the cavalry had arrived!

Talan. Chel. Ambriel. And a horde of others with an aura so energized and pure they had to be eudaemon.

And they were all fighting. For her.

The little hairs on her arms and legs stood on end as a flare of energy swirled around the room. A mountain of a man turned, sword in hand and yelled a question as a single name.

"Gabriel!?"

A being that flickered back and forth between battle form and pure light responded, "Yes! Now! Do it!"

Together Larien and the owner of the booming voice that must be Abaddon lifted their arms, palms out. They raised a battle cry that sent all her internal organs scrambling for the sky. A dark flash of purple left their fingertips, swirled around the room and sank into the flesh of each and every demon in the room.

And then they were simply...gone.

Almost as quickly as it had begun, it was over and Jayla was topside again, sucking wind like she'd run for her life. And she guessed she had.

* * * * *

Leaning against the sheer rock wall at the bottom of a ravine Larien took a quick look around. They were back where he'd started, Huashan Mountain. With his woman in his arms, Larien sucked in a relieved breath as Talan and Isthus appeared. They were just as winded, though with far fewer bruises.

The wind shifted. Larien looked up and froze. An angel landed just out of reach, his brilliant white wings curved against the wind as he touched down with ease.

"Ambriel, what are you doing here?"

Even though he and Jayla asked the question with the same baffled tone, Larien knew the answer. This angel was the missing piece of the puzzle. Larien cocked his head and listened, felt the air around them. And there it was—a familiar hum of energy so faint he'd obviously missed it the past however-many times. It was the same borrowed power that burned in Larien's own gut.

"You?" Larien said. "You've been the one unmaking angels? How's that possible?"

Ambriel grinned. There was a gleam in his eye that hadn't been there before. Actually, it seemed like more of a crazed light. Then it was gone as he straightened and said, "Same as you, Larry."

Talan cut in. "Wait. So the two Fallen inquisitors that stormed my apartment that day? You're the reason they came apart at the seams?"

Ambriel nodded.

"What about Improbael?"

"Him, too," Ambriel said in a sing-song voice.

"But why dust him?" Larien asked.

"You and Talan were about to walk into the very room that Improb-my-ass was recovering in."

"But he was no threat. He was down," Larien said.

"Says you, Larien. Besides, I must protect my charge."

"What charge? I've always been your charge." Jayla said, obviously as confused as he was.

Rather than answer, Ambriel simply pointed Talan's way.

"What?" Talan's mouth dropped open as he and Jayla scrunched up their faces, looking from each other to Larien, to

265

Ambriel and back again. "Why me and since when?" Talan asked.

Ambriel shuffled his feet as if he were having a hard time standing still. Then he started...humming? Quietly, but humming just the same. What the hell?

Finally Ambriel blurted, "For me to know and you to find out."

Larien blurted, "My cousin is a total basket case."

"Your cousin?" But Jayla's attention wasn't on Larien for more than a second before she turned to Ambriel. "But how can Talan be your charge? You came when I called." Jayla wondered aloud and her head tilted even further right than it already had.

"Yes, I came when you called. But that doesn't mean I have to stay. When Larien's on the scene, it's all on him. Those are the rules."

"Well there are too many rules that I don't know about!" she snapped.

Larien couldn't have agreed with Jayla more. Sure he knew the rules...but even this little secret hadn't been shared with him. Oh the intricacies of celestial law. And celestial games.

Then Ambriel, along with the faint humming, swiveled his hips in a very bad rendition of...Elvis?

"Oh, I know that song!" Talan, who seemed to have recovered from all the surprises they'd just become privy to, piped in merrily.

Ambriel kept right on dancing. A vision of him twirling around in a yellow Speedo to the tune of All Shook Up popped into Larien's head. It was too ghastly for words.

At that moment, Chel popped in, took one look at the current company and charged like a bull in full rage. "He was the one who came to me on the train! He was with Luc and offered me a crappy deal to sell out Jay."

Jayla's mouth dropped open in shock along with everyone else's as she simply gasped, "Ambriel?"

"Oh stop," the goofy angel said, waving them all off as if they'd just said the most outrageous thing and he was the only one sane. "I was undercover for God's sake. Literally."

"So each time they found me it wasn't because they knew where I was? It was because they knew where you were and you knew where Talan was because Talan, being a better friend than you, was usually wherever I was!" Jayla's volume increased until it was one big shout by the time she reached the final word.

"I was on assignment. If you want to be mad, be mad at Gabriel." And Ambriel kept right on dancing around as he changed to a more appropriate song. "Will it go 'round in circles? Will it go 'round like a bird up in the sky?"

Gabriel and Abaddon both chose that moment to arrive. Perfect fucking timing.

"You sons of bitches," Larien said. "Jayla could have been killed at least four times over because of your fucking games."

Gabriel said, "Yes, but it was on your watch."

Larien's fist connected with the square of Gabriel's jaw just as Chel's landed with a loud thwack on Ambriel's.

"Dammit Larien!" Gabriel spat. "That was the only one you get so I suggest you calm down. It was your job to make sure Jayla was not harmed while Ambriel's job was to keep Talan in one piece. It was all under control. Even Abaddon played his part."

All eyes swung left. Abaddon stared right back, half-smiled at them all and crossed his arms over his double-wide chest like the badass he was.

The rage on Chel's face transformed to sheer admiration. Abaddon's hard expression never wavered, but to Larien's surprise, the big angel colored under her doting gaze. "Death will be so glad to know you were here, Chelriad. That you're safe."

"Death?" Jayla asked.

"Uh, yeah. The Archangel Azrael, he's my cousin," Chel answered.

"Azrael? I thought he was a bad guy," Jayla gasped.

"Common misconception," Gabriel responded.

Jayla's eyes went wide with a mix of disbelief and awe. After all, she'd seen Death. And damn he was fine...though she had to admit she never wanted to see him again if she could help it.

While Larien and Gabriel argued back and forth, Jayla eavesdropped on Chel.

"I'm so sorry I made such a stupid choice way back when."

"I know. I can never condone your rebellion. It's so foreign a concept, I can't even fathom not doing what I was created to do. But I will never stop loving you, Chelriad."

"Really? Truly?"

"Truly. Oh, and don't tell him I said anything but you've got my brother hooked on Ralph Lauren. Just sayin'."

"Oh my God, not Azrael! You're kidding me."

"Not kidding. The cool thing about being an angel is that he can look in the magazines and fashion whatever he wants. If he had to buy it, he'd do nothing but complain about the cost of the stuff until I was tempted to unmake him."

After some companionable chattering, Chel was pulled against a body so large it seemed to engulf her.

"I love you, Ab."

"I love you, too, Chel. We can catch up on old times or start over with new ones. Or both. It's been quite long enough, but in the end it's your call, okay? Come see me in Aegypto sometime?"

"I can do that?" Chel asked, wiping her now tear-stained face on Abaddon's shirt.

"Of course you can," Abaddon said. "I'm in charge." And with a smile that managed to look both scary and assuring, he powered up and vanished.

Jayla let the tears run unchecked down her cheeks. Where her friend had been so ashamed, there was now some closure and a bit of understanding with her family. Though things could never be the same—it went against every law that governed them—Abaddon had a bit of leeway that none of the other angels did. And he was obviously willing to flaunt it where Chel was concerned.

Jayla kept the smile to herself. After all, Chel wouldn't appreciate being the center of attention just now.

Gabriel's smooth mid-tenor voice broke into her thoughts.

"Now that the niceties are dispensed with, Jayla and Larien, are you ready to finish this?" Gabriel asked, rubbing his jaw.

"No." Larien was adamant.

"Yes." Jayla was so ready to be done with it all.

"Where is the Seal?" Gabriel asked.

"Safe," Jayla responded. "It's on another plane."

"Part of Larien's mission was to bring it to me." Gabriel's human skin slipped just a bit. The man was so glorious to look upon it took everything in her to keep her knees steady and her voice from cracking.

"It is my family's legacy given to us by Michael himself. I decided what should be done with it. Larien had no say in the matter." She didn't bother revealing that he'd had no say because he'd insisted she make the decision. It was times like this she was glad angels were not all knowing, all seeing creatures.

"All right then. I'll ask you to accompany me to my captain and explain."

"Not without my friends, my family," Jayla said. "All of them."

"Done."

CHAPTER TWENTY-EIGHT

That familiar flash of energy that heralded Larien's presence made her suck in a delighted breath. She'd never get sick of feeling him arrive. She'd been visiting on the First Tier for three days. Everything was oversized. Big buildings with tall columns and high ceilings. Wide, majestic avenues with even more majestic beings moving along them. She could understand why people would describe this place as heaven. But it didn't change the fact that even in a place where everything was perfect, she sorely missed Larien's presence and was quite ready to go home.

Her man had appeared in her living room where she'd been curled up reading a very different take on human history given to her by none other than Ankarel, the angel of History.

She jumped up, wrapped her arms around Larien's neck and buried her face in his shirt. The weave of the cloth was soft against her cheek. A deep breath was released on a relaxed sigh as she snuggled in.

"Where've you been, big guy? Missed you. Now that this is done, I want a vacation." She knew she was rambling, but she was so happy to see him and get on with the next phase of whatever this was between them that everything just came spilling out all at once.

"Talan has been flitting around this place like he was born here. Amazing how the laws of physics don't apply on this plane. He says it's sort of like when he goes to visit Isthus in the fae realm, but the energy feels a bit different. Oh, and he thinks many of the eudaemon are stuck up dandies in bad boy clothes! Can you believe that? And Talan got a neat gift from Raphael that enhances his healing abilities. It's pretty cool and—"

"Jayla, I just came to say goodbye."

Larien's words brought her up short. Each whispered syllable was knife-edged and sharp against her heart. Lungs seized in a strange mix of panic and disbelief as he unwound her arms from around his body and took a very clear step back.

"Goodbye? What? Why?"

"Jayla, I can't stay here. I gave up that right a long time ago. I'm only here now because Gabriel has allowed it in order to conclude our…business."

"But—"

"No, sweetheart." Fingers twirled gently around a lock of her hair as he spoke. "I don't belong here anymore. I do believe this is the only time in my life I have truly regretted the decision I made so long ago, because it means I can't stay here with you. Just know that I love you, and I will always hold you in my heart." He pressed a kiss to the inside of her palm. "Always."

"You—" She sucked in a deep breath as her mind swirled with disbelief. "You love me?"

"I do. With everything in me."

"But you're leaving me?"

The man was doing a wonderful job of putting up a front for her sake. His face held tenderness, but not an ounce of sadness. His bearing was straight and sure as always, but his energy was off. Sad. Bereft. No matter how accepting he appeared on the outside, Larien's heart was breaking. She felt it as sure as she felt her own begin to crumble into fine dust inside her chest.

"Larien—"

"Jay, listen, this is a rare gift you've been given." He forced a smile and a light conversational tone. "There are only two humans I can think of since I was created that were brought here without the typical prerequisite of death. If this is what you want, I don't want you to give it up because of me. Here you'll have everything you ever needed or wanted."

Except for you.

With that he kissed her until her toes curled into the thick loops of the plush carpet. Then he was gone.

In her pristine gold, cream and white house, in her gold, cream and white pajamas, Jayla fell to her knees and wept uncaring as her gold, cream and white china coffee cup toppled from nerveless fingers to leave a glaring black stain on the pristine carpet.

* * * * *

Stiff, angry and hurt, Jayla listened as Gabriel shared.

"Jayla, I know there are things you do not understand. I felt your sorrow and came in hopes I could help explain how things have come to be this way."

She pulled her knees up on the couch and wrapped her arms around them. Her heart remained on the floor though she tried her best to be strong. Talan pressed a warm cup of fragrant fruity tea into her hands. She looked up at him before taking a sip.

"There's nothing in it but honey, Jay. Promise." Talan's smile was bittersweet. She tried to give him one in return but she just couldn't make her lips cooperate. She really, really needed the rest of the story.

Gabriel continued.

"At the time of King Solomon's death, his dying prayer was that the magic of the Seal be woven into the very fabric of his family, into the blood, the marrow and the bone of his progeny. It was to be passed down through the ages, awakened and commanded by those who were wise enough to call on it."

"So there are others out there like me?"

"There are. And we would like you to find them. Teach them who they are. For example, you have found one already."

"I have? Who?"

Gabriel's gaze slid to Talan.

"What? Who, me?" Talan sputtered.

"Indeed. What's more is that we know that the demons had been keeping track of Descendants for millennia, but for some reason they stopped caring around the year six hundred. Now, they have a reason to begin keeping up with where Descendants are again, and perhaps even trying to influence them. Those who are not aware of what they can and cannot do could be caught up in the fallout. They need your help."

Whoa. Now that was enough to snap her out of her baffled longing-for-Larien state. For the first time since her lover had walked out that door this morning, Jayla's mind was on something other than the big hole in her heart and the anger that simmered below the surface. How dare he sacrifice their love for some misguided notion of what was best for her. The bastard.

"Jayla, this is a huge responsibility and we will not ask you to make a decision right now."

"There something you're not telling me, other than learning that Talan is a Descendant like I am. And given that he's a red-headed Irishman, I'm dying to hear that story."

"If you do this we will need to make some changes," Gabriel said.

"What kind of changes?" But he didn't immediately answer. She so didn't have the patience for this right now. "Look, Gabriel, stop hemming and hawing with me and get to the point. You're pissing me off."

"You will need a team, and you will need a partner."

"I thought Talan was my partner. Isn't that why he's here?"

"No. Not exactly."

Jayla rolled her eyes in exasperation. "No wonder Larien always wants to zap you in the ass with that big gun of his," she mumbled not quite under her breath. Then she slapped her hands over her mouth. It just wouldn't do to sass the Messenger. It just wasn't smart. "I'm sorry, Gabriel."

"No you're not," Gabriel laughed. "But I can be patient with you. You have been through quite a lot for us. I will overlook it. This time." He stood. "Talan I would ask you to be part of this. Not only do you need to learn to tap into your power as a Descendant, but Larien told me during his debriefing that you were invaluable to him during his mission. Your skills must be honed as both a fighter and a healer."

And then he turned back to Jayla. "Jayla, if you agree to lead this team, I will ask you to transform. To become ageless."

"Ageless?"

"Immortal, Jay," Talan whispered.

"I know, doofus," Jayla grumbled back. "Spill it all, Gabe. Now. Or I'm out of here." Which she'd already planned, but the threat sounded good and soothed her inner-bitch, at least momentarily.

Gabriel simply gave her the side-eye and said, "Talan has already been given a partner, but if you want to form one single team instead I will leave that to you."

"Who is Talan's partner?"

"Ambriel. He is Talan's Watcher and has been since Larien revealed himself to you. That is why he was not around when you needed him at certain times. He was watching over Talan."

"So that's why he'd leave even after I'd called him into place?"

"That is why. I do not wish to separate you from your friends and family, Jayla. If you do this, you may have a Watcher of your choice to team with you. Or you may all work together. Whatever you wish. However, I will insist that you have at least one member that is good with strategy and planning."

"Larien."

"What about him?" Gabriel asked, genuinely baffled.

"I want him on my team," Jayla said without hesitation.

Gabriel began making his way to the door with an easy grace. Obviously the conversation was coming to an end.

"And while we're on the subject, if you can make a deal with one Fallen, you can make a deal with two. I want Chelriad, too," Jayla said.

"It is completely up to Chelriad what part she wants to play in this. She is free to choose."

Jayla sent her summons out into the ether. Moments later Chel was at her door. She and Talan filled her friend in on the new missions. After reminding them that she'd only been allowed on the First Tier long enough to be debriefed, Chel asked to be part of it before Jayla could even form the question. Jayla hadn't realized she'd been afraid Chel wouldn't want to do it until the knot in her guts unfurled.

Jayla thought herself into a clean, outdoor-fresh sundress and a pair of sandals—yep, this was an ability she'd surely miss once she got back home to Saturday chores with her washer and dryer. She downed the rest of her tea and said, "Well, let's get going then. First stop, home. Next stop is where, Gabriel?"

After getting their plans together it was decided that Chel and Talan would both spend a couple of weeks getting their affairs in order as this new mission was going to be a fulltime job. Chel kissed Jayla on the cheek and said, "Something's bothering you. I can tell. I'll leave you alone about it for now, but when we meet up again in a couple of weeks I want to know what's up. You're my girl, Jay and I love you."

"I love you, too, sweetpea."

And Chel was gone just as Ambriel showed up to escort Talan.

Talan gave her a kiss and a hug and then looked her in the eyes. He frowned for a moment but said nothing other than, "See you in a couple."

Jayla kissed Talan back with a peck on the cheek and then she watched her friend and Ambriel vanish.

Gabriel took Jayla's hand and when next she blinked she stood in her own backyard with the roar of the Pacific Ocean playing its typical soothing rhythm.

Reaching out with her senses brought home how alone she really was. There was peace, calm and the muted roar of the water. But no Larien.

And she wouldn't call him either.

"A moment, Jayla."

A gentle palm curled beneath her chin and a faint but noticeable warmth spread from the spot where Gabriel touched her clear down to the red painted toes peeking out of her sandals.

"You are an immortal now."

She opened her eyes. "That's all? No big ceremony or anything?"

"We are very efficient, Jayla. You will learn this about us. Because of the gift just given to you, as granted by the creative Source, you cannot be killed unless you literally lose your head or your heart. You are not an angel and you do not have an angel's powers, or even a daemon's gifts. But the power of the Seal embedded in your very bones is enough. Understand?"

"Yes, I understand. And thank you for everything, but I need just one more thing." And she pressed her lips together in a determined line even as the Archangel, Gabriel the Messenger, granted her request.

* * * * *

"Jay? What are you doing in here? How did you get in?"

"Guess your 'can't-get-in rule' doesn't apply to the Messenger?"

"The Mess—"

She cut him off with a chuckle, "Yep, he is a mess, isn't he?"

"Woman, why are you back on this plane?"

She closed the distance between them, grabbed Larien by the front of his plush bathrobe... Oh. Was he naked underneath? The possibilities of what she could do to him right here and now momentarily knocked her off kilter.

Focus, woman. Focus. You have a job to do here.

But her fingers went on an exploratory journey of their own as she raised herself on tip-toe for a kiss she'd told herself she would not take.

"And why aren't you kissing me back already?" The man was so thunderstruck he didn't even resist when she simply took what she wanted and continued to kiss him until they were both breathless and trembling.

Wonder how I can get him to be cooperative like this all the time? Heh. Right.

"I have a message for you, Larien."

"From who?" He asked, his expression still a bit bewildered, brushed with a tad of lust.

"The Messenger, who else?"

She snapped the folded bit of parchment into his open palm and stood quietly as he read it. Eyes grew wide, head tilted a hard left in disbelief and then his gaze snapped back to her.

"Is he serious?"

"Yep. You are my guardian from now until I die...and since I'm immortal, I do believe that's quite a while." Jayla was sure she'd never seen his mouth hang open like that. Mr. Unflappable was definitely, well, flapping. "So, we're hunting and training Descendants while kicking demon ass."

"Together? You and me?"

"With Chel and Talan, too, since Talan is a Descendant."

"Chel is Talan's guardian?"

"Uh, no."

"Who is it, then?"

She hedged.

"Jayla?" he warned.

"You're going to think it's the worst thing ever."

"Worse than Chel? What could be worse than that temperamental, permanent PMS-ing, high fallutin', shoe-whore of a bi—"

"Ambriel."

"Are you fucking kidding me?"

"Nope," she chuckled.

Larien knew his expression showed as less than enthusiastic. In truth, he was horrified. Then again, Jayla would be by his side. She was worth putting up with both Ambriel and Chelriad.

"You game?" she asked.

He sobered. "Do you really need to ask, Jayla? I didn't think to ever see you again, let alone have the chance to be with you. Even if I have to deal with…wait. Did you say you can't die?"

"Took you awhile to catch that one, but yes. Gabriel did some witchy woo-woo, though quite anti-climactic, thing and made me immortal. I'm not an angel like you, so I can still die but only if my head or heart leave my body. Anything else will heal."

But he still hadn't answered. Just stared because he couldn't really believe what his eyes told his brain—that she was here. In the flesh. Forever.

"So you accept this mission from Gabriel or what? Larien, did you really just roll your eyes at me?"

"You know that it is physically impossible for one to roll one's eyes, right? And besides, it was a stupid question."

"I'll take that smart-assed remark as a yes, Larien." Her smile lit him up inside as she said, "And a couple more things."

"Sure, Jay. Anything."

"First off, you owe me an apology with your whole 'I'm leaving you because I don't belong here' bullshit. Especially considering I'd had no intention of staying up on the First Tier, which you would have known if you'd bothered to ask me."

One side of his mouth tilted up as he said, "Point taken. I humbly apologize." Though he knew he didn't look like he was sorry at all. In fact, he let his head fall forward and graced her with the most rakish grin ever.

"Good. Apology accepted. And second, will you marry me?"

His heart stuttered in his chest.

"Excuse me?"

"Larien, Principality and Angel of the Art of War. Will."
She untied the belt of his robe.

"You."

The fabric rasped against his skin as she pushed it past his shoulders.

"Marry."

She ran the backs of her fingers over his pecs. His body went taut. Well, tauter than it was already.

"Me?"

He closed his eyes against the wash of excitement mixed with awe and a healthy bit of adrenaline-laced fear—all normal emotions when faced with life-changing events...and a beautiful woman running her hands over his naked body.

His male ego started to rise at not getting to ask her to marry him first, but he was so damn happy to have her back in his life he shoved his ego to the backseat. He reveled in her squeal of delight as he snatched her off her feet and ran naked for the stairs.

No time like the present to give her an early honeymoon. Jayla deserved it, and more. She'd given all of herself to him, without hesitation, without fear. By that, she'd given Larien back himself as well.

This woman had faced death, taken on the most unimaginable foes and walked out the other side of each ordeal with a heart full of love for him. He may not deserve her, but he would do everything within his power to become worthy.

This woman was everything. His heart. His home. His Seal.

His Destiny.

CONTINUE READING
for an exclusive sneak peek of chapters from
Wind and Fire, Gathering of the Storms Volume I
by T.J. Michaels

WIND AND FIRE-SNEAK PEEK
GATHERING OF THE STORMS BOOK ONE
VOLUME ONE

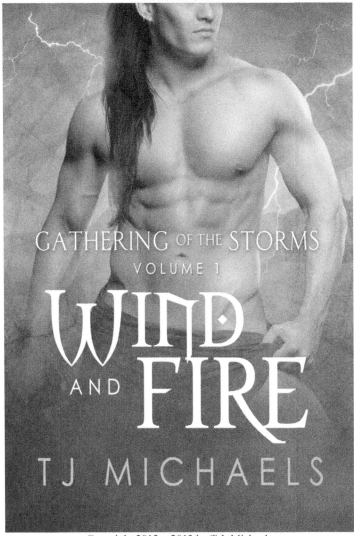

CHAPTER ONE

"Grandfather, if you must summon me from my pleasant dreams you could at least fashion a place more interesting," RuArk said softly into the darkness.

The room was stark, dimly lit, and completely empty—no windows, no doors. RuArk leaned against a rough wall with one foot propped up behind him, arms crossed over his chest. He smiled at the image of his favorite relative—an Elder known to all their clan as the Grandfather.

RuArk's brow furrowed as he watched the ethereal essence of the Grandfather's body shift and shimmer. Strange. It was as if he had difficulty staying with RuArk in a place where all was typically at the Elder's command. The Dream was a place where one was not confined to the body; able to move through time and space without the inhibition of flesh and bone. There was nothing to fear, though things appeared vividly real. It was one of several places to seek wisdom and direction, or face your greatest challenges. As he gazed at the roiling image, he noted the deep frown marring the old man's ancient features.

When he finally spoke, the Grandfather's urgency-laced words formed as ice in the pit of RuArk's stomach. Gifts lost to all, except the Gaian, since the Breaking of the world gave protection to the wielder. Those without were vulnerable in this place. If they lost their way, their physical body remained in a state of deep sleep until they either managed to escape or someone guided them out.

Unseen forces ruled this realm, and not all were friendly.

"The High Counsel of Draema sought us out in the Dream. Alone."

"Why would he do such a thing? He knows the risks better than anyone."

"He searched for your father to ask for your help," said the Grandfather. "Thank gods it was I who found him as he wandered."

"But why didn't he just come to me directly? I departed the High City not more than three days past. Negotiations were completed, and I am on my way home."

"Not any longer. You must return. This danger is focused on his daughter."

The coldness in RuArk's gut transformed into a 'berg, though it should be no surprise to learn 'that' particular female—Rhia Greysomne—was in trouble. He hadn't seen her while he'd been in the High City this time. In fact, he hadn't seen her on any of his journeys to Draema Proper over the years. Though he hadn't sought her out, surely he would have heard of any threat to her?

RuArk tensed and pushed away from the wall. "Focused on Rhia? By who?"

"The High Counsel believes one of his own is responsible. He is wise enough to accept that he needs someone outside of his own province. Now, I have told you all I can. You will have to find the rest of your answers in the *Seeking*, and quickly."

The urgent energy that rolled off the Elder's image spiked.

"What aren't you telling me, Elder?"

The Grandfather usually epitomized calm...but not today. His anger-infused growl was cut off with a thick, veil-like silence as he took an uncharacteristic moment to gather himself. Not good.

Finally, he ground out, "There is a taint, a strange darkness in the *other*realms. When the Realmwalkers first noticed, it was quite subtle. Now it seems to have found a focus. It grows bolder, and nearer to the High Counsel's daughter. If you are not in the appointed place at the appointed time, the bringer of this taint will prevail."

"Prevail over what, Grandfather? Over who?"

"I cannot say. It is no longer safe here, even for our kind. But know that I have faith in you, *akicita*. As such, your Gift of Vision will not fail you."

RuArk's head tilted a hard left.

What Gift of Vision?

The ability to enter the Dream or go on a *Seeking* quest didn't count as a Gift considering any Gaian could do it. But the Gift of Vision? That was something different. In fact, RuArk had never manifested such a Gift. Or any Gift for that matter. While some of his kin had been late bloomers in this regard, RuArk's bud had been on the tree so long, surely it had dried up and fallen off by now. He opened his mouth to ask.

With a warm smile and twinkling dark eyes that crinkled in the corners, the shifting misty presence of The Grandfather shattered before snapping whole once again.

"Go. I will get word to the High Counsel to expect your return to the High City. I will guard over Rhia as best I can until then."

The Elder's shimmering image lost the battle of holding its form and winked out just as RuArk was tossed headlong out of the Dream and slammed back into his own body.

* * * * *

Rama Collaidh sat in his official offices. His fingertips itched to roam over the smooth desktop, to trace the rare veins of gray and silver threaded throughout the polished, white stone. At well past midnight, the window coverings were locked down tight. The dimmed iozene lamp over his workspace gave off the only light in the room. He liked the darkness. It offered a sense of comfort, sitting there surrounded by shadows.

Carefully laid plans were flipped back and forth in his mind— turned sideways and upside down in his mind as he examined them for any holes. Many of his fellow Council members considered him an ambitious, middle-aged nuisance. He could care less what his peers thought. He was in the prime of his life; wily and determined enough to achieve the impossible. *And* he had the High Counsel's ear.

Yes, his board was set and the pieces were finally moving. Just as he noted a possible strategic problem, gooseflesh plumped just under the surface of his skin from scalp to fingertips. Sweat beaded between his shoulder blades before slipping coldly down his spine.

In spite of the urge to shudder, Collaidh forced his stylus to move smoothly over the viewer embedded in the top of his desk.

He didn't bother to turn towards the source of his discomfort. There was only one person, one *thing*, that could make him break out in a cold sweat. Could enter his offices unseen. How long had the creature been standing there watching? Collaidh quickly dismissed the concern. His determination to have what he wanted was stronger than fear or foe.

"So, you've finally come," Collaidh muttered.

The words hung in the gloom for what seemed like eons.

"You summoned me, did you not?" The tone was flat, uncaring, and alarmingly similar to his own.

"Have you succeeded in reaching Rhia Greysomne?" Collaidh asked coldly.

Now the deep, silky voice took on a harsh edge of impatience. "Someone is protecting her now, warding her while she sleeps. I cannot summon her into the Dream at all. Yet before the warding began…"

"Get to the point, Behn. And step out where I can see you, damn it."

Collaidh forced himself to look directly into the white eyes of the thing's too-pale face. The only true color on the creature was its clothing. Even the thick, billowing tresses of his shoulder-length hair were white as full moonlight. Everything about him was unnatural. Yet for all that, how did he manage to be so bloody handsome?

Once he was fully into what little light there was, Behn smiled.

The grin chilled the blood. Collaidh's lip curled at the sight of gleaming, elongated incisors—longer than any normal man's. And slightly yellowed.

Must be from endless cycles of feeding.

The thought turned his stomach.

Yes, Behn spoke with sophisticated diction, but he was *far* from civilized. And only a fool would forget it.

"When asleep," Behn said, "a person without the Gifts is vulnerable once inside the Dream. Strangely, Rhia does not have this vulnerability. The most I could do was deliver the most fantastic nightmares. I believe I was slowly wearing her down, though I could not directly manipulate her."

"So what. Get to the point."

"We have encountered a problem. I am unable to touch her dreams at all now. She is either Gifted, or someone with the Gifts is protecting her."

"That's impossible!" Collaidh shot to his feet. Palm slammed against the sturdy desk hard enough to sting. "Her father is the High Counsel. The man is Draeman, through and through."

"What of her mother? Rhia is half-Gaian, is she not? Perhaps the mother has passed on a Gift?" Behn insisted calmly.

Collaidh frowned. Hell. He hadn't thought of that. Hadn't anticipated any of these delays. But he had to keep the upper hand. Behn had proven to be keenly intelligent, single-minded and ruthlessly ambitious—a creature that would take advantage of any perceived weakness. No one could know he'd enlisted the aid of a creature that shouldn't exist—one that had rediscovered how to manipulate magick long lost...

But then, who would believe it? After all, this was Draema Province. Science ruled all.

With a smile that felt venomous even to himself, Collaidh pushed the thoughts away, deciding to force his point with his unwelcome, but much needed visitor.

"Look, the only people with Gifts are Gaian. Rhia's mother was, and remains, the only Gaian woman to marry outside her province since who knows how long. The woman is long dead, and certainly not around to teach her daughter anything about Gaia, Gifts, or anything else. And we all know the High Counsel hasn't tried in the least to teach Rhia anything about her mother's people since the girl was eight years old. Perhaps you're simply not capable of getting the job done?"

"Careful, old man."

Behn's feral growl sent Collaidh's heart into a stutter, but he was unwilling to give any ground. Collaidh ground his back teeth. This was his show to run, damn it. No way would he allow Behn to take control. He painted his face with a calm façade and refused to look away from the gleaming, white eyes. Eyes that seemed to bore right through his forehead.

"I said forget the High Counsel. We need that woman. We need Rhia, period." Settling back again into the plush cushions of his chair, Collaidh turned and unlocked a small drawer. "Perhaps this will help," he said as he held out a small amber vial filled with a milky looking fluid.

Collaidh steeled himself as perfectly manicured, long, semi-translucent fingers reached toward him. Little blue veins made various patterns underneath the smooth white skin. It made Collaidh's skin crawl when the lukewarm fingers touched his palm to retrieve the vial.

"What is this?" Behn asked.

"Don't worry about what it is. I called in a favor from a friend in the Society of Physicians. It won't harm her. Since the Dream business is no longer an option, you'll need to be more direct. This will make Rhia more cooperative."

"Fine. I will deliver it to someone who can get close to her. It must be done discretely if we are to avoid suspicion."

"I agree. You can't be seen here," Collaidh sniffed.

"If there is one thing I am good at, it is concealing myself from friends and enemies alike. And if I choose to be seen, I will simply be mistaken for my brother, would I not?

The sneer in Behn's voice was unmistakable. Collaidh grimaced at the bitterness in those words. Was it justified? Definitely. But he couldn't afford to be moved by it. Not now. Not ever.

"Perhaps," Collaidh responded, but didn't think it possible that Behn would ever be mistaken for his brother—a man who looked fully human, while it was obvious that Behn was…not. "But don't take any chances. I don't want anyone to become aware of your presence here. Besides, those teeth and eyes of yours would give you away for sure. You'd be shot on sight. What good would you be to me then? Unfortunately we need each other so let's make the best of it, shall we?"

"You promised to give Rhia to me. You will keep your promise, old man."

"Yes, yes, yes," Collaidh said, waving his hand dismissively. "I said you could have her once she's served my purpose. Now leave me alone. I have work to do."

Collaidh turned his back and ignored the wave of anger emanating from behind him. He didn't hear Behn leave, but was vastly relieved when the little hairs on the back of his neck finally stopped dancing.

* * * * *

Sara rose and donned a warm fluffy robe. She crossed the dark room to turn up the delicate-looking iozene sconces mounted on the walls. As she reached out her hand to adjust the brightness, her skin went cold. She was no longer alone. *He* was here. She expected no greeting and received none. He didn't care for niceties, only obedience.

"You will put this in the First Heir's teapot this morning. Do you understand?"

"I understand." Sara replied softly, her head tilted down in a genuinely terrified posture. "But her companion brings her breakfast in the mornings. How am I supposed to do this?" she asked on a shaky whisper.

"You will find a way, Sara."

She nodded quickly as he gave instruction and pressed a small glass vial into the center of her sweaty palm.

"Do you want to know what it is, sweet Sara?"

"N-No, sir. No, I don't." Sara clutched the vial firmly against her breast. Knowing too much simply wasn't a good thing with this man. He moved closer, his long, dark coat swished against her bare ankles as he shifted behind her. His breath was both warm and cool against the nape of her neck. Darkness radiated from him.

She shivered uncontrollably.

"Good girl, Sara. Very good indeed," he crooned against her skin as his fingers skimmed lightly over her shoulders. Her mind said she should run screaming from this creature, but her body wanted him—wanted to feel the thick mass of snow-white hair slide over her skin. To feel his teeth scrape against her shoulder as he took her roughly. Her sex warmed and softened in need of the thick erection pressed against her backside. Ashamed, Sara closed her eyes against her physical reaction to such an unnatural man. When she opened them again, she was in bed.

Blinking into the darkness, a wave of relief swept over her. It was a dream. It always seemed so real. Even the sensitive buds of her nipples puckered at the false memory of his breath wafting over her skin. She rose, wrapped her robe closely about her body, and went through the motions she could have sworn she'd already done. Slipping her hands into the warm pockets, Sara went dead still when her fingers wrapped around a small glass vial.

"How in blazes does he do that?" She almost wished she had the courage to ask him. Almost.

She washed up quickly. Dressed in her Houseman's uniform, she slipped the vial into her trouser pocket. As she rushed to the kitchens, Sara pushed away guilt for what she was about to do. Failure equaled pain—lots and lots of brilliantly delivered pain—courtesy of a much too-handsome devil that was supposed to exist only in dreams. Unfortunately for her, he didn't seem inclined to stay there.

CHAPTER TWO

By the time Rhia made it to the dining hall, she looked and felt like every description of hell she'd ever read about in the old story books. In addition to the sweat and dirt stains that covered her tunic, her leggings sported a long, jagged rip. The fabric flapped annoyingly as she walked, baring a good amount of thigh. She'd almost had her leg sliced open in the middle of teaching the final knife-fighting session of the day. Good thing she hadn't been instructing laser whips instead. Geesh.

She pushed the thoughts away, and instead focused on what awaited her upstairs in her rooms—a blasted bath, and she couldn't wait to sink into the warm…ewww!

She sniffed and then sniffed again. Was that rank smell her, or the filleted protein on her plate? Not wanting to offend, Rhia ate quickly at a table closest to the wide double doors and headed up to her apartments.

The twitchy burn in her legs made her hiss out loud as she climbed the tower stairs. Wiped out, and absolutely tired of being so damn tired, she forced herself to trudge on. Why did her place have to be on the only floor that couldn't be accessed by a lift?

Finally at the top of the tower stairs, she reached for the key around her neck. Her hand brushed the sharp corner of a note she'd completely forgotten about. Removing the crumpled piece of paper from her breast pocket, Rhia immediately recognized her father's bold, flowing script. Even bolder words had her bristling before she was halfway through the short missive.

To: Rhia Greysomne, First Heir to the Seven Colonies of Draema Province

Consider this a formal reprimand from the Office of the High Counsel. I don't have time to run all over the City looking for you as you take on more and more responsibilities. I had to send a Houseman to find you to deliver this note. I'm sure he's just catching up with you and it's probably well past dinner time as you're reading it.

"Damn it, how does he always know?" she wondered aloud.

You are hereby relieved of all duties except for the diplomatic responsibilities of the First Heir. In addition, you may teach one, and only one, combat or blade class. All of your other duties related to the Society of War have been assigned to other officers. Further, you are to leave at first light for Harbor Station to inspect the two new airships built for the coastal patrols. You will also inspect the troops stationed there under your brother's command. Joan Rouillard and Brita Shae will accompany you. To make the journey shorter, I've assigned you a hover driver. He'll take you to the train, where you'll board for Harbor Station. And no, you may not take the outmoded form of transportation you prefer—that damned horse of yours.

It was bad enough he was making her take the train to the harbors, but she wouldn't be allowed to even transport herself to the station? Not that she knew how to operate one of the hover things anyway, but that wasn't the point. And Moonlight was *not* outmoded, damn it!

With an annoyed huff, she finished reading.

I advise you to find time to enjoy yourself while you are at Harbor Station, young lady. You will come to my offices before you leave to pick up a message for your brother. When you return to the High City, your life will change considerably.

Regards,

Grey Greysomne, High Counsel of Draema Province

Commander in Chief, Society of War

Her father had sent a note to tell her off. This was a new experience. Grey Greysomne usually delivered any displeasure directly to her face. But a note? Geez, how impersonal could you get? And what did he mean her life would 'change considerably' when she returned from Harbor Station? And why did she need to go inspect a ship or troops? Her younger brother was the Harbormaster for a reason. That man knew all there was to know about the blasted vessels. What a total waste of time. But as one of the highest-ranking officers of the Society of War, she had her orders and would obey them. Of course she wouldn't admit to being secretly pleased with the opportunity to visit her brother and his family. Perhaps she'd rest better there.

Rhia cringed as she recalled the weeks of nightmares so terrifying, so *wrong,* that she'd jerked herself awake with a scream on her lips. There'd been several nights where she'd awoken with sweat-soaked bed linens stuck to her body as she sat huddled in the center of the bed. She was sure her skin had tried to crawl away and hide a time or two.

But last night everything had changed. Sleep had been peaceful and strangely calm with the presence of an old man. Her dream had been simple—the man seemed to enjoy nothing more than keeping her company, and the nasties had stayed away. It would be nice to drift off and not wonder what was in store. Maybe some rest and a change of scenery would do just that. Perhaps Harbor Station was the ticket.

Rhia read the note again, stuffed it back into her pocket, and fumbled with her key tag. The flat, square fob gleamed dully in the bluish light of the iozene lamps set into the walls. Holding the tag to the center of the panel next to the door, a familiar click indicated the release of the lock.

One step into her private domain, Rhia felt the cares of the day melt away. This space was uniquely hers. It was strategically unsound to have walls an enemy could hide behind, so there were none in this space. Instead, it was large, airy, and tastefully arranged so she could see from one end of the suite to the other without obstruction.

The sleeping area was dominated by a huge, curtained bed, but it was the floor that defined the space. It was covered with soft, gray, hand-knotted carpets. Where the carpets ended, so did her sleeping area. A large mosaic of tiny gray and white tiles in the shape of the sigil of the House of Greysomne covered the dining area floor. It was centered by a large table; its base of polished marble was topped with a thick, smoky glass pane. Off to the left was the mantel covered with awards and weapons, over a wide, and thankfully blazing, iozene fireplace.

A few steps past her large, four-post bed, a chilly wind sent the silky bed curtains billowing. The mid-winter breeze flowed through the glass doors that led to her private balcony... Only she was sure those doors were closed and locked this morning. Brita would have been the last person out of these rooms, and she would never have left them unsecured.

Shivering from the whoosh of cool air, Rhia dropped her blade and belt down on top of the dining table with a loud clunk as she passed. She pressed the little switches that controlled the wall of thick, beveled panes and waited impatiently as the glass slid silently along the tracks.

The moment the balcony doors closed, her trouble meter tipped off the scale. Turning ever so slowly, she peered into the darkness. Sharp senses tried to see and hear everything at once as her eyes adjusted.

The open curtains let in the glow of a half-moon, whose light was obscured by a passing cloud. Looking past the mantle, Rhia peered toward the bathroom entrance. The sheer curtains that gave her privacy were pulled open as usual.

However, what was *un*usual was the shadowed figure standing there. A black cloak swirled around a body as it took a step forward, and the "it" was revealed as a man.

"Hello, Rhia."

Bryan Collaidh? Aw hell. She hadn't seen him since she'd made First Blade, cycles ago. The haunted look on his face, and the dark shadows under his eyes, made it obvious those cycles had not been kind. His pale skin stood out in stark contrast against lackluster, shoulder-length black hair. Didn't he know greasy hair was out of style in Draema? And what was with the all-black garb?

The creep hadn't left the province under the best of circumstances. As far as she was concerned, he was still unwelcome in the High City, and certainly unwelcome in her personal space.

"What the hell are you doing here?" she asked, not bothering to hide the contempt in her voice.

The lines of his mouth hinted at the cruelty she knew he was capable of. A malevolent black gaze followed her steps. Deep set, and round as old-fashioned playing stones, his eyes seemed too large for his face. He looked like an overgrown guppy, complete with thin, pouting lips. An image popped into her head of this unwanted guest, complete with gills and fins. His lips glub-glub-glubbed as bubbles floated up towards the surface of the river she wanted to drown him in.

Her amusement faded quickly as she considered the situation. It took a bold man to break into her apartments with no fear. Why would he take such a risk? The answer was obvious—he still didn't have any goddamn common sense.

Rhia watched him closely as she walked across the room. The glowing fireplace halfway between them cast his smooth, black clothing with an eerie, orange tint.

"I asked what you're doing here, Bryan." At the mantle now, she stretched her hands toward the warming flames, appearing completely at ease.

"I've come to visit you, old friend," he drawled, moving slowly toward her. He attempted to smile, but it must have made his face hurt. The skin appeared to freeze just around his mouth in the middle of the feeble attempt.

"Old friend? What are you, nuts? I haven't seen you since the day you decided to use my face as a punching bag."

"I'm a changed man, Rhia. Cycles of surviving on the borders can do that to a person." He ground out the words as his gaze seemed to focus on something far, far away. Some called the borders "Hell's Eastern Seventh Level." Judging from the menace rolling off of her nemesis, like dust clouds of choking malintent, the name must be pretty accurate.

She took a deep breath, then another. Blast it, she'd always been calm when meeting a foe. But she'd never faced a known enemy whose very presence dragged one of the worst moments of her life out of the locked dungeon of her mind.

But her typical pre-fight calm was nowhere to be found. No, she was torqued the hell off. And this wasn't going to end nicely.

She almost smiled.

Biding her time, Rhia leaned against the smooth mantle with one arm draped casually atop the ledge. Her fingertips brushed the hilt of the specially commissioned blade her father had given her on her sixteenth birthday. For a few seconds she considered pulling the razor sharp work of art down off the mounting, but changed her mind. The blade was too special to dirty on the likes of Bryan Collaidh. Too bad she didn't have a laser pistol handy. At least those left wounds that didn't bleed much. Rhia was sharp enough to know that this little conversation was going to end in a fight, and the less blood on her tile, the better. She hated cleaning blood out of crystal grout.

Then she noticed that Bryan wasn't moving. Simply stood there, wasting her time.

"Look Bryan, I'm tired. I had a long day, and I really don't feel like being bothered. I was so busy this evening I was two hours late to dinner. Now I'm two hours late for bed. Can't you just go away? Perhaps we can talk in the morning." Knowing she didn't mean a word of that last part. After all, there was nothing to say.

"You have grown into a beautiful woman, Rhia. And I think I'd rather talk now. Besides, I've returned to Draema Proper for one purpose. To claim you."

Laughter bubbled up out of her throat before she could stop it. She just couldn't help it. Claim her? Ridiculous! Her smile was genuine, but her thoughts took another turn, and her insides turned with it. What if he was serious? A serious lunatic, that is. He wanted her? Why? He certainly didn't love her. She didn't think he even *liked* her.

Sigh.

Okay, he had about an inch on her in height, and maybe twenty pounds in weight. The calculations only took a moment. She could take him down fast, then call in a favor to a couple of the soldiers who roomed on the floors below. The advantage of living in her father's Citadel – it only took seconds to get someone up here to help drag the body away.

But Bryan still hadn't moved. Not even to blink. Perhaps a reminder that she outranked him would push him over the edge so they could get this over with.

She rolled her eyes and said sleepily, "Get out, you idiot. Otherwise, as the highest ranking officer in the Society of War, I'll personally have you assigned to the iozene mines with all the other miscreants."

Then she waited for him to lose it like he had long ago, when he'd taken a closed fist to her face. Her offense—a rank promotion ahead of him. Angry and full of jealousy, he used his failure as an excuse to abuse her. In his mind, the anger had been all her fault. Personal responsibility? Puh. Those two words weren't in his vocabulary.

Hands raised in surrender, he headed toward the door. Halfway there, he changed direction.

Damn it.

He looked back and forth, between her and the katana lying on the table. The metal under the black leather, which crisscrossed elegantly over the handle, gleamed dully in the moonlight. Bryan picked it up, testing the weight of it in his hand.

Calculation flared in those cold, black eyes as he took a single step, pivoted and threw the weapon clear across the room. It bounced off a wall near the front door with a loud clang. She had no doubts now—the man was definitely nuts.

From rage to cool civility in a blink, he crooned, "I hear you've made Blademaster well before the usual ten cycles. But it doesn't matter whether you're a Blademaster or not, we're going to reinstate our former engagement."

Bullshit.

One hand on her hip, she took an angry step forward. "My father didn't approve of you back then, and he certainly won't approve now. Besides, if you were on the up-and-up, you wouldn't have broken in and waited for me in the dark. What the hell do you really want?"

"Give me a minute. I'm sure you'll figure it out." He lunged.

* * * * *

Rhia was ready, and ducked past him so fast he found himself facing the fireplace with nothing but air where she had been seconds before. A clean kick to his kidneys from behind slammed him chest-first into the mantle. The wind whooshed from his lungs. After a few wheezing breaths, he faced her with eyes drawn tight in an angry frown. And a bit of...shock?

"Surprise, asshole."

He hadn't expected her to be able to defend herself without a weapon. Well good. But she'd rather have a blade between them. Rhia ran for her steel.

Bryan dove, taking her feet out from under her. She went down hard, skinning her cheek on the smooth, hard mosaic under the dining table. But stinging cheeks were a relief. If she'd landed a few more inches to the left, her jaw would have made solid contact with the glass and marble of the table.

She rolled over with a groan and was happy to be in absolute pain rather than knocked out cold.

Then he was on her, trying to capture her hands as they connected with his eyes, cheeks, and lips. Rage, thick and palpable filled the bit of air between them.

"I'll have what I want whether you agree or not, Rhia." Pant. "Once I fuck you." Snarl. "I'll present evidence to the Council."

What the hell?

"Your honor," he sneered as if she had none, "will require you to declare me your mate. Our houses will be joined one way or another. Good thing you were altered at the Age of Consent. Without a hymen, at least it won't hurt. Much."

Whoa. How did he know when she'd been altered? And what the hell else did he know? The records of every member of the Society of War, especially hers as First Heir, were classified. No one knew her secret other than her father, and her friends, Brita and Joan.

Her mind screeched to a halt. The law was clear. As female First Heir, she'd had her hymen painlessly removed at the Age of Consent as required. But afterward, Rhia didn't have the Draeman privilege of screwing around.

While mates, lovers and Sensuan were carefully recorded for all members of the Society of War, for Rhia the rules were a bit different. She had two choices—she could take an assigned lover for a time, whose identity and time of service were carefully determined and recorded.

Or she could take a mate. Period.

Her mate's identity would remain secret for a time until she declared the union to the Council, or proof of consummation was given. Vows could be taken in the presence of her father and a witness, or she could elope. This was to keep the First Heir's mate from being assassinated before he could actually say, "I do."

No one, especially Bryan Collaidh, should know that her records were clean – no assigned lover, no mate. If he managed to prove he'd had sex with her, she was screwed. And not in a good way. No recourse. No way out.

Except to get free. Right now.

Rhia jerked her hand loose. A fist connected with the side of Bryan's head, sending it sideways with a wicked snap. The jeweled dagger always strapped to her thigh was almost in her hand when the bastard dropped his full weight down on top of her. She just couldn't get a full breath. Her head spun. Wriggling black spots swam around her field of vision.

Ugh, she was going to throw up.

A backhand to the jaw didn't help. She hadn't seen the blow coming and now both her hands were above her head, held securely in his grip. His free hand brutally squeezed and twisted a tender breast. And he had an erection? Ewww.

She swallowed hard as more bile surged and her dinner bubbled threateningly at the base of her throat. Frustrated and angry, Rhia let out an ear-piercing scream when Bryan pushed his hand roughly underneath her tunic searching for the top of her leggings.

When the skin of a clammy hand touched the flesh of her belly, she went completely still.

"That's more like it, bitch," Bryan growled, yanking on her already ripped and torn clothing to expose her underwear. "I knew you would see things my way, Rhia. You always were a mewling little puke. It's your fault I ended up on the borders all those cycles. Your fault! If you hadn't run to your father blaming me for your making me angry, I would have surpassed your rank by now. You deserved a beating then, and you deserve one now."

Wasn't there an old proverb in the ancient books that said pride goes before destruction? Obviously the man wasn't much of a history reader.

In his haste to dip into her goodies, he released her hands to get a better grip on her bottoms. Her elbow crashed into the middle of his throat. Suddenly *he* was the one having trouble breathing.

Now wasn't that just too bad?

Knee to the groin preceded a full-contact left hook. He rolled completely away, eyes watering as he gasped through his bruised windpipe. It seemed he couldn't decide whether to hold his throat and gag, hold his balls and moan, or soothe his swelling eye.

On her feet, she yanked up her leggings and retrieved her blade from the carpet near the door. The corner of her mouth lifted at the exact moment Bryan realized the only way out was through her securely locked balcony windows or the front door. The first option was a no go. But a four story fall wasn't high enough to knock any sense into his hard head anyway. And unfortunately, Rhia and her blade stood in front of option number two.

There was a third option—part him from the family jewels he'd tried to force on her moments ago.

"You wouldn't kill a man in cold blood. You don't have it in you." But the quaver in his voice said he didn't believe his own words. He knew she'd do it. Knew she'd shred him. Sweat dripped from his brow and trailed down his clammy pale skin like wax down a spent candle.

Neither of them heard the door open.

CHAPTER THREE

His party had shown none of their discomfort or concern in their expressions at the suddenly pressing journey back to Draema Proper. In fact, if not for the chilling mounds of snow piled along the roads and the biting winds, it would have been a good time under clear, and amazingly vivid, blue skies.

They'd moved quickly through the buffer zone that separated Draema Seine from the capital of the province, Draema Proper. In the distance, the High City had been a welcome sight, rising from the heart of these lands. Built in the middle of its seven colonies, this was the most advanced area in the world. The dawning sunlight had reflected various shades of pink and purple off both the inner, and outer walls; all of which were built with the famous, silvery-white Draeman stone.

Sleek buildings were shaded by tree-lined walks, which led into vast, city squares. The High City boasted a mix of rolling hills, and neatly-groomed pastures alongside well-kept roads. Some were laid with cobblestone, while others were covered by a smooth, dark, magnetized substance that allowed the passage of small conveyances called 'hovers'. Horses were still used here for sport, but inner-to-outer city travel typically meant a ride in one of the neat little vehicles, or a spot on the train. RuArk preferred the wild, open spaces of his own province, but didn't hesitate to admit this place held wonder for those who appreciated such things.

He'd brought more than thirty men on this journey, but only RuArk and a single fireteam of six warriors had passed through the open City gates this morning. There were very few of his people in this place, yet he'd been immediately recognized. The advantage of being son of the ruler of the neighboring province was being waved through the towering gates quickly. Well, that, and the reputation of being a ruthless bastard that took down enemies hard and fast with no promise to ask questions later.

Through a second set of lower walls that surrounded the Citadel, the High Council's right-hand, Mannon, had greeted them and rushed them into a meeting. From this morning's arrival, until leaving the High Counsel's chambers moments ago, they'd worked through one planning session after another until everything was in place.

Though so tired his muscles weighed down his bones as he dragged himself toward the guest apartments, RuArk could not ignore the flash and tensing of excitement that tapped at his gut. As if something long dead was waking inside him, stretching and unfurling itself in anticipation of seeing where this new turn in life would lead.

And Rhia was smack in the middle of this, this...whatever it was.

And in spite of the intrigue surrounding the danger to the woman, what would occur between them would be hot as the mid-Summer sun. He'd known from the *Seeking*, had felt it as he'd replayed that vision over and over in his mind. Damn near ached for it now that he knew the woman was somewhere near. Strange, he still hadn't seen the flesh and blood star of his *Seeking* vision. But he would soon enough.

RuArk steered his First Commander, Sharyn, toward a wide archway that opened into a large, starlit atrium. The space was filled with lush green trees, shrubs and a little stone bench where one could sit and enjoy the sun or moon overhead. At the rear of the atrium, two sets of mirroring staircases took off up the tower walls to a landing; where tall arches led opened to wide hallways. The stairs continued up the walls, winding their way upward to another landing, and yet another.

belongs to my family so Isthus, if we find it, I give it to you of my own free will. Everyone in this room must vow to keep the location of the artifact and the secret of the true Seal to themselves."

"What about Gabriel? Isn't he going to wonder what's up given he sent Larien here to find the Seal of Solomon and Larien will come up empty?" Talan asked.

"I'm sure Gabriel had an idea of what I would find when he sent me on this mission." Larien's arms tightened around her as he spoke. "Though for the life of me I'm unsure why he chose me rather than one of his eudaemon. Let me worry about Gabriel. In the meantime, I vow never to reveal the whereabouts of the Seal."

With a solemn nod all of them agreed to the same.

They arrived in Xi'an under cover of darkness, picked up the gear that Isthus had somehow arranged for them, and then vanished from the hotel into a restricted part of the Qin Shi Huang tomb.

Even with Larien's snapping out orders of 'you take that side' and 'you, over there' Jayla took a few moments to admire the exquisite workmanship of the Terracotta warriors. She stood nose to nose with them, took in the shape of their eyes, the detail of the armor, the contours of their bodies. Noticed how the men in front of her, their features cast forever in clay, were all different from one another just as they would have been in life.

Nerves kicked around her gut—a mix of fear and excitement. The last thing they needed was for the Chinese government to discover them here in the dead of night with no plausible explanation, no papers, no nothing. Sure they could get away but who in their right mind wanted to cause an incident when what they were doing was supposed to be a secret?

Finally, after an hour of digging around in the off-limits unexcavated part of the tomb, Jayla was beyond grateful for Isthus. With his earth magic, the fae unearthed various bits of ancient history, searched for what they needed and then buried it again as if the dirt had never been disturbed. The job was so thorough there weren't even any extra motes floating about even though dust was everywhere.

"Let's move on to the next space," Talan whispered.

Finally they were at the top. There were no hallways or arches—only two doors separated by a ten-meter wide, colorful mural of the Draeman countryside.

He'd just pressed the key against the wall lock of the rooms he would share with Sharyn when a panic-inducing yell rang through the tower. He looked toward the sound and cursed.

Sharyn's gasp of surprise, followed by her quiet chuckle made him grimace. He hadn't meant to say that out loud, especially in the presence of a lady. The High Counsel put him in this part of the Citadel to keep an eye on Rhia. He'd hoped the job could wait until she returned from the made-up errand they'd created for her at Harbor Station.

"Apparently not," RuArk muttered and moved quickly towards the source of the noise. Through her slightly open door, two voices were clearly heard, both of them yelling. Not wanting to be mistaken for an intruder, he opened the door carefully, just enough to peek inside. The scene that met him was...wrong. On too many levels to list.

A greasy looking fellow had Rhia flat on her back on the thick carpets, trying to rip her trousers off. She was obviously not cooperating. The man's fist connected with her jaw. The blow should have knocked her out, but Rhia was moving and moving quickly. Her next breath saw her up off the floor and brandishing a wicked, long blade. A katana made in the old style.

Her intent was clear—skin the greaser.

Rhia's hair was dark, fire streaked and tangled all over her head. But the blood. There was so much blood. It was on her face, streaming down her neck from her eyes, nose and mouth to soak the collar of her top.

RuArk kept his expression neutral, but he really wanted nothing more than to rip the greaser in half. Hell, he might not love Rhia yet, but it was only a matter of time considering the Ancestors clearly meant for him to have her. The moment he'd accepted the *Seeking* she'd been given into his care. And this man dared to threaten her? Not bloody likely.

His first thought was to kick the door in the rest of the way, stride across the room and grab the idiot by his scrawny neck. But he'd be a fool to simply stroll into the room and surprise a woman with a sharp blade in her hands and hellfire in her eyes.

In spite of the obvious injuries, her fighting form was perfect; her handling of the blade smooth and experienced. She held no fear and knew she was in position to deliver a killing blow. And he couldn't blame her one bit. In truth, it was Rhia's ability to handle her *visitor* that helped keep RuArk's anger in check.

RuArk anticipated her move, knew the exact moment she'd decided to slice open the greaser's chest. What was she thinking? The scandal it would cause—a man in her rooms this time of night, and a dead man at that. Not to mention all the blood and guts that would have to be cleaned up.

And it would ruin his investigation.

One step through the door, RuArk called out.

"Excuse me. Is there a problem here?"

* * * * *

Rhia glanced away from the groveling swine on the floor and looked into a pair of eyes of such a wondrous mix of gray and silver, they reminded her of the waters off of Draema's southern coast.

RuArk Miwatani—the bane of her childhood existence. A bane she hadn't seen in so long she was surprised she recognized him. It was the eyes. Stormy sea, silver-as-fog, captivating eyes. Simply unforgettable. Ever. She had to look up a bit to meet his gaze, but once she caught it, Rhia was stuck right there.

Blazes, he was simply breath-stopping. Gone were the boyish good looks and mischievous expression. In their place was an angular jaw, high cheekbones and the confidence of a man.

A long, thick, black-as-sin braid was pulled forward over his shoulder to brush against the middle of his stomach. His skin, though quite a bit fairer than her own, was such a warm bronze that even now, at the end of mid-winter, he appeared to have spent a good deal of time under the glorious sunshine. He wore an unadorned, dark gray, fine gauged tunic, with dyed-to-match trousers. The outline of thick, roped muscle was visible beneath the supple material.

He closed in on her with a step so light she still didn't hear his footballs even though she was looking right at him.

And how the hell was she noticing this in the middle of a life or death struggle?

And what the hell was *he doing here?*

As far as she was concerned he was yet another man in her space without her damn permission. Enough gawking. Back to business.

Rhia returned her attention to the weasel groaning on the floor and raised her katana for the final blow. But before she could take a step, RuArk grabbed Bryan by the collar of his finely appointed cloak, and the back of his finely appointed trousers, hauled him out the door, and tossed him down the closest staircase.

While Bryan tumbled, Rhia's attention remained on RuArk. Sure, his expression was firm but she could tell he was totally enjoying this.

She looked him dead in the eye—or tried to, given his typical tree-like Gaian height—and proceeded to tear his head off with her tongue.

"Look, asshole. I know you warrior types are used to throwing the muscle around, but this is Draema. Here, people don't interfere unless they're asked to interfere. If I'd needed help I would have…"

Mouth snapped shut. The most beautiful woman she'd ever seen stood directly behind the most ruggedly handsome man she'd ever known. Humph.

Bone straight, thick, and black-as-midnight hair was partially covered with a length of translucent silk that could only be described as sensual. Actually, her entire outfit seemed to be one big wispy scarf. Her skin reminded Rhia of the summer fruits that, according to the histories, used to grow in the now non-existent southern locales so long ago.

"Peaches," Rhia whispered, though she truly hadn't meant to.

And if this female had stood here the whole time, then she'd seen Rhia act a complete fool.

"Blasted hell," she muttered.

Rhia knew her hair was a tangled mess. Her face was swelling and surely beginning to display various colors in addition to sweat and blood. She wasn't sure why she cared that this man might compare her raggedy, torn appearance to this exotic woman. Nope, she shouldn't give a bloody goddamn...but she did. In fact, she flew past 'caring' and skidded to a halt at 'mortified'.

She scowled. Maybe the blows Bryan had landed on her face had shaken her brain loose because there was no way she should notice how ridiculously delicious RuArk's lips looked with that bit of a smile spread over them. Gah.

"What do you want? Aren't you far from home?" she snapped, forcing a blizzard into her words.

"You screamed. Loudly," he said quietly as he stepped toward her slowly, carefully. His words may have been just as frosty as hers, but the look he gave was equal parts 'smoking hot' and 'royally pissed'. "I can't resist taking care of such a beautiful lady, especially if she's in distress."

RuArk's voice slid over Rhia's frazzled nerves like warm, honey syrup while his expression took on a mysterious quality; like he could see through her funky-assed mood straight into her head, to uncover all the secret thoughts swirling around in there. Thoughts of him.

"Anything else I can do to assist you?" he asked quietly, though no less firm and as bossy as ever. And he was entirely too close now and looking at her as if he knew something she didn't. Her ice began to melt. Fast. She shivered, but not from fear nor an adrenaline crash.

It was anticipation? But of what? And who? Not RuArk, for sure.

After all, she'd known this man forever. Though he'd been a boneheaded, spoiled, king's son, she'd carried a torch for this particular pain-in-the-ass for years. Memories she'd pushed to the very fringe of her mind peeked its head up and over the ragged edge of her conscience.

She remembered RuArk, putting straw in her hair. RuArk besting her at wooden blade practice. RuArk pulling stupid pranks on her, and getting her in trouble with both their fathers.

Sigh.

RuArk holding her hand at her mother's funeral, wiping the tears from her cheeks and telling her it would be okay. RuArk wrapping her in his cloak while she huddled in misery as they left the burial grounds so far away in Gaia province.

RuArk singing to her—quite badly at the top of his lungs—on her tenth birthday after talking his father into bringing him on an unscheduled visit, just to give her a birthday present he'd made with his own hands.

RuArk telling her he was going away to train for his role as Protector of the Realm of Gaia.

RuArk, staying away for years.

But it didn't matter now. Since then, Rhia had made a couple of trips to her own personal hell and back. She'd become her own woman—a woman who would never need saving by anyone. Ever.

And that included the gorgeous man towering over her.

"You should visit the Physicians, Rhia. It's getting late. I will escort you, if you wish."

So he was trying to save her, *and* tell her what to do? *Not.* Her out-of-whack-ness dissolved, replaced by a wash of hot anger. And a bit of unexplainable fear. Rather than dealing with the latter, she squashed her emotions into the toes of her blood-spattered boots and straightened her already-ramrod spine.

"Fuck. Off. RuArk."

She nudged him out the door with the tip of her katana, and practically punched a hole in the wall lock panel. The door slammed shut. So what if her behavior was irrational. Who cared? Besides, nobody asked the big guy to appear out of nowhere? To toss that pig, Bryan, down the stairs when she would have rather given him a few choice cuts?

Did it matter she'd been a shrew to a man who'd always set her pulse racing and put her senses on edge? Or that she'd bled all over the place in front of an exotic looking woman in a daringly sexy outfit, all after learning via a stupid note that she'd been stripped of everything that made her who she was?

Rhia stomped around her apartments hurling every curse word she'd ever heard her soldiers use, then switched over to a couple of different languages just to draw it out a bit longer. She soon found that growling and cursing weren't enough. She yelled her frustration to the top of her lungs.

* * * * *

"She was so grateful for your help. Really, I could tell just as she slammed the door in your face."

RuArk turned to scold a not-so-amused Sharyn, but snapped his mouth shut at Rhia's cursing, loud enough to hear through the thick door. Sharyn scowled but didn't say another word, choosing instead to disappear into their suite across the landing and head to her own bedroom.

As for RuArk, it had been a long time since he'd had a reason to see humor in anything but a good fight, yet here he was smiling, then laughing outright. The sound rumbled up through his chest in a deep, full timbre. And all because of the fate the Ancestors handed him, a fate named Rhia.

Door secured, he slipped his blades underneath his pillow and burrowed down into the thick, downy bedding. Keen senses detected no danger as he relaxed and closed his eyes to meditate.

The rest of his men had slipped quietly into the City and settled into the non-descript, seldom used quest quarters on the far side of town. At dawn, Rhia would depart for Harbor Station on the errand they'd made up for her, and RuArk would visit the High Counsel to finalize the details of their plans.

After her behavior tonight, he almost wished the High Counsel was going to be the one breaking the news to the hellcat next door. Almost.

He and Rhia's first meeting after so many seasons had been far from expected. He'd expected happiness, and light, and fun...then again, he had enjoyed tossing the greasy fellow down the steps. In the end, it didn't matter whether Rhia liked that he was here for her or not, he had a job to do—keep her safe and make her his.

As he drifted off, the *Seeking* quest he'd taken after his visit from the Grandfather flashed to the forefront of his mind.

Carried on the arms of the Wind, RuArk looked down upon the land with admiration. The beautiful, rolling hills were covered by a spectacular white, snowy blanket that sparkled like diamonds and luminescent pearls. The bright, full moon reflected off the frozen meadows. And there were so many stars. They filled the pre-dawn sky, twinkling their greeting to the Wind as It passed, carrying its companion.

Off in the distance RuArk spotted a faint glimmer on the ground. The light appeared to be a small campfire, out in the middle of the ice-covered lands. What would anyone be doing way out here in mid-winter? They circled around as RuArk searched for any signs of life. The place was deserted.

"What's going on here?" RuArk asked on a whisper.

The Wind gave no answer, but instead settled directly over the small flames, whipping them up into a firestorm. It flared wildly in spite of the snow covering the ground. The energy from the fire joined itself to that of the Wind, and the Wind became a great storm also. Side by side, the firestorm and the windstorm grew together, reaching up into the starlit sky until it seemed brightened by a second sun.

Then RuArk felt it, just as the Grandfather said. A taint. A subtle hint of foul aura just out of reach, focused on the flame. It faltered until it ceased to give as much energy to its union with the Wind. As the flame wavered, the windstorm and the firestorm were both diminished. The mighty forces of nature became nothing more than a slight breeze and a small campfire once more.

Here, just as in the Dream, he didn't experience true physical sensation, but only a fool would ignore the trickle of apprehension slipping up his arms. He turned to the North, but saw nothing. South, East and West, all was silent. But he knew something, someone, was out there. Perhaps multiple some ones.

After endless moments, he spotted a woman alone in the night, gliding along the snow-covered meadows. The sleek outline of her body was shrouded in shadow. She moved with easy grace. Careful yet confident, she possessed an inner strength that made her appear more hunter than prey. Who was this woman, now almost as near as his own skin?

Looking more closely, RuArk almost tumbled out of the Seeking and back into his physical body in surprise. The glow from her amber eyes pierced his soul—Rhia Greysomne, daughter of the High Counsel of Draema Province.

Oh, he remembered Rhia, stubborn and headstrong as a young girl. He was now being set on the path back to her as a woman. There was danger, yes, but he sensed that she needed something more than protection. But what could she need more than her own life?

It had been endless seasons since he'd seen her, yet even after all this time, and in this place, his body reacted strongly to her *presence. Gods, her essence was exquisite; her aura strong and clean. She was not the source of the foulness on the air. But whoever, or whatever it was, seemed to follow her, long for her, covet her from a distance. Strange.*

RuArk reached out but she didn't respond. Didn't seem to sense him at all.

Flashes of himself and Rhia in a loving embrace danced before his eyes. They were smiling at one another. Touching. Arms twined around each other as he loved her fiercely. Then they were sharing stolen moments, a few quiet words.

My gods, she was his? A woman he'd thought of often, but hadn't pursued? Had longed for, but believed was out of reach? RuArk had no idea how things would develop, but it wasn't his to worry about. All he needed to do was find and stay on the path that had obviously been chosen for him. A path that led to Rhia Greysomne.

RuArk rolled over in his bed and let the memory of the *Seeking* continue to wash over him and fill his mind even as sleep claimed him. After accepting what had been shown to him, he'd been returned to his physical body. And there he'd sat until gooseflesh had risen on his bare arms and legs. In fact, he'd watched the sunrise through the opening of the *Seeking* place and breathed in the lingering scent of sweet, warm female until it had completely faded away.

And now, the woman of his *Seeking* was just across the landing. Just out of reach. She was his, and he would protect her from whatever danger lurked here in Draema.

And RuArk couldn't wait to begin his new job.

ABOUT THE AUTHOR

TJ is an award-winning author of several romance genres, including paranormal, fantasy, sci-fi and urban fantasy romance. Writing like a madman, TJ hasn't lost steam. Her mind? Yep, that's gone, but steam there is a-plenty.

No matter the genre TJ is penning, her favorite thing to do is build worlds. To take you somewhere extraordinary. To transport you to a place where you can close your eyes and slip into your fantasy...

Connect with T.J. at www.TJMichaels.com
and
www.facebook.com/The.Real.TJMichaels

ALSO BY AUTHOR T.J. MICHAELS

Carinian's Seeker—
Book One in the Vampire Council of Ethics series.
Serati's Flame—
Book Two in the Vampire Council of Ethics series.
Hatsept Heat—
Book Three in the Vampire Council of Ethics series.
Seeker's Solace -
Book Four in the Vampire Council of Ethics series

Niah's Pride (Pryde Ranch Shifters)
Spirit of the Pryde (Pryde Ranch Shifters)

Jaguar's Rule
On The Prowl
Egyptian Voyage

Death and Roses (Hunters for Hire)
Entwined Hearts (Hearts of Fire)
Shards of Ecstasy (Hearts of Fire)

Caramel Kisses
Forever December

Wild Winter Anthology
Feral Fascination Anthology
Doing it the Hard Way Anthology

Made in the USA
Monee, IL
12 October 2021

79854231R10184